D0211457

Ace Books by Jack Campbell

THE LOST FLEET: DAUNTLESS
THE LOST FLEET: FEARLESS
THE LOST FLEET: COURAGEOUS

Praise for
THE LOST FLEET: FEARLESS

"Straightforward, solidly written military space opera . . . It's all good fun, and Campbell has actually given some thought to the problems of combat in space."

—Don D'Ammassa, author of
Encyclopedia of Fantasy and Horror Fiction

"Another satisfying [Campbell] cocktail to slake the thirst of fans who like their space operas with a refreshing moral and an intellectual chaser . . . *The Lost Fleet* deserves to find a home on your bookshelf." —*SF Reviews.net*

"A great and gripping read. It's a fast-paced roller coaster of action and intrigue, with realistic characters and situations."

—*TCM Reviews*

Praise for
THE LOST FLEET: DAUNTLESS

"A rousing adventure."

—William C. Dietz, national bestselling author of
When All Seems Lost

"Jack Campbell's dazzling new series is military science fiction at its best. Not only does he tell a yarn of great adventure and action, but he also develops the characters with satisfying depth. I thoroughly enjoyed this rip-roaring read, and I can hardly wait for the next book."

—Catherine Asaro, Nebula Award–winning author of
The Fire Opal

"Black Jack Geary is very real, very human, and so compelling he'll leave you wanting more. Jack Campbell knows fleet actions, and it shows . . . [*The Lost Fleet: Dauntless* is] the best novel of its type that I've read."

—David Sherman, coauthor of
the Starfist series

continued . . .

"A slam-bang good read that kept me up at night . . . a solid, thoughtful, and exciting novel loaded with edge-of-your-seat combat."   —Elizabeth Moon, Nebula Award–winning author of
Command Decision

"[*Dauntless*] should please many fans of old-fashioned hard SF."
—*Sci Fi Weekly*

"Readers will admire and like [Geary], who believes in honor, teamwork, and civilized behavior . . . This is a hard military science novel with space battles out of *Star Wars*. The battle scenes are so intricately described that readers will be able to visualize them . . . A fast-paced but intricate story line and fully developed characters turn this novel into a fun reading experience. Fans of David Weber, Elizabeth Moon, and Peter F. Hamilton will find *The Lost Fleet: Dauntless* thoroughly enjoyable."   —*SFRevu*

"This is an amazing piece of military science fiction writing, with a protagonist who is remarkable and memorable . . . Campbell writes well. Period. The book flows well, with an excellent mix of action and philosophical debate . . . Overall, this is just a plain good read with memorable characters and scenes, and a writing style that is aimed at people who like to think and ponder while enjoying the action. Bravo."   —*Rambles*

"*The Lost Fleet: Dauntless* is well written, with a hero who's all too human and battle weary. There's much here that will remind readers of *Battlestar Galactica* . . . The battles are well-done, but it's the characters who drive the story."
—*Fresh Fiction*

"[Campbell's] space operas [seek] to add new layers to the conventions of military SF."   —*SF Reviews.net*

"Lots of fun, and I devoured it in a day. I can't wait for the sequel."   —*The Weekly Press (Philadelphia)*

"Campbell's book takes a sharp look at military discipline (and the lack thereof) in wartime . . . engaging and interesting."
—*Romantic Times*

THE LOST FLEET

COURAGEOUS

JACK CAMPBELL

CONTRA COSTA COUNTY LIBRARY

3 1901 04571 6539

THE BERKLEY PUBLISHING GROUP
Published by the Penguin Group
Penguin Group (USA) Inc.
375 Hudson Street, New York, New York 10014, USA
Penguin Group (Canada), 90 Eglinton Avenue East, Suite 700, Toronto, Ontario M4P 2Y3, Canada
(a division of Pearson Penguin Canada Inc.)
Penguin Books Ltd., 80 Strand, London WC2R 0RL, England
Penguin Group Ireland, 25 St. Stephen's Green, Dublin 2, Ireland (a division of Penguin Books Ltd.)
Penguin Group (Australia), 250 Camberwell Road, Camberwell, Victoria 3124, Australia
(a division of Pearson Australia Group Pty. Ltd.)
Penguin Books India Pvt. Ltd., 11 Community Centre, Panchsheel Park, New Delhi—110 017, India
Penguin Group (NZ), 67 Apollo Drive, Rosedale, North Shore 0632, New Zealand
(a division of Pearson New Zealand Ltd.)
Penguin Books (South Africa) (Pty.) Ltd., 24 Sturdee Avenue, Rosebank, Johannesburg 2196,
South Africa

Penguin Books Ltd., Registered Offices: 80 Strand, London WC2R 0RL, England

This is a work of fiction. Names, characters, places, and incidents either are the product of the author's
imagination or are used fictitiously, and any resemblance to actual persons, living or dead, business
establishments, events, or locales is entirely coincidental. The publisher does not have any control over
and does not assume any responsibility for author or third-party websites or their content.

THE LOST FLEET: COURAGEOUS

An Ace Book / published by arrangement with the author

PRINTING HISTORY
Ace mass-market edition / January 2008

Copyright © 2008 by John G. Hemry.
Cover art by Peter Bollinger.
Cover design by Annette Fiore DeFex.
Interior text design by Kristin del Rosario.

All rights reserved.
No part of this book may be reproduced, scanned, or distributed in any printed or electronic form without
permission. Please do not participate in or encourage piracy of copyrighted materials in violation
of the author's rights. Purchase only authorized editions.
For information, address: The Berkley Publishing Group,
a division of Penguin Group (USA) Inc.,
375 Hudson Street, New York, New York 10014.

ISBN: 978-0-441-01567-2

ACE
Ace Books are published by The Berkley Publishing Group,
a division of Penguin Group (USA) Inc.,
375 Hudson Street, New York, New York 10014.
ACE and the "A" design are trademarks belonging to Penguin Group (USA) Inc.

PRINTED IN THE UNITED STATES OF AMERICA

10 9 8 7 6 5 4

If you purchased this book without a cover, you should be aware that this book is stolen property. It was
reported as "unsold and destroyed" to the publisher, and neither the author nor the publisher has
received any payment for this "stripped book."

To David Sherman,
who has kept the faith.
Semper Fi

For S., as always.

ACKNOWLEDGMENTS

I remain indebted to my agent, Joshua Bilmes, for his ever-inspired suggestions and assistance, and to my editor, Anne Sowards, for her support and editing. Thanks also to Catherine Asaro, Robert Chase, J. G. "Huck" Huckenpohler, Simcha Kuritzky, Michael LaViolette, Aly Parsons, Bud Sparhawk, and Constance A. Warner, for their suggestions, comments, and recommendations. Thanks also to Charles Petit, for his suggestions about space engagements.

THE ALLIANCE FLEET

CAPTAIN JOHN GEARY,
Commanding (acting)

As reorganized following the losses suffered immediately prior to Captain Geary assuming command in the Syndic home system.

Ship names in bold are those lost in action, with the name of star system of their loss given afterward.

SECOND BATTLESHIP DIVISION

Gallant
Indomitable
Glorious
Magnificent

THIRD BATTLESHIP DIVISION

Paladin
Orion
Majestic
Conqueror

FOURTH BATTLESHIP DIVISION

Warrior
Triumph (lost at Vidha)
Vengeance
Revenge

FIFTH BATTLESHIP DIVISION

Fearless
Resolution
Redoubtable
Warspite

SEVENTH BATTLESHIP DIVISION

Indefatigable
Audacious
Defiant

EIGHTH BATTLESHIP DIVISION

Relentless
Reprisal
Superb
Splendid

TENTH BATTLESHIP DIVISION

Colossus
Amazon
Spartan
Guardian

FIRST SCOUT BATTLESHIP DIVISION

Arrogant (lost at Kaliban)
Exemplar
Braveheart

FIRST BATTLE CRUISER DIVISION

Courageous
Formidable
Intrepid
Renown

SECOND BATTLE CRUISER DIVISION

Leviathan
Dragon
Steadfast
Valiant

FOURTH BATTLE CRUISER DIVISION

Dauntless (flagship)
Daring
Terrible (lost at Ilion)
Victorious

FIFTH BATTLE CRUISER DIVISION

Invincible (lost at Ilion)
Repulse (lost in Syndic home system)
Furious
Implacable

SIXTH BATTLE CRUISER DIVISION

Polaris (lost at Vidha)
Vanguard (lost at Vidha)
Illustrious
Incredible

SEVENTH BATTLE CRUISER DIVISION

Opportune
Brilliant
Inspire

THIRD FAST FLEET AUXILIARIES DIVISION

Titan
Witch
Jinn
Goblin

THIRTY-SEVEN SURVIVING HEAVY CRUISERS IN SEVEN DIVISIONS

First Heavy Cruiser Division
Third Heavy Cruiser Division
Fourth Heavy Cruiser Division
Fifth Heavy Cruiser Division
Seventh Heavy Cruiser Division
Eighth Heavy Cruiser Division
Tenth Heavy Cruiser Division

minus

Invidious (lost at Kaliban)
Cuirass (lost at Sutrah)
Crest, **War-Coat**, **Ram**, and **Citadel** (lost at Vidha)

SIXTY-TWO SURVIVING LIGHT CRUISERS IN TEN SQUADRONS

First Light Cruiser Squadron
Second Light Cruiser Squadron
Third Light Cruiser Squadron
Fifth Light Cruiser Squadron
Sixth Light Cruiser Squadron
Eighth Light Cruiser Squadron
Ninth Light Cruiser Squadron
Tenth Light Cruiser Squadron
Eleventh Light Cruiser Squadron
Fourteenth Light Cruiser Squadron

minus

Swift (lost at Kaliban)
Pommel, *Sling*, *Bolo*, and *Staff* (lost at Vidha)

ONE HUNDRED EIGHTY-THREE SURVIVING DESTROYERS IN TWENTY SQUADRONS

First Destroyer Squadron
Second Destroyer Squadron
Third Destroyer Squadron
Fourth Destroyer Squadron
Sixth Destroyer Squadron
Seventh Destroyer Squadron
Ninth Destroyer Squadron
Tenth Destroyer Squadron
Twelfth Destroyer Squadron
Fourteenth Destroyer Squadron
Sixteenth Destroyer Squadron
Seventeenth Destroyer Squadron
Twentieth Destroyer Squadron
Twenty-first Destroyer Squadron
Twenty-third Destroyer Squadron
Twenty-fifth Destroyer Squadron
Twenty-seventh Destroyer Squadron
Twenty-eighth Destroyer Squadron
Thirtieth Destroyer Squadron
Thirty-second Destroyer Squadron

minus

Dagger and *Venom* (lost at Kaliban)
Anelace, *Baselard*, and *Mace* (lost at Sutrah)
Celt, *Akhu*, *Sickle*, *Leaf*, *Bolt*, *Sabot*, *Flint*, *Needle*,
Dart, *Sting*, *Limpet*, and *Cudgel* (lost at Vidha)
Falcata (lost at Ilion)

SECOND FLEET MARINE FORCE
Colonel Carabali commanding (acting)

1,560 Marines divided into detachments on battle cruisers and battleships.

ONE

THE captain of the Syndicate Worlds merchant ship approaching the jump point out of Baldur Star System might have been having a good day—right up until the point that several squadrons of Alliance fleet destroyers appeared coming out of that jump point. He might have had a few minutes to wonder if he could somehow run past the Alliance destroyers and jump out of the system to safety, before many more destroyers appeared and before squadrons of light cruisers materialized behind the destroyers. He and his crew had definitely run for the merchant ship's one escape pod by the time divisions of heavy cruisers, battle cruisers, and battleships emerged from the jump point.

Syndicate Worlds authorities on the one habitable world orbiting Baldur would see the annihilation of the merchant ship and hear its crew's calls for rescue in about six hours, about the same time the light from the jump point reached them and they saw that the Alliance fleet had appeared in their backwater star system.

They wouldn't be having a good day, either.

• • •

"*RAPIER* and *Bulawa* report destruction of the Syndic merchant ship. One escape pod noted leaving the merchant ship. *Singhauta* reports destruction of the automated traffic management buoy monitoring the jump point." The watch-stander's voice rang calmly and clearly across the bridge of the Alliance battle cruiser *Dauntless*. "No minefields detected or suspicious anomalies sighted."

Captain John "Black Jack" Geary nodded to acknowledge the words, his attention focused on the display floating before his command seat. He could have picked out from the display every piece of information the watch-stander had just provided, but experience had proven that humans remained the best filters for highlighting important data. If some other human handled that, Geary could concentrate on the bigger picture. "Which one of our ships is in the best position to pick up the escape pod from the merchant?"

"Wait, sir. *Battleaxe*, sir."

Geary tapped the proper communications control without having to search for it, relieved that the unfamiliar equipment of this future was finally becoming second nature to him. "*Battleaxe*, this is Captain Geary. Request you pick up the Syndic escape pod. I want to interrogate that merchant crew."

The reply took a minute, naturally, since the destroyer *Battleaxe* was about twenty light-seconds distant from *Dauntless*. It took her twenty seconds to receive the transmission and another twenty seconds for the answer to make the return journey. "Yes, sir. Who should we deliver them to?"

"*Dauntless*," Geary advised.

He was still awaiting *Battleaxe*'s acknowledgment when a cool voice spoke from behind him. "What do you hope to learn from the crew of a merchant ship, Captain Geary? The Syndic leadership wouldn't have entrusted them with any classified information."

Geary glanced back, seeing that Victoria Rione, co-president of the Callas Republic and a senator of the Alliance, was giving him a curious look. "That ship was about to jump out of the system. That means they likely jumped into the system within the last few weeks instead of being a purely in-system trader. They'll have news from other Syndic star systems. I want to know what they've been told about this fleet and about the war in general. I also want to see if we can get them to cough up any rumors they've heard in their travels."

"You think that information will be valuable?" Rione pressed.

"I have no idea, but if I don't get it, I won't know, will I?"

She nodded, giving little clue to her opinion. Not that Geary found that unusual. He and Rione had been lovers for a few weeks, in the physical sense of the word, but she had been distant since just before they had left Ilion Star System, and he had yet to learn why. "Then perhaps you should have the prisoners delivered to *Vengeance*," Rione added. "That battleship has the best interrogation facilities in the fleet, or so I've heard."

Captain Tanya Desjani, sitting to one side of Geary, jerked her head around and spoke coldly. "*Dauntless* has excellent interrogation facilities and can ensure Captain Geary receives every measure of support he requests." Desjani wasn't about to let anyone imply that any other ship in the fleet was in any way superior to *her* ship.

Rione gazed back impassively at *Dauntless*'s commanding officer for a moment, then inclined her head slightly. "I did not mean to imply that *Dauntless* could not carry out the mission effectively."

"Thank you," Desjani replied, her voice no warmer.

Geary tried not to frown. Desjani and Rione had apparently been just one step shy of going for each other's throats ever since Ilion, and he hadn't been able to find out the cause of that, either. Bad enough he had to worry about the Syndic fleet without also trying to figure out why there was bad blood between two of the best advisers he had. He refocused on the display, where the fleet's sensors were busy adding newly detected information, then muttered a curse.

"What's the matter, sir?" Desjani asked, instantly alert as her own eyes scanned her display. "Oh. Damn."

"Yeah," Geary agreed. He knew Rione was listening and wondering. "There's another Syndic merchant ship almost at the jump point on the other side of the system. It'll have time to see us before it jumps out and will carry that news to the Syndic authorities elsewhere."

"It's a good thing we don't intend to linger here," Desjani added. "There's nothing in Baldur that we need. It's just another second-rate star system."

Geary nodded, his thoughts going back. Back a century, to before the war, to before he'd fought a desperate battle against the first Syndic surprise attack, before he'd barely escaped in a damaged survival pod to drift for a hundred years in survival sleep, before he'd found himself suddenly in command of a fleet whose survival depended on him. Back when he was just John Geary, a typical fleet officer, not the mythical hero Black Jack Geary, who these descendants of the people he'd known had been taught to believe could do anything. "People used to go to Baldur before the war," he remarked in an almost absentminded way. "Tourists, even from the Alliance."

Desjani stared at him in amazement. "Tourists?" After a century of bitter warfare, the idea of pleasure trips into what had been enemy territory for her entire life seemed to be incomprehensible to her.

"Yeah." Geary shifted his gaze to the display of the primary inhabited world. "There's some spectacular scenery down there. Even with all the worlds humanity has settled, there was something unique about it, something you had to be there to appreciate. That's what everyone said, anyway."

"Unique?" Desjani sounded simply doubtful now.

"Yeah," Geary repeated. "I saw an interview with someone who had been there. He said there was something awesome about it, like your ancestors came to stand beside you while you looked around. Maybe something happened to it, though, since Baldur didn't get a hypernet gate." He glanced over at Desjani, who still seemed baffled but also, as usual, willing to take the word of a man she believed had been sent by the living stars to save the Alliance.

She indicated her display. "Do you want to avoid bombarding the primary planet, then?"

Geary almost choked. After a century of trading atrocities with the Syndics, even Alliance officers could be remarkably cold-blooded. "Yes," he managed to get out. "If at all possible."

"Very well," Desjani agreed. "The military facilities seem to be primarily orbital, so if we have to take them out, it won't require surface bombardment."

"That's convenient," Geary agreed dryly. He settled back, trying to relax nerves that had been on edge as the fleet entered Baldur.

"Syndic combatants identified orbiting the third planet," *Dauntless*'s combat watch-stander announced as if on cue. "An additional Syndic combatant has been located in spacedock orbiting the fourth planet."

Geary, hoping he hadn't too obviously jerked to attention at the announcement, zoomed his display in on the enemy ships. Anything that hadn't been seen until now had to be pretty small. They were. "Three obsolete nickel corvettes and an even older light cruiser." The cruiser was older than him, too, Geary reflected. *And here we both are still fighting a war far beyond the time either of us ever planned on. At least I'm in better physical shape than that ancient cruiser probably is.*

"Five and a half light-hours distant," Desjani confirmed. "Orbiting between the third and fourth planets. They'll see us in roughly five more hours." She smiled. "They obviously weren't expecting us."

Geary smiled back, feeling relieved. Every time the fleet left jump, he had to worry about encountering a Syndic ambush. The only way to avoid that was to keep the

Syndic leadership guessing as to where the fleet would be next. The lack of even picket warships posted near Baldur's jump points meant the Syndics had no idea the Alliance fleet would be showing up here, or at least hadn't figured it out as a possible destination in time to get a courier ship to this star system. "Odds are they'll run, then. If they don't run, I want an analysis of what they might be concerned with protecting."

"Yes, sir," Desjani acknowledged, gesturing to one of her watch-standers. "Is there something else, sir?"

"What?" Geary realized he was staring tensely at the display and deliberately relaxed his breathing again. "No."

But Desjani had figured out his worry. "The fleet seems to be holding formation."

"Yes." *Seems to be.* If any of the outermost combatants took it into their minds to charge toward the Syndic warships, *Dauntless* wouldn't see it for almost half a minute. But everyone appeared to be holding formation. "Maybe what I'm trying to show the officers in this fleet about discipline in battle is really getting through to everyone." That was a cheerful thought.

Rione promptly threw a bucket of reality over him. "Or maybe they're holding formation because the Syndic combatants are five and a half light-hours distant. Even at full acceleration, an attempted intercept would take quite a while."

Desjani gave Rione another cool look as she had the navigation system run the intercept. "If the Syndics held course and didn't run, an intercept would require about twenty-five hours at maximum acceleration and deceleration," she confirmed reluctantly. "But I assure you, Madam Co-President, that before Captain Geary assumed command, we would still have had ships already launching themselves on that charge."

Rione smiled thinly and nodded. "I have no reason to doubt your assessment, Captain Desjani."

"Thank you, Madam Co-President."

"No, thank *you*, Captain."

Geary took a moment to be grateful that his officers didn't wear ceremonial swords. From the look in Desjani's eyes, Rione should be grateful for that as well. "All right," he announced out loud to distract the two women. "To all appearances, this star system is totally unprepared for our arrival. That means we should have a chance to intimidate them into avoiding doing anything stupid." Desjani nodded immediately, followed a noticeable few seconds later by Rione. "Captain Desjani, please broadcast to all Syndic installations that any actions taken to hinder or attack this fleet will be met with overwhelming force."

"Yes, sir. With your name on the end?"

"Yeah." Geary had never aspired to have a name that would frighten people, but apparently more than a few Syndics also believed in the legendary Alliance hero, Black Jack.

Victoria Rione spoke again. "Your messages are usually longer."

Geary shrugged. "I'm trying something different. They'll have no idea what our intentions are, which will keep them guessing and worried. Maybe enough so that they'll sit tight and not try to mess with us." *Not that I'm planning on doing anything but getting to the next jump point.* He studied the display, seeing the course leading to the jump point for Wendaya as a long arc passing above the plane of the Baldur Star System. The fleet wouldn't have to go anywhere near any Syndic installations, and the Syndics didn't have anything in-system that could be used to go after the fleet.

It all looked so perfect that Geary found himself double-checking, unwilling to trust a situation without an overt threat.

But nothing looked wrong. He finally relaxed again, pondering his formation, then calling up the individual ship status readouts. Very little information could be exchanged in jump space, but ever since the fleet had arrived here, automatic reports had been flowing in to *Dauntless* with information on the current state of every ship. If Geary had been so inclined, he could've found out exactly how many sailors on any one particular ship had head colds at the moment. He had known commanders who had concentrated on things like that, somehow expecting the business of actually running the fleet to happen on its own while they dug ever deeper into trivial details.

What he was seeing wasn't trivial, though. Geary couldn't prevent a gasp of exasperation as he looked at the primary status readouts, drawing glances from the others on the bridge. "Logistics," he explained very briefly to Desjani.

She nodded. "*Dauntless* is getting below recommended fuel cell reserves, too."

"I knew that. I didn't appreciate how much of the rest of the fleet was also at or below those levels." Geary shook his head as he checked another report. "And expendable munitions. We used a lot of mines at Sancere and Ilion, and specter missile stockpiles are low on most ships." He leaned back again, taking a long, calming breath. "Thank the living stars for the auxiliaries. Without them along to manufacture new fuel cells and weaponry, this fleet would have been trapped and helpless a few star systems back."

That simplified his plans for getting through Baldur Star System. Keep the fleet close together, keep fuel expenditures to a minimum, avoid using weapons, and give the auxiliaries plenty of time to replenish the fuel and munitions supplies on the warships.

Geary's feeling of satisfaction vanished as he checked the status of the four fast fleet auxiliaries, which weren't fast except in the imaginations of whoever had chosen that name for them. Difficult to protect and slow as they were, the self-propelled manufacturing facilities called auxiliaries were vital to getting this fleet home. As long as they could keep the fleet supplied, that is. "Why am I seeing critical shortage reports on the auxiliaries?" Geary wondered out loud. "We looted every raw material we could possibly use back at Sancere. The auxiliaries' supply bunkers were supposed to have been topped off."

Desjani frowned and checked the figures herself. "According to these reports, all of the auxiliaries will have to stop manufacturing fuel cells and munitions soon due to shortages of critical materials. That doesn't make sense. The auxiliaries certainly loaded a lot of *something* at Sancere."

The situation had looked too good to be true. So, of course, it had been. Muttering curses under his breath, Geary put in a call to the flagship of the auxiliaries division. *Witch* was a healthy fifteen light-seconds distant, causing a very aggravating delay in communications as the message crawled to the other ship at the speed of light, and the reply crawled back. Only in the vast distances of space did light seem slow.

The image of Captain Tyrosian finally appeared, looking the very model of someone bearing bad news. But all she said was, "Yes, sir."

At least the delay in message times had given Geary time to phrase a diplomatic question. "Captain Tyrosian, I'm looking at the status reports for your ships. All of them show shortages of critical raw materials."

Another wait. Finally, Tyrosian's image nodded unhappily. "Yes, sir, that is correct."

Geary fought down a grimace as it became clear that Tyrosian's reply wasn't more enlightening. "How is that possible? I thought all of the auxiliaries filled their stockpiles with raw materials at Sancere. How could we have ended up with shortages of critical materials this soon?"

The seconds crawled by, too long to ignore and too brief to allow time to do anything else. Tyrosian looked even unhappier as she nodded again. "The reports are accurate, Captain Geary. I've been trying to determine the cause of the problem. I'm fairly certain it's because of the shopping lists provided by the automated logistics system."

Another pause. Geary barely refrained from pounding

the arm of his seat in frustration. "How could the automated systems have made such a serious misjudgment of which supplies the auxiliaries would need to manufacture items critical to this fleet? Didn't your ships follow the recommendations from the logistics system?"

He spent the time waiting for a reply imagining the sorts of things he could do to Captain Tyrosian for screwing up something this important. It didn't help his temper that Tyrosian kept proving the old adage that engineers weren't the best people in the world when it came to verbal communications. Tyrosian kept telling him things that left critical information out as if expecting he would know everything she did.

When her reply came this time, Tyrosian spoke in the time-hallowed manner of engineers everywhere as they recited their professional opinions. "We did follow the system recommendations. That was the cause of the failure, Captain Geary. The systems provided flawed recommendations."

Geary hesitated, taken aback by the statement, despite his growing anger. "Explain that. Why would the systems have provided flawed recommendations? Are you saying the system was sabotaged somehow so that it didn't provide good information?" The implications of that were very serious indeed. If the automated systems that helped run the fleet became unreliable or were somehow hacked, it could cripple the fleet as badly as a lack of fuel and weaponry.

But Tyrosian shook her head as her reply eventually arrived. "No, sir. There wasn't, and isn't, anything wrong with the logistics systems. They're functioning exactly as they should. The problem lies in the underlying assumptions the logistics system used in extrapolating the needs of the fleet." She swallowed, clearly uncomfortable but bulling ahead with her report. "The logistics systems base future needs on projected usage and losses. Those projections are in turn constructed from historical patterns."

Tyrosian grimaced. "Under your command, the fleet

hasn't been experiencing usage of munitions or losses of ships in accordance with historical patterns. As a result, the logistics systems assumed we would have much fewer ships requiring resupply and that fewer munitions and fuel cells would be required."

It took Geary a moment to figure that out. "I should have been losing more ships every time we fought? I shouldn't have been using so many munitions or maneuvering so much?"

Seconds dragged by until Tyrosian nodded again. "Essentially, yes. We've been fighting more frequently and losing much fewer ships than called for by the underlying assumptions of the logistics systems. Battles have been more complex, requiring the use of more fuel cells. More long-range weapons have been used than is usually the case. None of us caught how that would change projected requirements. As a result, the logistics systems assumed a higher level of need for battle damage repair materials and a lower level for resupply of surviving ships. We have plenty of what we need to patch the holes in *Warrior*, *Orion*, and *Majestic*, but we're short on some critical raw materials that are used in small quantities in things like fuel cells and specter missiles."

Wonderful. Absolutely wonderful. Accustomed as he was to the perversity of the universe, it was still astounding to realize that he was facing problems because he had been doing too well in battle. Geary looked over at Desjani. "We're in trouble because the fleet hasn't been losing enough ships when we fight."

To his surprise, Desjani took only a moment to figure it out. "We need to adapt the systems to you, sir. I should've realized that, too."

Geary gave her a grim smile. It was just like Desjani to immediately accept a measure of responsibility, whether she bore any or not. Unlike, say, Captain Tyrosian, who seemed at a loss on what to do, waiting expectantly for Geary's orders and not offering any suggestions. "Tanya," he asked, using Desjani's first name to emphasize his confidence in her, "what do you recommend?"

"All of the auxiliaries are low on the critical materials?" Desjani checked the detailed status reports again and rolled her eyes. Her feelings about engineers running ships were clear. Then again, practically every other one of Geary's ship captains would agree with her on that count. "*Jinn*'s stockpiles of those materials are in slightly better shape than *Witch*'s," Desjani noted out loud, "*Goblin*'s slightly worse, and *Titan*'s stockpiles are in about the same condition as those on *Witch*." Geary tried not to think about all of the materials they had looted at Sancere, how easily they could have loaded much more of all of those critical materials. "We need more," Desjani concluded.

"So I assumed," Geary replied, trying not to go ballistic on Desjani over the obviousness of her observation. "Where do we get it?"

Desjani gestured to the system display. "The Syndics have mines in this star system, of course. They'll have what we need."

Geary grinned with sudden relief. *My mind was still stuck back in Sancere. Thank our ancestors that Desjani's was here in Baldur.* "Madam Co-President," he began.

She forestalled his question, frowning. "We've encountered sabotage from the Syndics before, Captain Geary. Asking them for the materials we need, even letting them know we need them, could be a serious error. I don't see any way diplomacy can be counted upon in this case."

Desjani reluctantly nodded in agreement. "That's almost certainly correct, sir."

Geary pondered that, then faced the window where Tyrosian's image waited. The engineering captain was visibly nervous but holding herself ready for the tongue-lashing, or worse, she probably expected. The sight helped drain the anger from Geary. Maybe Tyrosian wasn't the smartest or most capable officer in the fleet, but she knew her job, knew engineering, and had been a solid performer. She hadn't foreseen the problem, but automated systems bred dependency in their users. Everyone knew that. He was lucky Tyrosian had been able to identify the problem instead of just blindly clinging to the flawed output from the logistics systems.

So Geary forced himself to give Tyrosian a confident look, as if he had never doubted her ability to handle this. "Okay, to summarize, all four auxiliaries are facing serious shortages of a few critical raw materials. Unless we stock up on critical materials as soon as possible, we'll have to cease production of vital components. Are those raw materials available in this system?" Remembering the increasingly annoying time delay in answers, he added a further question. "Would they be available at any particular locations among the mining activity we've spotted?"

About thirty seconds later he saw Tyrosian's face light up. "Yes, sir. Mining activity on asteroids and near the gas giants has already been detected and analyzed by the fleet's sensors. The most likely location where we'd find what we need is . . . um . . . at this site on the fourth moon of the second gas giant." A secondary window popped up, revealing the place that Tyrosian had designated.

"What's your assessment of the wisdom of demanding that the Syndics supply us with those materials?"

Tyrosian's alarm was obvious. "That wouldn't be wise at all, sir. They'd know why we need those particular materials. They're all trace elements, found and used in small quantities. The Syndics could easily contaminate or destroy whatever stockpiles exist, since they wouldn't be large."

It just kept getting better. Geary's eyes went back to the display. He had to surprise the Syndics with a raid on a mining facility, which would have been a lot easier if the Syndics hadn't been able to see every one of his ships coming for days before they reached their objective. "Is there anything else I need to know, Captain Tyrosian? Anything else the auxiliaries need? Anything else that might impair their ability to keep this fleet in fuel cells and expendable munitions?" Not that he really wanted to hear any more bad news, but bad news never got better just because you didn't listen to it. Usually, it got worse.

Tyrosian shook her head again. "No, sir. Nothing of which I'm aware. I'll have each department on every auxiliary do a worst-case assessment, just to be certain."

"Good." Now, what to do about Tyrosian? She had screwed up mightily and left Geary to find out instead of telling him. The mistake had quite literally put the entire fleet at greater risk, and with the entire fleet fleeing for its life deep in Syndic space, increasing that risk took real effort.

But she had done a good job, or at least a decent one, up until now. And who did he choose in her place if he relieved her? The captain of *Titan* was enthusiastic but too young and inexperienced. In a fleet heavily focused on honor and seniority, elevating him to command of the auxiliaries division would create a lot of resentment, and there wasn't even any guarantee that he could handle that much responsibility this soon. *Goblin*'s captain had a service record remarkable for its bland mediocrity. *Jinn*'s commanding officer had only recently assumed the position after Geary had relieved his predecessor. And that predecessor, Captain Gundel, had been so aggressively uninterested in serving the needs of the warships that he might as well have been deliberately helping the ends of the enemy. Gundel was parked in a small office somewhere on *Titan*, under orders to produce an exhaustive study on the fleet's needs, whose sole purpose was to get him completely out of Geary's hair, even if it took years to get this fleet home.

Remembering Gundel made Geary's decision easier. Tyrosian might not be perfect, but the alternatives all seemed worse. *And, damn it all, as far as I can tell, she's tried her hardest.* "Captain Tyrosian, I'm unhappy that we're faced with this situation, and I wish you had brought it to my attention sooner, but you have analyzed the cause of the problem and I trust are taking measures to

ensure it doesn't happen again." At least, he was confident
she would be taking such measures as soon as she heard
Geary saying that. "I need your best estimate for a shopping list of what we need, and I want a team of engineers
ready to physically land at any Syndic mining facilities
and assess the stockpiles. Get both of those things ready."

Tyrosian blinked as if surprised. "Yes, sir." Had she realized she was in danger of being relieved? Probably. She
might not be among his best officers, but she was good
enough to be among those who understood the concept of
responsibility. Unlike his worst officers. If only the real
idiots among his captains were willing to offer their resig-
nations when they made big mistakes. But of course they
wouldn't, even if they did manage to realize they'd messed
up badly. That was one of the main things that made them
idiots.

Geary favored Tyrosian with another confident look. "I
also need a plan for replenishing and refueling the fleet's
ships with what the auxiliaries were able to manufacture
on the way here, with priority for those with the lowest
fuel and expendable munitions stockpiles."

"Yes, sir. That's not a problem. Can the fleet formation
be adjusted?"

"Yeah. I want the resupply done as quickly and effi-
ciently as possible."

"You'll get that," Tyrosian promised. She hesitated.
"I'm sorry, sir."

Geary paused, too. This time he felt sure his expression
was genuine as he nodded to Tyrosian. "Thank you, Captain. I already knew that. That's why you're still in command of *Witch* and the auxiliaries division, and that's why
I'm confident you'll perform well in both of those positions."

He closed his eyes for a moment after Tyrosian's image
vanished, hoping he had handled that right, trying to figure out if he had truly meant what he had said or just been
playing political games. Presenting a false face to the
enemy could play as big a role in winning as divisions of

battleships. Geary was comfortable with that. But he sometimes had to do the same with his own officers, and he had never managed to be at ease with it. Did he really believe in Tyrosian, or did he just regard her as the least bad of the choices available to him? *But even if I did feel that way, what purpose would it serve to tell her that?*

There's work to be done. Stop brooding. Geary's eyes opened and swung back to the display of Baldur System. He wasn't at all sure how they'd manage to get those raw materials from the Syndics, but he was certain who he needed to do it. Geary tapped his controls to bring up another window. Within moments, the image of his Marine commander appeared. "Colonel Carabali, we have a job for your troops."

HERE we go again. Geary braced himself, then entered the compartment where he held meetings with his fleet captains. It wasn't very large, and the table within could only comfortably seat perhaps a dozen people in reality, but the fleet's virtual conferencing software made the room and the table apparently big enough to hold every captain in the fleet. After enduring numerous meetings in here, Geary was still trying to decide if that was a blessing or a curse.

He took up position at the head of the table, looking down along both sides. Apparently seated nearest him were the most senior officers, the lines of captains running into the distance in decreasing seniority until the most junior ship commanders waited at the end. Only one other person was physically present, Captain Desjani, who seemed as unenthusiastic about the meeting as Geary himself, though Geary hoped he was doing a better job of hiding it.

The absence of Captain Numos and Captain Faresa, both normally "seated" close by him and both serious thorns in his side, didn't offer much comfort. The former commanding officers of *Orion* and *Majestic* were both under arrest but a constant source of disruption even now. Geary only had to look down the table to see eyes that were either wary or hiding whatever emotions they might hold. Fortunately, there were also many officers who clearly displayed near-worshipful (though discomforting) belief in Black Jack Geary as well as those who believed less in the legend of Black Jack and more in the man who had led the fleet this far. He couldn't help wondering how long it would be before he screwed up so badly that their growing faith would be crushed by the reality of his own human fallibility.

"Welcome to Baldur," Geary began. As he said the words, he realized that had been the title of a popular documentary over a century ago. No one else showed any reaction, though, so he was probably the only person in the fleet who remembered it. There wasn't anything unusual about that, of course. "I'd planned on just taking us above the plane of the system to the next jump point, but as usual our plans have changed."

A ripple of interest ran around the long, long virtual length of the table as Geary called up a display before him. A representation of the glowing yellow star Baldur floated in the center, positioned around it the several significant planets the star system boasted, and scattered through the system were symbols that marked Syndic activity or installations. "We need to pay a visit to the Syndic mining facility on the fourth moon of the second gas giant." That symbol flared brighter. "The auxiliaries require restocking of certain critical materials, and we're going to acquire those materials there. Or rather, our Marines are going to acquire them." Geary nodded toward the image of Colonel Carabali.

Carabali, like Geary, had ascended to command when her superior was murdered by the Syndics during negotiations. Being a Marine, she hadn't let that intimidate her in the least while dealing with the fleet officers around her. Now she spoke in the dry, precise cadence of a briefing officer. "There's concern that the Syndics could either sabotage the stockpiles we need or contaminate them," she began.

"Why?" someone interrupted.

Geary fixed his eyes on the speaker. Commander Yin, acting commanding officer of the *Orion* and doubtless a protégée of Captain Numos. Yin appeared slightly nervous but still belligerent, her attitude perhaps an unconscious imitation of Numos's own. "If you'll let Colonel Carabali finish presenting her information, you'll hear the answer to that," Geary stated, realizing his voice sounded harsher than he had intended.

Carabali glanced around, then continued speaking. "The materials in question are trace elements. The fleet has been able to confirm the existence of the stockpiles we need at that mining facility by analyzing the message traffic in this system and assessing what we can see of the mining facility from this distance. Since the relatively small size of the stockpiles makes sabotage or contamination easy, Captain Geary asked me to plan a raid designed to surprise anyone occupying or possibly defending the mining facility."

Carabali paused, and Captain Tulev of the battle cruiser *Leviathan* gave her a questioning but not hostile look. "Surprise? How will we achieve surprise?"

Geary answered. "We need to misdirect the Syndics, mislead them as to our intentions. They'll see us coming, but we have to convince them that we're swinging by purely to destroy the facility, not to take anything from it." He tapped controls, and a series of arcs appeared in the representation of Baldur Star System, curving from point to point among planets and asteroids. "We're going to start at the outer edges of Baldur and work our way inward, passing close to Syndic facilities on the way and destroying them with hell-lance fire at close range."

This time Captain Casia of the battleship *Conqueror* spoke up, frowning as he did so. "That doesn't make sense. Not even the Syndics would believe that we'd take the time to engage fixed targets at close range when we could just launch kinetic rounds at them from a distance."

Geary checked to confirm his suspicions, that *Conqueror* was part of the Third Battleship Division, which included both *Orion* and *Majestic*. Captain Casia hadn't stood out in earlier meetings, perhaps overshadowed by the presence of Numos or Faresa. He couldn't recall any grounds to assume Casia was like those two others, so Geary answered without assuming any antagonism. "It's not unreasonable that our fleet would be low on kinetic projectiles. As a matter of fact, we *are* low on them because of all the rounds we launched at Sancere. There's also no significant threat to us in this star system. Under those circumstances, it makes perfect sense to conserve kinetic rounds and employ hell-lance fire. The Syndics will believe we're even lower on kinetic rounds than we actually are, which might benefit us in the future in other ways."

Casia chewed his lip, a scowl just barely visible. The image of Captain Duellos of the battle cruiser *Courageous* caught Geary's eye and made a dismissive glance at Casia in a wordless assessment of the other officer. After a long moment that might have been attributable to nothing more than the distance separating *Dauntless* and *Conqueror*, Casia shook his head. "We're all low on kinetic rounds? What have the auxiliaries been doing?"

"Manufacturing fuel cells, Captain Casia," Duellos advised in a drawl that brought a flush to Casia's face. "I assume you prefer to be able to maneuver your ship, or do you want to drift through space with a full inventory of kinetic rounds on hand?"

Geary could easily judge Casia's status in the fleet by the reactions of the other officers. Many grinned at Duellos's put-down, but others seemed more unhappy with Duellos than with Casia. Odd, since Geary couldn't recall the man causing him any trouble before this. Why had the malcontents chosen him to rally around?

Geary thumped the table with his fist to forestall any

other comments. "Thank you, Captain Duellos. Do you have any further questions, Captain Casia?"

"Yes. Yes, I do." Casia stood to emphasize his words. "I understand we need these materials because the auxiliaries didn't stock up properly at Sancere. The entire fleet has been hazarded, but nothing has been done to those responsible."

He paused, while Geary glanced toward Captain Tyrosian and saw her stiffen. "Is that an observation or a question?" Geary asked Casia.

"It's . . . both."

"Then I will assure you," Geary stated evenly, "that I have discussed the matter with Captain Tyrosian, and she retains my confidence as commander of the auxiliaries division."

"What did you say to her?" Casia demanded.

Geary couldn't stop a frown; in fact, he let it stay in place as he gazed back at Casia. He recognized what was happening, the sort of debate that would have been unthinkable in the fleet he had known, not simply arguing courses of action but actively challenging the fleet commander and trying to manipulate the level of support the commander could count on. Any moment now Casia would probably call for a vote insisting that Geary remove Tyrosian from her job.

And that wasn't going to happen while he was in command. "Captain Casia," Geary said in his coldest voice, "I am not in the habit of discussing in public my private conversations with other officers. What I said to Captain Tyrosian is between her and me, just as anything I say to you in private will remain between us."

"We deserve to know that you'll take effective action—" Casia began.

"Are you challenging my authority to command this fleet, Captain Casia?" Geary demanded in a voice that rang through the room.

Silence reigned for a moment, then Captain Tulev spoke as if to himself, though his voice carried. "The Syndics have learned at Kaliban, at Sancere, and at Ilion that Captain Geary is a very effective commander."

Commander Yin's voice wavered slightly as she jumped back into the conversation. "The traditions of the fleet call for open debate and consensus among the captains. What's wrong with wanting to continue that tradition? Why wouldn't Captain Geary be in favor of maintaining the traditions that have kept this fleet fighting?"

Captain Desjani had kept herself quiet up until now but finally erupted at the direct attack on Geary. "Captain Geary believes in our traditions! He's reminded us of traditions we'd forgotten!"

"Captain Geary established those traditions a century ago!" another voice insisted. To Geary's surprise, it was Commander Gaes of the *Lorica*. "He fights! And more importantly, he knows *how* to fight! He hasn't sent this fleet into any Syndic traps!"

The clear reference to the disaster at Vidha brought a momentary stop to the debate. Both Casia and Yin were giving Commander Gaes hard looks, but she didn't seem to care. After choosing to follow Captain Falco in a rebellious force of Alliance fleet ships and then watching that force get cut to ribbons at Vidha, Gaes probably had little tolerance for anyone who might be advocating the sort of challenge to Geary's command that had led to that disaster.

Casia finally shook his head. "We're in a difficult position. The fleet can't afford to be at the mercy of those who've positioned themselves as favorites of the fleet commander, regardless of competence."

"That's enough." Geary saw that everyone had turned to stare at him and realized that must have been his voice speaking in those tones. He changed his tone with an effort, trying to sound more like a commander and less like an enraged deity. To sound less like Black Jack. "Captain Casia, this fleet has too much experience with officers incapable of carrying out their responsibilities. I won't tolerate anyone like that in a command position. Is that clear?" Casia flushed but remained silent. "Now, do you intend charging any officer present here with being incompetent to command their ships?" He was bullying the man, forcing him to publicly back down. Geary knew it. He shouldn't use his authority this way. He had to lead these officers, not drive them before him. But right now he was sick and tired of politics and of senior officers who seemed to enjoy politics even when it threatened the survival of the fleet. "Do you?" Geary pressed.

Casia's voice sounded strangled as he answered. "No."

"I'm the fleet commander and your superior officer, Captain Casia."

"No . . . sir."

"Thank you." *Just relieve him for cause. Right now. Lock up Casia along with Numos and Faresa and Captain Kerestes and crazy Captain Falco. Toss in Commander Yin as well. Why do I need to keep tolerating these idiots? This fleet will be far safer if they aren't around to interfere with me. If they'd stop challenging—*

Geary took a long, slow breath. *Damn. I'm losing it. Where would that road end if I started down it? How many officers would I sack, making sure that only those loyal to me were in command? And once I'd sacked enough, the rest wouldn't dare speak up to me, tell me when I was mistaken or wrong. And this fleet would die, because my ancestors know how often I make mistakes, how often I'm wrong.* "Colonel Carabali. Please continue."

The Marine colonel nodded as if nothing untoward had happened and continued her briefing. Nothing fancy or elaborate. The fleet would cruise past several other Syndic installations on its way in-system, blowing each apart in turn, using hell-lance charged-particle cannon. But as the fleet got close to the fourth moon of the second gas giant, it would begin braking, and shuttles would launch, carrying a Marine strike force. With good timing of the maneuver, the shuttles would have less than half an hour of flight time before the Marines set down. "Even if the Syndics somehow figure out exactly why the Alliance fleet wants to occupy this facility, that hopefully won't leave enough time for them to organize an effective defense or damage the stockpiles we need," Carabali concluded.

"We'll use the scout battleship division for close support in case the Marines need it," Geary added. "*Exemplar* and *Braveheart* have proven their skills in that work." They were also the only two surviving scout battleships, but nobody brought that up.

He indicated the arcs of the courses the fleet would follow, each leg curving through part of Baldur Star System like sabers aimed at Syndic installations. "This will take more time than just heading straight for our objective. But we'll also slow to point zero five light speed to simplify the task of resupplying the fleet. You'll all receive the transit and resupply plan within the hour."

"We could do more damage if the fleet was divided into a few subformations," Captain Cresida of the battle cruiser *Furious* suggested. She had somehow remained silent through the debate but now couldn't resist arguing for more combat action if possible.

Geary nodded to acknowledge her point. Along with Tulev and Duellos, Cresida was one of his best ship commanders. "That's true. But I want to keep fuel cell usage to a minimum until we have those trace element stockpiles in our hands, and I don't want to break up squadrons and divisions to ensure everyone gets appropriate resupply."

"What about the Syndic warships?" Commander Neeson of the battle cruiser *Implacable* asked, not quite able to hide his disappointment at not being part of a fast-moving strike force this time around.

Captain Desjani pointed to the display. "They've broken up. Two of the corvettes are heading for one of the jump points out of Baldur that we might use and the remaining corvette and the light cruiser are heading for the other."

Captain Duellos nodded. "Picket ships. One corvette will probably jump from each when they reach it to report our presence here, while the others wait to report which jump point we actually used."

It wasn't at all hard to read the dissatisfaction around the table at that, but there simply wasn't any way for the fleet to engage any of those Syndic warships. Even though the corvettes were slower than any ship in the Alliance fleet except the four auxiliaries, they just had too great a lead. "We're going to do a significant amount of damage to Syndic facilities in this star system," Geary pointed out. "And once again the Syndics are going to provide the raw materials our auxiliaries need to keep us going."

He could easily sense the lack of enthusiasm. Even his closest allies weren't thrilled, but what was there to be thrilled about? Baldur was just a waypoint in a long journey home. After Baldur they'd have to fight their way through Wendaya, then another star system, then another, then another . . .

They'd thrown the Syndics off their tracks with the lunge back into Syndicate Worlds' space to hit Sancere, but how much longer could they keep the Syndics from correctly guessing their next destination and mustering overwhelming force there?

TWO

HELL-LANCE batteries hurled their charged-particle spears at the Syndic military base and minor dockyard that had orbited this outlying gas giant in the Baldur System for centuries. Most of the facilities seemed to have been mothballed, probably for decades, and not many Syndic personnel remained as caretakers to manage the few systems remaining operational. Right now those Syndic personnel were fleeing in-system in escape pods, while behind them both active and inactive parts of the base and dockyard were shredded by hell-lance fire at point-blank range.

Geary had decided to spread out among the fleet the fun of annihilating Syndic facilities on their way toward the mining site. In this case, he'd let the Eighth Battleship Division have the honors. *Relentless*, *Reprisal*, *Superb*, and *Splendid* swung past the Syndic base, their massive firepower ripping apart equipment, stockpiles of supplies and spare parts, and the dockyards, which might still have offered occasional support for those obsolete corvettes.

The next target would be the mining facility they

needed to capture intact. Given humanity's apparently unceasing drive to build and preserve things, Geary couldn't help ponder the irony that in human wars it always seemed far easier to destroy something than it was to try to take it in one piece.

"Enjoying yourself?"

Geary looked over from the display showing the battleships smashing the Syndic installation and saw that Victoria Rione had entered his stateroom unannounced. She could do that, since he'd set the room's security features to allow her access, a legacy of the days when she'd been sharing his bed. He had thought about changing the settings again, given Rione's distance, but had avoided the step.

Now he shrugged in response to her question. "It's necessary."

Rione gave him an enigmatic look and sat down opposite him, maintaining the distance she'd kept from Geary since Ilion. " 'Necessary' is a matter of choice, John Geary. There's no bright, clear line dividing what must be done from what we choose to do."

Somehow he thought Rione was referring to something unspoken. Damned if he could figure out what that was, though. "I'm aware of that."

"I think you usually are," Rione conceded, an unusual step for her. Then she studied him for a moment before speaking again. "Usually. The commanding officers of the ships belonging to the Callas Republic and the Rift Federation have spoken to me about your latest fleet conference."

Geary fought down a flash of irritation. "You don't need to keep reminding me that those ships will follow your recommendations since you're co-president of the Callas Republic."

"No," Rione replied sharply. "I don't imagine Black Jack enjoys challenges to his authority. I understand you faced some more of that and dealt with them severely."

"I need to maintain control of this fleet, Madam Co-

President! I could've reacted much more strongly than I did, and you know it."

Instead of hurling his anger back at him, Rione grimaced and sat back. "You could've. The important thing isn't that I know that; it's that you know it. You're thinking about the things you could do, the things you could get away with, as Black Jack. Isn't that so?"

Geary hesitated. He didn't want to admit that, but Rione was the only person he could possibly be open with about it. "Yes. Those options are occurring to me."

"They didn't used to, did they?"

"No."

"How long can you stop him, John Geary? Black Jack gets to do whatever he wants because he's a legendary hero. Because he's won dramatic victories in command of this fleet."

Geary glared at her. "If I don't win victories, this fleet dies."

She nodded. "And if you do, your legend grows. Your power grows. Every new victory carries a hazard, because it would be so much easier for Black Jack. He wouldn't have to convince others to do what he asks; he can just command them and punish those who disagree. He wouldn't have to worry about rules or honor. He could make his own."

Geary sank back as well, closing his eyes. "What do you suggest, Madam Co-President?"

"I don't know. I wish I did. I fear for you. None of us are as much in control of ourselves as we'd like to think we are." Geary's eyes flew open, and he stared at her, startled by the admission of weakness. Rione was looking away, her face bleak for a moment; then she gathered her composure around her like a warship reinforcing its shields and gazed back at Geary with a cool expression. "What will you do if the mining facility doesn't have the materials this fleet needs?"

Geary made an exasperated gesture. "Hit another one. We need that stuff. I hate being slowed down in this system, but we can't enter jump without restocking the auxiliaries. Even after all of the fuel cells manufactured to date are distributed, the fleet will still average only about seventy percent fuel cell reserves, and that's way too low for a fleet facing as long a journey home as we do."

"Is that all that's bothering you?"

"You mean besides you?" Geary asked bluntly.

She met his eyes steadily. "Yes."

He'd have better luck interrogating Syndic prisoners than he would getting anything out of Victoria Rione that she didn't want to reveal. For some reason, Geary felt his mouth curve in an ironic smile. "Yeah, there's more." He looked back at the other display he'd been studying when she came in.

"What?" Victoria Rione stood up, walking to sit beside him and lean in slightly to view the same display, her head near his, the soft scent of her conjuring up memories of being enfolded in her arms. It wasn't a distraction that he particularly welcomed when she had avoided further physical contact for weeks without explanation. Not that she owed him her body, but surely Rione owed him a reason. Except that neither he nor she had given any promises, so it wasn't like she had broken any. But it still felt like it to him.

Geary frowned, angry at himself and at her. "I'm worried about the condition of my ships."

She gave him a slow look. "You're actually upset more about the losses." Rione's tone was matter-of-fact. She, along with Captain Desjani and a few others, knew how little Geary was accustomed to the deaths of ships and their crews. A hundred years ago, the loss of a single ship had been a tragedy. In the bloodbaths that battles had degenerated into since then, a single ship was easily lost, only another name to be revived when a replacement ship was rushed into commission. But Geary's feelings still remained where they had been a century ago for these people, and only several months ago for him, thanks to the survival sleep that had kept him unchanged during that span of time.

"Of course I'm upset about the losses," Geary stated shortly, trying to rein in his temper.

"That's to your credit." Rione sat, her face turned toward the list of ships. "I still fear the day when Black Jack will be comfortable with such losses."

"Black Jack isn't running this fleet. I still am." Geary glared at her, unhappy that the subject had been raised again. "Black Jack isn't running me. I don't deny he tempts me. It'd be a lot easier to just believe I'm this godlike hero whose every action is justified because the living stars will it and our ancestors bless it. But that's total nonsense, and I know it."

"Good. Then you should also know that our losses would have been far more severe under another commander. Do you need to hear me say that? I haven't denied your skills at command since Sancere."

He hadn't realized it, but that was true. "Thanks. I wish that made a difference."

"It should, John Geary."

He shook his head. "Because it could've been worse? Fine. I can accept that intellectually, even if I can't emotionally. But that's not the point. We can't sustain these losses." Geary pointed at the readout of his ships and their status. "Look. Our battle cruisers that survived the Syndic ambush in their home system were reorganized into six divisions. Normally, a division should have six ships. These divisions were only four battle cruisers strong to begin with, and the Seventh Division only had three. Twenty-three battle cruisers survived after the ambush. Of those, we lost *Repulse* getting out of the Syndic home system."

Geary had to pause then. *Lost.* A short, simple word. The epitaph for a ship, her crew, and her commanding officer, a man older than Geary who had been Geary's grandnephew. He swallowed, knowing Rione was watching, then continued. "*Polaris* and *Vanguard* were lost at Vidha, and then *Invincible* and *Terrible* at Ilion. Five out of twenty-three, and we're still a long way from home. That's not counting significant damage sustained by the ships in Tulev's Second Battle Cruiser Division at Sancere, some of which still hasn't been repaired."

Rione nodded. "I see your concern. Especially where *Dauntless* is concerned. Getting the Syndic hypernet key this battle cruiser carries back to Alliance space is critical to the Alliance war effort." She paused. "How many people in this fleet now know that *Dauntless* carries the key?"

"I don't know. Probably too many." A supposed Syndic traitor had provided the key, a means for the Alliance fleet to launch a surprise attack on the Syndic home system and win the war in one stroke. Irresistible bait for the recklessly aggressive leaders of the Alliance fleet. The Syndics had known they'd take the bait and waited in ambush when the Alliance fleet arrived. *Disaster* was too kind a word, but at least this much of the fleet had escaped to survive this long, and the Syndics had to be terrified that their hypernet key was on one of the remaining Alliance ships. "I've wondered why the Syndics killed all the most senior officers in this fleet when they went to negotiate. It would have made more sense to keep a few alive to interrogate."

"They may have," Rione noted. "Video can be faked. I've no doubt most of those officers we saw being murdered actually did die, leaving you as the senior officer in the fleet, but I wouldn't be surprised to learn that at least one or two who had supposedly been killed were in fact kept alive for just that purpose."

Which would mean the Syndics might also know that *Dauntless* carried the key and needed to be destroyed by them at all costs. "It just keeps getting better," Geary mumbled sarcastically.

"Excuse me?"

"Nothing. Just talking to myself."

Rione gave him an annoyed look. "We're supposed to be talking to each other. The battle cruiser losses are worrisome as well as tragic. We've lost almost no battleships, though."

"Yeah." Geary stared at the names. "*Triumph* at Vidha, and *Arrogant* at Kaliban." Technically *Arrogant* had been one of three scout battleships with the fleet, something halfway between a heavy cruiser and a battleship, and it had taken some work for him to stop thinking of them as cruisers. Geary wondered what strange bureaucratic impulse had led to their design, since it left them too small to operate as battleships and too large to function as heavy cruisers. "But *Warrior*, *Orion*, and *Majestic* are beat to hell. Getting them back into shape for battle is going to take a long time. If we can do it at all. They may require major shipyard repairs." He didn't need to add that the closest major shipyards that could do the job were in Alliance space. The fleet needed every battleship it had to get home safely, but it likely couldn't get the badly damaged battleships back into full operating condition until they got home safely.

Another nod from Rione. "I understand *Warrior* took almost as much damage at Vidha as *Invincible* did. Wouldn't it be wiser to just abandon and destroy *Warrior*, as you did *Invincible*?"

Rione's spies in the fleet had obviously been keeping her informed. Geary gave another grimace. "*Warrior* didn't suffer the propulsion system damage that *Invincible* did, so *Warrior* can keep up with the fleet. I won't abandon *Warrior* lightly. I can't explain why, but it hurts morale more to scuttle a ship ourselves than it does to have that ship die in combat. Besides, I've been keeping an eye on their repair progress. *Warrior*'s crew is working their butts off to get their ship back in shape. At this point, if worse came to worst, I'd consider cannibalizing *Majestic* to help get *Warrior* and *Orion* back into shape. *Orion* is making some progress on repairs, but *Majestic* is dragging. Neither of them will be fighting in the line of battle for a while. I'll have to keep all three of those battleships with the auxiliaries, which won't do their pride any good."

"They have little ground for pride." Rione's voice had

gone low and hard. "Running from this fleet, then running and leaving their comrades at Vidha—"

"I know that," Geary broke in, his own voice rough with anger. "But I can't write off those ships and crews! I need to rebuild not only the ships but also the crews, and that means they need to believe in themselves, and that means their pride matters."

Rione sat silent, her face flushed.

"Sorry."

"I deserved it," she shot back, her anger seeming directed mostly at herself. "I'm a politician. I should understand the importance of what people believe." She took a long, deep breath, calming herself. "I'm not oblivious to the pain of losing ships as large as battle cruisers, or any ships at all, but you should take comfort that you're not losing battleships in equal numbers."

Geary shook his head. "No. If I keep losing battle cruisers, then the battleships will start taking more losses."

This time Rione looked puzzled. "Why?"

"Because the battle cruisers do certain jobs," Geary explained. "They have the firepower of battleships but can accelerate, maneuver, and decelerate like heavy cruisers. They *don't* have the shields or armor of battleships because they trade that off in favor of the ability to move faster. That makes battle cruisers very useful for certain tasks requiring speed as well as firepower. But if I lose enough battle cruisers, I'll have to use battleships for those tasks, and battleships are too sluggish. They'll get caught by Syndic battle cruisers, and even though one battleship can outfight one battle cruiser, it can't handle four or more backed up by lighter combatants. Or I can use heavy cruisers and have them take even heavier losses until they're all gone and I have to fall back on the battleships anyway."

Rione finally frowned in understanding. "Losses will accelerate if we're forced to use warships for tasks they're not designed for."

"Yeah." Geary gestured at the display. "And if the major combatants, the battleships and battle cruisers, hold back at all, then the light cruisers and destroyers will get torn to pieces. It all ties together. I can't get replacements for lost units, so I have to avoid being forced to expend what I've got." He stared at the names of the ships, his mind filled with an image of the remains of the *Terrible* after it collided with a Syndic battle cruiser at Ilion. Or rather, an image of the flash of light that was all that remained of both ships after they struck each other at a decent fraction of the speed of light. Not just a ship but its entire crew blown to hell in an instant's time. "Ancestors help me," he whispered.

Geary felt Rione's hand rest on his shoulder for a long moment, offering the comfort of a firm grasp, before it was withdrawn again. "I'm sorry."

"Victoria—"

"No." She stood up abruptly, her face averted from him. "Victoria isn't here. Co-President Rione offers her condolences and her support. I'm sorry, Captain Geary." She rushed out before he could say anything else.

"WHAT have you got?" Geary asked. He was gazing through a one-way screen at the interrogation room where the captain of the Syndic merchant ship they'd destroyed upon arrival in Baldur sat sweating with fear despite the slightly cool temperature of the compartment. Readouts and displays around the screen revealed everything about the Syndic's physical state and the thought patterns in his brain. If the Syndic lied, it would be immediately obvious on the brain scans, and just being able to confront someone with that often produced results.

The intelligence officer, Lieutenant Iger, made a face. "Not much. The Syndics don't tell their civilian population any details about military operations or losses."

"Kind of like the Alliance?" Geary suggested dryly.

"Well, yes, sir," the lieutenant admitted. "But worse,

actually, and the Syndics don't allow a free press or open discussion, so it's harder for their citizens to figure out what's actually going on. About all the merchant crew has been able to tell us is what they've been told in Syndic propaganda. Victory is certain, Syndic losses light, and this fleet was totally destroyed."

"He knows that last certainly isn't true," Geary observed. "Where did his ship come from?"

"Tikana. Another system bypassed by the hypernet. His ship did trade runs on the margins, working for a Syndic corporation that lives off the economic scraps bigger corporations don't bother with."

"Not a lot of good, recent news or observations, then?"

"No, sir." Lieutenant Iger gestured toward the figure of the Syndic merchant captain. "Scared to death, but he doesn't seem able to tell us anything despite that."

"I take it he hasn't heard any rumors about this fleet?"

"No, sir," the intelligence officer repeated. "He's showing truthfulness when denying hearing anything like that. When we prompt him with names of systems we've been in, like Corvus or Sancere, he showed some recognition of the star system name but nothing more."

Geary spent a moment wondering whether to actually speak with the Syndic, then decided he should. "I'll go on in. What's his name?"

"Reynad Ybarra, sir. His home world is Meddak."

"Thanks." Geary went through the three hatches leading into the interrogation compartment. Once inside, he saw the Syndic merchant captain staring at him. The Syndic seemed too frightened to move, but even if he had been inclined toward suicidal attacks, it wouldn't have mattered. The interrogation facility had enough stun weaponry aimed at the prisoner to knock him out before he took a full step toward Geary. "Greetings on behalf of the Alliance, Captain Ybarra," Geary stated formally.

The Syndic didn't move or say anything, just stared nervously at Geary.

"How's the war going?" Geary asked.

This time the Syndic paused, then began reciting something he had obviously heard often enough to commit to memory. "The forces of the Syndicate Worlds continue to go from victory to victory. Our triumph over the Alliance aggressors is ensured."

Geary sat down opposite the man. "Do you ever wonder why you haven't won the war yet if your forces have been going from victory to victory for the last century?" The Syndic swallowed but said nothing. "The Alliance wasn't the aggressor, you know. We were attacked without warning. I know because I was there." The Syndic's eyes widened with disbelief tinged with fear. "I'm sure you've been told that I'm Captain John Geary." The fear grew. "Would you like this war to end?" More fear. Not a topic the man was comfortable with. Doubtless even discussing it could get a Syndic citizen accused of treason.

How to get the man to say something? Geary fell back on an old standby. "Do you have a family still at Meddak?"

The Syndic hesitated, as if trying to decide if the question was safe to answer, then nodded.

"Are they okay?"

That finally got something. "My parents only. My sister died when Ikoni was bombarded," the Syndic choked out. "My brother died five years ago when his ship was destroyed in battle."

Geary grimaced. A brother and a sister dead in the war. An all-too-common circumstance in a war characterized by bloody battles and bombardments of civilians. "I'm sorry. May they rest in the arms of their ancestors." The Syndic gazed back in confusion at the courteous offer of sympathy. "I'm going to tell you something, and then we're probably going to let you and your crew go. I won't bother saying that what you've been told by your leaders is a lie, because the fact that you're on a ship that was supposedly destroyed should tell you that already. No, I want you to realize that we'd like to end this war, too. There's been too many deaths, which aren't accomplishing any-

thing. Your home is safe from the fleet I command. Go to
any system we've been in since we left the Syndic home
system, and you'll see that only military or military-
related targets have been destroyed. The Alliance will
keep fighting as long and as hard as we have to in order to
ensure the safety of our own homes, but we'll do so with
honor. Tell that to anyone you want."

Standing up, Geary left the Syndic staring after him.
Once back in the observation room, he found the lieutenant eyeing the readouts. "Anything?"

"He doesn't believe you," the lieutenant observed.

"No, I didn't expect him to. Do you think we can get
anything useful out of them?"

"No, sir."

"Then put them back in their escape pod and launch it
toward safety."

"Yes, sir." Lieutenant Iger hesitated. "Captain Geary,
the personnel who went over the escape pod reported that
it had a couple of serious system failures due to use of
cheap materials and what looks like poor quality control."

"You check for that?" Geary asked, impressed.

The lieutenant grinned. "Yes, sir. This ship was sort of
an economic bottom dweller, but even its physical condition can tell us something about the state of the Syndic
economy as a whole."

Geary nodded. "I don't recall anything about the Syndic military escape pods we've captured having those kind
of problems."

"No," the lieutenant agreed. "They give the military
first pick at everything and priority on everything. Only
the leadership gets higher priority when it wants things."

"I guess that shouldn't surprise me. Can we fix the broken systems on that merchant ship's escape pod?"

"Yes, sir, I think so."

"Then I want that done before the pod is relaunched,"
Geary directed. "They'll know they only made it safely
because of our help."

The intelligence officer saluted, showing off his skill

with the gesture of respect that Geary had reintroduced to the fleet. "Aye, aye, sir. But this merchant crew is only a single tiny drop in the Syndic ocean, so even if they feel grateful, it won't help us."

"Maybe not." Geary turned to go, then paused and looked back. "Then again, enough drops add up into waves. Maybe in time we can rock the Syndic leadership's boat a little. Besides, sometimes our ancestors like to see us doing things for others that we don't expect to benefit us, don't you think?"

GEARY sat on the bridge of the *Dauntless* again, watching the images of the Syndic mining facility as his fleet rushed toward it at point zero two light. They'd had to brake down the fleet's velocity even more to ensure the shuttles would be able to slow to landing speed without overshooting the assault targets. Next to the image of the mining facility, a virtual window revealed Colonel Carabali, her face sober. "The landing force is embarked and ready, sir."

"Thank you, Colonel." Geary took a good look at Carabali. "Do you want to go in with them?"

Carabali hesitated, clearly torn by the offer. "I should remain on a ship, coordinating the battle from the landing force control center, Captain Geary."

Strange, Geary thought. For fleet officers, gaining rank didn't do much to change the risk of combat. Even the highest admiral in a combat assignment would be facing the same risk from enemy fire as the lowest ranking sailor, because they rode the same ships into battle. But it was different for the Marines. When the landing forces went in, their overall commanders had to have the discipline to avoid diving into personal combat so they could oversee the entire battle. It was odd to realize that in the case of the Marine commanders not rushing into combat required more discipline and, in a way, courage than simply accompanying the landing force would need. Facing death could be easier than watching your troops die while you floated above it all.

But all he said was, "Very well, Colonel. Should I address your people before they go in?"

Carabali hesitated again, this time for a different reason. "They're about to launch, sir. Any distraction at this time might be unwise."

Geary almost laughed. A distraction. If only that were the worst problem he could cause. "All right, Colonel. Let me know immediately if you need anything. Otherwise I'll leave you alone now so you can run your battle."

"Thank you, sir," Carabali replied with a grin. She rendered a precise salute to him. The Marines had never abandoned saluting like the rest of the fleet had, naturally, and so hadn't had to relearn the gesture. "I'll notify you when we have the facility in hand, Captain Geary."

The colonel's image vanished, and Geary leaned back in his command seat with a sigh. There was a sense of helplessness at times like this. Ships had been committed to their courses and speeds, Marines prepared for their assault, and now all he could do was watch it happen and hope nothing went wrong. *Commander of a fleet, and I'm still subject to the laws of time and space. I knew a few commanders in my time who thought their rank allowed them to ignore those things, but I imagine those commanders died early on during the war. While I floated in survival sleep and the Alliance turned me into a mythical hero. I wonder which of us was luckier?*

"Nothing's leaving the mining facility," Captain Desjani noted.

Geary switched his attention back to the display and nodded. "No escape pods, and even that old tug is still just sitting there. Whoever's there is staying instead of evacuating."

"They probably fear we'll blow away anything trying to escape," Desjani suggested in a way that told Geary such practices had been common before he assumed command.

He refrained from asking what honor there was in shooting defenseless escape pods. Practices that Geary found abhorrent had become commonplace over a century of war, as the Syndics had committed increasingly worse atrocities and the Alliance had responded in kind. Over time a lot had been forgotten by the descendants of the officers and sailors whom Geary had known. Forgotten until the revered Black Jack Geary had awakened and reminded the present of the things the past had believed in. Desjani had been among the first to realize what had been lost in trying to match Syndic inhumanity, so there was no sense in making an issue of it with her again. Instead, Geary nodded once more. "Or maybe when we slowed down they figured out we were coming to take the place instead of just destroying it. But they can't hope to repel our attack."

"No," Desjani agreed. "But they might inflict losses; they might slow us down. Syndic leaders would be willing to trade the workers in a mining facility for that."

"Yeah." They'd already seen evidence of that in almost every system they'd passed through. The Syndics had risked entire surplus worlds for the chance to strike blows at the fleeing Alliance fleet. He studied the image of the facility again. "They've got maglev rails for moving ore."

Desjani nodded. "Taking them out from a distance would risk hitting the stockpiles."

"What are the odds the Syndics could turn them into weapons?"

She shrugged. "They could try. But we'll see them elevating the tracks to turn the maglevs into weapons aimed at our ships or the shuttles."

Geary nodded, checking to see that his two surviving scout battleships, *Exemplar* and *Braveheart*, were braking to slide into position right over the mining facility, matching their movements precisely to that of the facility so they could fire down at it from very close range using their hell lances. In theory, a small kinetic projectile could be aimed accurately enough from a long distance to take out

even a little target in a fixed orbit, but Geary wanted to
conserve his supply of what the Marines called "rocks."
Besides, in practice he adhered to the old theories that the
closer you were to the target, the better the odds of hitting
it square, and that there wasn't any sense in using too
much weapon for the target, so hell lances would work
fine.

He'd learned that the new theory, born of a century of
war, was to just use a large kinetic projectile and blow
apart not only the target but a substantial area around it,
which after all belonged to the enemy anyway, even if it
did include things like schools, hospitals, and homes.
Geary had no intention of ever succumbing to that logic.

Neither scout battleship was firing yet, since neither
had targets. But they'd be positioned close overhead when
the Marine shuttles came in to land.

"Launching assault force," a watch-stander reported.

A dozen shuttles separated from their ships, their
courses arcing down toward the mining facility.

"Why only a dozen?" Co-President Rione asked from
her seat behind Geary. "It's unlike Colonel Carabali not to
employ as much force as possible."

Did she mean to imply that Geary had limited Carabali's forces? He turned to look at Rione. "It's a small facility, Madam Co-President. There's not enough room to
land and employ a larger force."

Turning back, Geary saw Captain Desjani with a lowered brow in apparent annoyance at Rione's question. But
Desjani kept her voice even as she spoke. "Movement
around the maglevs."

Geary twisted back and focused on the magnetic-
levitation rail lines that were used to move ore, containers,
and other materials around the facility. The full-spectrum
and optical sensors on the Alliance ships were precise
enough to track small targets on the other side of a solar
system. This close to a target, they could easily count individual grains of dust if required. Human-sized targets
were exceptionally easy to see.

Sure enough, a group was clustered around one of the end rails, raising one end toward the shapes of *Braveheart* and *Exemplar* above. "Stupid," Geary couldn't help muttering.

Desjani nodded. "*Exemplar* is firing hell lances."

Fire control systems designed to get hits on targets moving at thousands of kilometers per second during firing opportunities measured in fractions of a second didn't have much trouble getting a perfect hit on a close target almost at rest relative to the ship. On the visual display, Geary couldn't see the charged particle beam that tore through the maglev segment, but he did see the results. The segment shattered, the workers around it being blown back by the force of fragments hurled at them, a neat hole punched in the surface of the moon where the hell lance had kept going, barely slowed by the minor obstacles it had hit.

Then another segment of the maglev line shattered, then another. Geary cursed and hit his communications controls. "*Exemplar*, *Braveheart*, this is Captain Geary. Fire only on identified threats."

"Sir, they're using those maglevs for weapons," *Exemplar* protested.

Before replying, Geary checked to ensure the bombardment had stopped. To his relief, it had. "They tried, and you did a great job taking them out. But our own engineers might need the rest of that line." He paused. "Good job. Excellent accuracy on your weapons."

"Thank you, sir. Understood. *Exemplar* will fire on threat activity."

Fair enough. Geary checked his fleet status for information on *Exemplar*'s commanding officer. Commander Vendig. Very good marks. Recommended for command of a battle cruiser. *Why not a battleship?* Geary frowned as he put together for the first time that every one of his best commanders was a battle cruiser captain. Conversely, many of his problem officers were battleship captains, including the most serious pains like Captains Faresa and Numos and new problems like Captain Casia. *I hadn't realized that, hadn't seen the pattern, and whatever it is may be obvious to officers in the current fleet. There weren't that many battleships in my time, and they were then seen as the command that every good officer aimed for. Something happened in the last century that seems to have changed that. I'd better find out what.*

The shuttles were approaching the mining facility now, swooping in like birds of prey heading for their targets, their engines firing hard to match velocity with the mining facility as fast as possible. Geary kept switching his gaze from the overall fleet display showing the entire light-seconds-wide span of the Alliance formation, to the close-in display showing the area around the mining facility, to the tactical view the Marines would use. Symbols representing enemy forces were popping up on the tactical display now, here and gone as individual defenders were spotted dodging among the mining equipment and facilities.

Geary tagged one of the threat symbols, and a frozen image flashed into existence along with helpful explanatory text. *Damn near idiot-proof,* Geary thought, admiring the simplicity of the system, then frowned as more windows popped into existence, multiplying too fast to follow their information as they provided exhaustive details on estimated enemy weaponry, endurance time, power usage and power systems, defensive armor, and dozens of other pieces of trivia that a fleet commander had no real need for. Somebody had set the default for all this junk to flood his display, though. *But then there's always plenty of idiots to figure out how to screw it up anyway.*

Geary cursed as he painstakingly closed window after window of meticulous data until he could actually view the image and a few essential pieces of information. He studied the picture, seeing a glimpse of someone in what appeared to be a survival suit, not battle armor. The text confirmed that, noting that the individual's appearance matched that of someone wearing an obsolete version of the standard Syndic survival suit. The weapon being carried by the defender was some sort of pulse rifle with too little power to seriously threaten Marines in battle armor, the text told Geary, and was probably intended for internal security. *Internal security? At that small a facility? Oh. They'd need people to keep the Syndic citizens on this installation in line. With those maglev rails it wouldn't be smart to let any rebels get their hands on a facility that could launch rocks at the inhabited planet in this system.*

He checked the other threat symbols and confirmed they were all the same. "No actual soldiers. Internal security forces and occupants of the mining facility handed weapons and sent out to fight. What the hell is the sense of that?"

Desjani frowned over the same image projected before her seat. "All they can hope to do is slow us down. Unless the Syndic commanders in this system are completely delusional, that has to be their intended mission."

Slow us down. Geary checked the tactical display again, wondering what ought to be there but wasn't. Then he realized. "They're not sabotaging anything. Why hasn't stuff been blown? We're not even seeing equipment shutdowns that would accompany wiping their operating systems."

"A trap?" Desjani wondered.

"It wouldn't be the first time." Geary tapped his screen for Colonel Carabali. "Colonel, this is looking like a trap."

Carabali nodded, looking harassed. "Yes, sir. It bears all the signs of that. My assault forces have been ordered to search for any and every thing that might blow up in our faces. There should be lots of small-scale demolitions on hand, but my experts say a mining facility like this shouldn't have the means to generate a huge explosion, especially not in the limited warning time they had to work with."

"That doesn't seem to be reassuring you, Colonel."

She gave Geary a quick, humorless smile. "No, sir. By

your leave, sir, I'd like to get back to overseeing the assault."

"By all means, Colonel. My apologies." Geary tried to relax, annoyed with himself for violating one of his own rules by bothering an officer who was trying to carry out the orders that Geary had given her.

"Admiral Bloch always kept the Marine commander on his screen," Desjani noted in a low voice. "The admiral liked to offer comments and suggestions, and of course wanted any questions answered right away."

"You're kidding."

Desjani shook her head.

Geary laughed shortly. "At least I'm not that bad."

"I just thought you should know that Colonel Carabali probably isn't all that upset with the way you deal with command, sir."

Of course, as far as Captain Desjani was concerned, Geary could do no wrong. But he still shuddered at the idea of working for a commander who kept him on-screen during an operation, demanding attention that was needed for the battle.

Speaking of which, the shuttles were sliding into landings, bay doors opening and Marines in battle armor tumbling out as the shuttles kept moving so that the ground troops were spread out instead of being clumped together into a mass target. Twelve shuttles deposited twelve lines of Marines, then accelerated upward again. "Nice job on the delivery," Geary observed. "Were the flight paths automated?"

Desjani frowned, gestured to a watch-stander, then waited for the reply. "No, sir. The shuttle pilots prefer to use personal control. The Marines have a deal with them. As long as the shuttle pilots do a good job, the Marines let them fly their birds."

"That's a reasonable arrangement. And if any pilot screws up, then the Marines require them to use automated controls on the next drop?"

"Uh, yes, sir," the watch-stander confirmed. "After any

Marines who survived the failed drop catch the pilot and beat the hell out of him or her. Not that they've ever been caught doing that, sir."

"Of course not," Geary agreed, suppressing a smile. The lines of Marines were moving into the mining facility, dodging from cover to cover, moving in sections to provide covering fire for each other.

Not that the precautions seemed needed. Geary watched the display with growing uneasiness as clusters of enemy symbols fell back faster than the Marines were advancing. Leading elements of the defenders were already vanishing into some of the mine shafts littering the surface of the moon. "What the hell?"

A moment later, Colonel Carabali called him. "Captain Geary, the defenders aren't really trying to hold. They're falling back fast into some of the mine shafts."

"I just noticed that. Any guesses as to why they're not fighting?"

"Sir, I'd guess they want to evacuate the installation before something happens. We'd already speculated that this looked like a trap."

The defenders are getting out of a blast zone? "What do you recommend, Colonel?"

"Sir, as much as I hate to do so, I think we need to pull back until we scan this rock atom by atom and find out what the Syndics have planted."

Geary hesitated. How could they delay as long as that would require? And it would mean slowing down the main fleet even more, costing more fuel reserves. But he couldn't send Marines farther into what was increasingly looking like a death trap. "Colonel—"

A sharp voice sounded behind Geary. "It's a bluff." He turned to see Co-President Rione leaning forward in her observer's seat, her expression demanding. "Don't any of you gamble? The Syndics have created a situation that looks like a trap. Yet they haven't actually demonstrated any ability to blow up the entire facility, and in fact have left it intact behind them. If we run, they've saved their mining facility and we haven't gotten whatever we wanted. If we slow down and take our time, it causes further delay in this star system. Either way, the Syndics come out ahead."

Colonel Carabali appeared uncertain. "Co-President Rione's assessment does sound logical, but—"

"Colonel," Rione demanded, "do the Syndics routinely display high regard for the well-being of low-level personnel such as these miners?"

"No, Madam Co-President. They don't."

"Then why were the mine workers not ordered to die delaying your actual occupation of the facility, thereby also drawing more Marines into the supposed trap? Why were they withdrawn into the mine shafts where they cannot hinder us and in fact are now sitting ducks if we choose to fire weapons down into the shafts?"

Captain Desjani spoke in carefully controlled tones. "With all due respect, you're not down there with the Marines, Madam Co-President."

Rione's eyes narrowed as she gazed at Desjani. "Lest you think I'm making this call lightly, I'll point out that some of the Marines participating in this assault are from the Callas Republic. I would not place them in extra peril if I believed it existed."

Carabali frowned. So did Desjani. Both looked at Geary. *Yeah, okay, Rione believes in what she's saying, but can I go with her belief? She's not military, after all. She's also not in command, which is why everybody is looking at me. It's my call. I want to believe that Rione is right because if she is, it will make things happen the way I want them to. Am I too eager to believe she's right because of that? What if she's wrong? What if this isn't a bluff?*

We lose a bunch of Marines and everything we came to this facility for.

But why would the Syndics suddenly display such high regard for the welfare of low-level workers and then order them into a hopeless position?

*I have to make this decision. If I'm wrong, I could see
a lot of Marines die. Or if I'm wrong the other way, I
could see this fleet needlessly delayed even further while
the Syndics gather forces in surrounding star systems.*

Ancestors, please give me a sign.

If they did, Geary couldn't see or feel it. He glanced at
Desjani and saw her utter confidence that he would reach
the right decision. Whatever that was. Rione was eyeing
Geary, her expression stern, almost challenging him to believe her. Colonel Carabali simply waited, her feelings unreadable behind a professionally emotionless mask. The
longer Geary waited, the more likely the decision would
be taken out of his hands by developing events. He had a
duty to those Marines, a responsibility to make a call, to
make it clear who was accountable if the worst happened.
Odd, it was usually Rione warning him about the worst
that could happen . . .

That *was* usually the case. Rione the politician never
liked having any part of the fleet running risks. Yet here
she was urging a course of action that had his Marine
commander and one of Geary's hardest-charging ship captains recommending caution. Either Rione had gone
crazy, or his ancestors had sent a sign. Through her.

Geary breathed a quick prayer. "I think Co-President
Rione is right. Keep the Marines in there and occupy the
entire facility."

Carabali, her face rigid, saluted. "Yes, sir." Her screen
blanked as she passed on the orders.

Geary looked down, hoping he hadn't let a sense of urgency override his own common sense. When he looked
up, the tactical display showed Marines swarming deeper
into the installation, segment after segment of the Syndic
facility glowing green to show it had been cleared and occupied.

Nothing had blown up yet.

He gave in to temptation and called up a view from one
of the Marine junior officers. Now he had a window floating before him showing the view from that officer's hel-

met. This part of the facility was open to the surface, so
the Marines were moving through an area with no atmosphere. An occasional light illuminated part of the equipment the Marines were moving past, the sharp-edged
beams centered on whatever needed to be lit, since the
light didn't spread at all without any air to do the job. The
shadows were just as sharp-edged and as black as the lit
areas were bright.

There was always something spooky about abandoned
places, a sense that the former occupants hadn't really left
and were somewhere just out of sight, watching these in-
truders come into their world. Because so little changed in
abandoned facilities on airless worlds, a place deserted
moments before could feel just as haunted as one left
empty centuries ago. Had someone else walked here an
hour ago, or yesterday, or a hundred years in the past?
Even though he'd seen the defenders moving through
these areas a short time before, the mining facility felt
like that, empty and silent on the outside, even though inside the buried buildings equipment still functioned.

An airtight hatch loomed before the Marine officer.
Geary watched as two enlisted Marines attached physical
taps to the air lock locking mechanism and overrode the
coded entry system. Weapons leveled at the hatch as it
began to swing open, one Marine near the hatch tossing a
small object in through the growing gap and then huddling
back as the magnetic pulse charge detonated inside the
lock to fry the circuits on nearby weapons, enemy survival
suits, and detonators for booby traps.

Then the Marines were inside, moving through empty
passageways, kicking in or blowing open doors, searching
for anything out of place, anything that even looked like a
bomb.

Geary rapped his forehead in exasperation as he realized he'd forgotten something that could really help, then
slapped his communications circuit. "Captain Tyrosian.
Your ships are now being given access to the views from
the Marine landing force occupying the mining facility. I

assume the engineers on the auxiliaries know the sort of
equipment we're dealing with and will be able to identify
anything that doesn't belong. Get some of them watching
the Marines as fast as possible."

Tyrosian's reply took a bit longer than it should since
the auxiliaries were now in the center of the Alliance formation. "Sir," she replied hesitantly, "my personnel don't
usually play any direct role in operations."

Fighting down an urge to yell, Geary spoke firmly.
"They are this time. I want qualified people observing
those feeds as quickly as you can get them on there, and I
want to know immediately if they see anything they regard as suspicious."

Before Tyrosian's reply could come in, Geary saw another window pop up with Colonel Carabali in it. "Someone's sending my assault force's feeds to the engineers on
the auxiliaries," she reported, frowning.

"That someone is me, Colonel."

"I must protest, sir. They're noncombatant support personnel without a need for direct real-time access to my assault force."

Geary tried not to let aggravation show. "They won't
do any harm."

"With all due respect, sir," Carabali stated stiffly, "engineers are capable of wreaking total havoc in the real
world if not closely supervised, and I do not have the luxury of the time to be able to so supervise them."

On the heels of Carabali's words, Captain Tyrosian's
reply came in on her window. "Captain Geary, we don't
have a list of specifications as to what we're supposed to
look for."

His earlier tension replaced by a growing headache,
Geary spoke through gritted teeth. "Wait, Colonel. Captain, your engineers are supposed to look for anything that
shouldn't be in a mining facility." Tyrosian nodded, but
her eyes remained puzzled. "Bombs. Booby traps. Things
that will blow up."

Tyrosian's puzzlement increased. "A lot of equipment will suffer catastrophic failure if improperly—"

"Captain Geary," Colonel Carabali declared, both her face and voice rigid with disapproval, "I advise against this in the strongest possible—"

"My people need to talk directly to the Marine officers in the facility about what they're seeing," Tyrosian suggested hesitantly. "Without detailed guidance—"

"All right!" Geary interrupted both of them. *Bad idea. I can tell them to just go ahead and do it, or just cancel the whole thing. I'm mad enough to say, "Just do it," which tells me I probably shouldn't. Serves me right for trying to improvise something between two such different mind-sets.* "Cancel my previous direction. The feed from the assault force will be available to the engineers but on a receive-only basis. If they see anything they regard as *suspicious*, you are to contact *me* without delay, Captain Tyrosian. Colonel Carabali, please continue your assault, and my apologies for the distraction."

Both officers looked startled by Geary's orders, as if they'd expected a different outcome; then Carabali saluted hastily just before her window blanked out again. Tyrosian nodded. "Yes, sir. The, uh, shuttles with the engineering exploitation team and equipment have launched."

"Good. Make sure everyone on those shuttles understands that they are under the control of the Marine assault force commander."

Geary slumped back as the other comm window closed, rubbing his forehead to help with what was now a raging headache. Desjani, who couldn't have heard Geary's private communications with the other officers, gave him a sympathetic look. "Engineers?"

"And Marines," Geary replied sourly. "Why does it sometimes seem I have to spend more time fighting my own officers than I do fighting the enemy?" His gaze went back to the display showing the assault on the mining facility. The Marines continued to penetrate the objective, occupying almost the entire facility now and posting forces to guard the mine shafts where the Syndic defenders had withdrawn. Arcing down from above came the shuttles carrying the engineering exploitation teams, preparing to drop their skilled personnel directly onto the facility's main landing pad.

If something was going to explode, it would probably happen any moment now.

THREE

ALLIANCE Marines entered the main control room of the mining facility, spreading out, using portable gear to check for booby traps. Green lights shone on the many panels in the room, indicating the mining equipment was in full operating condition. The Marine officer who Geary was monitoring stepped close to one panel with multiple red lights blinking. "Maglev rails," the Marine reported to his superiors, Geary hearing the transmission, too. "That's the only equipment showing failures. Everything else is up and running." Instead of sounding happy about that, the Marine seemed worried.

A window popped up in front of Geary, showing Captain Tyrosian frowning. "They didn't shut down their equipment."

"No," Geary agreed.

"This is going to cause a lot of delays," Tyrosian complained.

"I would have thought powering up the equipment would have taken a while."

Tyrosian seemed surprised at the question. "Well . . .

yes. If the equipment had been shut down, then we'd have to power up slowly to make certain none of the equipment had been sabotaged mechanically or in its software. You know, worms and such embedded in the operating systems. But it's *already* operating, sir."

Meaning any worms or other destructive programming were also running. Never trust gifts from Syndics. "I see."

Colonel Carabali's face reappeared, frowning in tandem with Tyrosian. "Sir, we're going to have to do a controlled shutdown of everything, do a clean sweep of all systems, then bring them back up one by one."

Geary exhaled heavily, wondering why this had to be the one thing both his Marines and his engineers agreed upon. "What's the worst case if we try to operate the systems now?"

"Catastrophic failure of all systems, destructive shutdowns of equipment, fatal damage to the operating environment, individual injuries and fatalities, and loss of all mining facility capabilities," Tyrosian replied.

"Everything blows up," the Marine colonel noted succinctly.

Geary nodded. *Okay. Bad things happen.* "How long to do what we need to do?"

"Estimates will vary widely because of the many factors involved—" Tyrosian began.

"This fleet cannot linger around this mining facility, Captain Tyrosian!" Geary snapped.

"How much of this stuff do we need?" Carabali asked. "To access the stockpiles of elements we require and get the rocks analyzed and loaded?"

Tyrosian made an angry gesture. "You need the mining subsystems. You have to have the main operating systems to issue commands to the mining subsystems. If the safety systems aren't activated and monitoring activity on the main operating systems and the mining subsystems, then the safety interlocks won't allow anything to happen."

"Damn near everything, then," Geary noted.

Tyrosian nodded.

"We can't—" He paused as a high-priority message alert blinked, indicating someone wanted to join in his conference with Carabali and the engineer. He took a look at the message alert, seeing the communication was from *Titan*. Messages from *Titan* tended to be bad news. Frustrated by the delays, Geary almost slapped the Deny command. *I don't need anyone else complicating things. Hell, how much more complicated can they get? What I need is better options, and maybe whoever this is will have some ideas.* Geary paused, counted to five, and tapped Accept instead.

Commander Lommand's face appeared. Captain of the *Titan*. Young for his position, but Geary had already learned that Lommand tended to make up for lack of experience with initiative and enthusiasm. Now Lommand appeared slightly regretful. "My apologies for breaking in, Captain Geary, but I was told Captain Tyrosian was tied up in this meeting with you, and I thought she'd want to know immediately that the two Mobile Mining Units on *Titan* are loaded on heavy-lift shuttles and ready to launch."

Geary glanced at Tyrosian, who was unsuccessfully trying to look as if she weren't surprised to hear the news. "Mobile Mining Units?" Geary asked. "Can those help?"

"They can if the equipment at the Syndic mining facilities can't be used," Lommand stated innocently. "It seemed a good idea to have them ready in case that happened."

"Yes," Tyrosian interjected just as if she had ordered Lommand to do that. "There's a risk in deploying them, because the two on *Titan* are all we have left in the fleet, but the MMUs can locate, analyze, and load the Syndic stockpiles of the trace elements we need."

"What's the flight time?" Geary demanded, scanning his controls for the right ones to give him the information.

Commander Lommand answered immediately. "Thirty-one minutes if we launch now."

Colonel Carabali was checking something herself. "We

can't risk having critical equipment down here while the Syndic systems are still operating and capable of executing some Trojan horse action. Carrying out a safe shutdown of the Syndic gear will take approximately ... twenty minutes."

Geary nodded. "What about everything else needed to use the Syndic gear? Should we employ these, uh, MMUs instead?"

"Sir, it'd take at least a couple of hours to go through the Syndic systems and scrub them clean, then maybe another half a day or more to bring them up in a controlled fashion—"

"How quickly can the MMUs start operating once they're on the surface?" Geary asked the engineers.

"Immediately, sir," Commander Lommand responded. "Start-up is carried out on board the shuttles. Once the shuttles land, the Moo-Moos roll off the ramp and start grazing."

Nice. One more little thing that Geary had to depend upon hearing about from his subordinates. Fortunately, one of those subordinates was Commander Lommand. Geary was about to order Lommand to launch his shuttles from *Titan* when he caught himself and faced Captain Tyrosian, Lommand's immediate superior. Commander Lommand had jumped the chain of command again, but this time at least he'd done it in a way that looked legitimate by pretending he was updating Tyrosian. "Captain Tyrosian, have *Titan* launch those shuttles, and get them to that facility. I want them working when they hit the surface. Commander Lommand, thank you for the status update. Colonel Carabali, have your system geeks shut down everything the Syndics left working. I want it all off when *Titan*'s shuttles get there."

"Yes, sir," Carabali replied, smiling thinly. "Do you want us to proceed with scrubbing the systems for sabotage?"

"Not unless it's needed for the safety of your troops. I don't intend powering up those systems while we're there, and as soon as we leave, we're going to flatten every piece of equipment in the facility."

Carabali's smile widened. "Yes, sir."

As the Marine's image vanished, Captain Tyrosian gave Geary a confident look, as if this was a plan she'd developed. "I've ordered *Titan* to launch her shuttles, sir."

"Thank you." At least Tyrosian had thought on her feet and reacted properly when Lommand broke into the conference. "Good work. Let's get those rocks and get out of here."

The windows vanished, leaving just the system display floating in front of Geary. He watched the symbols marking his fleet racing past the moon holding the Syndic mining facility, looping around the gas giant to come past the moon again, then ran some quick calculations to see if he would have to slow the fleet even more due to the delays on the surface.

It looked okay at this point. Not great, and with way too small a margin of error left, but if the mobile mining gear could do the job quickly, he wouldn't have to burn off further fuel cells braking the fleet's velocity more.

Geary leaned back, noticing Captain Desjani trying not to look curious. "The Syndics left the equipment running at the mining facility," he explained to her.

"Bastards," Desjani replied with a frown. "They knew we'd have to assume it was laced with soft and hard booby traps."

"Yeah. But *Titan* has a couple of portable mining things they're sending down to take care of getting the stockpiles." Geary looked back to include Rione in the conversation. "The Marines are shutting down the Syndic gear."

Rione shook her head. "Odds are the Syndics didn't have time to plant elaborate booby traps in the systems, but we have no choice but to act as if they did."

"They've laid traps everywhere we've encountered Syndics." Geary watched the shuttles from *Titan* arcing down toward the moon, wishing the enemy was a little less devious and his own fleet's situation a lot less perilous.

THE voice of the chief petty officer supervising *Titan*'s Mobile Mining Units seemed startled and awed when he heard Geary. "Sir. It's an honor to speak with you, sir."

Geary tried not to let his unhappiness at the hero worship show in his voice. The sailors in the fleet were more likely than the officers to believe that Geary had been sent by the living stars themselves to save the Alliance, and this fleet in particular. They were also more likely to believe that Geary really was the mythical hero of the past. But he owed them respect for their faith even as he tried his best not to believe in it himself. "Do you have a moment, Chief? To talk about your gear?" Nothing was happening elsewhere, but Geary felt that he had to stay on the bridge until this mess was over, and anyway Geary was curious about the MMUs.

The view from the chief's helmet showed one side of the Syndic facility. Big doors giving access to stockpiles of mined and refined minerals had been blown off their hinges by Marines happy to get a head start on wrecking the Syndic installation. The hulking shapes of the two MMUs had crawled on treads across the surface of the moon, crushing or shouldering aside some Syndic safety barriers, and now crouched in front of the accesses.

"Yes, sir," the chief replied. "The crews on the Moo-Moos are operating their own cows, and I'm just here if needed."

Cows. The nickname made as much sense as any other for a piece of equipment with the official designation of MMU. "I'm not familiar with your gear, Chief. What can you tell me about it?" He'd already tried looking up information in the online library on *Dauntless*, only to be submerged by a huge mass of documents, none of which seemed to have a single simple, clear diagram or discussion about the capabilities of the MMUs. After unsuccessfully trying to wade through a mass of complex data, Geary had decided to follow his training as a junior officer; when you needed to know something, ask a chief petty officer.

This particular chief sounded disbelieving that the great Black Jack Geary would really need to be told anything. "The technology hasn't changed much since . . . uh . . . since . . ."

"In the last century?" Geary asked dryly. "I didn't know much about it then, Chief. No need arose in those days for me to worry about it."

"Oh, uh, yes, sir. Well, like I said, the tech hasn't changed much. It's simple and robust. Everything that's been tried as a replacement is more complicated, more expensive, breaks more and, uh, you know."

"I certainly do, Chief," Geary agreed, recalling many of the "improvements" to ship systems that had bedeviled him a hundred years ago by creating new problems with equipment that had worked perfectly well before being upgraded into temperamental, buggy pieces of junk. "I'm glad they've let you stick with something that works well. What are your cows doing now? Waiting for clearance to enter the facility?"

"No, sir! They won't have to go any farther in. The cows are sending in worms, sir. Once the worms—"

"Worms?"

"Uh, yes, sir." The view from the chief's helmet changed, focusing on the front of one of the Moo-Moos and zooming in. What looked like a nest of very fine wires extended out, the wires leading into the storage buildings. "Do you see the leashes, sir? Every one connects to a worm. We call them that because they're about the size of worms and work the same way. They eat dirt. Or rock."

"How do they get through rock?" Geary asked.

"What amounts to really tiny shock cannon mounted around the front mouth. The worm analyzes the rock structure and sends out vibration pulses that shatter the rock right in front of it. Of course, in this case this stuff

has already been mined, so they're going through stocks
of solid metal. The worms eat the dust and move on, constantly doing the same thing. As the dust runs through the
inside of the worms, molecular-level sensors analyze the
content. Then it goes out the back. Just like a worm, like
I said, sir."

"What are the wires for?"

"Command and control, and power. A mining worm
has to move a lot faster than a real worm and keep doing
it, so they need a lot more energy than a real worm-sized
object could hold. And we don't want stray radiation
being emitted in a mining environment—you know, because of explosive gases and detonators and stuff—or
have our links to the worms blocked by metals or other
stuff, so all the communications to and from the worm run
through the line." The chief's view pivoted and focused on
where the lines ran into the building. "In a normal mining
operation the worms go out, dig in below the surface, and
find the ore or veins of material you need. In this case, we
know where the stockpiles are, so right now the worms are
tunneling through the stockpiles, identifying what's in
each one, and looking for contamination or nano-bugs."

Nano-bugs. Geary knew that much. Tiny devices planted
to cause problems in equipment once triggered by heat or
pressure. "I thought nano-bugs were outlawed since they
were so hard to keep contained."

He could see the motion caused by the chief's shrug.
"Yes, sir. But there's a lot of stuff that's been outlawed, if
you know what I mean, sir."

"Yeah, Chief, I do." Outlawed didn't mean it wouldn't
be used. Not in the case of the Syndics, and not in the case
of the Alliance either, as Geary had been shocked to learn.
Century-long wars too easily bred contempt for life and
law. "Any problems identified so far?"

"No, sir. We're giving the worms time to do a decent
sample check, then we'll send in the moles."

"Moles?"

"Yes, sir. The moles actually go out and dig down to

the stuff, load it on board, then bring it back to the cow. The cows have big moles and little moles, depending on how much you want to recover. And we can hook up a monster mole to a cow if we have to, but *Titan*'s only got one monster mole. It just digs a big hole and feeds the stuff back through a conveyor tube on its ass." The chief went silent for a moment, then spoke in a slightly choked voice. "Excuse me, sir, the material is expelled through the aft matter-expulsion portal."

"I get the idea, Chief." Geary paused to consider the information, watching as shapes scuttled away from the cows and into the Syndic storage area, each shape trailing its own wire. "Everything looks good, then?"

"Yes, sir. That's a mix of big and little moles because we've got orders to get this stuff loaded and the cows back on the shuttles as fast as possible."

"Right. Thanks, Chief. I appreciate the rundown." Geary broke the link, blinking to focus his own eyes back on the display showing his fleet. So far, so good, which was the first time in a while he felt like saying that.

Desjani yawned. "Excuse me, sir."

"I feel the same way. At least I got to learn about the cows the engineers are using."

"Cows?" Desjani gave Geary a skeptical look.

"Yeah. Cows with worms and moles."

She grinned. "Are you sure you weren't talking to the cooks about what the fleet is feeding us?"

Food. How long had he been on the bridge, anyway? Geary's stomach rumbled.

Desjani smiled again, dug in one pocket, and offered him a ration bar. "I always carry a few."

"Thanks. Remind me to say something about your ability to plan ahead when I write your next evaluation." Geary took the ration bar, debated whether he should read the label or just guess what it contained, then decided he'd rather not know. That was something else that hadn't changed in a century. In a misguided attempt to satisfy individual tastes and reflect the diversity of the Alliance

member worlds, the ration bars were allegedly formulated
to fit the widely varying cuisines of many planets and re-
gions. Instead, the flavors the fleet came up with somehow managed to revolt everyone, regardless of place of
origin.

He opened the wrapper, took a bite, shuddered, then finally glanced at the label. "Forshukyen Solos? What the
hell is that?" Geary checked the fine print. " 'A favorite
meal on the worlds of the Hokaiden Star System.' I bet."

"Try to avoid the Danaka Yoruk bars," Desjani advised.

"They still make those? When they came out, we
wanted them to be traded to the Syndics, but—" *But we
were afraid the Syndics would start a war if we did. That
joke was a lot funnier before the Syndics* did *start a war.*

Desjani had the sense not to ask about the way Geary
had broken off his sentence. "I think they stopped making
those bars a long time ago but are still trying to get rid of
the ones they made." She laughed, the lines worn by years
of war easing and her face looking younger than usual.

Geary grinned back at her, grateful that even with
someone who thought him a mythical hero he could com-
plain about the fleet's food. The familiar banter made him
feel less out of place, offering a connection to the people
and places he'd once known.

The trace elements his auxiliaries needed were rapidly
flowing into *Titan*'s cows. Geary studied the movement of
his fleet, feeling a headache rising again as he saw how
close the timeline was now. Even the smallest delay would
require him to waste time and fuel cells in a braking maneuver.

As if on cue, an alert pulsed on his display tracking the
situation on the moon's surface. Even as Geary was focusing on it, Colonel Carabali's face appeared again. "The
Syndics in the mine shafts are trying to come out. They're
exchanging fire with the Marines guarding the exits from
the shafts."

The last thing he needed was a ground engagement.
Maybe the Syndics had figured that out and were willing

to expend some of their people just to slow the Alliance fleet down a little more. Geary took a deep breath, leaning back to think, and his eyes came to rest on the fleet display. *Oh, hell. For once this is easy.* "Colonel Carabali, prepare to pull your Marines back toward the shuttles. Make sure *Titan*'s cows remain covered until they're loaded and their shuttles take off."

The Marine colonel frowned slightly. "Cows, sir?"

"The Moo-Moos." That sounded ridiculous. "The Mobile Mining Units."

"Oh. Yes, sir. Sir, the moment we start pulling my Marines back, the Syndics are going to come out of those holes."

"I don't think so, Colonel. Not with *Exemplar* and *Braveheart* throwing hell lances at them. How big a no-fire zone do you need to be comfortable with those ships firing near your Marines?"

Carabali's frown deepened. "With all due respect, sir, we prefer to be as far away as possible when the fleet is bombarding an area."

Understandable, perhaps, but not too helpful. Geary looked over at Desjani. "How accurate should hell-lance fire from *Exemplar* and *Braveheart* be if they start shooting at the Syndics on the surface again? The Marines are worried."

Desjani snorted. "With those two ships that close to the targets and at a dead stop relative to them? It'd be impossible under those circumstances for a hell lance to miss a target by any meaningful margin of error, by which I mean something measured in less than a centimeter. Those Marines could be ten meters away from an aim point and be perfectly safe."

Geary didn't think he'd personally be willing to stand ten meters from a hell-lance aim point but didn't say so aloud. "Colonel, how about two hundred meters for a no-fire zone between your Marines and the bombardment from the ships?"

"Could you make it three hundred, sir?"

*Oh, for—Then again, I did order the Marines into the
facility in the face of the possibility it was a trap. I owe
them one.* "All right. Three hundred. Once your closest
Marine is three hundred meters away from the mine shafts
occupied by the Syndics, *Exemplar* and *Braveheart* will
open fire on any Syndics trying to leave the shafts."

The Marine's face brightened. "Could you make it a
rolling barrage, sir? As my people pull back, the ships can
walk their bombardment through the facility behind them,
getting a head start on demolishing it and discouraging
pursuit."

"Excellent suggestion, Colonel. I'll pass those orders
on to *Exemplar* and *Braveheart*." Another message popped
up. "The cows have picked up everything we need and are
on the way to their shuttles."

"I'll prepare my Marines to fall back toward them."
Carabali's image saluted and vanished.

Geary called up the two scout battleships, ensured they
understood their orders, and added a requirement to ensure the facility was wrecked except for one small set of
rooms and their associated life support. Life wouldn't be
easy for the Syndics left behind until the inhabited world
in this system sent ships to lift them off, but since they
could easily have been slaughtered to the last individual
by the Alliance ships, Geary didn't think they had any
grounds for complaints.

Things were finally happening again, though at a seem-
ingly glacial pace as the symbols marking Marines and
the cows fell back toward their respective shuttles. Used
to dealing with velocities measured in tenths of the speed
of light, Geary found himself amazed at how long it took
something on the surface to go a few hundred meters.

It took the Syndics a very short while to figure out that
the Marines were withdrawing; then scattered figures
began pouring out of the exits from the mine shafts. But
the nearest Alliance Marines were still within three hundred meters. Geary crossed his fingers, but both scout bat-

tleships held their fire as the Syndics moved in pursuit of the slowly withdrawing Marines.

At this rate the Marines would never get three hundred meters from the enemy.

But maybe that wouldn't matter. *Exemplar* and then *Braveheart* opened fire, their hell lances dancing across the area near the mine shaft exits, the charged-particle spears slashing through metal, rock, and human bodies. Geary stared as symbols marking Syndics simply vanished in quick succession as hell lances scored direct hits on the individual enemies and vaporized them as well as everything else in the immediate area.

The Syndics closest to the Marines were still within three hundred meters, but their movement halted as they saw the havoc being wreaked behind them. A natural reaction, and exactly the wrong one. The Marines kept withdrawing, the nearest enemies fell outside the three hundred meter no-fire zone, and the hell lances blew the Syndic defenders to atoms.

No more enemy shapes could be seen on the surface by the fleet's sensors. It was possible a few members of the Syndic pursuit force had survived, hidden under the wreckage of the facility as *Exemplar* and *Braveheart* enthusiastically pounded it into scrap. But it didn't matter, since nothing moved in the firing zone now but structures collapsing and debris flying away from the sites of hits.

Safely separated from the devastation, the shuttles carrying the cows lifted from the surface. Around them, the last Marines were falling back by sections into their own shuttles. As Geary watched, the Marine shuttles leaped into space behind the heavy-lift shuttles loaded with the cows, escorting the trace elements needed back to *Titan*, from which they could be distributed to the other auxiliaries.

Another two minutes and Geary would have had to slow the fleet down to allow the shuttles to catch up. But the shuttles could still manage an intercept now.

He let out a long breath. One more crisis surmounted. *I wonder what the next one will be.*

• • •

"**CONGRATULATIONS** to everyone who helped make the last operation a success." Geary nodded toward Colonel Carabali, Captain Tyrosian, and Commander Lommand, and the commanding officers of *Exemplar* and *Braveheart*. "Captain Tyrosian informs me that the necessary trace elements are being distributed among the four auxiliaries as we speak. Expendable weapons and fuel cells the auxiliaries have already manufactured have been delivered to warships. As soon as the final deliveries have been made and the shuttles recovered, we'll head for the jump point out of Baldur."

Not everyone seemed to share Geary's sentiments about Tyrosian and Lommand. Captain Casia from *Conqueror* and Commander Yin from *Orion* smiled approvingly at the commanding officers of the scout battleships but bent lowered brows toward the two engineering officers. Geary took a moment to scan down the very long virtual table, trying to gauge how many other commanding officers were following the lead of Casia and Yin. There didn't seem to be many, but it wasn't easy to tell, and Geary suspected his most dangerous opponents within the fleet wouldn't be as obvious about their hostility as Casia and Yin.

Still, it was both aggravating and important to know that those who disapproved of Geary's command of the fleet were trying to use the engineers as a wedge issue with the other ship commanders.

"Captain Geary," a new voice spoke up. It took Geary a moment to realize who it was, aided by the meeting software, which helpfully highlighted a name not far down the table. Captain Badaya of the *Illustrious*. He was also commander of what was left of the Sixth Battle Cruiser Division, which now consisted only of *Illustrious* and *Incredible*. "Captain Geary," Badaya repeated slowly, as if still thinking through his words, "before we discuss other matters, there's something I wanted to bring up. We face major difficulties to get back to Alliance space and can't spend much time considering means of harming the Syndics where it will hurt them the most. The sort of thing we did at Sancere. I've been thinking about what happened at Sancere."

That could mean many things, and Badaya didn't seem to be challenging his authority, so Geary just nodded to acknowledge the statement and waited.

"The hypernet gate at Sancere," Badaya suggested. "When it collapsed, there was an energy pulse that strained the shields of our ships. I understand that the actions of *Dauntless*, *Daring*, and *Diamond* prevented the pulse from being even worse." He paused.

Badaya's words were straying onto territory that Geary preferred to avoid, but he couldn't think of any way to shut down the other officer without drawing even more attention to the topic. For once, Geary was grateful that Victoria Rione wasn't present in the meeting. If she had been, he probably couldn't have avoided a quick look her way that might have conveyed to others that she and Geary shared information that they hadn't provided to the others present. "That's correct," Geary stated calmly.

"Could we use that?" Badaya wondered. "It might offer the means to inflict serious damage on enemy star systems as we make our way home, and in a small fraction of the time required to reduce a system using conventional means."

It might indeed. It might also trigger the genocidal warfare that Geary feared. He was searching for an answer, knowing that whatever he said might have very serious repercussions, when Captain Cresida answered in regretful tones. "Captain Geary asked me about that," she stated, "and I had to tell him that the energy output seems to be unpredictable. It might amount to a lot less than we experienced, or even nothing."

Captain Tulev nodded judiciously. "And we hope to use such a gate to get home." No one disagreed with that. Instead of having to skip from star to star using the old jump drives, the hypernet could not only take them directly to a

Syndic star system bordering on the Alliance but also do it far faster than travel through jump space. "If we destroyed it instead, we couldn't use it."

"Loss of benefit to us and the chance of no damage to the Syndic star system," Captain Duellos observed. "An interesting suggestion, Captain Badaya, but it may not be practical for us."

Badaya frowned but nodded as well. "That's true. I guess it's not a viable option right now. We should keep it in mind, though."

Geary tried to look thoughtful. "Thank you, Captain. That's an intriguing possibility. I appreciate you bringing it up." *Like hell. I wish you'd never said a word. Forgive me the lie, ancestors. It's not to benefit me but to possibly save uncounted others.* He lowered his head for a moment, thinking and wondering at the way both Cresida and Tulev had jumped in to quash the idea of using hypernet gates as weapons. Cresida knew, of course, because she'd developed the targeting algorithms that had kept Sancere's hypernet gate from putting out a nova-scale blast. But Tulev didn't. Or did he? Was there a group of officers aware that hypernet gates could be used to wipe out the human race in a mutual burst of genocide, and determined to help Geary suppress that knowledge as long as possible?

What would they do with that knowledge in the long run if they decided Geary wasn't using it properly?

He had to move on, get the subject out of the minds of the officers present. Fortunately, he had just the topic guaranteed to do that. "I've been considering our next course of action. As you know, I intended taking the fleet to Wendaya from here. I've been reconsidering that."

A ripple of reaction ran around the virtual table. Geary studied the expressions of his commanding officers, not liking what he was seeing. Enthusiasm seemed nonexistent, even among his firmest supporters. But only Captain Casia spoke out. "We're barely closer to Alliance space now than when we left the Syndic home system," he complained.

"I didn't bring this fleet to the Syndic home system," Geary reminded Casia. "It's a long way home. I can't help that." He paused, gauging reactions again. Too many officers were gazing at the star display with resigned or worried expressions. "We need to try something different, though. We've been avoiding jumping along a straight line to Alliance space to avoid Syndic traps, but the Syndics are starting to figure out that we're doing that."

He had them again, every officer listening closely, but Casia swept a hand toward the display. "We're not going to retreat *again*, are we?"

The question was perfectly phrased, so perfectly that Geary wondered if Casia had come up with it himself or if a more capable officer opposed to Geary had fed him the line. It was exactly the sort of query that would undermine Geary and any plan he suggested.

But it appeared he'd been able to outmaneuver his adversaries in the fleet this time. "No," Geary informed Casia, his eyes hard. "I intend taking the fleet on a dash toward Alliance space, seeing how far we can get before the Syndics figure out what we're trying and attempt to tighten the noose around this fleet again. We should be able to make substantial distance toward home and throw off Syndic plans based on the assumption that we won't act that way."

Faces brightened all along the table, though this time Geary noted that Captains Duellos, Tulev, and Cresida seemed a bit wary, as if concerned that he had conceded to Casia. There wasn't anything he could do to make everyone happy, it seemed.

Then again, it wasn't his duty to make people happy.

Geary pointed at the display. "Instead of jumping for Wendaya, from here we'll go to Sendai, then straight through to Daiquon, and if everything seems clear, on to Ixion." Bright lines appeared on the display, forming a slightly bent arrow aimed at Alliance space.

"That'll take us almost a third of the remaining distance home!" Commander Neeson noted with a smile.

"Surely the Syndics will figure out our path before we reach Ixion," Captain Mosko of the battleship *Defiant* replied with a worried expression.

"I would think so," Captain Tulev agreed. "Captain Geary, do I understand properly that we will evaluate the situation in each star system before jumping to the next?"

"That's correct," Geary confirmed. "I expect the Syndics to figure out we've changed our approach to getting back to Alliance space. Once they do so, they'll be able to use their hypernet system to shift forces more rapidly than we can move and set up blocking forces again. But I think we've got a very good chance of making Daiquon without serious opposition, and a decent chance of being able to get to Ixion."

He seemed to have them. Geary felt a momentary rush of annoyance, angry that he had to convince them rather than just tell them what to do. It wasn't like he'd made endless mistakes since reluctantly assuming command of this fleet. But it seemed he had to prove himself again every day to the doubters. "We'll take advantage of the times in jump space for the auxiliaries to manufacture more fuel cells and expendable munitions, and distribute those among the other ships during our transits of Sendai and Daiquon. If we proceed on to Ixion, I want us to be ready for anything."

Captain Casia was still frowning. "And after Ixion? Will we continue toward home?"

Geary fought down an intense desire to wrap his hands around Casia's neck. Fortunately, just the mental image of Casia's face turning purple as Geary squeezed cheered Geary enough to calm him before he replied. "This fleet's course is ultimately always toward home," he stated evenly. "But I'm not making detailed plans four star systems ahead. We will have to take into account what the Syndics are doing by the time we reach Ixion."

"If we maintain the initiative—"

"The Syndics can move faster than us, Captain Casia. They have the advantage of a hypernet they can use." Why did he have to explain something so simple?

Commander Yin spoke up again as if she had been encouraged by some sign Geary had missed. "Returning this fleet to Alliance space as quickly as possible is critical to the war effort," she noted as if uttering a profound observation.

"If this fleet doesn't survive to reach Alliance space," Captain Duellos drawled, "it won't do much for the war effort."

"We're fighting our way home," Captain Desjani added with a glare at Yin. "We're inflicting damage on the Syndics every step of the way home."

Instead of replying, Commander Yin bent one corner of her mouth as she looked at Desjani, as if her words were somehow amusing. Desjani obviously caught the expression, too, her face hardening. But before she could say anything else, Captain Tulev spoke up. "We're also tying up most of the Syndic fleet trying to find us and stop us," Tulev tossed in blandly. "They can't take advantage of our absence from Alliance space to attack the Alliance, because they need to use almost everything they have to hunt us."

Commander Yin glanced around, didn't see whatever she was looking for, and subsided with a dark expression.

It was past time to say something to remind everyone that they were part of the same fleet. "The Alliance needs us home," Geary stated in a quiet voice that required all of the other officers to listen closely. "The Alliance ships that didn't accompany this fleet and are now holding off the Syndics are surely counting on us getting back. The Syndics are just as desperately trying to stop us from getting home. Every day this fleet continues to operate behind Syndic lines is a victory for the Alliance and a defeat for the Syndics. *When* we get home, we'll do so with our heads held high and with a Syndic fleet that's a lot smaller, thanks to the victories we've already won and

will continue to win. Our ancestors will be proud of us."
He paused. Everyone was watching him, but there didn't
seem to be anything else he should add. "Thank you.
You'll get maneuvering orders for the jump to Sendai
within the hour."

The images of ship commanders disappeared like a
flurry of soap bubbles vanishing under a strong wind.
Captain Desjani, still glowering toward the place where
Commander Yin had appeared to be seated, stood up and
with a mumbled, "Excuse me, sir," quickly departed the
room.

That left one image still seated, now leaning back,
boots resting on the table surface. If he hadn't known it
was a projection reflecting the actions of a man on another
ship, Geary would have sworn the other officer was actually here with him. "Captain Duellos," Geary greeted the
image of the man. "Thanks for staying."

Duellos's virtual presence smiled. "It's not that much
of a hardship."

"I'm still grateful." Geary sat down again and sighed.
"There were a couple of things I wanted to ask you."

"Is something wrong? Or perhaps I should ask, is
something *else* wrong?"

Geary made a twisted smile, and he nodded to acknowledge the point. "Nothing that didn't come up at the
meeting, I think."

"The usual subsurface intrigue and counterproductive
debate," Duellos observed, examining his fingernails.

"Yeah." Routine not-quite-disrespectful-or-mutinous
behavior from some of the fleet's officers. "I am curious
about something."

The figure of Duellos stood up, walked over to the seat
opposite Geary, and sat down. "Policy issues? Personnel?"

"Both. First, what can you tell me about Captain
Casia?"

Duellos's lip curled. "An officer of very modest gifts,
so modest that he was even outshone by Captain Numos.

Are you wondering why he was so big a pain at the last fleet conference and now this one?"

"Yeah."

"Because both Numos and Captain Faresa are currently under arrest. That leaves an abuse-of-power vacuum within the Third Battleship Division," Duellos noted. "As you may have guessed, that division has been a dumping ground for problem commanding officers."

Geary pondered that. In his time, with so few capital ships available, the idea of devoting a division of battleships to isolating problem officers would have been unthinkable. "How serious a problem is Casia?"

"Hard to say," Duellos admitted, his image frowning. "Alone, he's most likely to do damage by messing up badly. But if he serves as a rallying point for those who want to contest your command, he could be a dangerous figurehead for more capable officers who want to keep their true motivations hidden."

Unfortunately, that assessment matched Geary's worst fears. "Would you feel comfortable speculating on who those other officers might be?"

Duellos let his discomfort show. "I would prefer not to do so, sir. If I had evidence or direct knowledge, it would be one thing. But I'm very hesitant to accuse others based on speculation."

"I understand. Frankly, I don't want to be the sort of commander who tries to spy out subordinates who might be troublemakers." He'd never imagined being that kind of commander, actually, because a century ago the fleet's culture wouldn't have accepted such behavior.

"It's not exactly unheard of," Duellos suggested. "As I'm sure you've figured out by now, you're going against the common practice for a fleet commander by not conducting espionage against your own subordinate commanders to find out who can be trusted and who cannot."

For some reason, that brought an ironic smile to Geary's lips. "A century ago a fleet commander was expected to be qualified to make such judgments without spying on subordinates."

"A simpler time. Like much else, current practice is excused by the fact that we're in a war for survival."

"It makes a great excuse, doesn't it? But I can't imagine our ancestors look upon it with favor." Geary shook his head. "I refuse to conduct a witch hunt among my officers."

Duellos eyed Geary for a long moment. "And if the price for your honor is the loss of this fleet and the loss of the war for the Alliance?"

"Are you trying to convince me to act against my own officers based on suspicions?" Geary asked. "I'm surprised."

"And disappointed?" Duellos waved one hand in a dismissive gesture. "I happen to believe that if this fleet makes it home, it will be because we remembered the honor of our ancestors." His gaze shifted to the star field on one bulkhead. "It seems so obvious, really. Deplorable practices adopted during the last century were repeatedly declared necessary if regrettable in order to win the war. Oddly enough, we've yet to win. You'd think somebody would have asked before this why the regrettable but necessary measures haven't actually produced the promised results. Not until you came along and started us really thinking about it instead of just accepting it." Duellos sighed. "No, I'm just playing devil's advocate, Captain Geary. Every commander needs someone like that, don't they?"

"At least one," Geary agreed.

"And you have not only me but also Co-President Rione." Duellos gave Geary a speculative look. "How's that going? If I may ask."

"Your guess is as good as mine."

"She's a strong woman, and a hard woman, and as respected as any politician can be among the fleet."

"I have plenty of experience with the first two descrip-

tions, and I don't doubt the last." Geary shrugged. "She's
been distant since Ilion. I don't know why. She won't say."

"The commanders of ships from the Rift Federation
and the Callas Republic have confided in me that Co-
President Rione has been uncharacteristically disengaged
lately," Duellos observed. "She seems to be more distant
with them as well."

"That's odd." *I've been assuming I did something. But
then why would Rione be acting the same way to the ships
from her own republic? From all I've seen of her, Rione
has a lot of personal concern for those ships and their
crews.* "I'll see what I can find out. It's certainly puzzling
to see that kind of behavior from someone like Rione."

Duellos nodded.

"Speaking of puzzles, though, I've noticed something
that I don't understand. My latest thorn in my side, Captain Casia, is a battleship commander," Geary noted.

"Yes," Duellos agreed, clearly wondering why Geary
had brought that up.

"So are, or were, people like Numos, Faresa, and Kerestes. Meanwhile, I've got commanders like you, Desjani, Tulev, and Cresida who are excellent officers and all
command battle cruisers." Duellos spread his hands in a
self-mocking gesture of humility and nodded. "Why?"

"Why?" Duellos repeated, perplexed now.

"Why are my battleship commanders of lower quality
than my battle cruiser commanders?" Geary asked bluntly.

Duellos had the look of a man who'd just been asked
why space was dark. "That's the way the fleet works. The
most promising officers go to the battle cruisers. Those
who aren't judged good enough to command battle cruisers go to battleships."

Geary waited, but Duellos seemed to think the arrangement didn't require further explanation. "Okay, that's how
things work. But why? In my day, battleships were seen as
the highest and most prestigious command. Battle cruisers
were important, too, but ranked *below* battleships."

It may have been the first time that Geary actually startled Duellos. "Are you serious? But battleships are slow. Ponderous. They're powerful, but they don't lead the fleet into battle!"

"Lead the fleet?"

"Yes!" Duellos made a sweeping gesture. "Battle cruisers are fast. They lead the charges, they make the first contact with the enemy—"

"They die faster and more frequently because they lack the same level of protection that battleships have," Geary interrupted.

"Naturally," Duellos agreed, still seeming baffled. "We don't go into battle to hide behind armor. We go to fight. And the battle cruisers are in the forefront of the fight."

It suddenly made sense. A fleet culture that valued combat above everything else, that saw the highest virtue in coming to grips with the enemy as fast as possible, that had grown to disdain anything that could be called defensive in favor of always seeking to be on the attack. Of course the best officers would aspire to command the most offensive-oriented ships, and the least regarded officers would be sent to the ships that emphasized defensive capability along with their massive armament.

But there was a serious problem with that way of thinking. Geary wondered if he had finally discovered one of the things that had worked to cripple leadership in the fleet. "Captain Duellos, think about what the fleet is doing. It's been putting its best officers on the ships most likely to die and keeping its worst officers on the ships that are most heavily protected. Doesn't that strike you as a fairly insane way of doing business in the long run?"

Duellos frowned in thought. "I hadn't considered it in that light. But the fleet needs its best in the fastest and less heavily armored ships. A less-capable officer can survive in a battleship because they're much harder to kill, you see."

Geary couldn't help a sudden laugh. "The system is designed to protect less capable officers?"

This time Duellos's frown was deeper. "I've never

heard it put that way. The usual way of thinking is that the defenses of a battleship can compensate for any shortcomings in its commanding officer."

That almost made sense in a strange way. "Do the Syndics do the same thing?"

"I don't know," Duellos admitted. "I assume so."

If so, at least both sides had been working to wipe out their best officers as quickly as possible. Once again Geary wondered why an intelligent alien race would need to take measures against humanity when the human race kept demonstrating great skill and enthusiasm at working against itself. "At least now I understand something important. Just between you and me, I think this is a crazy way of doing things, but for now I obviously can't change it." If he kept losing battle cruisers, he'd also keep losing his best senior officers. But there wasn't any way he knew of to keep those battle cruisers out of combat when the fleet clashed with the Syndics. Even his best officers wouldn't accept that. It was too contrary to the way they'd been trained, the way they believed, the way they'd always fought. *But I'd better think of a way to preserve my battle cruisers, or this fleet is doomed.* "Is there anything else I should know that I haven't figured out already?"

Duellos frowned and seemed to hesitate. "You're aware that your opponents in the fleet continue to spread rumors in an attempt to diminish your standing."

"Yeah. Old news. Are they saying anything new?"

Another, deeper, frown. "I'm of two minds about telling you, Captain Geary. But you surely noticed the byplay between Captain Desjani and Commander Yin toward the end of the conference."

"Yes, I did. What was that?"

Duellos spoke with clear reluctance. "I doubt that Captain Desjani has heard, unless someone claiming to be a friend has passed on the rumors, but you should probably be aware that some of the rumors claim that you and Captain Desjani enjoy a close relationship."

It was Geary's turn to frown. "I take it you mean something more than a close *professional* relationship."

Duellos nodded, his expression reflecting distaste at having to discuss the matter.

"Are they claiming I'm cheating on Rione? I thought the whole fleet knew about her."

"Apparently you're able to keep two women happy," Duellos replied, then quirked a sardonic smile. "One man allegedly able to keep the likes of Rione and Desjani contented. By all rights that should enhance your reputation, I'd think."

"It's not exactly funny," Geary responded.

"No. It implicates not just your honor but also Captain Desjani's, and for that matter Co-President Rione's." Duellos shrugged. "Anyone seen as your ally is fair game for those who oppose you."

"Including you?"

Duellos nodded silently, and Geary shook his head. "I shouldn't be surprised. But I'll watch my step with Desjani, ensuring there's nothing that even the most twisted mind could warp into some kind of improper action between us."

"Twisted minds are enormously inventive," Duellos pointed out. "If you were on my ship, they'd probably be spreading the same rumors about you and me."

"No offense, Captain Duellos, but you're not my type."

"None taken," Duellos replied with a grin. "Besides, my wife would look askance on such a relationship."

"Women can be like that," Geary agreed, recalling that Duellos had a family back in Alliance space, then couldn't help a small, derisive smile. "For a guy allegedly with two women, I'm sure not getting lucky very often."

"Look at the bright side," Duellos offered. "If you really were cheating on Rione with Desjani, or vice versa, one or both of those women would surely kill you and laugh as they watched you die. Women can be like that, too."

"They can indeed. Especially women like Rione and

Desjani. Thanks for the heads-up on those rumors. I don't want anyone's honor questioned on my account." Geary hesitated as another question came to mind along with memories of Rione. "That stuff that Captain Badaya brought up, about the hypernet gates . . ."

Duellos nodded calmly. "We managed to defuse that."

"How much do you *know* about that?"

"Species extinction." Captain Duellos leaned back again, closing his eyes for a moment. "Supernovas or novas going off in every star system with a hypernet gate in it. Commander, pardon me, *Captain* Cresida has let a small group of us know of the potential threat. She anticipated you might need backing up on the matter." Opening his eyes, Duellos gave Geary a serious look. "I hope you won't be angry with her. I think Cresida was wise to tell a few of us, as you saw during this conference when the subject came up."

"I did see that," Geary admitted. "You're right. She was smart to do it. I'm frankly afraid for anyone to know, but if we're to prevent the worst from happening, some people have to know."

"Who else have you told?"

"Only Co-President Rione."

"Ah. An Alliance senator." Duellos grimaced. "The Alliance Senate would vote to use the gates, to explode the ones within Syndic space. You know that, don't you?"

"That's was Rione's assessment, too. And the Syndics would have time to figure out what we were doing and retaliate in kind."

Duellos nodded, suddenly looking older. "If you get this fleet home, you carry with it the knowledge to wipe out the human race."

"Yup." Geary slumped and rubbed his forehead. "Do you want to take over command?"

"Not on your life." Duellos's eyes strayed to the star display. "Perhaps the living stars have decided humanity is a hopeless case."

"The living stars didn't create the hypernet gates," Geary replied, his voice harsh.

"If they guided us, it's the same—"

"Someone . . . some*thing* else gave us that technology. I'm sure of it."

Duellos pondered the words for a long time before answering. "Some thing. Nonhuman?"

"That's my guess. Rione agrees with it. We think they're on the far side of Syndic space."

"An interesting idea." Another long pause. "They gave us poison wrapped in candy and are just waiting for us to pop it into our mouths?"

"Maybe." Geary made a gesture toward the star display. "We can only guess at their motivations. They're right that humanity is just stupid enough to take their gift and wipe itself out, but they forgot something else about people."

Duellos raised a questioning eyebrow. "And that would be?"

"We hate being told what to do, and we're very unpredictable."

The other officer smiled. "True. May I share this information?"

"Yeah." Geary thought a moment. "Tell the same people who know about the hypernet gates. I've been so afraid of what might happen if the wrong people hear that I forgot to make sure more of the right people know what's going on. Just in case something happens to me."

Duellos frowned again. "Bad as we've become, assassination of superior officers has never been a path to advancement in the Alliance fleet."

Geary couldn't help laughing. "Sorry. I didn't mean that. But, you know, there's a war on. People get hurt."

"So I've heard." Duellos stood slowly, his face thoughtful. "The stakes keep rising, and the responsibility ultimately rests on you. How are you doing?"

"Lousy."

Duellos nodded. "If worse comes to worst, and you are

lost in combat, I'll do my best. With everything. You have my word on the honor of my ancestors."

Geary stood as well, reaching to grasp the shoulder of the image and remembering in time to just mimic the gesture. "I never doubted that. Thank you, my friend."

Duellos saluted, Geary returned the gesture, and the image vanished, leaving Geary truly alone again.

FOUR

NO matter how bad it got, no matter how lonely and isolated he felt in command of this fleet, there were always his ancestors.

When the fleet finally reached the right point around the sun of Baldur and entered jump space en route to Sendai, Geary watched the external display change from endless star-spangled black to endless dull gray shot through with occasional lights that bloomed and faded. No one had known what the lights were in Geary's time, since it had been impossible to explore jump space, and with the advent of the hypernet, interest in jump space had faded. Or maybe the lines of research that might have explained the lights in jump space had been forestalled by the need to support the war with all the scientific, technical, and monetary means available.

Captain Desjani caught Geary gazing at the lights, realized that Geary had noticed her noticing him, and looked away quickly. She'd told him soon after he assumed command that many sailors believed that Geary had been one of those lights, his spirit resting in the otherwise unchanging expanse of jump space until the Alliance's need was so desperate that the legendary Black Jack Geary would return to save his people. Did they still believe that, after learning that Geary had actually been drifting in a damaged survival pod orbiting the star named Grendel at the edge of Alliance space for all those years, the beacon inoperative, the survival sleep equipment barely keeping him alive until this fleet stumbled across him?

Would he ever see Grendel again? He didn't particularly want to. It was pretty much a useless star, the sort of place ships and convoys had once passed through on their ways to important places. Geary had been told the system had been abandoned because it was too close to the border with the Syndicate Worlds, and there wasn't anything really worth defending in it, the wreckage of dozens of battles orbiting the star the only remaining signs of humanity's former presence. But some of that wreckage had belonged to his old ship, the ship destroyed while covering the retreat of the rest of the convoy. A lot of his crew had died at Grendel. He owed them a respectful visit to the place where they had fought and died under his command.

Unfortunately, a lot more people had already died under his new command, including almost certainly his own grandnephew, whose ship *Repulse* had been destroyed covering the fleet's retreat from the Syndic home system. Michael Geary probably rested with Geary's ancestors now, ancestors he hadn't paid respect to for too long. "Captain Desjani, please hold everything but emergency calls for me for the next hour or so."

She nodded, her own face weary from time spent on the bridge while in enemy space. "There's not much chance of an emergency while we're in jump. Jump space might be boring, but at the moment boring sounds pretty nice."

Geary turned to leave the bridge of the *Dauntless*, his eyes resting for a moment on the empty observer's chair. Co-President Rione had normally occupied that chair even for something as routine as entering jump space. *I need to find out what's going on with her. I've needed to do that for a while, but I could find excuses not to while we were in Baldur Star System.*

He left the bridge, but instead of heading for his stateroom went deeper into the ship, toward a set of compartments buried as deeply within the battle cruiser as possible, protected as well as anything on the ship from enemy fire or accident. With all else that had changed since Geary's time, finding those compartments still on ships had been a major relief.

Sailors and officers in the passageways made shows of saluting Geary as he passed, smiling at him with looks of admiration and hero worship. He smiled back, even though inside Geary wanted to shake all of them and ask why they couldn't see that he was as human and as prone to error as each of them. He returned the endless salutes, his arm tiring rapidly from constant use and causing Geary to wonder if maybe he shouldn't have reintroduced saluting to the fleet after all.

There were a few sailors standing near the worship spaces, but they all cleared a way for Geary when he arrived. After he'd passed them, he heard the murmur of whispered conversations. The crew liked knowing that he talked to his ancestors, liked knowing that he sought their advice and comfort just like anyone else.

Geary entered a small room, pulled shut the privacy door, then sat down on the wooden bench facing a small shelf on which a candle rested. Picking up the nearby lighter, he set the candle's wick ablaze, then sat a little while, relaxing his mind as he waited for his ancestors' spirits to gather.

Finally, he started talking. "Thank you, my ancestors, for bringing this fleet safely through another enemy star system. Thank you for guiding me in my decisions and for your help in ensuring we lost no people at Baldur." Geary paused, his thoughts straying to places he hadn't let them go for a while. "I hope Baldur hasn't changed. I'd still like to see that world someday, see if it's really what everyone used to say. But nobody in this fleet but me remembers that. Nobody else in this fleet remembers Baldur as anything but another enemy star system."

Another pause while Geary let his thoughts drift. "I hope I'm making the right decision by going to Sendai and the stars beyond. If I'm wrong, please find a way to show me. These people trust me. Well, most of them do. Some of them think . . . hell, I don't know what they think. It's not like I want this job."

He looked beyond the candle at the bulkhead, mentally seeing the emptiness outside of *Dauntless*'s hull. "It's a great temptation. You know what whispers to me. Just be Black Jack Geary. Just do whatever I think is right. It'd be so much easier. Don't try to convince people. Just show them how it should be done. I have to keep reminding myself that I'm not who they think Black Jack is, some perfect hero. If I start acting like someone I'm not, it could be a disaster for not just the Alliance but for all humanity.

"Is that okay? I can't believe I'm asking, but is it okay to see the Syndic people as people? Their leaders are horrible, and their warships and other armed forces have to be stopped, but if I start thinking all Syndics are monsters whose deaths don't matter, wouldn't I be wrong? If there truly is a nonhuman intelligent race on the other side of Syndic space, one that's tricked humanity into planting unbelievably destructive mines in every important human-occupied star system, don't we need to remember the good things that tie humanity together? We might have a common enemy now."

Might have. Those two words hung in the air for a moment. "I wish I knew. I can't even be certain the aliens exist. What do they want? What are their plans? Can I bring this fleet home safely without triggering truly genocidal fighting between the Alliance and the Syndicate Worlds?"

He spent a long while just sitting, not trying to think, letting his mind wander so he'd be open to any messages.

Nothing appeared in a burst of inspiration, though. Geary sighed and prepared to stand up, then spoke one more time. "I don't know what's bothering Victoria Rione, but something is, something she won't share with me or anyone else. I know she's not family, but if there's anything I can do for her, show me how, if that's permitted. I honestly don't know how I feel about the woman, but she's given a lot to others."

Reaching to snuff out the candle, Geary recited the old, old words. "Give me peace, give me guidance, give me wisdom."

Leaving, he felt considerably better.

"THERE'S some interesting material among the records recovered by the Marines at the Syndic mining facility at Baldur."

The message from Lieutenant Iger in intelligence didn't reveal much, but then intelligence types enjoyed sounding cryptic and mysterious, as if they always knew a little more than they'd actually ever tell you. In this case, the message succeeded in getting Geary down to the intelligence section. "What have you got?"

Lieutenant Iger and one of his petty officers offered a portable reader to Geary. "It's on here, sir," Iger explained.

Geary read the first document. *"Dear Asira"* . . . *It's a personal letter.* He started skimming, then slowed down. *"We can't get the parts we need to keep everything running and have had to cannibalize some of the mining equipment to keep the rest going . . . rations ran short again last week . . . there's rumors of another draft call, please tell me they aren't true . . . when will this war end?"*

He looked up. "Is this from the files of the security police on that facility? I assume whoever wrote this was under arrest."

Iger shook his head. "It was queued for transmission, sir. The security reviewers had already passed it."

"You're kidding." Geary frowned down at the letter. "I assume you didn't ask me down here to tell me that the Syndicate Worlds are a lot freer than I've been led to believe."

The lieutenant and the petty officer both grinned. "No, sir," Iger replied. "They're still a police state. But this is just one letter. There's a whole bunch in there, all pulled off the Syndic transmitter queue, and most of them contain the same sort of sentiments. We bounced the names on the letters against the files the Marines lifted from the security offices, and aside from routine entries, there's nothing on these people."

"Why not?" Geary held up the reader. "Isn't this the sort of thing that gets people sent to labor camps in the Syndicate Worlds?"

"It is, sir." Iger was serious now. "Or it should be. But to all appearances, open complaints were being tolerated to an unprecedented degree at that facility. Either the security force was extremely lax, or unhappiness with the state of affairs is bad enough that these kinds of sentiments are too common to be suppressed." He indicated the reader. "The files at the installation also included some mail from the habitable world not yet delivered to miners and other workers at the facility. Many of them say pretty much the same thing. Not enough of anything and worries about more people or resources being demanded to meet war requirements."

"Do any of them directly criticize the government?" The few Syndics who Geary had met since assuming command had all been thoroughly frightened of saying anything wrong or against their leaders.

"Only one, sir. The others carefully tiptoe around criticism of the Syndicate Worlds' leaders." Iger reached to push a couple of commands. "Here's the exception."

Geary read carefully. *"What are our leaders thinking? Somebody must be making serious mistakes. But nobody pays except you and me. This can't go on.*" "Was this one flagged by security at the installation? It must have been."

"No, sir." Iger barely suppressed another smile. "The person who wrote it is the chief of security at the installation."

"You're joking." Geary looked down at it again. "It's not fake? Some sort of trick designed to mislead us?"

"As far as we can tell, it's the real deal, sir."

"I've talked to Syndics we've captured. You've interrogated them. None of them have said this sort of thing."

"Not to us, sir," Iger agreed. "It's one thing to discuss this sort of thing among themselves, but saying it to us would be suicidal for any Syndic who ever got home again and was debriefed. 'Did you tell the Alliance anything?' 'What did you say to Alliance personnel?' That sort of thing. They'd pop positive for deception and be subjected to, um, harsher methods of interrogation and then find themselves charged with treasonous statements to the enemy."

That sounded reasonable. "What do you think the fact that Syndic civilians are saying this among themselves means, Lieutenant?"

Iger paused, getting solemn again. "We ran it by our expert-based social analysis systems. They said if these messages were authentic and accurately reflected the state of public sentiment in Baldur System and were not resulting in punitive actions or arrests, then the Syndic political leadership is on shaky ground. The stresses of the war must be making it harder and harder to keep a lid on dissent and dissatisfaction with the leadership. Some of the other letters discuss official announcements of Syndic victories over the Alliance, almost always in dismissive terms. Granted, this is just one hypernet-bypassed system, and sentiment in other Syndic star systems may well vary in intensity and degree of expression, but there's no reason to think Baldur is completely unique."

"We didn't find anything in Sancere like this," Geary observed.

"No, sir, but then Sancere is . . . or rather *was* a wealthy system packed with military shipyards before we hammered the hell out of the place. Lots of government contracts, good jobs, priority on resources, linked to the hypernet, and the great majority of the people probably in critical war-related jobs that exempt them from drafts. Not many grounds for complaint in a place like that." Lieutenant Iger made an apologetic face. "I come from a star system like that in the Alliance, sir. Marduk. Life is pretty good in that kind of star system. Better than anywhere else during this war, anyway."

Geary regarded the lieutenant. "But you joined the fleet anyway instead of taking one of those good, draft-exempted jobs?"

"Um . . . yes, sir." Iger glanced at the petty officer, who was grinning again. "People like to joke that's why I ended up in intelligence, because I demonstrated I didn't have much."

Jokes about intelligence officers obviously hadn't changed in a century. Geary focused back on the letters from Baldur. It seemed too good to be true, enemy morale finally cracking. "What do they say about the Alliance?" Nobody answered for a moment, and Geary looked up at the lieutenant and the petty officer. "Do they say anything about the Alliance?"

Iger nodded, unhappiness obvious. "It's mostly repeating Syndic propaganda, sir. One of the last messages in the queue was after our fleet had been sighted, and it's almost a last testament. There are a few other partially finished but unsent messages like that, all assuming our fleet would wipe out everything within Baldur System, that we wouldn't distinguish between civilian and military targets, expressing worries about the safety of their families. One individual talked about a relative who'd been captured by us and expressed the belief that they'd been killed. That sort of thing."

"Propaganda?" Geary repeated. "Lieutenant, I know that Alliance military forces have been bombarding civilian targets for some time. I know that prisoners were being executed."

Iger appeared shocked. "But that was situational, sir! Driven by necessity. It was never Alliance *policy* like those actions are Syndic policy."

"The Syndic population doesn't seem to have recognized the distinction, Lieutenant." Geary pointed to the reader. "They may be unhappy with their leaders, but they are afraid of us. Is that a fair assessment?"

"I . . . Yes, sir, it may be."

"Which would mean the main thing keeping the Syndic population supporting their leaders and the war is fear of the Alliance, fear our own actions have created."

The petty officer finally spoke. "But, sir, we only did those things because we had to."

Geary tried not to sigh. "Assume that's one hundred percent true, and I have no doubt that Alliance personnel sincerely believe that. Do the Syndics know that? Or are the people on Syndic worlds judging us by our actions and not our justifications for them?"

Lieutenant Iger was staring at Geary. "Sir, you stopped bombarding civilian targets and allowing prisoners to be killed as soon as you took over. Every Syndic star system we've been through knows that under your command this fleet isn't a threat to their homes and families. How did you know how they felt? How did you know what to do?"

Remember that the lieutenant and the petty officer and every man and woman in this fleet have spent their entire lives at war with the Syndics. Remember that their parents spent their entire lives at war. Remember the atrocities, the revenge attacks, the endless rounds of provocation and retaliation. Remember that I didn't have to endure that and have no right to condemn them for thinking differently. "I did what I did," Geary stated softly, "because it was right. The sort of thing I'd been taught was right, what our ancestors demanded of us, what our honor demanded of us. I know what you've been through, what the Alliance has endured in the course of this war. Under that kind of pressure, it's possible to forget why you're fighting in the first place."

The petty officer nodded, looking stricken. "Like you told us in Corvus, sir. Like you reminded us. Our ancestors had to tell us we'd taken the wrong path, and they sent you, because they knew we'd listen to you."

Oh, great. He couldn't simply be reminding them of what they had been; he also had to be a messenger from their ancestors.

Though in a way he actually was, bringing with him from a hundred years ago the ways their ancestors had thought.

Because he was one of their ancestors. He didn't like remembering that, recalling that his world had vanished into the past, but it was true.

Lieutenant Iger planted a fist on the table, staring down at it. "We need to convince the Syndics it's different now, that we're no longer a greater threat to them than their own leaders. We can do that if we keep demonstrating it. Right, sir?"

"Right," Geary agreed.

"And if their morale is starting to break, and they decide they have *less* to fear from us than from their own leaders, it could finally break the Syndicate Worlds."

"That'd be an outcome to be hoped for." Geary turned the reader in his hands, thinking. "Let's keep our eyes out for anything else like this, and if your expert-based systems have any recommendations for how we can exploit the sort of Syndic morale problems we see in these letters, I want to know them."

Maybe, just maybe, there really was a light at the end of the tunnel. The Alliance had no hope of defeating the Syndicate Worlds as long as the Syndic leaders could keep drawing on the resources of all the worlds under their sway. But if even a good percentage of those worlds began to rebel, to hold back their people and their resources from the Syndic war effort, it would finally provide the advantage the Alliance had needed and had been unable to achieve for a century.

VICTORIA Rione successfully avoided Geary during the six days needed to reach Sendai. Geary spent the time going over possible battle scenarios, trying to figure out how to avoid losing his battle cruisers and their commanding officers and coming up with nothing. There simply wasn't a good excuse for holding those ships out of battle.

He sat on the bridge of *Dauntless* again as the fleet left jump space. The odds the Syndics had been able to plant mines here or even guessed that the Alliance fleet was headed to Sendai were very small, but Geary wanted to be ready to react, just in case the Syndic leaders had been able to make a very lucky guess.

His guts wrenched as the transition to normal space occurred, and the dull gray of jump space disappeared as the infinite stars became visible.

Geary couldn't waste time admiring the view; his eyes locked on the star system display, watching for any sign of Syndic ships or mines.

"Looks completely empty," Desjani remarked. "Not even picket ships. You were right, sir. The Syndics had no idea we'd head for Sendai." She gave him an admiring smile.

"Thanks," Geary muttered, feeling uncomfortable. "There's not even any satellites monitoring the system?"

"No, sir," a watch-stander reported. "Because of that." He pointed to the center of the display, seeming nervous.

Normally the display would be centered on a star, the object with enough mass to warp space around it and create the conditions necessary for jump points. Sendai had been such a star, once. A very large star. It had certainly had many planets back then, unknown millions of years ago.

Until it ran out of fuel, exploded in a supernova that turned its planets into burnt fragments, then collapsed into itself, the matter making up Sendai crushing tighter and tighter together, denser and denser, until all the mass of a huge sun was compressed into a ball of matter the size of a small planet so dense that the gravity from it kept even light from escaping.

Captain Desjani nodded, then swallowed in apparent nervousness as well. "The black hole."

Nothing was visible to the naked eye where the remnants of Sendai still existed. But on full-spectrum displays, a riot of radiation shot out from the black hole in two tight beams from the north and south poles of the dead star, the death screams of matter being sucked into the black hole at incredible velocities.

Geary looked around and saw every man and woman on the bridge staring at their displays in the same edgy way. Veterans of unnumbered battles, they seemed unnerved by the black hole. "Do ships ever visit black holes anymore?"

Desjani shook her head. "Why would they?"

Good question. When using the jump drives, ships had to go to every star intervening between themselves and their destination. But the hypernet let a ship go from any gate to any other gate. Black hole star systems, which weren't really star systems anymore because the holes ravenously sucked down all of the matter that had once orbited them, offered nothing for ships and held peril from the radiation being pumped out into space. Even modern shields wouldn't stand up indefinitely to that sort of radiation barrage.

But still, it was just a black hole. They weren't going to linger here but just transit quickly to the next jump point, while avoiding those jets of radiation at the black hole's poles. Geary leaned close to Desjani. "What's the matter?"

She looked down, then spoke reluctantly. "It's . . . unnatural."

"No, it's not. Black holes are perfectly natural."

"That's not what I mean." Desjani took a deep breath.

"They say if you look at a black hole too long you . . . you develop an overwhelming urge to dive in, to take your ship below the event horizon and see what's on the other side. That which was once the star calls to you, seeking to consume human ships just as it does everything else."

He'd never heard such stories, and the sailors Geary had served with as a junior officer had enjoyed regaling him with all manner of ghost stories and tales of mysterious threats that devoured ships and people in the cold reaches of space. But then a hundred years was plenty long enough to develop new stories. "I haven't been around a lot of them, but a few. I've never felt that."

"I'd wager that no one in this fleet but you has ever been around a black hole," Desjani replied.

The unknown. Still the most fertile ground for human fears. And as Geary took another look at the display, now aware of the beliefs of those around him, he could almost feel a tug from the invisible mass at the heart of Sendai. Something more than simply gravity so great it held light itself hostage.

"That's why the Syndics aren't here," Desjani announced suddenly. "They knew if they tried to order ships to be pickets here that the crews would revolt rather than stay around a black hole for a long time."

"Good guess." Geary raised his voice and spoke calmly. "I've been around black holes before." He could tell everyone on the bridge was listening. "There's no threat as long as you don't get too close. And we won't. Let's get this fleet to the next jump point."

He realized that giving the order to jump out of Sendai would probably be the only order he'd give that even his worst enemies in the fleet would approve of unconditionally.

"**DAMN.**" Three more Alliance battle cruisers had just exploded.

Geary killed the simulation with an irritable punch of

the controls. The tactic he'd tried had seemed a little crazy, and apparently it really was. It certainly hadn't worked worth a damn. Instead of reducing the risk to his battle cruisers, it had led to them being pinned between superior Syndic forces and blown apart. Granted, the simulation might have smarter Syndic commanders than the Alliance fleet would actually encounter, but officers Geary had once known and respected a century ago had warned him never to base his plans on the assumption that the enemy was stupid. A clever trap worked far better than one that assumed the enemy was too dumb to see the obvious. *Now all I need is a clever trap.*

His hatch chimed to announce a visitor to Geary's stateroom. Captain Desjani, saluting, her face professional. "We're two hours from the jump point to Daiquon, sir. You asked to be informed."

"Yes, but you didn't have to come down here in person to tell me."

Desjani shrugged, letting discomfort show. "You're . . . reassuring, sir. Surely you've noticed how much the crew appreciates seeing you being so calm around the black hole. I assure you that word of that has spread to every ship in the fleet and helped keep everyone calm."

"Huh." It seemed odd to be praised for not being spooked by a black hole. But Geary had found himself increasingly reluctant to view the thing himself, influenced by the superstitions of those around him. "Thanks, but I don't mind telling you that I won't miss this place."

"Not you and not anyone else in the fleet," Desjani replied with a brief smile. "I'm sorry I disturbed you, sir."

"Don't worry about it. I was just running a simulation that wasn't going right." Geary leaned back and sighed. "Sit down. I'd appreciate the chance to just talk about something other than tactics and strategy and Syndics and the war."

Desjani hesitated, then came in and sat down opposite Geary, sitting at attention the way she usually did when in his stateroom. "Those topics have dominated life in the

Alliance for much longer than I've been alive," she confessed. "I don't know what we'd talk about if we didn't have them."

"There are other things. Things that keep us going when the war seems to be all the universe contains." Geary's eyes rested on the still-distant stars of Alliance space. "What'll you do when you get back to Kosatka, Tanya?"

Desjani seemed startled by the question, her own gaze going to the starscape. "My home world," she murmured. "I haven't been back for a long time. There's no guarantee I'll get a chance even if—even when we get back."

"I understand. The war isn't going to stop just because we make it home." Geary sat silent for a moment. "Are your parents still there?" *Are they still alive*, he'd meant, but he wouldn't phrase the question that bluntly.

She knew what he meant, nodding. "They're both there. My father works in a manufacturing plant supplying the orbital shipyards. Mother is part of the planetary defense forces."

A wartime economy, of course, even on a planet as far from the front lines of battle as Kosatka. What else could you expect after a century of war? "How do they feel about you being the captain of a battle cruiser?"

Captain Tanya Desjani, hardened veteran of dozens of space battles, actually blushed and looked down. "They're . . . proud. Very proud." Her expression changed. "They knew the risks that being a fleet officer entailed. I'm sure they've been waiting for the notification that I died in battle ever since I went to my first ship. So far I've beaten the odds, and they've been spared that, but they may believe I'm dead now, along with the rest of the fleet."

That brought a grimace to Geary's face. "Surely the Alliance government wouldn't have told the population that? It's not that the people don't have a right to know, but governments tend to believe they have a right to lie about bad news." He'd examined an official history of the war soon after assuming command of the fleet and discovered it contained a relentlessly positive and upbeat account, chronicling alleged victory after Alliance victory but remaining silent on the question of why such victories had yet to result in winning the war. Distressingly similar to the nonsense the captured Syndic merchant officer had told him, Geary realized. The government that wrote that history wasn't likely to confess that its main fleet had disappeared behind enemy lines and had very likely been wiped out.

"Certainly," Desjani agreed, "but the Syndic propaganda broadcasts would've announced it. They jump automated broadcast units into border star systems and pump out as much of their lies as they can before our defense systems can destroy them." Geary nodded, thinking that the Alliance probably did the same thing to broadcast its side of things to Syndic border star systems. "Officially," Desjani continued, "no one's supposed to repeat what they hear from the Syndics, but word gets around. Unlike Syndics, citizens of the Alliance can still express opinions and don't believe everything their politicians say." She shrugged, her expression grim. "My parents have surely heard that the Syndics are claiming our fleet was lost deep in Syndic space. They won't believe the Syndics, but they won't be too comforted by official Alliance government denials. They have to be worried."

"Sorry." The single word was inadequate, but Geary couldn't think of anything else for a moment. "I guess they'll be doubly happy, then, when you come home."

Desjani grinned. "Yes. Oh, yes." She gave Geary an almost shy glance. "And when my home world hears that their daughter's ship carried Black Jack Geary himself, that he commanded the fleet from the bridge of my ship as he brought us home against all odds, they'll be the most famous people on Kosatka, I'm sure."

Geary laughed to cover up his embarrassment. "I've thought about going to Kosatka once we get back." The words Victoria Rione had once said came to him. *Kosatka isn't big enough to hold you, John Geary.* "To visit, I mean."

"Really?" Desjani seemed awed.

"I told you I was there once. A long time ago." Geary managed not to slap his forehead in exasperation with himself. Very few things in his life didn't fall under the heading of "a long time ago." "I wouldn't mind seeing it again."

"I'm sure it's changed, sir."

"Yeah. I guess I'll need a guide."

Desjani hesitated. "We could, I mean, if you wanted to come along when I, that is—"

"That'd be nice," Geary replied. "Maybe I'll do that." Having a familiar face along, a known presence, might be a very good thing indeed. And he had already started to wonder how he would feel once he got this fleet home and walked away from it, having done his duty and more. Because what had once been a collection of strange ships and unknown people was increasingly becoming *his* fleet, populated by people he knew and in some cases liked and admired. Hell, after seeing the crews of *Dauntless*, *Daring*, and *Diamond* stand firm while the hypernet gate at Sancere collapsed, Geary had developed a fierce pride in the courage and dedication of these sailors. Did he really want to exchange that for the unknowns of a civilian world in which the worship of Black Jack Geary would be even harder to escape?

Should he even be asking himself that question? He couldn't remain in command of this fleet when it returned to Alliance space. It wasn't just that he didn't feel competent to the demands of the position; he feared that Victoria Rione might have been right when she spoke of the temptations he would face then. Black Jack Geary, mythical hero, back from the dead to save the Alliance, the fleet under his command. Anything he wanted could be his. He need only reach out and take it.

"Sir?" Desjani asked, eyeing him curiously. "Did I say something wrong?"

"What? No. I'm sorry. I was thinking about something

else." Geary smiled reassuringly again. "Let's go to the bridge and get ready to say good-bye to Sendai."

Everyone on the bridge was studiously avoiding looking at the display where the black hole dominated space. As Geary entered the bridge, he noticed everyone giving him those looks, hope and trust mingled together. Like Desjani, they apparently thought him a sort of talisman against whatever demon lurked inside the black hole.

Too bad *he* didn't have a talisman.

An hour and a half until the fleet reached the jump point. Geary took a moment to order his thoughts, then tapped the controls so he could speak to the entire fleet. Once within jump space, communications would be extremely limited, with only messages a few words long able to be exchanged among ships. There were things he needed to say while the fleet was still in normal space. If space around a black hole could be called normal, that is.

"All ships of the Alliance fleet, this is Captain Geary," he began, speaking with deliberate calm. "We don't know what awaits us at Daiquon. The Syndics didn't expect us to come to Sendai, but they've surely figured out by now that we didn't go to any of the other places reachable from Baldur. They may well guess Daiquon is a possible objective of ours in time to position forces using the advantage of their hypernet. I want all ships ready for battle when we leave jump space at Daiquon. We may face an immediate engagement, and if so I want whatever Syndic warships we encounter to get kicked into Daiquon's sun so fast they'll still be trying to figure out what happened." He paused again, trying to think of the best ending for his transmission. "To the honor of our ancestors."

Then it was just a matter of waiting. Geary occupied the time going over fleet readiness data again. The auxiliaries had been manufacturing new fuel cells and expendable weapons at a furious pace, as if the engineers were determined to make up for the errors that had led to shortages of trace elements. Even without those new items, the fleet's warships were in good shape for an engagement if the Syndics were waiting at Daiquon. Except for *Orion*, *Majestic*, and *Warrior*, of course. But most of the damage that Captain Tulev's battle cruisers had sustained at Sancere had been repaired now, and *Leviathan*, *Steadfast*, *Dragon*, and *Valiant* were fully combat-ready again.

If the Syndics were waiting at Daiquon, this fleet was ready for them.

"Captain Geary"—Desjani broke into his train of thought—"the fleet has reached the jump point for Daiquon."

"Good. Let's get the hell out of here." He tapped the communications controls again. "All ships in the Alliance fleet, jump for Daiquon now."

As the fleet entered jump space and the black hole named Sendai vanished, the feeling of relief that ran through *Dauntless* was so powerful that Geary could have sworn the ship itself sighed with satisfaction.

Four days and a few hours to Daiquon. Victoria Rione managed to avoid him the entire time, so Geary spent his time working on more simulations, watching his battle cruisers explode and getting steadily more frustrated in every sense of the word.

THE Syndics were at Daiquon.

Right in front of the jump point.

Staring at the enemy ship symbols popping into existence on the star system display, Geary first focused on two battleships and two battle cruisers, apparently tracking across the front of the jump point.

"They're laying mines!" Desjani warned.

And the path of the Alliance fleet would sweep partly across areas where those mines had already been laid. Geary did the maneuvering solution in his head. "All units in the Alliance fleet. Immediate execute, turn starboard four zero degrees, up two zero degrees." Turning toward the watch-standers, he snapped out another order. "Get a minefield marker displayed along the track those Syndic ships must have followed!"

Four major warships. Geary's eyes raced across the display, adding up the rest of the Syndic force. Three heavy cruisers, five light cruisers, a dozen Hunter-Killers. Probably sent here to lay mines in front of the jump points and then leave a few light units behind to report if the Alliance fleet passed through the system. Instead, they'd been caught in the middle of laying the minefield. The Syndic warships weren't a major threat to the Alliance fleet, not if he had time to set up an engagement. But the fleet was right on top of the Syndic warships, both formations tangling in a melee without time to plan or execute a careful plan of action. "All ships, engage nearest Syndic warships."

A squadron of destroyers had emerged from the jump point almost in the laps of the two Syndic battleships. The light warships swung away frantically, firing their few weapons, which sparkled futilely against the massive shields of the enemy battleships. The Syndic battleships fired back, their heavy armament shredding through the light shields of the destroyers and into the little armor the destroyers boasted. *Kheten* exploded under the barrage, and *Epee* was torn apart, its pieces tumbling away.

The only thing that saved the rest of the destroyers in the squadron was the arrival of a squadron of Alliance light cruisers, flashing out of jump space and right into the arms of the Syndic battleships. The battleships greedily shifted fire to the new targets, ripping *Glacis* into fragments and smashing *Aegis* and *Hauberk*.

But now the heavy cruisers and battle cruisers of the Alliance fleet had reached the Syndic battleships, bearing shields heavy enough to engage the enemy and enough firepower to instantly shift the odds drastically against the Syndics.

Six of the Syndic Hunter-Killers had been escorting the battleships, and now five of them blew apart as a swarm of Alliance destroyers swept past the battleships and targeted their lighter counterparts. The last HuK tried to run but had no time to accelerate away before being pounded into scrap. Two light cruisers tried to hide behind the battleships but were pinned between three divisions of Alliance heavy cruisers and smashed. The single Syndic heavy cruiser with the battleships found itself facing Tulev's battle cruiser division and blew up after a single volley from the big Alliance warships.

"First, Second, and Fourth Battle Cruiser Divisions," Geary ordered. "Disregard Syndic battleships and engage the enemy battle cruisers and their escorts." He scanned the display, trying to figure out who else to order where. "Second, Fifth, and Seventh Battleship Divisions, get the Syndic battleships. All heavy cruisers attempt to engage the surviving Syndic escorts around the enemy battle cruisers. All lighter Alliance units engage targets of opportunity." It amounted less to tactics than to simply trying to overwhelm the enemy forces as fast as possible, but that seemed the best option at the moment.

And he also had to ensure against the Syndics trying a desperate counterblow. "Eighth and Tenth Battleship Divisions, guard the auxiliaries division. Make sure nothing gets through to them." He didn't know if all of those battleships would obey the command in the heat of battle, but if even a few did, it would provide necessary insurance.

Eleven Alliance battle cruisers swung their bows around and accelerated toward the two Syndic battle cruisers, followed by a tangle of heavy cruiser divisions mixed in with light cruisers and destroyers. "Accelerate to point one light," Captain Desjani ordered. "Up one five degrees, port zero four degrees. All weapons target the leading Syndic battle cruisers. Prepare to fire specters."

At the same time, the eleven Alliance battleships of the Second, Fifth, and Seventh Divisions bore down on the Syndic battleships. Geary saw the two surviving and combat-ready battleships of the Fourth Division also come around and swing toward the enemy battleships but didn't try to order them away. *Vengeance* and *Revenge* owed the Syndics for the loss of *Triumph* at Vidha and the terrible damage suffered by *Warrior* at the same battle.

Thirteen battleships tore into the Syndic battleships,

the range too short to fire specter missiles. Instead, several of the closest Alliance ships hurled out grapeshot, the metal ball bearings slamming into enemy shields and vaporizing from the impacts. Then all of the Alliance battleships unleashed their hell-lance batteries from three sides, causing the weakened shields of the Syndic battleships to flare and collapse almost instantly. The hell lances then punched through armor and into the guts of the Syndic ships, tearing holes through which gusts of atmosphere vented as the enemy ships shuddered under the blows.

Vengeance and *Revenge* ripped past at close range, firing their short-range null-field projectors. The glowing balls of the null fields met the hulls of the Syndic ships, causing atomic bonds to fail everywhere they passed. Sections of the enemy battleships vaporized inside the null fields, opening huge wounds in their hulls.

The two Syndic battle cruisers could have tried to run as the Alliance battle cruisers bore down on them, but their commander apparently hesitated. The brief delay doomed both ships. "Fire specters," Desjani ordered. As *Dauntless* fired a volley of missiles, the other Alliance battle cruisers followed suit, sending a flock of the autonomous missiles accelerating toward the enemy battle cruisers.

The Syndics fired back, the surviving HuKs, light cruisers, and heavy cruisers placing themselves between the battle cruisers and the onrushing Alliance missiles. Despite their evasive maneuvers, speed, and stealth, a lot of specters flared and died short of their targets. But by concentrating their fire on the specters, the Syndic ships let the lighter Alliance ships close to firing range.

HuKs flared and burst under the fire of Alliance destroyers and light cruisers, while the three Syndic light cruisers were riddled by fire from the heavy cruisers accompanying the Alliance battle cruisers.

Then the Alliance battle cruisers reached engagement range for their hell lances. The leading battle Syndic cruiser seemed to glow as its shields absorbed hit after hit;

then the shields collapsed and the hell lances began ravaging the ship itself.

Geary held his breath, trying not to betray his concern as Desjani led *Dauntless*, *Daring*, and *Victorious* in a close pass against the stricken Syndic battle cruiser, firing null fields as they raced past. *Here I was worried about risking any battle cruisers, and I'm throwing them into the thick of a battle, led by the one battle cruiser that I can't afford to lose. If we lose* Dauntless, *we lose the Syndic hypernet key it carries. I have to come up with a solution to this problem.*

Not that the leading Syndic battle cruiser was a threat anymore. The null-field hits on top of the torrent of hell-lance fire had riddled the warship and left it a drifting wreck from which survival pods were bursting spasmodically as the surviving crew tried to find safety.

Geary searched for the second Syndic battle cruiser, clenching his teeth as he saw that the battle cruiser's commander had wrenched the big warship around and was accelerating toward the Alliance auxiliaries.

"He doesn't stand a chance," Desjani observed.

As the battle cruiser tore through the Alliance formation, it took hit after hit from destroyers, light cruisers, and heavy cruisers along its path. Each individual blow did little damage, but they kept adding up as the Syndic battle cruiser kept accelerating in an attempt to confuse the Alliance targeting systems. But without enough time and distance to get its speed high enough, the battle cruiser took more and more hits. It sliced past *Illustrious* and *Incredible* and staggered as the two Alliance battle cruisers poured fire into its port side.

The Syndic battle cruiser kept going as the damage accumulated, running into wave after wave of fire.

By the time it reached the battleships of the Tenth Battleship Division, the Syndic battle cruiser had taken so many hits that it was probably running blind, its sensors smashed, its remaining weapons flashing out futilely and gaining no hits. Only the battle cruiser's main drives at the stern remained relatively undamaged, bringing the Syndic warship up past point one light as it kept accelerating.

Amazon and *Guardian*, the closest Alliance battleships to the doomed Syndic battle cruiser's path, fired volleys of grapeshot almost straight down the enemy ship's course, the metal shot hitting the Syndic's hull at a combined velocity of close to point two light speed.

The front half of the Syndic battle cruiser vaporized under the impacts, the stern portion shuddering as it passed through the remains of the bow and then coming apart into a field of small fragments, some of which impacted harmlessly on the shields of *Amazon* and *Guardian*.

Desjani sighed. "The entire crew of that battle cruiser must be dead."

Geary nodded in agreement. "No one could've survived that."

"Too bad." Desjani looked toward Geary. "For the first time in my life, I really wanted to meet a Syndic. The commanding officer of that ship. He or she fought very gallantly." She'd come a ways from the officer who Geary had first met, to whom the Syndic enemy were inhuman and beneath contempt. "It's best he or she is dead, of course," Desjani added matter-of-factly. "I'd hate to leave a Syndic like that alive."

"You'd hate to leave alive a Syndic officer that you respect?" Geary asked.

Desjani lowered her brow slightly. "Respect? I couldn't respect a Syndic, sir. How could anyone? Though this one died well. I just wanted to see what such a Syndic was like."

Geary shrugged. "Right now, they're dead, blown into very small pieces along with their crew and their ship."

"Yes, sir." Desjani smiled in reply.

Maybe she hadn't come that far. But then, Desjani was the daughter of a hundred years of war, a century of tit-for-tat atrocities. The enemy was as alien to her as the intelligences that Geary suspected lurked beyond Syndic space. "Let's get this fleet straightened out. All units, well done." Geary's eyes locked on the display, where in one corner names in red told of Alliance ships lost: two destroyers and three light cruisers. A lot of other ships had taken damage during the melee. Some of the surviving destroyers might not be repairable and might have to be abandoned here, and at least one heavy cruiser had taken serious damage. "Assume Formation Delta One unless engaged in recovering Alliance survival pods." He would have to figure out which warships were so badly hurt that they'd have to fall back with the auxiliaries to simplify repair efforts, joining the torn-up battleships *Orion*, *Majestic*, and *Warrior* in what was becoming a formation of crippled ships.

Geary switched circuits and called down to the intelligence section. "See if you can find out if any of those Syndic survival pods have high-ranking officers in them." He needed to know what the Syndics were doing and how the war was going along the border with the Alliance. Given the Syndic obsession with secrecy and keeping their own officers under tight control, odds were that even if the commander of the entire Syndic force had survived, he or she wouldn't know the answers to that. But the longer Geary went without knowing, the more the questions gnawed at him. How long could he evade an enemy, most of whose movements were invisible to him?

If the Alliance fleet had arrived in Daiquon half a day later, it would have run right into that minefield outside the jump point, and the Syndic picket ships would have escaped to tell their high command the path the Alliance ships were following.

Any elation in the victory vanished as Geary stared at the names of the dead ships and the nearby reports of damage and crew casualties from other ships. It had been a small victory, dearly purchased.

FIVE

ALL things being equal, the transit through Daiquon to the jump point for Ixion should have required about five and a half days. The five substantial objects in orbit about the star Daiquon consisted of four barely planet-sized rocks and one massive supergiant that was just shy of enough mass to become a star in its own right. The small Syndic installations that had once occupied one of the rocks were all cold and had probably been mothballed long ago. There was absolutely no reason to linger in Daiquon and nothing capable of delaying the fleet.

But the Alliance heavy cruiser *Brilliant* had been so badly hurt during the brief engagement that Geary had to slow the entire formation while *Brilliant*'s main propulsion units received emergency repairs. The only alternative to that was leaving *Brilliant* behind, and he wasn't about to do that.

But there wasn't any choice when it came to the destroyers *Sword-Breaker* and *Machete*. Both had been so badly chewed up that only a major shipyard could have repaired them. Geary had the crews taken off and the ships' power cores set to overload, turning both destroyers into slowly expanding balls of wreckage to join those already littering Daiquon as a result of the destruction of the Syndic warships. His other ships could use the officers and sailors from the lost destroyers, but it still hurt morale to have to scuttle two ships.

A score of other destroyers, three more light cruisers, and one more heavy cruiser had joined the three battleships in the makeshift division of badly damaged ships near the auxiliaries division. Geary tried to salve the pride of those ships by officially designating them a close support escort force for the auxiliaries, but he feared their unhappiness with being assigned to a place far from the front of any battle would breed further problems down the line. *They'll be upset, even though it's the only decision that makes any sense. But then what about war has anything to do with making sense?*

Geary closed his eyes, trying to block out the images of dying ships and their crews. His stateroom was very quiet, only the faint sounds that spoke of *Dauntless* being a living ship penetrating the bulkheads to provide familiar comfort. Vent fans humming as they distributed and cooled air, pumps churning as liquids went here and there, barely audible voices of members of the crew passing near, perhaps accompanied by the low rumble of a transport cart. For how many centuries had sailors heard those sounds around them? Before that there had been the creaking of wood and rigging on ships that used sails to carry them across planetary oceans. Ships were never completely silent, not while they lived.

"Captain Geary? This is Lieutenant Iger in the intelligence section."

He hit the comm pad to accept the call. "This is Geary. What've you got?"

"We've analyzed the communications between the survival pods from the Syndic warships we destroyed, and as far as we can tell, all of the senior officers died on their

ships. None of the pods seem to contain anyone who's trying to assert authority or coordinating activity."

No sense in diverting any of his own ships to pick up
prisoners who wouldn't know anything useful. "Are they
all still headed for the mothballed installation in this system?"

"Yes, sir," Iger confirmed. "There's no place else for
them to go."

"How long can they survive on what's in the pods and
whatever's at that base?" So far, the Alliance fleet had
found either emergency rations or simply food abandoned
in place, frozen on airless worlds, at every derelict Syndic
facility they'd examined.

"The pods contain enough provisions for a couple of
weeks, assuming they're all full of survivors. They can stretch
that, of course. Even if most of the ships were supposed
to stay here to see if we showed up, Syndic procedure is
to send a courier ship to report mission completion, in this
case laying the minefields. When the enemy leaders in the
nearby systems don't hear from the warships in Daiquon,
they'll send someone to check on them. There may already be a ship on the way."

"Okay. Thanks." No sense in diverting a ship to pick up
any pods containing Syndic sailors. He could make sure
this fleet sent a message to the Syndic authorities on the
inhabited world in Ixion Star System when they got there,
ensuring the Syndics knew they had people awaiting rescue here.

Geary tried to drop back into his reverie, but an instant
later his hatch alert chimed. "Come in," Geary called re-
signedly without opening his eyes.

After a short interval, he heard a dry voice. "Congratulations on another victory."

Geary's eyes shot open. Victoria Rione stood in the
entry. As she saw him gaze at her, she stepped inside, the
hatch sealing in her wake, and came to sit across from
Geary. Unlike Desjani, Rione leaned back, almost casual,

but in the manner of a cat who could spring at any moment. "What's the occasion?" Geary asked.

"I told you. I came to congratulate you."

"Like hell." Geary gestured angrily. "You've spent weeks avoiding me. Why'd you decide to finally show up here again?"

Rione looked away. "I have my reasons. We lost a ship from the Callas Republic in that battle you just fought."

"I know. *Glacis.* I'm sorry. We lost about half of her crew but were able to rescue the rest. The survivors were distributed among other ships from the Callas Republic."

"Thank you." Rione's jaw clenched. "I should have seen to that myself. It's my responsibility."

"No, it's mine, as fleet commander, but I would have welcomed your assistance in the matter. And, to put it bluntly, Madam Co-President, the ships of the Callas Republic are wondering why you haven't been in closer contact with them."

"I have my reasons," Rione repeated after a long moment of silence.

"You could share them," Geary suggested. "Didn't you once advise me to talk about my problems?"

"Did I? Have you been lonely?" she added abruptly.

"I missed you, yes."

"I'm not the only woman on this ship, Captain Geary."

"You're the only one I can touch," Geary replied sharply. "You know that. Everyone else in this fleet works for me."

She gazed at him, her feelings hidden as usual. "You had no one else to talk to?"

"A few times. Captain Duellos. Captain Desjani."

"Oh?" It was still impossible to tell what Rione was feeling. "Captain Desjani? Did you discuss various ways to slaughter Syndics?"

That almost sounded like Rione's old, acerbic teasing. Geary weighed his response, then decided to be open about it. "Mostly just operational things, yes. But we did talk about Kosatka once. I told her I'd like to visit there when we get back."

Rione raised one eyebrow.

"Why not? It's a nice place. Maybe I couldn't stay there, but I'd like to see it again."

"It's changed, Captain Geary."

"That's what Desjani said." Geary shrugged. "Maybe I want to see how it's changed, to help me absorb the fact that a century has passed since I last was there."

"You'd scarcely be allowed to wander around, you know." Rione twisted her mouth. "Black Jack would be mobbed."

"Yeah. Desjani offered to show me around. She could help me avoid the crowds, maybe. Her parents are still alive. They'd help us keep a low profile, I think."

Victoria Rione stayed silent again for a moment, her face unmoving. "So," she finally observed, "Tanya Desjani has invited you home to meet her parents."

It hadn't even occurred to him that Desjani's offer could be read that way. "What's the matter? Are you jealous?"

This time both of Rione's eyebrows arched upward. "Hardly."

"Good. Because the last thing I want is anyone thinking I'm interested in her or vice versa." Had Rione heard the baseless rumors about him and Desjani that Duellos had referred to? How could she not have heard them with her spies keeping track of events inside the fleet?

This time Rione smiled slightly. "Oh, surely not, John Geary. Think of the advantages of having a woman who believes you were sent by the living stars to save us all. Many men pray for a woman who would worship them. You've got one ready and waiting."

Geary stood up, anger stirring. "I don't find that funny at all. Tanya Desjani is a fine officer. I don't want anyone thinking she would engage in unprofessional behavior. My enemies in this fleet are already trying to stir up trouble and undermine me by alleging that Desjani and I have an unprofessional relationship. I don't want any more rumors that we're involved with each other. I won't do that to her."

Rione's smile vanished, and she looked down for a moment. When she raised her head again, her face was composed. "I'm sorry. You're right."

"Well, damn," Geary couldn't help saying, "I've got a woman who just admitted I was right. A lot of men pray for that, too."

"Just because I'm being a bitch doesn't mean you have to be a bastard."

It was Geary's turn to look away and nod. "That's true."

"Besides," Rione continued, "I'm much better at it than you are." She sagged back in her seat, her expression a mix of weariness and unhappiness.

Geary leaned forward. "What the hell's going on, Victoria? I can tell something is bothering you, and I don't think it's me. I've been trying to imagine why you'd neglect your duties to the Alliance and the Callas Republic and, quite frankly, I'm baffled." She sat silent, her expression revealing nothing. "Is it me? You haven't touched me since Ilion. We never made any promises, but I honestly don't understand what happened to change things."

Rione shrugged, her face averted. "I'm a bitch. You knew that. It was only physical, anyway."

"No, it wasn't." Rione didn't look up, so Geary continued. "I said it before, and I'll say it now. I like talking with you. I like being around you."

"I notice you're not denying that I'm a bitch."

"And you're trying to change the subject." He caught her frown. "Is this related to why you and Captain Desjani are at sword's point whenever you're together?"

She laughed mockingly. "Such an observant man. If Desjani and I were two formations of Syndic warships you'd have figured out what we were doing a long time ago."

Geary refused to rise to the bait. "I respect you both. I

like you both, though in different ways. I also respect the way both of you think. That's why it worries the hell out of me that I don't know why you two seem to hate each other since Ilion."

Rione looked away for some time before answering. "Captain Tanya Desjani is afraid that I will hurt the man she idolizes."

"Dammit, Victoria—"

"I'm not joking, John Geary." She sighed heavily and finally looked back at him. "Use your head!" Rione demanded harshly. "What did we pick up at Sancere?"

"A lot of things."

"Including an outdated but large listing of Alliance prisoners of war." To Geary's shock, Rione seemed to be trembling slightly as she spoke. "You know the Syndics stopped sharing lists of prisoners with us long ago. You know many of the names on that list were presumed dead. You should have realized that some of the names on that list would be people that were thought to be certainly dead!" She almost shouted the last.

He finally got it. "Your husband. His name was on the list?"

Her fists were clenched, and she was visibly shaking. "Yes."

"But you said you knew he was dead."

"Those who escaped from the ship said he had died!" she yelled, though Geary somehow knew Rione wasn't yelling at him. She calmed herself, taking long, slow breaths. "But the list we captured gives his name and identity number. It says he was badly injured but alive when captured."

Geary waited a moment, but she said nothing more. "That's all?"

"That's all, John Geary. I know the Syndics captured him alive. I know he was seriously hurt. I don't know if he lived for even another day. I don't know if he survived whatever medical treatment the Syndics offered. I don't

know if he was sent to a labor camp. I don't know if he
died after that." She paused. "I don't know."

Victoria Rione, normally so in control, was radiating
pain. Geary moved over and held her close, feeling the
tremors inside her. "I'm sorry. Damn, I'm sorry."

Her voice was slightly muffled now. "I don't know if
he's alive. I don't know if he's dead. If he somehow survived, if he's in a labor camp somewhere, the chances that
I'd ever learn of it, the chances that I'd ever see him again,
are so tiny as to be zero. Yet he could be alive. My husband, the man I still love."

And, Geary realized, she had learned this within weeks
of coming into his bed for the first time. The ugly irony of
it left him wondering why the living stars had done such a
thing to Rione. "Okay. You don't have to say any more."

"Yes, I do. After ten years of staying true to his memory, I gave myself to you, and then learned he might still
live." Rione pushed Geary away and stared off to the side.
"Fate had its joke, didn't it? I thought I had done the right
thing, John Geary. I thought I had honored my dead husband and done as he would have wished. Now I find I may
have dishonored him. Myself as well, but mostly him."

"No." His reply came out without thinking. Geary
paused to order his words. "You've dishonored no one.
Tell me the truth. If he showed up at a labor camp in the
next star system we visit, would you go with him or stay
with me?"

"Go with him," she answered without hesitating. "I'm
sorry, John Geary, but that is the truth, and it will not
change. I've told you where my heart would forever lie."
Rione breathed deeply again, trying to control her emotions. "Desjani knows that, too. She found my husband's
name on the list and came to tell me out of a sense of duty.
Your Captain Desjani is very dedicated in her sense of
duty. She was also hurt for me, though I didn't give her
enough credit for that at the time, and shocked when I revealed that I already had seen the same thing and not told
you." Rione locked eyes with Geary. "She didn't think I

should keep it from you. She didn't want *you* hurt when you found out."

There wasn't any reason to doubt Rione. It sounded just like what Desjani would do. "And when you refused to tell me . . ."

"She wouldn't divulge my secret. Not the noble, honorable Captain Desjani." Rione grimaced and shook her head. "She doesn't deserve to be spoken of by me that way. She was just trying to protect you. Tanya Desjani has honor. If anyone deserves you, she does."

"What?" The conversation had shifted too suddenly. "Deserves me? She's one of my subordinates. She's never given the slightest sign of—"

"Nor will she," Rione interrupted. "As I said, she has honor. Even if she was willing to compromise her own honor, she'd never compromise yours. I, on the other hand, am a politician. I use people. I used you."

"You gave me no promises," Geary repeated. "Damn, Victoria, am I supposed to feel abused here? When you're the one who's been torn apart?"

"You were enticed into publicly sharing your bed with a woman whose husband might still live!" Rione yelled, losing control again. "I have stained your honor and left openings for your enemies to exploit! Why can't you get angry about that?"

"Who else knows about this?" Geary asked, startled.

"I . . ." Rione flung one hand out angrily. "You, me, and the noble Captain Desjani. For certain. Others may have found the same information and be waiting to employ it when it will harm you the most. You have to assume that's the case. You have to assume your honor will be questioned sooner or later because of me."

"I seem to recall you once telling me that you could look out for your own honor. I can do the same."

"Can you?" Rione took a long, deep breath. "If I'm supposed to be your example, you're not very convincing. Why are you trying to defend me?"

"Because any man worth anything wouldn't fault you for an honest mistake—"

"Any man? Will you speak for my husband now, John Geary?" Rione glared at him. "What would I tell him? What should I tell my ancestors? I haven't spoken with them since I learned of this. How can I?"

Geary looked silently back at her for a moment. "Do you want me to speak honestly?"

"Oh, why not? One of us should be honest," Rione answered bitterly.

"Then I'll tell you a few things." Geary kept his voice firm, speaking as if giving commands on the bridge. "First, my honor isn't stained. Neither is your honor. A stain requires *knowingly* doing a dishonorable thing."

"That is not—"

"I don't care how people see things now! A hundred years ago people understood that! Aren't your lives hard enough after a century of war? Do you need to make them even harder by holding yourselves to impossible standards?" Rione stared at him. "I don't have the right to tell you how to feel, but I'm telling you that's how I feel. Secondly," Geary continued, "you're not helping anyone by flaying yourself this way. Yes, in a perfect, ideal universe you could be held to some impossible standard of loyalty. Not here."

She shook her head. "That's unlikely to bring comfort to my husband or to my ancestors."

"What would you have wanted to happen if the situation were reversed?" Geary demanded. "If you'd been badly hurt, taken for dead, and perhaps forever separated from your husband? What would you have wanted?"

Rione spent a long time with her eyes lowered, saying nothing. Finally, she raised her gaze again and spoke calmly. "I would want him to be happy."

"Even if that meant finding someone else if he thought you were dead?"

"Yes."

"And if he then learned you could still be alive but still

possibly forever lost to him? Would you want him to blame himself?"

"Do not use my husband against me, John Geary," Rione spat. "You don't have the right."

He sat back and nodded, trying to stay calm. "That's so. Why not talk to your ancestors? Maybe they'll give you some sign of how they feel."

"Such as the word *adulteress* appearing on my forehead?" Rione asked, still angry.

"Since you already think it's there, why not?" Geary shot back. "But maybe they won't condemn you. They're your ancestors, Victoria. They were human, too. They lived imperfect lives. That's why we talk to them, because they can remember and understand and maybe, just maybe, they can show us some wisdom that we've not yet learned."

She shook her head, looking away again. "I can't."

"Even the most dishonorable can talk to their ancestors! No one can take that from you!"

"That's not what I mean." Rione stared stubbornly toward the opposite bulkhead.

He studied her profile, the set of her jaw, and slowly began to understand. "You're afraid to talk to them? Afraid of how they might react?"

"Does that surprise you, John Geary? Of course I'm afraid. I've done many things I'm not particularly proud of, but I've never done anything that I thought would shame my ancestors."

He considered that for a while. "You don't have to face them alone. There are—"

"I will not share my shame with another!"

"You've already shared it with Desjani and now me!" Geary yelled back.

"And that is where it will end," Rione muttered, her face grim and stubborn.

"I could—"

"No!" Rione visibly tried to calm herself again. "That

would have been my husband's role. I won't have you beside me when I face my ancestors."

That left only one option. "How about Desjani? Could you ask her to accompany you?"

Rione stared at him, plainly shocked.

"She already knows."

"And she detests me."

"Because you wouldn't tell me. Now you have." Rione's eyes wavered. "You said it yourself. Desjani has honor. Your ancestors can't object to her."

Rione shook her head, avoiding Geary's gaze again. "Why would she do that for me?"

"I could ask her." Wrong answer, as Rione's eyes blazed. "Or you could. Do you think Desjani would deny you that?"

She finally sighed. "Oh, no. Not the noble Captain Desjani. She'd even stand beside a politician if that person needed her, wouldn't she? Especially if she thought the great Captain Geary wanted her to do it."

"I think so, but you can leave the 'great Captain Geary' crap out of it. I'm trying to help you here, and Captain Desjani will help you if you ask, so you don't need to keep throwing verbal missiles at either of us."

Rione stood up, gazing down at Geary with a searching expression. "You won't be in command of this fleet forever. Someday you'll get it home. The living stars alone know how, but somehow you'll do it. You can retire the day after that if you want. No one in the Alliance would deny you that. On that day, when you no longer have the responsibilities of command, when regulations and honor no longer keep you from personal relationships with any other officers, would you want to be tied to someone like me, or would you like the freedom to learn the heart of someone like Tanya Desjani?"

"I've never—"

"No. And you won't. Damn you." Rione spun around and left.

•   •   •

GEARY started awake as his stateroom door opened, then closed. He slapped the light control, bringing the dim night lighting to life, and saw Victoria Rione standing there, watching him silently.

"Hello, John Geary." She walked a bit unsteadily toward him, then sat down on the end of the bed, staring at him. "Aren't you going to ask?"

He could easily smell the wine on her breath even across the distance still separating them. "About what?"

"How it went." Rione waved one hand grandly. "Me, my ancestors, and Captain Desjani. Surely you want to know."

"Victoria—"

"Nothing." She shook her head, slightly wobbly, her voice thick. "I explained what had happened. I expressed my remorse. I asked for guidance. Nothing. I felt nothing. They sent me nothing. My ancestors don't even want to acknowledge me anymore, John Geary."

He sat up finally. "That can't be true."

"Ask the noble Captain Desjani! Damn her and damn you." Rione shoved herself to her feet and started pulling off her clothes.

Geary got up, too. "What are you doing?"

"Being what I am." She dropped the last garment and half fell onto the bed, gazing up at him. "Go ahead."

"You must be crazy if you think I'd take advantage of you right now."

"Too honorable? Don't fool yourself. Just be Black Jack for a while. Do whatever you want."

He stared down at her, trying to find words.

Rione spoke again, her eyes looking past Geary now as if seeing other things. "I'll kill him if I have to, you know. If Black Jack tries to harm the Alliance and there's no other way to stop him, I'll kill him. Too many others have died to let their sacrifices be lost. Maybe that's when my honor disappeared, when I vowed to do anything it took to

stop Black Jack." Her eyes focused back on him with
some difficulty. "Anything."

It wasn't easy to say, but he had to speak the thought
that came to him. "Is that why you started sleeping with
me in the first place?"

Her mouth worked; then she shook her head slightly.
"No," she whispered. "I don't think even I would do that."

"Even you? At one point you spoke of things even I
wouldn't do, and now you're being just as hard on yourself." Geary reached down to pull the sheet over her while
she watched, unmoving. "I will not treat you badly, Victoria. You deserve much better, whether you believe that or
not."

He sat down nearby, his eyes on the starscape glowing
softly on one wall. "You're a hard person, a tough person,
but you're just as hard on yourself as you are on others.
Maybe harder. I don't think it's possible for your ancestors to forgive you when you refuse to forgive yourself."

A long time went by in silence, then he looked over
and saw that Rione had passed out. Even now, dead to the
world, her face was lined with distress.

When Geary had first been awakened on *Dauntless*,
he'd been too stunned to really pay attention to the people
in the fleet, the descendants of the people he'd once
known and lived among. After assuming command, he'd
quickly learned about some of the changes that a century
of time and ugly warfare had wrought, and he had been
left believing that he was among strangers who no longer
felt or thought like he did. As the weeks went by and he
learned more about them, Geary had decided he'd too
harshly judged these people and had begun to feel as if he
and they shared fundamental things. But now he felt doubt
again. Honor could be a burden and a sword. It could be
too easily misused. And it seemed the people of the Alliance in this time a hundred years from his own used
honor as a weapon against themselves, making honor so
unyielding and unreasonable that it could just as easily

harm them as their enemies, just as easily endorse injustice as integrity.

Geary sighed, stood up carefully to avoid making noise, then dressed silently. At the door he paused to look back at her. *I've felt so much pain from knowing everyone I once knew and loved was dead. But how many people in the Alliance are like Victoria Rione, not knowing if their loved ones are dead or alive, wondering how to live with their souls torn by uncertainty? How many in the Syndicate Worlds feel the same?* For the first time, he realized there was an advantage to even the cruel certainty he had been forced to deal with. At least it was a certainty.

He roamed the quiet passageways and compartments of *Dauntless*, greeting those members of the crew standing watches in the depths of the ship's night, trying to find comfort in living the rituals of command.

Rounding a corner, he found Captain Desjani doing the same.

"Captain Geary?" Desjani didn't hide her surprise. "Is everything all right?"

"Yeah. I'm okay."

His tone, his attitude, obviously conveyed otherwise. Desjani grimaced. "You've talked with Co-President Rione?"

Geary nodded.

"I had thought . . ." Desjani paused and tried again. "I'd been very angry with her. As you could tell. I thought she'd refused to tell you because she lacked honor. I didn't realize her sense of honor was in fact tearing her apart."

"How did it really go? Did her ancestors really reject her?"

Desjani lowered her head and thought some more. "I felt something. I don't know what. They were there. But she wouldn't accept that, I think."

"That was my impression, too."

"She . . . um . . ." Desjani seemed embarrassed and angry. "I saw her again a little while ago. She'd been drinking, and she said a few things."

"Yeah, I know."

"Sir, I hope nothing I have done or said has in any way led you to think that I would ever—"

He held up a hand to forestall her. "You've been completely professional. I couldn't ask for a better officer."

Desjani still seemed distressed. "Even if you didn't have a great mission to fulfill, even if the living stars hadn't sent you to us at our hour of greatest need, it would still be wrong for me to—"

"Captain, please." Geary hoped his own voice didn't sound too distraught. "I understand. We don't need to talk about it again."

"There are rumors, Captain Geary," Desjani got out between clenched teeth. "About you and me. I've been made aware of them."

"Groundless rumors, Captain Desjani. Created and passed on by officers who themselves lack understanding of honor. I'll do everything I can to act only professionally around you, as I'm sure you will continue to do with me."

"Yes, sir. Thank you, sir. I knew you'd understand." She nodded gratefully, then saluted and walked on. Geary watched her go, realizing that regardless of whether they ever talked about it again, it would still be looming over them constantly.

Eventually he ended up back at his stateroom. Rione was still unconscious, so Geary sat down and called up the simulations again. Three more days of passing through Daiquon Star System, and then the Alliance fleet would be at the jump point for Ixion.

Should he still take the fleet to Ixion? The Syndics had obviously guessed enough about his route to plant mines here. What might be at Ixion?

But then the alternative destinations weren't that attractive. And they definitely had surprised the Syndics by how fast they'd arrived in Daiquon. If the Alliance fleet could keep moving faster than the Syndics could react, they might clear Ixion before the Syndics could get a blocking force in place.

Or not. According to the newest Syndic records they'd been able to steal at Sancere, Ixion boasted a decent inhabited world and a number of off-planet colonies and facilities that could well still be active. It wasn't an empty or abandoned star system.

He'd have to be ready, really ready, when they arrived in Ixion. Assume the jump point they arrived at was mined, assume the Syndics were waiting in ambush. Make sure the Alliance fleet was ready to cope with that.

Put that way, it sounded simple. He wished he knew how to actually do those things.

Geary finally fell asleep in the chair, wishing Rione would get out of her funk and offer him advice again.

WHEN he awoke, stiff from sleeping in the chair, Geary saw Rione still lying in his bed, but she was awake and gazing at the overhead. Without a word, he stood up and went over to the stateroom's sink, pulling out some painkillers and some water, then bringing them over to her.

She accepted the offering, still not looking at him. Only after he had sat back down did she speak. "I don't recall everything I said last night."

"That's probably just as well," Geary noted in a neutral tone.

"I also don't recall everything I did last night."

"We didn't do anything, if that's what you're asking."

Rione nodded, then sighed, then winced as the gestures apparently brought stabs of pain. "Thank you. Now, if you'll do me the favor of turning your back, I'll gather my clothes and whatever shreds of dignity remain to me and spare you having to deal with my presence any longer."

"Suppose I don't want to turn my back on you?"

"Spare me the chivalry, John Geary. Unless you simply want to revel in my nakedness. I've no right to deny you that small pleasure." She looked and sounded defeated.

Geary felt himself getting angry with her, started to tamp it down, then realized sympathy hadn't produced any results so far. "Okay, Madam Co-President. Perhaps I haven't made myself clear." Rione frowned at his harsh tone. "I frankly don't care what you think of yourself right now. I am disappointed that someone of your intelligence and abilities is choosing to wallow in self-pity when I am in desperate need of her advice and good counsel in order to keep this fleet alive and keep my own head on straight. In less than three days we'll be jumping for Ixion, and I have no idea what will be awaiting us there. Have you decided that Black Jack doesn't need you to help him make the right choices?"

Rione's frown deepened, though Geary also spotted a flash of fear in her. Was she wondering what she'd said last night? Whether she'd actually told him straight out just how far she'd go to protect the Alliance from Black Jack?

Geary kept his tone hard. "You've told me time and again how important the Alliance is to you. The Alliance needs this fleet back. If I'm to get it back, I need you working to keep me honest. I'm getting more and more comfortable with being in command, and I'm finding it harder and harder to avoid simply doing things because I can. Because the legendary Black Jack Geary could get away with a lot of things that John Geary doesn't believe would be wise or honorable. What's more important to you, Madam Co-President? Your own misery or the welfare of the Alliance you claim to believe in?"

Rione sat up, the sheet dropping away from her. But she was apparently unaware of that as she glared at him through bloodshot eyes. "So much for the sympathy of the fleet commander," Rione spat at him.

"If you want to medicate yourself for depression, then you'd better try something more effective than alcohol," Geary continued, and this time Rione's eyes lit with fury. "You seem determined not to forgive yourself or to allow anyone else to forgive you. I can't make you change that. But I can insist that you provide me with the best support and advice that you can, and that you refrain from acting in ways that could bring harm to the Alliance as a whole and to the Callas Republic. I expect you to act in keeping with your positions as a senator of the Alliance and co-president of your republic."

She had one fist clenched and seemed ready to leap for Geary's throat. "Is that all, Captain Geary?" Rione snarled.

"No." He paused, realizing that as she sat there half-naked, eyes blazing, Rione resembled an ancient goddess ready to hurl vengeance on an unbeliever. Oddly enough, even through his anger she'd never looked more desirable to him. "Last night didn't happen, if you want it that way. Nothing has ever happened between us, if you want it that way. Whatever it takes to get you on your feet again."

She stood up, flaunting her body, even though she still broadcast fury. "Do I mean that little to you, then? Is that what you're saying?"

"No." He stood up as well, fighting to keep from grabbing her and pulling them both back onto the bed. "I'm saying you mean that much to me."

Not knowing if he could control himself any longer, Geary turned quickly and walked out of the stateroom.

AN entire battle cruiser at his disposal—no, a fleet of battle cruisers and battleships at his disposal—and he didn't have anyplace to go sit down where an audience wouldn't be wondering why Geary looked as if he'd slept in a chair last night. He finally realized the fleet conference room would be private and headed that way, closing the hatch behind him and sinking into the seat at the head of the table.

It felt odd being alone in here, no one else in any of the seats, the table and the room their normal dimensions rather than extending great virtual distances to accommodate all of the ship commanders in the fleet. Geary called up the star display, then the fleet formation, eyeing his ships. *Yeah. My ships. I'm responsible for them. And I know the Syndics will have something waiting at Ixion.*

They'll have something waiting no matter which star I jump to from here.

He hated not knowing how to arrange his fleet. *How can I do that when I don't know what's waiting for us at Ixion? I'm used to having hours at the least, and days or weeks at the most, to see the enemy forces and arrange my own fleet the way I want to deal with the enemy. I can't afford to keep having goat ropes like when we arrived at Daiquon.*

It was like not knowing where Rione was right now. He might return to his stateroom and find her there or run into her coming around a corner. And then what? He'd have to assume the worst and act first, because otherwise Rione might go for his throat after that little speech he'd given before leaving her.

Act first. Damn. It's so simple. I'm too accustomed to normal combat in space, where you have lots of time to plan for the encounter. I just need to assume the Syndics have a heavy force in place waiting for us. And a minefield in front of the jump exit. There's an ambush waiting. I know that. And I have to go there anyway. So have the fleet maneuvering and fighting as it comes out of the jump exit.

Why not? The old fleet in Geary's time couldn't have managed that. Not because it was beyond their skills but because it was too different from what they drilled and planned for. Everything had been more of a set piece then, more elegant, no chaotic melees allowed. But this fleet, these officers who liked nothing better than charging straight at the enemy, they not only could do it but would do it. They just needed a good plan to go along with their willingness to do whatever it took to kill Syndics.

Okay. What's the ambush in Ixion going to be like? Worst case. If it's anything less than that, I'll have time to react. So, worst case, mines right in front of the jump exit. Right behind them the main Syndic force, ready to hit us immediately after our ships take hits from the mines. They'll try doing what we did to them at Ilion, only setting up even closer to the jump point than we did. If they're farther back, fine. That's easier to handle if I'm expecting the worst.

Maybe, if they've been watching me operate, they'll have forces above, below, and to each side as well to catch this fleet in a crossfire as it heads for the main body. Maybe not. That requires a lot of ships. I need to mess up their plan by doing something ships normally don't do, something that this fleet normally hasn't done.

He manipulated the display, trying out different Alliance formations and movements, then, finally satisfied, headed for his stateroom, not sure if he wanted to see Rione there or not.

His stateroom was empty, though. Geary paused just inside the entrance, recalling the look on Victoria Rione's face when he'd left and seriously wondering whether he should have the stateroom swept for booby traps. His ancestors alone knew what kind of retaliation someone like Rione could improvise on the spur of the moment.

Don't get paranoid about her. It's bad enough having to be paranoid about my ship commanders. Geary sent out a message scheduling a commanding officers' conference in half an hour, then hastily got cleaned up and presentable. As he headed back toward the conference room, Geary wondered if rumors of his blowup with Rione had already reached around the fleet, and if so whether it would somehow be brought up.

Captain Desjani had already taken her seat, springing up respectfully when Geary arrived. "Something urgent, sir?"

"Sort of. Not a danger, just something I need to make sure everyone knows before we jump for Ixion."

They waited, watching figures begin to pop into existence as the start time of the meeting approached, the table and the room beyond it seeming to expand to accommodate each increase in numbers.

As the scheduled time arrived, Geary stood to speak, only to be forestalled by Captain Midea of the *Paladin*.

"Have you decided not to go to Ixion?" she demanded. "Are we running away from Alliance space again?"

Everyone around the table seemed to be holding their breaths, waiting for Geary's response. For his part, Geary felt a burst of rage that he had trouble controlling. Work his ass off figuring out how to kick Syndic butt and save Alliance ships and lives, and all he got was more grief from senior officers who should be grateful they weren't making big rocks into little rocks at some Syndic labor camp on a barely habitable world. It didn't help that Captain Midea, who had been a silent presence in fleet conferences up to now, wore a severe expression matched to a uniform so perfect in every aspect that she resembled the Syndic CEOs that Geary had seen.

It took him another moment, while he fixed a level stare at Captain Midea, to be reminded by the identifying data provided by the meeting software that *Paladin* was part of the increasingly infamous Third Battleship Division, home to Captain Casia and Commander Yin, where Captains Faresa and Numos remained under arrest.

The combination of her disrespectful question, his own fatigue from an uncomfortable night, emotional turmoil over Victoria Rione, and frustration with the Battleship Division from Hell almost made Geary explode right then and there. Fortunately, he remembered why he'd called the meeting and realized that either luck or his ancestors had provided the perfect rebuke to Captain Midea.

So, instead of going nova on Captain Midea, Geary gave her a grim smile. "We're going to Ixion, Captain. We're going to Ixion, and we're going to come out of the jump exit in battle formation, because I fully expect the Syndics to have an ambush in place there. I called this conference to ensure you all knew how we were going to fight that battle."

That threw her off, Geary could tell. She'd been expecting to engage him in a debate over his caution, but not only was the fleet charging ahead, it was doing so expecting battle. None of his opponents would dare object to that. Captain Casia, who had appeared poised to leap into verbal combat beside Midea, clamped his mouth shut and sat back.

Geary reached down and began entering commands. The display sprang to life over the table, showing the formation that Geary had worked out that morning. "We're going to get the fleet into Formation Kilo One before we jump. It's a combat formation, with the fleet broken into many subformations, each built around a battle cruiser or battleship division, and all of them arranged to provide supporting fire to neighboring subformations." He rotated the image of the formation on the display, making it clear that it consisted of a staggered series of blocks of ships, twelve blocks in total, arranged into the overall shape of a roughly rectangular box.

Captain Desjani studied the formation along with all of the other officers and spoke first. "In case we run into something like Daiquon again?"

"Right. See, each of these formations is self-supporting. None of our lighter units will be far from heavy support, and all of the heavy combatants will have light units close by supporting them. No matter what we encounter, these subformations will be able to defend themselves, and taken together will let us hit any Syndic formation we run into from multiple angles. It's not a perfect attack formation because we don't know how the Syndics will be arranged, but regardless of how they're set up, we'll be able to maul any Syndics at the jump exit and provide effective protection for our own ships until we get clear of the initial combat area and can adjust our formation to hit them again."

"You're assuming major combat at the exit itself?" Captain Tulev asked. "It happened at Daiquon by chance, but we've never worked that way."

"We will now." Geary smiled at Tulev, then around the table. "We'll come out of the jump exit ready to engage a major enemy force, and we will engage them and we will hurt them badly before they even realize we're there." He could see faces lighting up with enthusiasm. This fleet loved charging into action. Most of his work since assuming command had been slowly teaching these officers to think as hard as they fought. That usually meant avoiding headlong charges, which had been difficult for many of his ship commanders to accept. Now he was offering them something like a headlong charge into battle again, and they were as happy as could be at the prospect of mutual slaughter.

"All units will proceed to stations in Formation Kilo One at time three zero," Geary continued. "Formation assignments will be transmitted to all ships as soon as this conference is over. In addition, we will have maneuvering orders to take effect the instant your ships arrive in Ixion. We'll come through the exit at only point zero five light speed. The instant each ship and their subformation exits jump at Ixion, they are to alter course up six zero degrees."

"Mines?" Captain Cresida asked.

"Right. Changing course up that much should bring us clear of mines set to catch ships coming straight out of the exit. The Syndics were mining the exits here at Daiquon, so we have to assume they're doing the same at other systems they think we're within reach of. Once we clear the minefield, we'll change course down again and accelerate as necessary to engage the enemy."

"That's a lot of mines," Captain Duellos observed. "They must be sinking a lot of resources into that."

"It'll also disrupt their trade with systems not on their hypernet," Geary added.

"They're getting desperate," Captain Cresida concluded. "Everything they've tried to stop this fleet has failed, and we're getting closer to home."

The statement had enough evidence to support it that no one objected, though some faces frowned in thought.

"Are there any questions?" Geary asked.

"Where do we go after Ixion?" Captain Casia had recovered enough to ask.

Just relieve him of command and arrest him, Black Jack urged Geary. He took a deep breath and answered firmly but calmly. "I haven't decided. That depends on what we find at Ixion. There'll be four star systems within jump range of Ixion, five counting Daiquon, though I've no intention of coming back here. Are there any other questions?"

Commander Yin piped up. "Why doesn't Co-President Rione attend these conferences anymore?"

Rumors had flown just as quickly as Geary had thought they might. He wondered just who watched arrivals and departures from his stateroom and how. "You'd have to ask Co-President Rione. She knows she's welcome to attend, and I have every expectation that the ships of the Callas Republic and the Rift Federation keep her informed of events." Those commanding officers all nodded with varying degrees of hesitation.

"Why doesn't she register her opinions here, at the conferences?" Captain Midea demanded. "We know she offers her opinions to you in private."

His opponents had previously tried to generate trouble from accusations that a civilian politician was having too much influence on fleet actions. It looked like that same charge was about to be raised again. Rather than lose his temper, Geary decided to try handling it with humor. "Captain Midea, if you know anything of Co-President Rione, you know that nothing and no one is capable of preventing her from expressing her opinion whenever and wherever she desires to do so." That brought grins to a lot of faces. "Co-President Rione lets me know what she thinks and has in fact provided invaluable suggestions during operations."

Captain Desjani, her own expression carefully composed, nodded. "Co-President Rione is usually on the bridge during operations."

"Co-President Rione was openly offering suggestions during ground operations at Baldur," Colonel Carabali chimed in. "There was no attempt to hide her involvement."

"But why isn't she here?" Commander Yin pressed, her tone implying that something was being hidden.

"I don't know," Geary replied coldly. "A member of the Alliance Senate is not subject to orders from me. As a citizen of the Alliance you have the right to speak with a senator at any time, so why don't you ask her yourself?"

"A politician, with the ear of the fleet commander on a constant basis." *Resolution*'s captain spoke cautiously. "You can surely understand our concern, Captain Geary."

Geary tried to respond in an even voice, even though he wasn't liking where the conversation was going this time. "Co-President Rione is an *Alliance* politician, not a Syndic politician. She is on our side."

"Politicians are only out for themselves," the captain of *Fearless* suggested. "The military sacrifices for the Alliance, while the politicians make bad decisions and big money."

"Such a discussion involves politics, too," Geary suggested. "We're not here to debate the virtues of the Alliance's political leadership. I will state again that Co-President Rione does not and will not make decisions about employment of this fleet, but that she has every right and responsibility to inform me of her opinions and recommendations. Ultimately we work for her, because ultimately she works for the citizens of the Alliance." Did that sound pompous? He wasn't sure. But then he'd never imagined having to remind Alliance officers of those basic facts.

A moment's silence stretched, finally broken by Captain Duellos speaking in casual tones. "You believe the civilian government's authority over you is absolute, Captain Geary?"

A deliberately leading question, one he had no problem answering, but one he couldn't help wondering why it had to be asked at all. "That's correct. I follow orders from the government, or I resign my commission. That's how the fleet works." Not as many nods of agreement answered that as Geary would have hoped. In addition to all of its other damage, the long war had obviously harmed the relationship between the fleet and the Alliance's leaders. Geary's own experience with Captain Falco had revealed to him a belief in parts of today's fleet that military duty might justify going against civilian authority. Maybe Black Jack's mystique could help discredit that corrosive idea before it did even greater damage. "That's what makes us the Alliance. We answer to the government, and the government answers to the people. If any of you doubt the virtues of that system, I suggest you study our enemies. The Syndicate Worlds are what happens when people with power do whatever they want."

That was as close to a slap in the face as Geary could publicly administer to his opponents, and he could see it hit home in some of them. "Thank you. I expect to hold my next conference at Ixion."

Figures vanished rapidly, but this time the image of Captain Badaya remained in the room with Geary. Badaya glanced at Desjani, who gave him a measuring look back and excused herself.

Once Desjani had left, Captain Badaya faced Geary and spoke quietly. "Captain Geary, I've been among those who have had my doubts about you. Like the others in this fleet, I was raised to believe that Black Jack Geary was the epitome of an Alliance officer, the sort of beyond-comparison individual who had saved the Alliance once and might someday return to save it again in the future."

He hated hearing that. "Captain Badaya—"

Badaya held up one hand, palm out. "Let me finish. When the fleet found you, I was *not* among those who were willing to place full faith and trust in you. I didn't oppose you, but I wasn't a supporter, either. After so many years of war I have a hard time believing in miraculous saviors."

Geary smiled slightly. "I assure you that I'm not miraculous, Captain Badaya."

"No," Badaya agreed. "You're human enough. Which is what has led me to join with those who believe most fervently in you. I don't agree with their abstract faith in you, but I do agree that you have proven to be an exceptionally able commander. No other officer I've met could have brought the fleet this far or won the victories that you have. But that's what I must talk to you about. Should we reach Alliance space again, it will be because you brought this fleet there. You did something no one else could do."

Geary suddenly realized where this might be heading and desperately hoped he was wrong.

"How foolish would it be for someone of your talents, someone who could indeed finally win this war, to submit himself to the control of the fools in the Alliance Grand Council and the Senate, who have played such a distasteful part in prolonging this war?" Badaya asked. "You have the idealism of the past, which has served us well, but you need to see what has happened at home in the last century. Yes, the politicians are supposed to answer to the people of the Alliance, but they long since stopped doing anything but looking after their own interests. They've played politics with the fate of the Alliance and the fate of the military that defends the Alliance. How many have died, civilian and military, in a war that has had no end because thoughtless civilian politicians have meddled in the decisions that by rights should belong to those risking their lives on the front lines?"

Geary shook his head. "Captain Badaya—"

"Listen, please! You can make the difference. You can rescue the Alliance from politicians who the people of the Alliance no longer trust or believe in. When we reach Alliance space, you can claim the authority needed to make the decisions necessary to win this war, to end the ceaseless bloodshed. The people will follow Black Jack Geary if he calls on them." Badaya nodded, his expression solemn. "There are many commanders in this fleet who believe the same. I was asked to speak for them to assure you that this belief is not based solely on faith in your legend. And, yes, there are those who will oppose you no matter what. Those officers can be dealt with, for the good of us all."

The implicit opportunity to become a dictator had never actually been offered to Geary so explicitly. Just the statement of the offer constituted treason, and yet he needed officers like Badaya in order to get the fleet home. "I . . . appreciate your reasoning. I am . . . grateful that you think highly of me. But I cannot in good conscience consider what you offer. It goes against everything I believe in as an officer of the Alliance."

Badaya nodded again. "I didn't expect you to jump at the offer. You're far too capable to make such a leap without careful consideration. We merely want you to be aware of what you could do, of the backing you have, so that you may mull it over prior to our return to Alliance space. Once you've really looked over the misgovernment of the politicians in the Council and the Senate, you'll feel differently."

"Captain Badaya, similar sentiments were expressed to me by Captain Falco, though in his case he thought himself the natural one to seize power."

Badaya grimaced. "Captain Falco was always eager to express his confidence in himself. I never liked that. You're different, as different as the great victory you achieved at Ilion compared to the disaster that Falco presided over at Vidha."

Say it. Just say it clearly. He could not leave any grounds for anyone to believe that he would seriously consider the offer. "Captain Badaya, because I'm *not* Captain Falco, I cannot imagine any circumstances under which I would seize power from the civilian government of the Alliance."

Badaya didn't seem offended, just nodding once more. "We expected to hear that. You are Black Jack Geary, after all. But Black Jack Geary is devoted to the Alliance, isn't he? All we ask is that you consider the good you could do. The people of the Alliance need you, Captain Geary, to save them just as you're saving this fleet. I didn't believe that when we first recovered you, but you've made me believe that is true. And don't expect gratitude from the politicians when you bring this fleet home. They'll see you as a rival and try to destroy you. But I assure you that any arrest order will be resisted by the majority of the fleet. Thank you for your time, sir." Badaya saluted, waiting for Geary to return the gesture before his image vanished.

Geary collapsed into his seat and pressed his palms against his forehead. *Damn. "Think of the good you could do." Ancestors, save me from those who hate me and from those who admire me.*

When I found out the Syndic citizens on Baldur were unhappy with their leaders, I thought it was great news. Maybe the Syndics would finally act against their own government. And now I learn as clearly as possible that a lot of the Alliance's own officers are just as unhappy with their government.

Wouldn't that be ironic, if the governments of both the Alliance and Syndicate Worlds collapsed because of the frustrations of their people with this apparently endless war? To be replaced by what? Lots of small, squabbling, fighting gatherings of a few star systems?

What if I face a choice of seeing that happen or accepting the sort of dictatorship that Badaya and his friends want to hand me?

SIX

"I *need* to talk to you." Geary's voice was brittle as he spoke into the intercom. He knew it. He couldn't help it.

Rione didn't answer.

"Damn it all, Madam Co-President, this is about the Alliance. It's about Black Jack."

Her voice ripped into him like a dull knife. "I'll consider it. Now leave me alone."

Geary broke the connection, glaring at the bulkhead. Part of his fleet was ready to mutiny against him, part wanted to back him in treason against the Alliance, and part just accepted him as a decent commander. He couldn't help wondering what the last part would do if Geary gave in to the temptation offered by the second part. Would his fleet end up in a three-way fight against itself, or a two-way fight?

It'd be far different if he didn't know about the hypernet gates, about the very real chance that the Alliance government would learn about the destructive potential of the gates and vote to use them. It wasn't just about saving the

Alliance, but potentially about saving the entire human race.

And he didn't know if he had the strength to resist that, especially since he didn't know which course of action would be right when the survival of humanity was at stake.

Arrest order. He couldn't get that out of his mind. Would the political leadership of the Alliance actually order him to be arrested? And whether they would or not, the fact that an officer such as Captain Badaya believed they would told Geary some things that he didn't like at all.

He considered calling Captain Desjani to ask her about everything. But Desjani might endorse what Badaya had said, and Geary simply didn't want to deal with facing the reality that she believed in him that much. She'd never shown much regard for politicians, Co-President Rione being a notable example. Proper outward respect, yes, but it was clear enough that Desjani didn't trust the political leaders of the Alliance. And now it was abundantly clear that she wasn't unique at all in that respect.

Ancestors, what's happened? I thought I was getting a good grasp on how the people in this fleet thought, on the changes that a century of war had caused, but now I realize there's a lot more, some of it a lot worse, than I had thought.

He finally fell asleep without any answers to the questions plaguing him.

GEARY woke without knowing why, then glanced around his stateroom.

Someone was sitting nearby watching him. He squinted against the darkness, making out the figure's identity. "Madam Co-President?"

"That's correct." Her voice was calm, which was a considerable reassurance. "It frankly surprised me to see that you hadn't reset your security settings to bar my access to your stateroom."

He sat up, trying to clear the lingering traces of sleep from his mind. "It occurred to me that it might be a good thing to let you have continued access."

"I know some of what I said the night I was drunk, John Geary. I know what I told you."

"That you'd do whatever it took to stop Black Jack. Yeah."

"I said more than that," she insisted.

"You said you'd kill me if you had to," Geary agreed. "Maybe I think it's a good thing to have that threat hanging over me."

She sounded exasperated now. "You're either very trusting, very naïve, or very stupid."

"Try scared," he suggested.

"Of yourself?" Rione didn't wait for an answer. "I hear you received an offer."

Geary wished he could make out her expression. He'd wondered if Rione's spies in the fleet would somehow find out about that. "What else did you hear?"

"That your answer was that you'd think it over."

"No. My answer was that it wouldn't happen. Clear and unequivocal."

She actually laughed. "Oh, John Geary, you don't know the first lesson any politician learns. It doesn't matter what you say, it's what people think they hear. Anyone wanting to offer you control of the Alliance isn't going to hear you say no." Rione paused. "You needed to talk. You're tempted, aren't you?"

"Yeah," he admitted. "Because of the hypernet gates."

"You don't trust politicians with knowledge of those weapons? I can't say I blame you. I don't want the Alliance government to learn of them, either. But you don't trust yourself with that knowledge, do you? That's why you gave *me* the program for scaling up the energy released when a hypernet gate collapses."

"Maybe you should be the dictator."

"I think I've given you abundant evidence of my own human failings, John Geary." She paused, then sighed. "You gave me hard words, and I recognized their truth. You may now make another joke about a woman admitting you were right."

"No, thanks."

"By my ancestors, you have learned a little about women, haven't you? Why is the fleet going to Ixion?"

The sudden change of topic startled Geary. "Because it's the best of a lot of bad options."

"You expect the Syndics to be there in force."

"Yeah. I expect them to be present in force at any star we can reach." He tossed off the covers and turned to face her. "I can't stay lucky forever. Daiquon was so close. We might have lost the same number of ships to a finished minefield and not had any Syndic warships taken out to balance the scales. What else have your spies told you? I really need to know what you're hearing."

"Casia and Midea aren't leading the officers opposed to your continued command of this fleet. I haven't been able to find out who is, but they're answering to someone else. Despite being under arrest and guarded by Marines, Numos and Faresa have found ways to pass messages to those who still believe in them."

That shouldn't have been surprising. "But Numos and Faresa aren't the leaders of my opponents, either?"

"No." Rione's voice altered, becoming strained. "And you should know that rumor holds that I am intensely jealous of your relationship with Captain Desjani."

Geary slammed a fist onto his thigh. "My *imaginary* relationship?"

Rione took a moment to answer. "It seems the best counter to those rumors is for me to cease avoiding you and for me to act civilly toward Desjani again. Besides, as you pointed out, I've been neglecting my duties. If you've been honest with me, my advice has been of value to you. You can count on it once more."

"Thanks." Geary hesitated, not knowing how to phrase the obvious next question.

"What's done is done," Rione stated softly. "What I first told you remains true—my heart will always remain another's. But nothing has really changed. Even if my husband still lives, he's just as lost to me, and me to him, as if death had claimed him. My duty will be to the Alliance. I know you need me."

That sounded wrong. "Madam Co-President—"

"Victoria."

It had been a while since she was Victoria to him. "Victoria, I need your advice, and I value your companionship. There's nothing I can ask of you beyond that."

"My honor is already compromised, John Geary. I have to do what I think best from this point on. And I have missed you. It's not entirely a matter of duty."

"That's nice to hear."

"I didn't mean to make it sound so impersonal. Will you have me? I'm not drunk. I . . . need you."

He regarded her in the dimness, barely seeing the shape of her face. She sounded sincere. Yet if Rione's highest priority was saving the Alliance from Black Jack, then she'd want to have him sleeping next to her again. She knew he'd received the offer that she had predicted he'd get someday. And she knew he felt tempted by that offer. Was it a coincidence that she'd finally unbent toward him again on the night of the same day on which Captain Badaya had offered him a dictatorship with the backing of what was claimed to be a majority of the fleet?

Did she truly want him, or was she willing to do whatever it took to be able to act if the time came, or was she hitching herself firmly to his power, an amoral politician ensuring she'd be the consort of the possible future ruler of the Alliance?

Victoria Rione stood up, her clothing falling down around her feet, then walked across the short distance separating them and molded herself against his body. As her lips met his, Geary realized that at some level he didn't care what the answer was as long as she was in his bed again. As she pushed him down and straddled his body, he realized he didn't care if she had a knife in her free hand at that very moment.

"ALL ships prepare to jump." The star Daiquon wasn't much more than a bright point of light to the naked eye now. The fleet had been in Formation Kilo One for days now, ready for anything when they arrived at Ixion. Or so he hoped.

Victoria Rione was in the observer's chair on the bridge of *Dauntless* again, watching the action as if there had never been an interval in which she avoided the bridge. Desjani had greeted Rione politely but with what Geary thought was an undercurrent of worry. For Rione's part, Geary had suspected he caught a gleam of triumph in her eyes as she acknowledged Desjani's welcome. But that was certainly just his imagination, wrought to a fever pitch by worries about what awaited them at Ixion.

"All units in the Alliance fleet, upon arrival at Ixion, immediately execute all preordered maneuvers and engage any enemy warships within range. Jump for Ixion now."

SLIGHTLY less than four days in jump space to Ixion. It shouldn't have been a big deal, but Geary found himself increasingly unhappy with the intervals in jump space. Given the risks they were running, he wished going to Ixion were bringing them closer to Alliance space than it was. Instead of offering a chance to rest and think without the pressure of an immediate Syndic threat, the jump space time felt more and more like wasted periods, the hours and days dragging by while nothing changed outside the ship. Nothing ever had changed outside a ship in jump space, of course, but now that bothered him. He wanted to do something. Confront the Syndics, beat them once and for all in battle, find out the truth about the alien intelligences he and Rione suspected lurked on the other side of Syndic space, and end this damned war.

The fact that he had no chance of actually accomplishing those things even in real space didn't seem to make a difference to the frustration he felt. And he was coming to recognize that in jump space he had more dreams about the past, dreams with people he had known who were now long dead. It wasn't pleasant to wake up from a dream holding a conversation with an old friend and realize the old friend would never speak with him again. Not in this life, anyway.

At least he didn't have to spend this interval in jump space making guilty and sporadic attempts to locate Victoria Rione to learn how she was doing. Rione came to his stateroom every evening and spent every night, her love-making seeming to mix passion and desperation in equal measure. When not in bed with him, though, she continued to hide her innermost self, revealing neither passion nor desperation nor anything else.

Geary distracted himself by running simulations, trying to guess what Ixion would hold, what the fleet would have to do there. But it was all guesswork, and only arrival at Ixion would reveal any answers.

GEARY tried to focus his attention on the display as the time to leave jump space at Ixion approached. Right now all it showed was what had been in the obsolete Syndic records they had looted a dozen star systems ago. The data, several decades old, showed a relatively prosperous system with a nearly ideal planet holding a very respectable population and a lot of off-planet activity and facilities. The records, intended for use by merchant ships, contained nothing about defense capabilities except various standard warnings to do exactly as told if contacted by military authorities.

"Is something wrong, sir?" Captain Desjani asked.

"Just wondering what's there," Geary confessed. "And wondering why a star system this well off didn't get a hypernet gate."

Victoria Rione answered from her position in the observer's chair, once again watching and listening to what happened on *Dauntless*'s bridge. "It could have been politics. In the Alliance, many more planets wanted hypernet gates than there were funds to construct them, and past a certain point, the practical differences between worlds were very minor. Then it became a question of whose politicians could outmaneuver the others."

Desjani, her face turned away from Rione but visible to Geary, rolled her eyes in silent commentary on politicians. Geary managed to keep a straight face, nodding in such a way that Rione but hopefully not Desjani would read it as agreement.

"Stand by to exit jump," a watch-stander called. "Five . . . four . . . three . . . two . . . one . . . exit."

Grayness was replaced by black space and white stars, quiet by pulsing alarms as *Dauntless*'s sensors picked up enemy warships nearby. Simultaneously, Geary felt himself pressed back as the battle cruiser's maneuvering systems executed the preplanned minefield evasion, shoving the bow upward and pushing so hard with the main drives that the inertial dampers couldn't quite block all of the effects on ship and crew.

Next time, the Syndics might try placing the minefield above the jump exit. But this time Geary stretched his mouth in a fierce grin as he saw his fleet angling upward in as tight a turn as the ships could manage at the fleet's velocity. Sensors doing full-spectrum scans of the space around the fleet picked up the small anomalies that marked stealth mines and marked out a minefield along the path the fleet would have taken straight from the exit. Geary did a quick estimate in his head and decided that if the fleet had come through at a higher speed, it couldn't have turned in time to avoid the mines.

Ignoring the rest of the star system, he focused on the

area within a few light-minutes of the jump exit. It took a
moment to believe what he was seeing: the worst case
he'd assumed wouldn't really happen in this form, even
though he'd prepared for it. Just on the far side of the
minefield, Syndic warships waited. Four battleships and
six battle cruisers, plus an even eight heavy cruisers but
only three light cruisers and barely a dozen HuKs, in a
concave-disk formation focused on the center of the jump
exit. Anything coming through the minefield would have
run right into those warships while shields were still
weakened, before damage could be completely assessed,
let alone corrected. But . . .

"They're only a light-minute away and at dead stop relative to the jump exit," Desjani gasped in amazement.

"They've seen Captain Geary breaking the rules," Rione
observed dryly.

Desjani shot Rione a look, then nodded. "The Syndic
high command has seen new ways of fighting, but doesn't
really understand them. Just as we wouldn't have understood what we were seeing if the Syndics had found a
commander with knowledge of past fighting methods.
Now the Syndics think the way to beat us is by doing similar things but pushing them past the points they've seen
the Alliance fleet using."

"You think that's what's happening?" Geary asked.

"I know it," Desjani stated. "We would have done the
same. I'm sure of that. But they're missing the point if
they go to extremes. It's one thing to be close to a jump
exit so you can charge into and hit an exiting enemy after
you've had time to size him up. It's another thing entirely
to be too close to have time to react and without any relative speed advantage!"

"Yeah," Geary agreed, pleased that Desjani had not
only analyzed the Syndic approach but had also displayed
awareness of the weaknesses her own side might have
had. "Our fleet has a speed advantage already. Not a lot,
but with the two forces this close, no one has time to ac-

celerate much before the opposing warships reach engagement range."

The leading boxes of ships in the Alliance formation were clearing the top of the minefield. Geary saw the Syndics begin to accelerate and rotate their formation so that it would center on the leading units of his fleet, and he called out commands to frustrate the move. "All units in the Alliance fleet, accelerate to point one light speed, alter course up two zero degrees. Immediate execute."

The Alliance formation angled even farther back, moving almost vertical now relative to the plane of the Ixion Star System. The ships farthest back in the formation, those just entering normal space and still in their initial turns, wouldn't be able to match the farther turn and would end up slightly out of position, but that wasn't important.

The Syndic disk was flattening out as the big warships in the center of their formation accelerated faster than the small vessels around the rim. "They should have had the battleships and battle cruisers around the rim," Geary remarked, "instead of in the center."

"But they expected us to come at their center," Desjani objected. "Their major combatants would never have accepted roles on the periphery of the formation, leaving the lighter units the honor of being the objects of our assault."

Okay, so even Desjani was still thinking in current ways about tactics focused on satisfying the honor of individual commanders rather than winning a battle. *Thank the living stars the Syndics have become as dumb about combat tactics as the Alliance.*

The Syndics, seeing Geary's maneuver, tilted their formation again, swinging it and aiming for where the lower corner of the Alliance formation would be. They were trying to do a glancing blow at the unsupported units just as Captain Cresida had done with Task Force Furious at Sancere, Geary realized, but without the high relative speeds that Cresida had taken advantage of. Just as Desjani had noted with the placing of ships close to the jump exit, the Syndics were trying to copy what Geary's fleet was doing but failing to grasp the basic concepts. At much slower relative speeds like this, the Syndics were setting themselves up to be hammered.

And he had every intention of doing just that. Geary waited as the trailing units in his formation cleared the upper edge of the minefield. "All units, pivot formation one one zero degrees down at time one seven. Alter course down one one zero degrees, port two zero degrees, time one eight."

The Syndics were still aiming for where the lower corner of the Alliance formation would be, their velocity still less than half that of the Alliance ships, when time one seven came and the Alliance ships brought their bows down, aiming the formation at the Syndics' planned track through space. As the Alliance ships accelerated onto their new course, the broad side of the box containing the Alliance subformations headed toward a point centered on the expected Syndic position.

The Syndic commander may or may not have been a fool, but the tactical situation left him or her few options now, and none of them were good. "Do you think he'll try maneuvering again?" Desjani asked cheerfully as *Dauntless*'s targeting systems locked onto an oncoming Syndic battle cruiser. With the changes in aspect of the formation, the block of ships containing *Dauntless* in the center of the Alliance box was now close to the point where the Syndic formation would pass through the Alliance formation, and it appeared certain that *Dauntless* would draw blood.

"If he tries weaving through our formation, he might confuse our aim enough—" Geary broke off. "What the hell?"

The Syndic formation began to pivot on its axis again, simultaneously altering course down and to one side, but a heavy cruiser and a battle cruiser missed their movements and had to dodge frantically to avoid each other. In its desperate avoidance maneuvers, the heavy cruiser sent another battle cruiser into a wild twist up and to one side, then stumbled directly across the path of one of the Syndic battleships.

There should have been time for even the massive battleship to avoid collision, but its evasive actions were late and too small. The battleship sideswiped the heavy cruiser at a fairly low relative velocity that still measured in hundreds of kilometers per second, turning the smaller ship into a ball of vapor and fragments, collapsing the battleship's shields and sending the heavier ship flailing sideways with its port side blown away.

A light cruiser, scrambling to avoid the stricken battleship, slammed into a HuK, annihilating both ships.

Within the span of a few minutes, the Syndic formation had lost three ships, seen a fourth crippled, and degenerated into a chaotic mess still accelerating to contact with the Alliance fleet.

"Don't any of them know how to drive a ship?" Geary asked, appalled at seeing even enemy ships wiped out that way.

"No," Desjani replied, jubilant. "They're barely trained. We've been inflicting so many losses on the Syndics that they've been rushing new units into action. Congratulations, sir."

Congratulations. It didn't seem the right term for what would have been a one-sided battle but would now be a slaughter. The Syndic warships weren't even trying to regain their formation but were instead attempting to scatter. If they'd been far enough away from the Alliance fleet, or if they'd had a good speed advantage, they might have succeeded.

But they were close, and the Alliance fleet was moving twice as fast as they were. "All units, engage targets of opportunity. Open fire as weapons enter engagement envelopes. Conserve expendable munitions."

The Alliance box swept across the scattered tangle of Syndic ships. A few volleys of specter missiles flashed away from Alliance ships, homing on Syndic targets. The battle cruiser being targeted by *Dauntless* tried accelerating straight through the Alliance formation, not even attempting any evasive maneuvers, which made it a perfect target for grapeshot patterns from *Dauntless*, *Daring*, and *Victorious*.

The impact of the grapeshot on the Syndic battle cruiser's bow shields created a series of incandescent flashes as the metal ball bearings vaporized on impact. The shields collapsed under the multiple blows, allowing the last part of *Victorious*'s grapeshot volley to hit the bow armor of the Syndic, pitting it with more flares of light, heat, and metal turned to gas. The follow-up volleys of hell lances from all three Alliance battle cruisers ripped lengthwise through the Syndic battle cruiser, knocking out every system and probably killing most of the crew.

Geary let out a breath he hadn't known he was holding, then cursed as he realized that he'd been focused on the single engagement with the closest battle cruiser instead of watching the wider battle.

Most of the Syndic warships had been crippled already. Three surviving HuKs were trying to clear the Alliance box, veering wildly to avoid fire coming from all sides. Two of the battleships had staggered through most of the Alliance box, their shields in rags and their armor penetrated by multiple hits. As Geary watched, one of the battleships took two specter missiles up the stern and lost its remaining propulsion capability.

He couldn't get the rest of the Syndics while holding his fleet together. Geary activated one circuit, broadcasting to the Syndics. "All Syndic units are called upon to surrender now. Drop shields and deactivate weapons immediately, or you'll be destroyed." He switched to another circuit to call his own ships. "All units in the Alliance fleet with the exception of Subformation Kilo One Nine and Subformation Kilo One Ten, general pursuit. Break formation and engage the enemy at will."

The damaged ships with the auxiliaries in Subformation Kilo One Nine and the battleships of the Second Battleship Division at the core of Subformation Kilo One Ten wouldn't like that, Geary knew, and within moments a call came in from *Indomitable*. "Sir, why aren't we being allowed to join in the pursuit?"

"Because I need you to ensure that no Syndics try a suicide charge at the damaged ships in Kilo One Nine. You're positioned to guard those ships, and they're counting on you." The auxiliaries were also counting on them, but Geary knew the battleships would be more likely to accept a role of escorting their fellow heavy combatants.

"*Orion*, *Majestic*, and *Warrior* can hold off anything the Syndics have surviving," *Indomitable*'s captain argued.

He really didn't want to debate the issue, especially since the Second Battleship Division was six light-seconds away, making the conversation drawn out by delays in every exchange of messages. He wanted to keep an eye on the battle. How to shut down the complaints? "There is greater honor in protecting an injured comrade than in seeking glory, Captain," Geary stated. "I believe that *Indomitable* and the other battleships of the Second Division are worthy of that honor and can be trusted to carry it out with steadfast courage."

Indomitable's captain blinked as if surprised. "I—"

"Thank you, Captain," Geary added quickly. "I assure you that the Second Battleship Division will be in the forefront of battle in the future, and thank you for carrying out this vital task now."

The Syndic battleship that had lost propulsion was still fighting, a few hell-lance batteries continuing to fire as Alliance warships made repeated passes, slowly reducing it to junk. The other Syndic battleship that had been near it hurled out a burst of escape pods, then blew up.

Geary felt himself jerked to one side as Captain Desjani took *Dauntless* into a tight turn in pursuit of one of the surviving Syndic battleships. *Tight* being a relative term for a ship traveling at close to point one light speed, of course, but even the wide arc of space that *Dauntless* swung through still required the inertial compensators to operate at maximum.

Two of the three fleeing HuKs were dead. The third reeled from a direct hit from a specter, then also began issuing escape pods.

Tearing his eyes away from the battleship that *Dauntless* was bearing down on below and to starboard, Geary tried to figure out which Syndic ships might still be problems. Heavily outnumbered to begin with, the Syndics had lost any hope of either escaping or inflicting significant casualties on the Alliance fleet when their own formation fell apart. Only a single light cruiser still seemed to have a chance at getting away, accelerating at a pace that made Geary look twice to be sure he'd seen right. *They're holding their propulsion units on full emergency thrust. How long can their propulsion systems and their inertial compensators handle that?*

Not long. As *Dauntless* lined up for a firing run on the Syndic battleship, Geary watched the fleeing Syndic light cruiser come apart, disintegrating as its inertial compensators failed and the full stress of its acceleration ripped the ship to pieces. He didn't want to think about what had happened to the light cruiser's crew.

Captain Desjani had her attention focused on the Syndic battleship, which had just endured a fast-firing pass from *Furious* and was now using its surviving weapons to try to hold off repeated blows from destroyers and light cruisers tearing past and getting off one or two hell-lance shots on each pass. "Targeting priority on remaining operational weapons," Desjani ordered. "Fire when within engagement envelopes."

Dauntless shot past the Syndic battleship in the blink of an eye, her automated targeting systems slamming hell lances into the battleship's weapons during the instant in which the two ships were close enough to fire on each other. Only a single Syndic hell lance hit *Dauntless*'s shields, being absorbed without effect.

But most of *Dauntless*'s shots had gone home. The Syndic battleship had only a single battery of hell lances still firing. As *Dauntless* rose past and away from the Syndic ship, *Paladin* came lumbering up and pumped several salvos into the enemy, silencing the last weapon and leaving it without any maneuvering control. *Surrender,* Geary willed the commanding officer of the stricken Syndic battleship, but even though escape pods began spitting out of it, the enemy ship didn't broadcast a surrender.

Despite the fact that the Syndic battleship was out of action, *Paladin* unleashed its null-field projector as the Alliance ship reached its closest approach to the enemy vessel. The glowing ball dug a hole deep into the now-defenseless battleship.

Behind *Paladin*, her fellow battleship *Conqueror* swung in, also firing hell lances into the slowly tumbling wreck as escape pods jetted frantically away from it. Geary watched, feeling his anger rise at the punishment being inflicted on a helpless enemy, and even Desjani seemed to find the overkill distasteful. After firing its own null field, *Conqueror* launched two specters into the derelict as she pulled away.

That gave Geary the opening he needed. "*Conqueror*, save your expendable munitions for ships that still constitute a threat," he snapped.

There weren't any of those left within weapons range of the fleet. A quick examination of the display confirmed that. Geary pulled out the scale, seeing the entire Ixion Star System again, and felt a stab of anger. "Now we know why those capital ships had so few HuKs with them."

Desjani took a look. "Nine more, in groups of three, stationed to use the other jump points out of Ixion."

Geary checked their positions. "The nearest batch of HuKs is three light-hours away. They don't even know we're here yet."

"They won't enjoy the show when the light from this battle reaches them," Desjani noted with a grin.

"I'm not sure this qualified as a battle. Okay, no threat within less than three light-hours. Let's get this fleet back into formation, assuming I can get the Third Battleship Division to stop pummeling dead ships."

"Give them the duty of sending teams to blow up the wrecks," Desjani suggested. "It's tedious work."

"Why should I punish the crews of those ships?" Geary asked. But somebody had to take care of ensuring the Syndic wrecks couldn't be salvaged. "Then again, it'll keep Casia and Midea occupied for a while." He prepared the order, then paused as he examined the damage reports. Very little to speak of, since the collapse of the Syndic formation had stripped all of the enemy warships of support while exposing them to concentrated fire from superior numbers of Allied warships. But—"Damn. How did *Titan* get hurt?" Of all ships to suffer damage, why did it have to be *Titan*?

"Mine strike," Desjani observed. "She couldn't turn tight enough to completely avoid the minefield."

"Captain Tyrosian warned me that *Titan* maneuvered like a pig when her bunkers were loaded with raw materials." Geary sighed. He braced himself and read the details of the damage. "Not too bad, but we need to keep the fleet's speed down so *Titan* has time to fix that damage." It was past time to return a semblance of order to the fleet. "All units, cease fire unless fired upon and assume Formation Delta Two, forming on fleet flagship *Dauntless*."

GEARY sat on the bridge of *Dauntless* watching his fleet re-form, trying to figure out exactly what was bothering him. It wasn't the remaining Syndic presence at Ixion. Annoying as the nine surviving HuKs were, there wasn't anything that could be done about them. Since their mission was clearly to track the Alliance fleet, they'd surely run if pursued rather than seek hopeless combat. Two of the groups of HuKs were so far off they hadn't even seen the arrival of the Alliance fleet in the star system yet. Nor was there any other shipping to worry about. The assorted merchant traffic in the system offered no threat, and as the light from the Alliance fleet's arrival spread through the system, that civilian traffic was fleeing for the nearest possible place of refuge.

The fleet had arrived in Ixion six light-hours from the star itself. Aside from a scattering of mining and manufacturing facilities farther out in the system, the Syndic presence was concentrated around the sole habitable world a mere nine light-minutes from its star. As expected, Ixion had suffered from not being on the Syndic hypernet, though not as badly as some of the places that Geary had seen. It still seemed moderately prosperous and from analysis of the planet's atmosphere and surface retained a large population and plenty of industry.

There was an orbital facility about the habitable world that had been tagged by the fleet's sensors as probably military, but it posed no danger at all to the Alliance fleet. He'd already sent off a brief message to all the Syndics in the Ixion Star System warning them not to attempt to interfere with the Alliance fleet's passage and letting them know about the survivors awaiting rescue at Daiquon.

So what was the problem? The main Syndic combat presence in the star system had been crushed with ease. Too much ease. That was it. "The crews of those Syndic ships were totally green and unprepared for combat."

Captain Desjani looked over at him and nodded. "That's clear."

"And yet they were positioned as if the Syndics clearly expected this fleet to arrive in Ixion."

"Yes, sir." Now Desjani frowned. "That's inconsistent, isn't it? If they believed you'd bring the fleet here, why did they have their least experienced units guarding the jump exit?"

"Good question. And not just a couple of sacrificial lambs, but battleships and battle cruisers. Why did the

Syndics throw away those ships by leaving them to confront us?" Geary looked toward the back of the bridge. "Madam Co-President? What do you think?"

"I think there's something I need explained," Rione replied. "You know those Syndic crews were inexperienced because of their behavior. I remember something like that at Sancere. Some Syndicate Worlds warships barely avoiding collision. But this was much worse."

"The formation at Sancere was made up of new ships with barely trained crews," Desjani pointed out. "Like the one we encountered here, but I'd guess a little better trained."

"So?" Rione pressed. "Why should that matter? How do the crews influence what the ships do when maneuvering orders are given? Aren't the motions of warships controlled by automated systems?"

Geary nodded, realizing that was a perfectly reasonable question. "Right. At the velocities warships move, it's almost always crazy to try maneuvering manually."

"Then why would their amount of training and experience make a difference?"

Desjani spoke like an instructor, apparently oblivious to Rione's obvious annoyance with her tone. "There are three stages of training and experience with maneuvering warships. The least experienced simply don't trust the automated maneuvering systems, since we all know any automated system can suffer errors. What creates the most problems is that as relativistic distortion effects come into play, human instincts are thrown off. We think the maneuvering systems are doing the wrong thing because our senses and our experiences in a much slower environment don't match what we seem to be seeing and feeling when moving at tenths of light speed.

"Crews at that most inexperienced stage are the most likely to panic, decide that the maneuvering systems are in serious error, and try to manage the maneuvers themselves." Desjani waved one hand toward the display. "You saw what happens then. It takes a good amount of time to learn enough to accept that the maneuvering systems know what they're doing and to understand what will happen if you override them. That's the second stage of experience. Those who last long enough come to realize that even automated maneuvering systems can suffer miscalculations and failures sometimes, and that they really do need to be overridden on rare occasions. Then you have to know when to override and what to do, which is the third stage of experience."

Desjani smiled at Geary. "Correct, sir?"

"That's how it was in my time, too. It takes a lot of time moving at point one and up to point two light to develop the instincts needed to correctly second-guess the automated systems." He gestured from Rione to the display. "I say instincts, because it has to happen below the level of conscious thought. There's not enough time for our brains to process it. And even then, only a fool would try to override the autos in a combat situation when two formations are passing through each other. By the time you realized you were going to hit something, you'd already be part of a ball of plasma from the collision."

"Thank you," Rione answered in a flat voice. "Then the answer to your question seems obvious. They thought you might bring this fleet here, but didn't consider it the mostly likely place. It may have been the least likely in their judgment. They left something in place just in case, but didn't really expect that force to end up confronting this fleet."

Geary glanced at Desjani, who nodded. "That seems plausible. But why assume this was the least likely destination for the fleet?"

Rione swung her arm in a grand gesture and spoke with broad exaggeration. "Because the great Black Jack Geary has repeatedly demonstrated that he doesn't make straight runs for Alliance space. He moves carefully, trying to avoid the obvious destinations in favor of ones that the Syndics are liable to judge unlikely."

That made sense. "They're trying to second-guess me

based on my patterns of movements so far, but in this case I did something uncharacteristic."

"Uncharacteristic is one word for it," Rione agreed sarcastically.

"It worked," Desjani noted in a sharp voice, instantly reacting in defense of Geary.

"But we can't count on it working again," Rione replied in a tone just as blunt. "You can see, the first of the Syndic Hunter-Killers is already heading for a jump point. It will carry news of where the Alliance fleet is, and then the Syndics will see a new pattern in the movements of this fleet."

"Yes," Geary broke in quickly to keep the argument from escalating. "You're both right." That didn't seem to make anyone happy, though. "I need to think about our next destination. Thanks for your insights, Captain Desjani and Madam Co-President." He stood up, stiff from sitting since the fleet's arrival at Ixion.

Rione stood as well, accompanying Geary off the bridge. She waited until they were temporarily alone in a passageway before speaking once more. "It won't work again."

"I told you I need to think about it," Geary answered, a little harsher than he had intended.

"It shouldn't take that much thought. I know the next star on the straightest possible line to Alliance space is T'negu. If we go there, this fleet will find a trap far deadlier than those poor fools we encountered here."

"You could be right."

"I *am* right! Even if I don't know all those little details of fleet operations that you and Captain Tanya Desjani enjoy sharing with each other!"

He stopped and glared at Rione. "Is that about the experience question? You asked, and we answered. And you're supposed to be working to disprove rumors that you're jealous of Captain Desjani!"

"Jealous?" Rione shook her head and smiled, but the humor didn't reach her eyes. "Not likely. I just want you

to remember that Captain Desjani worships the space you
sail through. That influences her advice to you. She doesn't
think you can fail."

"That's—" Geary reined in his temper. "All right, I'll
admit that's important to remember. I haven't forgotten it.
Now, I repeat, I haven't decided on where we'll go from
here. Please wait until I've reached a decision before in-
forming me how wrong it is."

"I'll be happy to wait until then." Rione sighed and ran
one hand through her hair. "I'm not trying to be a bitch
about this. I'm worried. This lunge toward Alliance space
has gone far smoother than we had any right to expect.
You're surprised, too, aren't you? Thank you for admitting
that. There's a fine line between the confidence needed to
command this fleet effectively and the overconfidence
that will doom it."

There wasn't any trace of mockery or anger in her now
that Geary could see, so he responded in the same reasonable tones. "I understand that. I know I need someone
whom I trust second-guessing me."

"Someone who knows you're human," Rione emphasized.

"I know I'm not what people think Black Jack is."

"I realize that. But . . ." This time Rione frowned. "Are
you jealous of *him*?"

That came as a total surprise. "What?"

"Are you jealous of Black Jack? The great hero who
can win any battle? Do you want to prove you could be
just as good as him?"

"No! That's ridiculous!"

"Is it?" Rione just watched Geary for a few seconds.
"Many of your most devoted followers, even certain captains, idolize Black Jack and not necessarily you. Any
human would find that frustrating."

"Certain captains know who I am by now." But Geary
couldn't help wondering. He did get angry when Black
Jack came up, almost as if the myth were a rival to the real
man. "I don't think I'm trying to prove anything."

"Thank you for qualifying your statement. All I can ask is that you be aware of the fact that envy of Black Jack might skew your thinking." Rione shook her head. "I still think this dash toward Alliance space was a dangerous thing to do. It worked out this far, but it's left us at Ixion with the Syndics drawing in again. And I wonder if you did it in part because it's what Black Jack would have done."

Maybe he had. After all, the fleet's captains had been restive again, wanting to see progress in getting home, wanting to do something not necessarily cautious but courageous. He'd known that, and he'd given them what they wanted. "I can't ignore what the fleet's officers expect and want. You know that."

"I do. But what they *need* is thoughtful, sensible Captain John Geary, not heroic Black Jack." She stepped back. "Think about what I said. Now, I need to catch up on how the ships of the Callas Republic are doing. I'll see you tonight, if all is quiet."

"Okay." He watched her go, then turned back to his own stateroom. *Have I been trying to outdo or match Black Jack? No. Aggravating as it is dealing with that legend, it has also given me the leverage I need to get the fleet this far. It's not about me trying to outguess Black Jack. No, I've been trying to outguess the Syndics since I ended up in command of this fleet. Now the Syndics have seen enough of what I'm doing to try to outguess how I'm outguessing them. How do I outguess myself and the Syndics at the same time?*

I need to talk to someone else. Who? Duellos, Tulev, Cresida, they'd all have good advice, but it would be the advice of officers trained to think in patterns the Syndics are familiar with. Rione is a very sharp politician, but when it comes to decisions about the fleet, she's got limitations. Desjani . . . Rione was right. Tanya Desjani doesn't think my decisions can be wrong.

Who else is there? I can't exactly ask my opponents in

the fleet for their advice, not that I'd respect advice from
people like Midea, Casia, Numos, or Faresa.
   Or Falco.
   Falco.
   Rione would scream bloody murder.
   But I wonder what Falco would advise. The man's a
fool and insane, but . . . if I'm looking for an opinion to-
tally different from what I would normally do . . .

SEVEN

"HOW'S Captain Falco doing?" Geary asked in a professionally brisk tone with an undercurrent of concern for a fellow officer in the fleet. He didn't want anyone saying that they'd heard him mocking Falco.

The fleet doctor on the screen frowned slightly. "He's happy."

Which could only mean that Falco remained completely delusional. If he had any idea that he was under arrest instead of being in command of the fleet, Falco would be furious. "Is he being treated?"

"He's being kept stable," the doctor replied. "Those are our orders and the usual procedure when a next of kin can't be contacted for a decision on further treatment. We're keeping the condition from worsening, and we're ensuring he doesn't turn violent or self-harming. He spends most of his time developing campaign plans and seeing to the administrative needs of a virtual fleet he can access."

"The last time I checked, the fleet doctors were still running tests and evaluating Captain Falco. Can you tell me now whether or not he can be cured?" Geary asked, not sure whether he really wanted to know the answer.

"Hold on while I review his record." The doctor's image vanished, replaced by a screen holder portraying fleet doctors at work. Geary tried not to get upset with the doctor's attitude, recognizing the same kinds of behavior toward laypeople that doctors had used in Geary's time a century earlier and had probably been using for quite a few millennia before that.

Finally the doctor's image reappeared. "A cure is possible. Probable, I'd say. Of part of the condition," the doctor amended. "We could reduce the delusions substantially, but from my review of Captain Falco's records and history, he was already suffering from a long-term ailment before being committed to my care. That condition probably has become habitual for him and merely correcting physical problems and near-term stress-related reality avoidance wouldn't change Captain Falco's well-established thought patterns."

"A long-term ailment? You mean something that Captain Falco developed while he was a prisoner of the Syndics?"

"No, no," the doctor corrected in the slightly annoyed way his profession had of dealing with the nondoctor parts of humanity who attempted to grasp the secrets of medicine. "Long-term. Even prior to his capture by the Syndicate Worlds, Captain Falco obviously suffered from a condition in which he believed himself uniquely capable and qualified to command the Alliance fleet and win the war for the Alliance. It's more common than you might realize," the doctor lectured, apparently having forgotten that he was speaking to the fleet commander.

"Really?" Geary asked.

"Oh, yes. The condition was common enough to be given a name several decades ago."

"A name?"

"Certainly! It's called a Geary Complex." The doctor paused, frowned, then gave Geary a close look. "That's you, isn't it?"

"The last time I checked," Geary replied, wondering just how many officers in the fleet had suffered from a Geary Complex over the last century of war.

The doctor nodded thoughtfully, eyeing Geary as if expecting him to start raving at any moment. "Well, then, you should know exactly what I'm talking about."

Geary started to laugh, then hesitated. He could imagine what Victoria Rione would be saying right now, and she'd be partly right. He did believe that he was best suited to command this fleet. But that was because his legend could be used to keep the fleet together and the training he'd brought with him from the past could win victories. It wasn't based on any exaggerated ideas of his abilities, on any belief that he alone could command the fleet to victory. And it wasn't about trying to match the legend of Black Jack.

I'm nothing like Falco, and don't want to be like Falco. The differences between us are why I want to talk to Falco.

He ended up shrugging. "Maybe, Doctor. But I don't really want to command this fleet. I don't have any choice. I'm the senior officer and have a duty to perform."

The doctor nodded in the manner of someone humoring a patient. "Naturally. They all say variations on that. Their duty. They have a responsibility to save the Alliance. And so forth."

Geary sighed, not enjoying the too-close-for-comfort conversation. "I have a responsibility to save lives, Doctor, and if you look up seniority information in the fleet database, you'll see that I'm the most senior captain in the fleet by a very wide margin." He'd been promoted to captain a hundred years ago. Posthumously promoted since he was believed dead at Grendel, but the fleet regulations didn't worry about that. Once he showed up alive, the seniority counted. "Can I order treatment for Captain Falco? To get him back to reality?"

"If you're the fleet commander you can order that. Your decision would be reviewed by Alliance authorities, of course."

It should have been easy to decide. Why let a man remain insane? But Falco was under arrest, facing a number of offenses against fleet regulations and Alliance law that carried the death penalty. Cure him, and he'd face a reality far less happy than the delusions he was enjoying. But what right did anyone have to decide not to make someone else well if they had the power? "It's not an easy decision," Geary finally stated heavily.

"I would recommend against it," the doctor replied. "Taking into account all of Captain Falco's circumstances, he could well turn both despondent and suicidal if forced to confront reality. He'd be much better off in a fully staffed and dedicated health facility when he faces those issues."

There was the out that Geary had been hoping for. He wouldn't have to decide on his own. "I see no reason to go against your recommendation, Doctor. Please make sure I'm informed if your recommendation changes, or if Captain Falco's condition changes or deteriorates significantly."

"I suppose I could do that. Yes, you are the fleet commander, so you're authorized to see that information."

"Thank you. I'd like to visit Captain Falco, in virtual mode."

"Visit him?" The doctor seemed startled.

"Doesn't Captain Falco have many visitors?"

"He's under arrest. Did you know that?"

"Yes," Geary explained patiently. "I'm the one who ordered his arrest."

"Oh. Yes. But you want to see him now?"

"See him and talk to him."

The doctor frowned in thought, then nodded. "It's not contraindicated for someone in Captain Falco's condition, and of course since you won't be physically present, there's no bodily risk to either of you. I would advise you not to forcefully confront him with his true status."

"I've no intention of doing that. I assume the software in the fleet conference room can handle a virtual visit by

me to Falco's stateroom. Give me the link and any necessary access codes."

That generated more frowns and warnings about medical procedures and privacy, but the doctor eventually
coughed up the information that Geary needed. He broke
the connection with a sense of relief and headed for the
conference room, trying to fight off a sense of gloom.

He didn't like contemplating what had happened to
Falco. Part of him wanted to hate Falco for causing the
needless deaths of ships and their crews. Part of him just
felt pity for the man. Part of him was afraid of how much
more damage Falco might cause if he were brought back
to reality, or at least the version of reality to which Falco
had long subscribed.

Geary made sure he sealed the hatch to the conference
room under his own access code, activated the meeting
software and its highest level of security, then entered the
data to access Falco.

A moment later the image of Captain Falco stood before him, impeccably attired in his uniform, looking as
if he'd just been engaged in something important. Falco
gazed around, then focused on Geary. "Yes?" After a
moment, Falco's expression shifted from annoyed to the
practiced, automatic smile of camaraderie that Geary remembered.

"Captain Falco, I was wondering if you had time to discuss a few things," Geary began carefully.

"Time? A fleet commander like myself has many responsibilities, you know," Falco lectured, then flashed the
smile again. "But I can always spare time for a fellow officer. I've instructed the Marine honor guard sentries outside my stateroom to ensure any officer who wants to see
me has access."

As the doctor had said, Falco still believed he was in
command of the fleet, even rationalizing the presence of
the Marine guards outside his door as sentries in keeping
with his status. Did he even recognize Geary? "It's an operational question, about movements of the fleet."

"Yes. Of course. I've been reviewing the situation. I haven't yet reached a decision on where we'll go from here."

That was close enough to what Geary had told Rione to make him want to flinch, but he managed to avoid showing it. "May I?" he asked Falco, then activated the star display showing the surrounding region. Falco gave the display a confident look as if he were already intimately familiar with it. "The fleet's at Ixion."

"Of course. The latest offensive is going well," Falco declared.

"Uh . . . yes. But we're heading back to Alliance space now."

"Hmmm." Falco studied the display, then appeared briefly confused for a moment. "Hypernet. The Syndic hypernet."

"We can use it," Geary stated. "But the Syndics will try to destroy any gate before we can reach it."

"Yes. Naturally." Falco pointed. "The most direct route to Alliance space is T'negu. But we're not going there."

Geary had expected Falco to say T'negu was the only reasonable choice. "We're not?"

"Of course not." Falco upped the brightness on his companionable smile. "It's a trap! Obvious, you see?" Geary nodded, not seeing at all. "Mines. The system will be carpeted with them." Falco's expression faltered again. "Mines." Geary wondered if Falco was remembering the damage a Syndic minefield had wreaked at Vidha.

Geary hadn't considered the possibility of the Syndics planting a huge number of mines at T'negu, yet it made perfect sense. The approach to Alliance space necked down here. To keep going in that direction, T'negu was the only option. The system had no habitable worlds and only a small Syndic presence left inside underground cities on one planet with too little heat from the sun and too little atmosphere. Every jump point in the star system could be provided not with just a single minefield but turned into a maze of minefields subject only to the limits of the Syndic mine inventory.

Falco was still staring toward the star display but not saying anything. "Where should we go instead?" Geary prompted.

"Where?" Falco blinked, his eyes returning to Geary, and then going back to the display. "Lakota."

"Lakota? There's a hypernet gate at Lakota. The Syndics will be easily able to reinforce the star system."

"Exactly! They know that we know that! Which means they don't need to reinforce it, because they think we'll be afraid to go there!" Falco grinned triumphantly. "We'll surprise them."

Geary tried to get his mind around Falco's rationale. It made sense, in a way. And it certainly wasn't what Geary would have thought of doing. Was Falco right? The Syndics were clearly feeling the effects of the losses the Alliance fleet had inflicted on them in the last few months. They'd lost a lot of ships. Would they risk leaving Lakota lightly defended believing that the Alliance fleet wouldn't dare go there?

Falco didn't know about the destruction of the hypernet gate at Sancere, didn't know that the Syndics had demonstrated the will to destroy a hypernet gate rather than let the Alliance fleet use it. But the Syndics knew that the Alliance fleet was aware of that.

"There will be a Syndic force guarding the hypernet gate," Geary pointed out. "They can't afford not to have a decent-sized flotilla in the system."

"Of course," Falco said again with a dismissive wave. "Nothing we can't handle. We'll be able to wipe out those defenders, bombard the inhabited world into rubble, then leave as we choose."

That could be so, though Geary had no intention of bombarding civilian targets. The materials from Baldur that Lieutenant Iger had shown him had merely confirmed his own beliefs that an Alliance strategy of unconditional warfare had seriously backfired. Average Syndicate Worlds citizens feared the Alliance, feared to have their home worlds devastated, and so fought all the harder to defeat the Alliance. But did the rest of Falco's argument make sense? Was Falco crazy like a fox in this case?

Geary studied the display. Using jump drives, Lakota did have access to three stars besides Ixion.

It might work.

"Thank you, Captain Falco. I'm sorry I disturbed you." Falco smiled again, and Geary felt a stab of guilt at deceiving a man who was mentally ill. "Are you doing all right?"

Falco frowned slightly. "All right? Yes, of course. Aside from the stresses of command. You know how that is. But I'm honored to be able to serve the Alliance in any way I can. It's my duty." The smile returned.

"Do you need anything?"

"We should have a fleet conference soon. Set it up, will you, Captain . . . ?"

"Geary."

"Really? Some relation of the great hero?"

Geary nodded. "Some relation. Yes."

"Marvelous. Now if you'll excuse me, duty calls." Falco stood and looked around uncertainly.

Geary broke the connection, and Falco's image vanished. *Damn. Damn, damn, damn.*

"LAKOTA!?" Victoria Rione wasn't quite screaming. "Where did you get that idea?" Her face lit with horrified realization. "You spoke with Captain Falco this afternoon. Did he suggest that? And you listened to him?"

"I—" Geary stared at her. "You know I talked to Falco? I put that conference under my tightest security seal."

"I don't know what you *said*, if that makes you feel better." Rione turned away, shaking her head. "Please tell me you didn't ask his advice."

"Not in so many words." Geary felt defensive and knew

that Rione had every reason to be incredulous with him. "I wanted to know what he would do."

"Something stupid! I could have told you that!"

"He didn't want to go to T'negu."

Rione spun back to face Geary and watched him with narrowed eyes.

"Falco thought T'negu would be a trap."

Rione threw her hands up. "And now I find that I agree with Captain Falco about something. I never thought that would happen."

Geary checked to make sure the hatch into his stateroom was sealed. He didn't want anyone overhearing any part of this debate. "Look, I wouldn't go to Lakota."

"Then *don't*."

"The Syndics probably know I wouldn't go there," Geary explained with all the patience he could muster. "They know where I'm likely to go, one of the other stars within reach of Ixion. They know where this fleet will go if it keeps on the straightest possible course toward home. Lakota doesn't match either of those."

"Because going there is *stupid*!"

"The Syndics know it'd be stupid for us to go there, and we know it'd be stupid for us to go there, so maybe that's the last thing they'd expect us to do!"

Rione stared at him. "You're serious."

"Yes!" Geary paced, then paused to turn on the star display in his stateroom and center it on Ixion. "T'negu is too clearly a possible objective for us. We can't go there without assuming every jump point is laced with far more mines than we found waiting for us here. Going back to Daiquon wouldn't achieve anything except hurting morale in this fleet and might land us in the lap of a Syndic force pursuing us through systems we've visited. Vosta takes us up and back into Syndic territory, and there are only two stars reachable using jump drives from Vosta. Kopara takes us off to one side, neither gaining nor losing much ground toward the Alliance, and has only *one* star accessible using jump drives. Dansik, according to our intelligence and the records we've captured, is a regional military headquarters and certain to be heavily defended. That leaves Lakota."

Rione looked from the display to Geary, her expression guarded, then back to the display. "Where would Captain Geary go?"

"Vosta." Geary scowled at the display. "To throw off pursuit."

"But the Syndics have already seen you backtrack that way more than once."

"Yeah."

"Would they think you'd go to Kopara?"

"Doubtful. They'd only have to place strong forces in two star systems to trap us. It'd be nice if they thought I was that dumb, but I can't count on it."

Her expression hardened. "You managed to get us to Ixion, where you don't like any of the options."

He almost snarled in reply but realized the truth of her statement. "I didn't think we'd make it to Ixion. I thought the Syndics would react faster, and we'd divert at Daiquon from the dash toward the Alliance."

"And you're basing your plan now on the hope that the Syndics won't think you're stupid? Listen to yourself, taking advice from Falco! Falco has always been an idiot, and now he's an insane idiot." Rione walked around the star display, burying her face in both hands. "John, don't do it. Don't take the fleet to Lakota."

She'd never called him by just his first name before. "The other options aren't that good. If Lakota works—"

The hands came down, and Rione glared at him. "If! What if it doesn't? What will your options be then?"

"We can avoid combat, proceed across the system, and jump to another objective."

Rione's head sagged. "Do you honestly believe that this fleet will allow you to refuse battle? Yes, it did so after the losses suffered in the Syndic home system, when everyone was so shocked their instinctive urge to suicidal charges was temporarily thrown off. But if you try to

avoid battle at Lakota, some of your ships will turn to engage, and then what will you do?"

That was something he hadn't considered. Geary stared
past her, thinking. "You really believe some of them would
do that? The ones who work against me, people like
Casia, don't seem the sort to risk themselves in heroic
charges against huge odds."

"They're not the ones you have to worry about! What
did the living stars give you for brains, John Geary?"
Rione stepped closer and grabbed his arms. "The ones
most dangerous to you are the ones who believe in you
enough to offer you a dictatorship but not enough to accept changing their own ways of thinking! Ask the officers
you trust most. Roberto Duellos. He'll tell you. Even
Tanya Desjani will tell you. If you don't believe me, then
ask them!"

It made a great deal of sense. "I guess there are advantages at times to thinking like a politician."

"Thank you. I think," Rione flung at him as she
stomped off and pointed at the display again. "If they'd
never believe you'd go to Kopara—"

"No! If we get trapped at Kopara, there's no way out!
Lakota leaves us options." He glared at the display, then
shifted his gaze to Rione. "Why haven't you said it?"

She glared back. "What?"

"Threaten to tell the ships from the Callas Republic
and the Rift Federation not to follow my orders anymore.
Why haven't you warned me that you'd do that?"

"Because I don't make threats I can no longer back
up," Rione replied angrily. "Please don't pretend that you
don't know the loyalties of my own commanders are now
split. No matter what I said, many would still follow you."

"Really?" His surprise must have showed. "I haven't
tried to subvert their loyalty to—"

"Aiyee!" Rione yelled in rage, stepped close again, and
thumped a fist onto Geary's chest. "Stop pretending that
you're that big a fool! They believe in you, John Geary!
Because you've brought the fleet this far and won some

notable victories along the way! They believe that you are
Black Jack and that you'll save them and the Alliance!
They believe that you're not a politician, and in that they
are certainly correct. But you've earned their trust." She
thrust an angry forefinger at the display. "Don't repay that
trust by taking them to Lakota!"

"Hell." Geary let himself drop into a nearby seat, feeling suddenly weary. "Do you think I don't spend every
minute of every day trying to do the best I can by the people who've placed their trust in me?"

Her rage visibly faded, leaving Rione eyeing Geary
with apparent helplessness. "What are you going to do?"

"Call a fleet conference. See how they react to Lakota."

"They'll love it. Just the sort of bold stroke that Black
Jack Geary would do." Rione sagged into a seat as well.

After a minute of silence, Geary looked over at her.
"Madam Co-President, have you ever heard of something
called a Geary Complex?"

Rione raised her head and bent one eyebrow upward.
"Yes. It was first mentioned to me years ago when a fellow senator was telling me about Captain Falco. You finally heard about it?"

"I'm curious as to why you never accused me of having one."

"You could scarcely be accused of imagining you were
Captain John Geary."

"I think there's at least one fleet doctor who suspects
that," Geary replied dryly. "I don't get it. You're different
this time."

"Why, thank you," Rione ground out. "What is that
supposed to mean?"

"Among other things, that you haven't given me any
warnings about the dangers posed by Black Jack, about
what might happen if I start believing I really am him."

Rione shrugged. "I've stated those warnings many
times, and you seem well aware of them. Saying them
again would probably be overkill."

"That's never stopped you before."

"Perhaps it's time I warned you about that misplaced sense of humor you have," Rione stated in a dangerous voice. "Is there some point you're trying to make?"

"Yes." Geary studied her before answering. "You're strongly opposed to the idea of this fleet going to Lakota. You think I'm mistaken; you think I may be trying to live up to the reputation of Black Jack. But you haven't exploded at me. You haven't stormed out of this stateroom or uttered barely veiled warnings about what might happen to me personally if I really start acting like Black Jack would act. Why haven't you done any of that?"

She shrugged, looking away. "Maybe I'm trying to be unpredictable. You think I'll do that, and I know you think I'll do that, so I'm doing something else. Though in my case what I'm doing isn't stupid."

"You've got quite a sense of humor yourself." Geary dropped any pretense or mockery from his voice. "Seriously. What's changed?"

It took Rione a little while to reply; then she finally looked back at him. "To put it bluntly, I have issued dire warnings before about the actions you planned to take. Every single time I was certain that I was right, and every single time it turned out that I was wrong and you were right. Sancere is only the largest of those misjudgments I've made. There's no way of knowing where this fleet would be if you'd listened to me, but I find it hard to believe that it would be in a better state or that our enemies would have suffered anything like the losses they have endured."

"You trust me?" His surprise must have been obvious.

Rione smiled wryly. "I'm afraid so. I think going to Lakota is a mistake. I've told you that, and I've told you my reasons. You've listened. Yes, I noticed that you did. Now, given our respective track records, I don't feel I have the right to work against your instincts. They've been right too many times." She paused, searching his eyes. "Yes, I know you're wondering if your instincts are right about *me*. You aren't sure why I returned to you, why I chose to share your bed in the first place, or why I came back to it."

He nodded. "That's true."

"And you won't ask me, because you don't know if you'd believe whatever I'd tell you. Don't deny it. I see the hesitation within you. I deserve it."

"I didn't say—"

"You don't have to." Rione spread her hands. "Do you want me to say I love you? I won't. You know where my heart is."

"Then why?" Geary demanded. "Why are you sleeping with me?"

"You're irresistible to women. Didn't you know that?" Rione laughed. "You should have seen the look on your face."

He smiled back at her, realizing that Rione would never actually answer the question but just provide more words, the sincerity of which he could never prove. "I'll think some more about it."

"About Lakota? Will you?" Rione's laughter faded, and she nodded. "Maybe that's why I came to you, John Geary. Maybe that's why I'll be with you tonight."

"What about when we return to Alliance space? Assuming we make it. Will you walk off this ship on my arm? Will you still spend the nights with me?"

She regarded him silently for a long moment. "You ask a politician what she'll do in the future? Yes. Do you believe me?"

"I don't know."

"Good job. I'll teach you a bit about politicians yet. You'll need that when you get home." She stood up and extended one hand. "Come on. Let's get something to eat. Publicly. Together. We need to let the fleet see that their hero is happy."

Geary stood up as well, still feeling tired. "I suppose I can try to pretend to be happy for a few hours."

"You'll do fine." She smiled again, differently this

time. "And then we'll come back here, and you and I will make each other truly happy for a while."

Even through the excitement that promise generated, Geary wished he could see what she was really thinking at that moment.

"IT hasn't been easy deciding on our next course of action," Geary announced to the images of the fleet captains gathered in the conference room. The tension was like that before a battle. Obvious opponents like Captains Casia and Midea and Commander Yin were poised to pounce if Geary suggested anything that could be construed as insufficiently aggressive.

His allies, like Captains Duellos, Tulev, and Cresida, were just as clearly worried that Geary would propose something designed to placate the fleet, which would also put it in serious danger. He'd talked to all of them, one-on-one, before this meeting, trying to assure them that he'd thought this out. He hoped he'd convinced them.

Near him, the real presence of Captain Desjani waited, her attention focused on Geary's opponents as if she were a bodyguard. Farther down the table, where the commanders of the ships from the Callas Republic were gathered, the virtual presence of Co-President Rione sat among them. She'd chosen that over physical attendance to ensure that the ships from her republic felt that Rione was still committed to them. But it left Geary wondering how much Rione might have held back in their discussion, whether she would really back him or stay silent or offer a telling word against Geary's plan when debate started.

The star display flared to life. "You're all familiar with our options, I'm sure. T'negu, attractive as it looks, is certainly a trap."

"We made it easily this far along a straight track for Alliance space," Captain Casia interrupted.

"And have thereby established a pattern the Syndics

can see with both eyes closed," Duellos responded. "T'negu is tailor-made for extensive minefields."

"My thoughts exactly," Geary agreed, then pinned Casia with a glare before he could speak again. "The other stars we can reach all offer various shortcomings, various degrees of threats. After long thought and consultation with others, I've concluded our best objective is Lakota."

Captain Midea made to speak, then choked off the words as what Geary had said got through to her. "Lakota?" she finally asked.

"Yes." Whether or not he ended up surprising the Syndics, he'd certainly surprised Midea. That was reassuring, since it meant his opponents' spies in the fleet hadn't been able to discover his plans earlier. "There *will* be a Syndic flotilla there to guard the hypernet gate in that system. But the Syndics may regard our arrival there as so unlikely that the flotilla will be too weak to stop us."

"Can we use the gate ourselves?" someone demanded breathlessly.

"If possible," Geary replied in an even voice. He couldn't afford for any illusions to exist about that. "But we know the Syndics are willing to destroy their own hypernet gates to avoid us using them, and the flotilla at Lakota will certainly have orders to do just that. If we're very lucky, we may catch that flotilla out of position and be able to reach the gate before the Syndics can. That's a very long shot, though. If the Syndics do start to destroy that gate . . ." He let the sentence hang, allowing each officer to bring up their own memories of what the collapse of the hypernet gate at Sancere had been like.

"We can still charge the gate, try to stop them," argued Commander Yin.

"Speaking personally," the captain of *Daring* said, "I'd really prefer not to be near a collapsing hypernet gate again."

"Me, either," the captain of *Diamond* added. "If *Orion* wants to take on the job, I'll gladly let her do so."

Commander Yin glowered at both of the other commanding officers but apparently had enough sense to realize that picking a fight with them would only expose her to further ridicule.

"How many Syndics might be at Lakota?" asked the captain of the *Warspite*. "We've hurt them a lot in the last several battles and torn up the ships under construction at Sancere along with the shipyards there. If the bunch we found waiting for us here at Ixion is any measure, the Syndics are desperate for ships right now."

Captain Tulev answered, his voice somber, "Recall our own serious losses in the Syndic home system. Every loss we have inflicted on the Syndic fleet since then has only gone to balance out the ships we lost in the ambush there."

Grim silence fell around the conference table. No one denied the truth of Tulev's statement.

"But the Syndic warships we destroyed here had totally green crews," Commander Neeson of the *Implacable* noted. "They shouldn't have been sent on an actual combat mission."

"True," Captain Duellos agreed. "Captain Geary and I have discussed this, and we believe the Syndics regarded our arrival at Ixion as unlikely and sent their most qualified ships to other star systems."

"But that means they are short of ships," Neeson argued.

"Short in the sense that they need to try to establish local superiority over us at more than one location, since they can't know exactly where we're going," Duellos pointed out. "They certainly have increasing difficulty doing that."

"And with any luck," Geary added, "that will affect the type of force we encounter at Lakota."

"Did you discuss this matter with Senator Rione?" Captain Midea asked.

Geary eyed her dispassionately, thinking that Midea looked more like a Syndic CEO every time he noticed her. "The proper title is Co-President Rione of the Callas Republic, Captain Midea, though she is also a member of the Alliance Senate. Yes, I did discuss it with her."

"Then going to Lakota is her decision?"

Backs stiffened all along the table. Geary had no difficulty measuring the reaction to that suggestion. He also knew that if Rione was going to object to the plan at this conference, she'd just been handed the perfect vehicle for doing that. "As I have stated before, Co-President Rione does not make decisions regarding the movements of this fleet," he stated firmly.

Rione spoke up, her voice flat. "As a member of the Alliance Senate, I have no command authority in this fleet, Captain Midea. Were you unaware of that?"

Midea's face reddened. "If *Co-President* Rione has a great deal of influence over the decisions of the commander of this fleet, it amounts to the same thing."

Rione smiled thinly. "I'm perfectly willing to swear on the honor of my ancestors that Captain Geary has rarely followed my advice regarding the movements of this fleet."

"The honor of a politician," someone muttered.

Some but not all of the commanding officers from the Callas Republic ships scowled. A number of other officers around the table reacted to the insult with small smiles. Most kept their expressions unrevealing.

Geary knew his own feelings were easy enough to read. "Does my honor satisfy anyone who doubts what Co-President Rione said?" he challenged. Rione hadn't used the opportunity to openly express her doubts in Geary's decision, leaving him both relieved and grateful.

Only silence answered him, until Captain Mosko spoke awkwardly. "You'd be expected to defend her, Captain Geary. Under the circumstances of your relationship. That's also the act of an honorable officer."

"Co-President Rione does not give orders to Captain Geary, and if she tried to do so, he wouldn't listen," Captain Desjani stated in a clear, emotionless voice. "That is my judgment from direct observation of Captain Geary on the bridge of *Dauntless*. I say this on my honor, and I trust no one believes that Co-President Rione and I have any relationship that would obligate *me* to defend her."

"You obviously feel obligated to defend Captain Geary," Captain Midea replied in a tone that implied that Desjani's obligation wasn't based on purely professional grounds.

Desjani turned a hard gaze on her fellow officer. "Captain Midea, I will defend any officer who can defeat our enemies, especially one who can do so as Captain Geary does. He is my fleet commander, and he has honor. *My* enemies are the Syndics and *anyone* who assists them."

The silence this time held an even sharper edge of tension. Captain Casia broke it, though with seeming reluctance to back Midea's intemperate words. "Discussion and debate among commanding officers are accepted within the fleet. They are not cause for accusations of treason."

"Did I accuse someone of treason?" Desjani asked.

Geary spoke in the awkward quiet that followed. "*Open* discussion and debate are accepted, though not once a course of action has been decided upon. I know there are some officers in this fleet who say things in private that they decline to repeat openly. I've said before and will repeat that I encourage suggestions and constructive comments, but I also repeat that as the commander of this fleet, I have the duty and responsibility to make the decisions and issue the orders."

Captain Badaya nodded. "That's what we've learned to expect of you," he stated with a scornful glance toward Casia. "If we can't use the hypernet gate at Lakota, what will be the next objective?"

Grateful for a chance to get back to discussing operational matters rather than real or imagined relationships, Geary gestured toward the display. "We'd have a couple of good options. Which way we go will depend partly on whatever we find in Lakota and how much combat results from that." He looked down the virtual length of the table toward Captain Tyrosian and the other auxiliaries' commanders. "Thanks to the outstanding efforts of our auxiliaries, we've been able to get fuel cell and expendable munitions stocks back up to decent levels, even though we're short of one hundred percent across the board. But doing that has used up a majority of the raw materials we've acquired to date. We'll need to find more to restock the bunkers in the auxiliaries. The urgency of that restocking will depend on how many fuel cells we have to burn at Lakota and how many weapons we have to expend."

"We seem to spend a great deal of time either guarding the auxiliaries or getting them restocked," *Intrepid*'s commanding officer grumbled.

"If we didn't," Captain Duellos pointed out in a cheerful voice, "you'd be in a Syndic labor camp by now, since it's hard to fight without fuel or weapons."

The commander of *Bracer* nodded. "My ship took a lot of damage at Daiquon. The engineers have been working themselves to exhaustion helping us on the repairs. My crew and I are happy to continue escorting them while we're being brought back to fully operational status."

A number of officers looked toward Commander Yin and the acting commanding officers of *Majestic* and *Warrior*. All three battleships were having extensive damage repaired, and none of their commanding officers had spoken up for the auxiliaries. "We're grateful, too," Commander Suram of *Warrior* stated quickly. "We may be operational in time for Lakota."

Revenge's captain smiled. "The Fourth Division hasn't been the same without you." The smile faded. "We still owe the Syndics for *Triumph*. We'll be glad to have *Warrior* helping us pay them back some more."

Damage. Geary frowned down at the table, trying to recall the details of his most badly damaged ships. *Titan* had repaired the mine damage it had suffered, and *Warrior* was coming along well, but both *Orion* and *Majestic* were still barely capable, and a number of lighter units were working hard to get back in shape. If he only had two months free of Syndic pursuit in a resource-rich star system . . . with a dockyard available . . . a big dockyard . . . *I might as well wish for an unguarded Syndic hypernet gate. That's about as likely to happen.* "We will continue paying back the Syndics," he added out loud. "The fleet will be adjusting its course for the jump point to Lakota. We'll enter the jump point a little slower than we did here and this time execute an immediate preplanned turn to port right out of the jump exit at Lakota to avoid any Syndic minefields. We'll be prepared again to fight coming out of jump, but I don't expect to encounter a very close blocking force at Lakota like we did here."

"Once the Syndics authorities here in Ixion report on how easily we wiped out the defenders of the jump point from Daiquon, I don't think the Syndic high command will be repeating that tactic," Tulev observed.

"They'll only repeat it if we're lucky," Geary replied, drawing some more smiles. "Are there any questions? Good. I'll see you all again in Lakota."

This time as the figures of the ship captains vanished rapidly, they left four figures in the conference room beside Geary. Captain Desjani, of course, but also Captains Badaya, Duellos, and Tyrosian.

Tyrosian gave surprised glances to Badaya and Duellos, then spoke rapidly. "I just wanted to thank you, Captain Geary, for appreciating the role we play. I've worked for a number of commanders who just see the difficulties auxiliaries create. It's good to work for someone who knows we're necessary."

"I'm very grateful to have *Witch*, *Titan*, *Jinn*, and *Goblin* in the fleet," Geary assured her. "They're invaluable, and the efforts of their crews have been extraordinary. Please pass that on to those ships."

Tyrosian nodded, saluted hastily, then vanished.

Captain Badaya frowned toward Captain Desjani. "You shouldn't have to put up with nonsense like that from someone like Midea. Three years ago she almost got court-martialed for inappropriate behavior with her executive officer, and now she's publicly implying misconduct on your part."

Desjani made a face. "The words of someone like her don't bother me."

"The fleet would be better off if Midea were relieved of command," Badaya continued. "Unless she has a firm hand on her, Midea has always tended to impulsive actions without thinking them through. There wouldn't be much objection to be her being relieved, Captain Geary. She doesn't have a good reputation. But then neither does Captain Casia."

"Nor did Captain Numos," Duellos pointed out. "Yet many listened to him."

"That's so," Badaya admitted. "But the numbers of such officers are not increasing. I'm not the fleet commander, I don't presume to tell him what to do, but I just want him to know that he need not tolerate Midea's nonsense. And I did wish to express my regret to Captain Desjani, though I suppose there's worse fates than to be thought of as Captain Geary's choice."

Desjani flushed, clearly not pleased at the last comment, though Badaya didn't seem to notice. "Thank you, Captain Badaya," she stated without warmth.

Badaya smiled, saluted crisply, and then his image left as well.

Captain Desjani shook her head, then exhaled heavily. "I suppose I shouldn't be left alone with you, sir," she told Geary in an exasperated and angry voice, "so I'll depart before Captain Duellos does."

Duellos stepped forward. "Tanya, those who know you pay no attention to the rumors."

She nodded. "My thanks. But I still care what those who don't know me think." Saluting as well, Desjani walked quickly out of the room.

Geary gazed after her, his jaw tight. "She doesn't deserve that."

"No," Duellos agreed, "though, contrary to the opinion of Captain Badaya, getting rid of Captain Midea wouldn't improve things. I think it more likely that such an action would merely spread rumors that you'd tried to silence her for speaking up."

"You're probably right. That thing that Badaya said about her needing to be kept on a tight rein, does that match your impression?"

Duellos nodded. "Ironic, isn't it? Captain Numos, who impresses few people as a capable officer, managed to control Midea so well that her recklessness wasn't even apparent when he was in command of that battleship division."

"That is ironic. I never thought I'd have grounds for thinking Numos had any leadership skills." Geary exhaled heavily, looking back toward where Captain Desjani had sat. "How can I put a lid on those rumors? All I can think is that the best thing I can do for Desjani is to keep treating her like a fellow officer and nothing more."

"I think so, though I don't believe it helped things when Badaya somewhat clumsily blessed the idea of her as your companion. Even though he didn't say it, having a politician at your side isn't nearly as desirable in the eyes of many."

"Who I have at my side is nobody's business but mine! As long as I'm behaving honorably and not violating regulations, that is," Geary added.

"I don't deny that. But you're not just any fleet commander, and politicians, even ones as upright as Co-President Rione is said to be, are not trusted. Those who think like Badaya doubtless see your leaving her in favor of Desjani as the best possible outcome, two fleet officers ruling the Alliance." Duellos paused before speaking again. "Would you do it?"

"What?" Geary stared at Duellos. "How can you even ask if I'd do that? I already said I wouldn't treat Desjani that way."

Duellos bent one corner of his mouth in a derisive smile. "Sorry. I accepted your statement about Captain Desjani. I was referring to the offer that Captain Badaya made to you recently."

"Oh." Geary's outrage subsided, and he shook his head. "No. I didn't and won't accept that offer, and I told him that. How many people know about it?"

"Probably every commanding officer in the fleet." Duellos gazed straight into Geary's eyes. "I'm glad you're so firm on the matter. I have my faults and my share of frustration with our political leaders, but I take my oath to the Alliance seriously. I couldn't support you in that. I'd have to oppose you."

Geary just nodded, thinking that of course Duellos would remain loyal to the government. "Is Badaya right? Would most of the fleet back such a move by me? I'm hoping you'll say no."

"Unfortunately, I can't say that. Most likely two-thirds of the fleet would accept you as dictator, though the exact reasons might vary from captain to captain." Duellos looked away for a moment. "And of those captains who wouldn't back the move, at least some would be deposed by their crews in favor of anyone you appointed."

Geary rubbed his forehead with both hands, trying to think. "I don't even want to ask Colonel Carabali for fear she'll believe I'm sounding her out."

"The Marines?" Duellos frowned in concentration. "Now, there's a wild card. Great personal loyalty to you, no doubt, but their loyalty to the Alliance is legendary." He shrugged. "It doesn't really matter. If the crews go for you, there aren't enough Marines to overwhelm them."

"I can't believe I'm talking about this." Geary shook his head, walking slowly to one side of the room and then back. He had to make a firm stand on this, both on the outside and in his own mind. "I won't accept Badaya's offer."

Duellos smiled. "Good. Not that I believed you would, but the stakes are so high, it feels comforting to be told so directly. I wouldn't want to be on the opposite side from you."

"That makes two of us," Geary replied with his own smile. "I think we'll always be on the same side."

"Tanya Desjani would follow you. She'd be torn, but she'd be loyal to you."

"Why are you telling me that?"

"Because I don't think you'd ever ask her to break her oath, and she surely wouldn't under any other conditions, but I wanted you to know that she would do what *you* asked."

"Thanks." Though Geary wasn't sure why Duellos had wanted him to know that. "How do you feel about going to Lakota now? Still worried?"

Duellos smiled slightly again. "Aren't you? It's a risk. Anyplace we go from here is a risk. I think it's a risk worth taking. Sooner or later, no matter how well we guess and plan, our luck will run out, and this fleet will find itself in serious trouble. We might as well die like warriors reaching for the stars rather than like mice hiding in shadows."

"Even if there's a lot of Syndics at Lakota, that doesn't mean this fleet will die."

"Hopefully not. But if it does, you've helped us even the odds after the disaster in the Syndic home system. If we take enough Syndics with us when we go, the Alliance will still have a chance." Duellos saluted. "I'll see you in Lakota."

"WE'VE got company, sir."

Geary jerked awake in his darkened stateroom at the sound of Desjani's voice, slapping the comm panel to acknowledge the message. "How many?"

"Eight Syndic capital ships have arrived in Ixion via the jump point from Dansik. Four battleships and four battle cruisers, accompanied by six heavy cruisers and a standard mix of light cruisers and HuKs. They're about two light-hours distant, relative bearing off of our starboard beam, moving at about point one light as of two hours ago."

"They've probably turned toward us since then."

"Yes, sir. Here it is. We're seeing the turn start now, but I don't think they'll try an intercept. We're four hours and ten minutes from arrival at the jump point to Lakota."

"No," Geary agreed. At point one light just covering two light-hours' distance would take twenty hours. Since the Syndics were coming toward the Alliance fleet at an angle as the Alliance ships kept moving, the distance to be covered would be even greater. "They'll trail us through whatever jump exit we use and come in behind us there." The enemy had been sighted, but there was absolutely nothing to do about it. Turning his own fleet to intercept the Syndics would be worse than useless, since the new flotilla would simply avoid action while awaiting more reinforcements. "Thanks for the information. Continue on course for the jump point to Lakota."

"Yes, sir," Desjani replied.

He lay back down, feeling guilty. Desjani was on the bridge, monitoring the situation and watching the enemy, while he was in his stateroom in bed. Of course there was nothing he could do on the bridge, but it still felt wrong.

One of Rione's hands snaked slowly over his chest. "They'll be coming after us to Lakota?" she murmured in his ear.

"Yeah. Sorry that woke you."

"That's all right. You'll probably have trouble getting back to sleep." Her hand slid lower. "There's no sense in wasting us both being awake, is there?"

News of Syndic warships arriving in this star system didn't seem to have upset Rione. Or maybe she was trying to distract him from his worries. Or maybe she was still very worried about what would happen at Lakota and really didn't want to waste any opportunities together.

After a few moments, he stopped caring about her motivation.

•   •   •

GEARY sat on the bridge of *Dauntless*, eyeing the display showing his fleet. He'd arranged it in an old formation known as Echo Five, consisting of five subformations resembling coins, each a disk facing forward with a little depth to it. Leading the fleet was Echo Five One, built around the remnants of Captain Cresida's Fifth Battle Cruiser Division plus the understrength Seventh Battle Cruiser Division. Two battle cruiser divisions totaling only five ships combined. That was depressing if he dared think about it. With the heavy cruisers, light cruisers, and destroyers attached, the vanguard had decent fighting capability.

On either side of the main body sat Echo Five Two and Five Three, Five Two containing the eight battle cruisers of the First and Second Divisions plus plenty of lighter units, while Five Three was built around the eight battleships of the Second and Fifth Divisions plus lighter support. In the rear of the fleet, Echo Five Five contained the four auxiliaries, the damaged warships with them including *Warrior*, *Orion*, and *Majestic*, plus *Indefatigable*, *Defiant*, and *Audacious* from the Seventh Battleship Division.

The remaining five battle cruisers, including *Dauntless*, the thirteen other battleships, and the two scout battleships, formed the core of the main body in Fox Five Four, the rest of the heavy cruisers, light cruisers, and destroyers escorting them. Taken all in all, the Alliance fleet should be able to handle anything it encountered coming out of the jump exit at Lakota.

"All units have slowed to point zero four light speed," Captain Desjani reported. "All units report prepared to jump."

Geary nodded slowly, hoping he wasn't finally making the mistake he'd dreaded since assuming command of this fleet. "All units, be prepared for combat upon exiting jump at Lakota. All units, jump now."

EIGHT

FIVE and a half days to Lakota. Another five and a half days of staring at the endless gray nothingness of jump space.

"Are you all right?" Rione asked him.

"Worried," Geary replied, keeping his eyes on the display.

She sat down next to him, her own gaze going to the display. "So tell me, how was it in the lights of jump space?"

"Very funny."

"I'm not entirely joking, you know." Rione took a deep breath. "Do you remember anything?"

He glanced at her. "You mean from survival sleep?"

"Yes. A hundred years. There aren't a lot of people who've been kept suspended that long and lived. Only one I know of, actually."

"Lucky me." Geary thought about the question. "I don't honestly know. Sometimes I think I remember dreams, but those could be memories of dreams before the battle at Grendel. I jumped into the escape pod as my ship was about to blow up without time to have thought about the battle or what had happened, and when the doctors in this fleet woke me up, it was as if I'd only been asleep for a few moments. I didn't believe them at first. Thought it was some Syndic trick. I couldn't believe that everyone I'd ever known was dead, everything I'd known lost a hundred years in the past."

"And then you found out you'd become Black Jack Geary, mythical hero of the Alliance," Rione added softly.

"Yeah. The only thing that saved me was having to take command of this fleet. It forced me to pull out of my defensive shell." He remembered the ice that had once filled him, the cold that had tried to wall out the world around him. "If not for that . . ." Geary shook his head.

"Lucky us, lucky you," Rione noted.

"And are you lucky?" he asked.

"Me?" Rione sighed. "I wonder if my husband is one of those lights. I wonder what my ancestors think of me. I wonder what Lakota holds, and what will happen to the Alliance. Is that luck, to live in such times and face such issues?"

"Not *good* luck."

"No. Definitely not."

AT least there was always paperwork to fill the time, to distract him from worries about whatever waited at Lakota, though so very little paperwork actually got printed on paper that he wondered where the name had come from. Geary frowned down at a message from *Furious*. Routine administrative personnel transfers between ships shouldn't be sent to him even as an information copy. He'd be buried in paperwork if that started happening.

Then he read the name on the transfer and called Captain Desjani. "I've got a transfer order from *Furious* and—"

"Yes, sir. I'll be right down to discuss it, sir."

Geary waited, wondering what was going on now, until Captain Desjani arrived. He waved her to a seat, where she sat at attention as usual. Since the rumors of something between them had started, Geary had stopped asking her to relax. He wondered if the transfer order was somehow related to those rumors. "This is an order to transfer Lieutenant Casell Riva from *Furious* to the *Vambrace*."

Desjani's expression didn't change as she nodded. "A heavy cruiser may suit him better, but the needs of the fleet take priority in any event."

"I see." *No, I don't.* "Were you aware of this?"

"Captain Cresida had informed me that she intended transferring Lieutenant Riva, sir."

"And you're fine with that?"

"Sir, I can't concern myself with the fates of junior officers on other ships."

Geary tried not to let his surprise show. "Normally that would be true. I shouldn't be worried about it, either, except that the last I heard, you had hopes that you and Lieutenant Riva would be able to reestablish a personal relationship." How long had it been since he'd talked to Desjani about that? He wasn't sure. So much time devoted to his own relationship with Rione and all the emotional fallout from that, plus the rumors of involvement with Desjani. It had obviously been too long since he'd expressed any interest in how Desjani's own life was going.

Desjani shrugged. "Co-President Rione and I do have some things in common, sir."

That came as a surprise to Geary.

She must have read his expression, because Desjani spoke carefully. "Ghosts from our pasts, churning up old emotions and leaving personal wreckage in their wake."

"I don't understand. I thought you and Lieutenant Riva—"

Desjani shook her head. "Lieutenant Riva developed a strong interest in a fellow officer on *Furious*, and he chose to act on that interest."

"But that's—"

"Yes, sir. Captain Cresida had to come down hard on him for violating good order and discipline. Which is how I heard of it. Lieutenant Riva had not seen fit to inform me of his new interest."

Lieutenant Casell Riva obviously wasn't "Casell" to Desjani anymore, not that Geary could blame her. *Hell. And I'm the one who suggested to Desjani that she send Riva to a ship like* Furious. "I'm sorry."

She shrugged again as if unconcerned. "It's his loss, sir."

"Damn straight."

"It's odd, though," Desjani continued, her eyes looking past Geary. "At times I felt it was as if Lieutenant Riva had been in survival sleep the entire time he was imprisoned. He had stayed the same, his career and his life on hold, locked in the places where they had been when he was captured, just as he was physically locked inside the Syndic labor camp. Everything about him except his age was the same as I remembered." She paused, thinking. "Once he got over the shock of being rescued, of finding me alive, I think it began to bother him that I had changed. I wasn't the lieutenant he'd last seen, the lieutenant he'd remembered during his captivity."

"If he spent that much time thinking about you in camp, I'm surprised he didn't stay faithful once he got out."

Desjani grinned without humor. "I didn't say he was faithful to my memory, sir. There were a lot of women in that camp. Lieutenant Riva availed himself of temporary relationships. He admitted that to me, and I didn't blame him, though I should have wondered why all of the relationships were temporary."

"Was he jealous, do you think?" Geary asked. "Of you being a captain, and having your own ship?"

"I began to sense that, too. It frustrated Lieutenant Riva to see so many officers younger than him who outranked him. I told him promotion would likely come rapidly, but he seemed to feel it should be *now*, that he should some-

how fast-forward until he caught up with the world that
had moved on without him." Desjani's mouth twisted.
"The officer he took up with on *Furious* was an ensign not
much more than half his age."

"That's usually not a smart way for a man to boost his
ego," Geary observed. "Well, I'm still sorry."

Desjani really did smile slightly this time. "I think I deserve better than him, sir."

"There's no doubt of that at all. Thank you, Tanya.
Sorry I bothered you with this."

"I appreciate your concern, sir." Desjani's smile turned
rueful. "I should know better than to expect room in my
life for a relationship. I already have a full-time commit-
ment with a lady named *Dauntless* who demands all of my
attention."

"I know that feeling," Geary agreed. "Being a commanding officer doesn't leave much room for a life.
You're a good captain, though."

"Thank you, sir." Desjani stood and turned to go, then
faced him again. "Sir, may I ask a personal question?"

"You've earned the right to that," Geary observed.
"We've been talking about your personal life. What is it?"

"How are you and Co-President Rione?"

Geary wasn't sure which expression was appropriate
and thought he ended up sort of smiling and lightly frowning simultaneously. "We're doing all right, I think."

"I . . . was surprised, sir. I didn't expect her to go back
to you."

He nodded this time. "Me, too."

Desjani hesitated. "Do you care for her, sir?"

"I think so." Geary laughed shortly. "Hell, I don't
know. I think so."

"And does she care for you?"

"I'm not sure." If there was anyone who Geary could
be open with about that, it was surely Desjani. "I don't
know. She doesn't give a lot of clues to what she's feeling."

"She did once, sir," Desjani stated quietly. "I can't tell

you what Co-President Rione is feeling right now, but I don't think discovering that her husband might be alive would have struck her so hard if she had felt nothing for you. That's just my opinion, of course."

It wasn't something that Geary had considered before. "Thanks for mentioning that. I can't always . . . well . . ."

"Can't always know if she's telling the truth?" Desjani asked with a slight smile.

Geary smiled back at her. "Yeah. Rione's a politician, but then I knew that going in."

"Some politicians are worse than others, which means some must be better than others. And bad as politicians may be, there are worse professions."

"Are there? Well, sure, like lawyers."

"Yes, sir," Desjani agreed. "Or literary agents. I might have become one."

"You're kidding." Geary stared at her, trying to imagine the captain of *Dauntless* sitting at a desk somewhere on a planet, reading and selling tales of adventure instead of living them.

"My uncle offered me a job with his agency before I joined the fleet," Desjani explained. "But aside from everything else, taking that job would have meant I had to work with writers, and you know what they're like."

"I've heard stories." Geary couldn't suppress a grin. "Is that one you just told me true?"

Desjani smiled back. "Perhaps, sir."

She left, but Geary sat watching the closed hatch for a while. It was nice to be able to relax a bit with Desjani. She shared experiences with him, some of those born of separate careers in the fleet, which, though one hundred years apart, still had the common elements every officer and sailor had dealt with from the beginnings of the human race. Others sprang from their time on this ship together, dealing with the strains of command, of fighting alongside each other. It was, Geary realized, easy to talk to Desjani.

I wonder what would have happened if I hadn't been in

command of Desjani and still been on this ship, if we hadn't been constrained by duty and honor . . .

Don't even go there. Don't even start to consider that. That's not how it happened, and that's not how it can ever happen.

HE woke up knowing it was not long after midnight of the ship's day. Ideally, the fleet would arrive at Lakota at some reasonable hour when everyone had the benefit of a good night's sleep and a leisurely breakfast. Assuming anyone could get a good night's sleep the night before arriving in an enemy system holding an unknown number of enemy warships, or stomach breakfast when their nerves were knotted over the thought of impending combat. Still, the opportunity to do those things would have been nice.

But even though humanity had figured out how to break some rules of the universe under certain circumstances, like using the jump drives to travel faster than light between stars, the ways to break rules had their own rules. Traveling in jump space between Ixion and Lakota took a certain amount of time, no more and no less. The Alliance fleet would emerge into normal space again at the jump exit in Lakota at about zero four hundred in the morning on the day/night schedules the ships maintained to keep human biorhythms happy.

Four hours was a long time to lie awake next to Victoria Rione, who seemed to be sleeping peacefully. That alone was unusual enough that Geary didn't want to disturb her. Whatever her thoughts and feelings actually were, at night they caused inner turmoil obvious to someone sharing his bed with her.

He got out of the bed carefully, dressed silently, then left, pausing in the entry to gaze back at Rione for a moment before starting to close the stateroom's hatch, only to hear her call out, fully awake, "I'll see you on the bridge."

"Okay." Damn. He couldn't even tell when she was really asleep. Or know why she'd faked sleep until he was leaving, only to let him know at the last minute that he'd been fooled.

Captain Desjani was clearly awake, sitting in her command seat on the bridge and going over her ship's preparations for battle. She flashed him a look filled with confidence. "You're a little early, sir."

"It's kind of hard to sleep." He spent a few moments going over the same fleet status readouts that he'd been studying for days, then stood up again. "I'm going to walk around the ship."

As he had guessed, just about everyone else in the crew seemed to be awake already as well. Even those who had come off the watches that ended at midnight had stayed up to mingle restlessly with others in mess areas or at duty stations. Geary fixed a hopefully calm and confident look on his face and walked among them, exchanging greetings and making small talk about homes and how they'd surely beat the Syndics again in Lakota System. Whenever conversations veered to when the fleet would get home, Geary tried to be honest. He didn't know when the fleet would once again reach Alliance space, but he was doing all he could to make it happen.

And they trusted him. They trusted him when he said that. They trusted him with their lives. In a very real way, they trusted him to save the Alliance, though saving the Alliance didn't always mean the same thing, depending on who they were.

He paid a little more attention to how the crew members of *Dauntless* talked about home, about the Alliance, trying to see if they expressed the same frustrations with politicians, the same feelings that the blame for the state of the war rested there. Perhaps he was hypersensitive to the issue now, but Geary thought he heard more of that sort of thing than he'd ever realized was being said. *Like Rione told me that time, it doesn't matter what you say as much as what people think they hear. I haven't been hearing this stuff.*

No wonder they welcomed the "miraculous" return of

Black Jack Geary so much. They weren't looking for just a military leader but for someone to lead the Alliance itself. Ancestors, help me.

He returned to the bridge with about an hour to go, finding that Rione was now there in the observer's seat, she and Desjani being outwardly polite when dealing with each other.

The only option left for killing time was calling up the local star systems display and trying to figure out where to go if the fleet couldn't employ the Syndic hypernet gate at Lakota, which was the most likely outcome. As usual, the lack of current intelligence on surrounding star systems ranged from being annoying to infuriating. Branwyn seemed relatively safe as stars went, but had its small human presence and associated mining facilities been abandoned in the decades since the latest reports available to Geary, or were the Syndics still there to complicate any attempt to get more materials for the auxiliaries? Going to Branwyn would also continue toward Alliance space. Had its jump points already been mined? Were Syndic blocking forces already moving into position?

Of the other options, T'negu was actually reachable from Lakota just as it had been from Ixion. Would the jump exit from Lakota be mined or left unobstructed, since the Alliance fleet wasn't supposed to enter T'negu from that direction? Seruta seemed average, bypassed by the hypernet system, with a single harsh but habitable world holding a population measured in tens of millions and a scattering of off-planet facilities. No special threat there, but going to Seruta angled away from Alliance space again. And of course Ixion, the place they'd left.

He didn't like the options, but they were better than in any other place he could have taken the fleet.

"Five minutes to jump exit," a watch-stander called, startling Geary out of his thoughts.

Captain Desjani tapped an intercom control. "All hands prepare for battle upon exit. Remember that the eyes of Captain Geary are upon us."

He tried not to flinch, but something made Geary look back to see Rione's reaction. She gazed back at him with an unreadable expression, but her eyes betrayed nervousness.

"One minute to jump exit."

Geary tried to calm his breathing, focusing on the display where a portrayal of Lakota Star System now hung before him, showing what the old records knew of that star and the Syndic presence there. In moments that display would begin frantically updating as the fleet entered normal space again and the fleet's sensors began spotting everything that wasn't in those old records.

"Stand by. Exit."

Grayness turned to blackness, then Geary felt himself being pushed to one side as *Dauntless* swung through the tight turn preprogrammed into the maneuvering systems. All around *Dauntless*, the rest of the ships of the main body swung together in the same turn. Up ahead, the vanguard was already well into the turn, and to either side the flanking formations were turning along with the main body. Moments later, the trailing formation flashed into existence, then began the same swing to port.

"Where are the mines?" Desjani demanded, then smiled grimly as warning markers sprang to life on the displays. Sure enough, a dense minefield floated along the straight path out of the jump point. The Alliance fleet had now turned so that the coin-shaped formations were moving in the directions of one of the thin sides, as if five coins were standing and sliding across a smooth surface edge first. Off to the starboard of the Alliance formations, the minefield drifted past impotently.

His gaze swinging away from the most immediate threat, Geary searched for enemy warships. None just outside the jump exit. None nearby. His eyes went farther and farther across the display, scarcely able to believe the lack of enemy warships, until they reached the hypernet gate.

The expected Syndic flotilla waited there, cruising slowly past the hypernet gate on what must be a fixed pa-

trol path. "Syndic Flotilla Alpha consists of six battleships, four battle cruisers, nine heavy cruisers, thirteen
light cruisers, and twenty HuKs," the combat systems
watch reported at the same time as the displays portrayed
the identical information.

"We've got them," Desjani exulted. "We can take that
force easily." She turned a fierce grin on Geary, the smile
of a fellow teammate when the other side has made a fatal
error and victory seems assured.

Geary tried to relax himself, scanning the displays for
any more Syndic warships in Lakota. But except for a
couple of HuKs moving down near the inhabited world
five light-hours from the Alliance fleet's current position,
everything seemed to be in the flotilla moving past the
looming presence of the hypernet gate.

"That would be more than enough Syndic firepower to
destroy that gate before we reach it," Rione noted flatly.

"Yeah." Geary nodded. But such a possible opportunity
shouldn't be thrown away. Couldn't be thrown away. Desjani wouldn't be the only officer in the fleet convinced
that the Syndics were easy prey. "A straight charge at the
gate would cause the Syndics to stay there and destroy it.
We need to try to lure them out of position, then get to the
gate before they can return."

"If we destroy them—" Desjani began.

"I know. But our overriding priority is getting to that
gate while it's intact."

Desjani nodded reluctantly.

"How will you lure them?" Rione asked.

"What would you suggest?" Geary replied.

Rione spent a moment thinking. "Offer them something? An irresistible target?"

"Yes," Desjani agreed. "Make them think we're not interested in the gate and present a target they'll have to go
after."

Unfortunately, there was only one Alliance target that
satisfied that need. "Formation Echo Five Five. The auxiliaries and the badly damaged warships." Like sick animals

at the rear of the herd. But he didn't want to lose any of those ships. The auxiliaries remained crucial to the fleet's continued survival, and the damaged warships with them were not only important for the combat capability they retained but for what their presence told the fleet: that Geary wouldn't abandon ships or crews. Using them as bait didn't exactly keep faith with that concept.

He took a long look at the entire situation again. Lakota Star System seemed wealthy after the sparsely populated stars the Alliance fleet had visited lately. The primary inhabited planet, nine light-hours distant on the other side of the star Lakota right now, showed every sign of being a growing and dynamic world. Substantial colonies existed on a couple of other planets, and facilities of various kinds dotted the system on stars, moons, and in fixed orbits. Between all of that a fair amount of civilian traffic moved, merchant ships plying within the system and heading outward from within it or inbound after arriving from other stars, and big ore carriers hauling resources from the mines on rich but uninhabitable outer worlds and asteroids. Fixed antiorbital defenses surrounded a few off-planet locations, but Geary paid them little attention. Those, and the military stations orbiting the inhabited world, were sitting ducks for long-range bombardment by his fleet.

If only they could linger here to haul some of the cargo from those ore carriers onto the Alliance auxiliaries.

The maneuvering systems had no trouble running the actions that Geary wanted. "Second and Seventh Destroyer Squadrons, you are to detach from the formation and intercept the Syndic ore carriers located near the gas giant one point two light-hours to starboard of the fleet. Take possession of the ore carriers and escort them to join the fleet so we can transfer their cargoes to our auxiliaries."

He paused to decide if that was all he needed to order now, then decided to simplify his problems in this system. Geary told *Dauntless*'s combat systems what he wanted destroyed by highlighting targets and how to achieve it by

choosing a weapon, and the combat systems presented a
reply after thinking about it for a tiny fraction of a second.
Geary studied the plan for a few moments himself, then
forwarded it to *Reprisal*. "Eighth Battleship Squadron,
conduct kinetic bombardment of Syndic military installations as laid out in attached plan of action."

As Geary ran his next course calculations, the four
battleships were already spitting out the solid chunks of
metal that would gain energy all the way to hitting their
targets. At the velocities the metal projectiles would be
traveling when they struck their targets, not only the projectiles but also a fair amount of surrounding real estate
would be vaporized. Ships could easily see kinetic projectiles coming and make the tiny alterations in course necessary to dodge something coming from millions of
kilometers away, but installations on objects in fixed orbits were stuck on predictable paths, which had made
them easy targets ever since mankind had weaponized
space.

"All units," Geary ordered, "turn starboard seven two
degrees, down zero three degrees, at time one six." The orders would cause every ship to pivot in place, the formations aligned the same way but now heading in a different
direction so that the broad sides of the coins once again
faced forward.

Desjani only took a moment to analyze the order.
"You're splitting the difference between the jump points
for Branwyn and T'negu?"

"I want to keep the Syndics guessing on our objective,"
Geary explained as he stood. "Ready for another fleet
conference?"

"If you can face them, I can," she replied.

Desjani followed Geary off the bridge, but as Geary
passed Rione, she stood up and came right behind him, in-
terposing herself between Geary and Desjani. "You're
going to be physically present at this conference?" Geary
asked, surprised out of his concentration on his alternatives.

"Perhaps," Rione answered with a frosty edge to her

voice. "I'd like to know what you're going to say before-hand, unless it's a secret."

"All right."

Rione walked alongside him as they headed for the conference room, Desjani trailing and remaining silent.

"I'm going to tell them that I intend trying to lure the Syndics at the hypernet gate out of position. The track we're on will keep them guessing as to our objective but lead them to believe we're just transiting the system and intend leaving as soon as possible."

"Isn't that what you really intend doing?" Rione pressed.

"Well, yes, though if we get that Syndic flotilla far enough out of position, we can make a run for the hyper-net gate. That's going to remain an option."

"Do you really think they'll risk leaving the gate?" Rione wasn't trying to hide her skepticism.

"They might. If they don't, we go on to Branwyn."

The conference room was already expanded by the vir-tual meeting software, most of the fleet's captains already in attendance. A small heads-up warning floated before Geary as he took his place at the head of the table, remind-ing him that because the fleet remained dispersed, there'd be noticeable delays in response times from ships at a dis-tance.

"Welcome to Lakota," Geary stated, realizing that he'd need to come up with some other way to start these meet-ings. "It looks like we outguessed the Syndics again."

"Why aren't we headed for the hypernet gate?" Captain Casia demanded.

Feeling very tired of having Casia interrupt him, Geary just stood and looked at the man for a long time, until Casia began fidgeting. "I'd appreciate it in the future," Geary stated in a voice as devoid of emotion as he could make it, "if you would wait until I have outlined our plans before commenting on them. Is that clear, Captain Casia?"

"I'm only—"

"Am I clear, Captain Casia? Did you understand what I

said?" Oh, yeah. Black Jack could do this. It felt good on
that level. He just had to make sure he didn't push it past
the point that John Geary would regard as appropriate.

"I understood you." Geary's face hardened, and Casia
added a final word. "Sir."

"Thank you." Gazing down the table again, Geary tried
to pick up where he'd left off. "There's only a small Syndic flotilla in this system, but one easily big enough to destroy that hypernet gate if we try to charge it while they
remain in position near the gate. As long as they're there,
we can't hope to access the gate."

He gestured to the display, where a representation of
the Alliance formation glowed, a long line arcing through
Lakota toward a point about midway between two jump
points on the other side of the star. "If we can't get those
Syndics away from the gate, we'll have to use jump points
again. If it comes to that, we'll head for Branwyn." That
brought smiles, since Branwyn led toward Alliance space.
"But we might as well keep the Syndics a little uncertain
until then about whether we might jump for T'negu instead."

"They won't leave that gate," Captain Tulev noted.
"The Syndics must have orders to ensure we don't use it."

"Probably," Geary agreed. "But there's a chance if
they're convinced we're heading for a jump point, and
they see an attractive enough opportunity, that they might
risk coming after us."

Far down the table, Captain Tyrosian flinched. The last
time Geary had needed a lure, it was one of the auxiliaries.
She'd be even less happy when she found out he intended
using all four this time.

Geary altered the display floating above the table,
zooming in on the depiction of the Alliance formation.
"The Syndics can tell the ships in Echo Five Five consist
mostly of our four auxiliaries and our most badly damaged ships. I've already positioned the formations so that
Echo Five Five trails the fleet. As we head across the sys-

tem, Echo Five Five will gradually lose ground on the rest of the fleet as if unable to keep up."

"How much ground?" Captain Midea asked. Her attitude was a bit different, Geary realized. In the absence of an immediate threat, she'd been extremely aggravating. But with the Syndics around in force, Midea seemed more professional, more focused on dealing with the enemy than with messing with Geary.

"Echo Five Five will remain within supporting distance of the rest of the fleet," Geary assured her.

"If so, the Syndics won't take the bait," Midea objected. "We need to be far enough away that the rest of the fleet seems too far off to render assistance."

Duellos was giving Midea a measuring look, Casia was frowning at her, and Captain Cresida was nodding. "She's right, sir."

Geary shook his head. "I can't risk—"

"*Paladin* can fight," Midea insisted. "Put her back there with *Orion* and *Majestic* and *Warrior*. Add in the ships from the Seventh Battleship Division, and we'll have seven battleships in that formation. That's enough to deal with the warships in the Syndic flotilla."

Commander Yin of *Orion* was staring at Midea with unsuccessfully concealed horror. *Majestic*'s commanding officer shook his head regretfully. "We're not front-line capable. Neither is *Warrior*."

"*Warrior* is prepared to engage in combat," Commander Suram corrected quickly and firmly.

Geary gave Suram a measuring look, impressed by his attitude and letting Suram see it.

"Since when does the Alliance fleet need superior numbers to engage the enemy?" Midea demanded. "*Warrior* is ready to fight, so even if you leave out *Majestic* and *Orion*, that would still give us half the number of major combatants the Syndics muster. Alliance ships can easily defeat twice their number of Syndics." She turned an accusing gaze on Geary. "Black Jack Geary defeated *ten times* his number."

Had he really been outnumbered ten to one at Grendel? Funny how he couldn't remember general things like that, just lots of details of the battle.

Geary suddenly realized that Captain Midea had the potential to be a thorn in the side of every fleet commander, not just him. When not facing an immediate threat from the enemy, she was difficult and challenging, and when facing the enemy she wanted to charge straight into battle. He couldn't fault her courage, but being reckless in every environment wasn't a good thing in an officer. He wondered how Numos had managed to keep her under control.

Was the chance of reaching that hypernet gate worth the chance of increasing the risk of losing one or more of his auxiliaries? After all, if the fleet could get home quickly through the gate, it wouldn't need the resupply capability the auxiliaries offered.

Hell, if he believed sacrificing ships like that was a good idea, then why bother attaching the three good battleships of the Seventh Division to the formation? Why not just send the auxiliaries and his crippled warships off alone and let them get wiped out while Geary took the fleet home?

Geary shook his head. "I want to lure the Syndics out, but I cannot expose the auxiliaries or the damaged ships in Echo Five Five to destruction. We need to ensure they have adequate protection."

"Alliance sailors are ready to die for their home worlds," Captain Midea insisted, which earned her a number of looks suggesting that not all Alliance sailors were all that eager to die, even if they were ready to do so.

"My objective," Geary stated, "is to make sure that any *Syndics* who are ready to die have that particular wish fulfilled." That brought him some smiles and some relieved looks. He wondered what he was doing, how he was acting, that those relieved officers thought he would sacrifice ships that way. "I'll run some simulations to check possible outcomes, but for now I don't want Formation Echo

Five Five to drop back more than three light-minutes behind the rest of the fleet. Is that understood?"

"May *Paladin* join that formation?" Captain Midea demanded. "Two of the ships from my division are already
there."

Geary switched his gaze to Captain Casia. "You're the
commander of the division containing *Paladin*. How do
you feel about that?"

Casia bent a dark look toward Midea. "Certainly. *Paladin* can join with *Orion* and *Majestic*."

"Captain Mosko?" Geary asked. "You're in command
of Echo Five Five. Do you need *Paladin*?"

Mosko shrugged. "Need it? No. But *Indefatigable*, *Audacious*, and *Defiant* are always ready to welcome a sister
ship alongside us, under my command." The last three
words were emphasized slightly, resulting in Midea nar-
rowing her eyes at Mosko. She didn't object to them,
though.

"What about *Conqueror*?" Captain Duellos asked innocently. "If she also joined Echo Five Five, then the entire
Third Battleship Division would be together again, fighting as one."

The look Casia gave Duellos would have killed if that
were possible. "*Conqueror* should remain in a position
to . . . to coordinate with the fleet commander."

Geary eyed the man, trying to decide if putting so
many of the bad eggs in the Third Battleship Division into
one formation again was just asking for trouble, and if
sending Casia there wouldn't create more problems. But
in a way Duellos was right. Sending *Paladin* to Echo Five
Five and keeping *Conqueror* in Echo Five Four didn't
make sense.

*No. If I send Casia back there, too, I'll have to keep my
eye on him constantly. I can't afford that distraction.*

Captain Mosko frowned slightly. "If Captain Casia
were also in the formation, it might create some confusion
about command arrangements in Five Five."

Geary nodded judiciously, grateful for another reason

to turn down Duellos's mischievous suggestion. "That's true. And we can't let Echo Five Five get too strong, or the Syndics won't be attracted to it. *Paladin* will ensure the formation is not too badly outmatched in terms of numbers. Are there any other questions?"

"What about the Syndics we left at Ixion?" said Commander Neeson of *Implacable*, not asking a leading question but a real one. "Four battleships and four battle cruisers. They haven't shown up yet, but they will."

"They're waiting," Captain Tulev announced. Everyone looked at him, clearly wondering at his reasons for the statement, so Tulev shrugged and continued his explanation, his face impassive. "Lakota wasn't the most expected destination for us. Correct? So they think maybe we're not going there for real but intend jumping there and jumping right back to Ixion to confuse the Syndics."

Duellos nodded. "So they wait."

"Yes," Tulev emphasized. "Jump takes five and a half days here, five and a half days back. They wait, say, twelve days total. We don't reappear at Ixion, they jump after us then."

"We could be clear of Lakota by the time they jumped in here," Captain Cresida objected.

"So? There's a Syndic flotilla at the hypernet gate. There's Syndic facilities and the inhabited world. If we just pass through and jump elsewhere, they know, but if we're here to create long-term trouble, they catch us anyway."

"They might also have been waiting for reinforcements they expect to meet them at Ixion," Captain Badaya objected.

Tulev frowned, then nodded. "True. Either way, they come here eventually, but not right behind us."

"That sounds like a good assessment," Geary agreed. "We can't forget about that force, but we don't know when they'll get here. We should be a long way from the jump exit from Ixion by the time they do, though. Anything else?"

Captain Tyrosian spoke with visible reluctance, as if
not wanting to draw attention to herself and the state of
the auxiliaries. "Raw materials stocks on the auxiliaries
are getting low, but we have new fuel cells and munitions
available for transfer to warships."

"Can we risk transferring supplies while the Syndics
are out there?" Tulev asked.

Geary tapped some controls and rechecked the status of
his warships. Not great, but okay. "Go ahead and transfer
their share of fuel cells and new munitions to the ships in
Echo Five Five," he told Tyrosian. "That activity will help
provide a plausible cover for you falling behind the rest of
the fleet and maybe make you look a little more vulnerable.
Captain Tyrosian, there are two destroyer squadrons rounding up some Syndic ore carriers not far from the track we're
following. Hopefully we'll be able to manage an intercept,
and you can bring some material off those ships for the
bunkers on the auxiliaries."

He thought that would be all, but then Midea spoke
again. "Captain Geary, if you wish to offer the Syndics an
inviting target, then transfer to one of the ships in the trailing formation in such a way that the Syndics know you've
done that. The chance to eliminate Black Jack Geary will
be a very powerful temptation."

There was plenty of truth to that. Especially since he
was asking other sailors to risk their own lives as bait. *But*
Dauntless *has the hypernet key on board. A lot of people
still don't know that, but I do. I have to stay with* Dauntless. Was he grateful that the hypernet key offered an out?
It wasn't that *Dauntless* was necessarily safer than a ship
in the trailing formation, but the battle cruiser and her
crew were familiar, the only truly familiar things Geary
had in this universe a century removed from his own. It
probably was a weakness, but he didn't want to go
through the emotional turmoil of trying to get accustomed
to another set of surroundings, not with battle looming
and so much else to deal with. Two big reasons for staying on *Dauntless*, neither of which he wanted to discuss

here and now. "Thank you for the suggestion, Captain Midea, but I feel I can best continue to command the fleet from *Dauntless* within the main body of the formation."

To Geary's surprise, Midea briefly revealed a flash of success, as if Geary had done what she wanted. Her next words explained why. "Is the fleet best served by a commander who's making decisions for the wrong reasons?"

Desjani was giving Midea a murderous look.

Geary shook his head. "Explain that statement, Captain Midea."

She shrugged lightly in reply. "We're aware that you have strong reasons for not wanting to leave *Dauntless*," Captain Midea stated, giving the name of the ship an ironic twist as if actually referring to something else.

Now Desjani flushed with anger, and Geary understood what that something else was. Yet in order to counter Midea's sly innuendo, Desjani or Geary would have to explicitly bring up the rumors of their being involved together.

Desjani's tone was as hot as her face. "I will not—"

Victoria Rione's voice, as cool as Desjani's was warm, cut across the conference like a saber forged from ice. "Captain Midea, do you know something I do not? Or are you referring to me?"

Midea might resemble a Syndic CEO in the perfection of her uniform and her attitude, but Co-President Rione had about her all the cold authority and aloofness that Geary remembered from his first encounters with her. *Intimidating* was an inadequate word to describe Rione at times like this.

Captain Midea obviously felt the same way, clearly groping for some way to avoid openly stating what she had previously implied. Casia was giving Midea the look of a superior whose subordinate had just royally screwed up. To Geary's annoyance, his closest allies among the officers, such as, Duellos, Tulev, and Cresida, were silently watching Midea's discomfort with ill-concealed satisfaction and not changing the topic, even though pursuing it would just generate more discontent.

Fortunately, Captain Badaya stepped in, speaking as if imparting a lesson that his students should already know. "Every officer in the fleet is surely aware that Captain Geary has developed a good *working* relationship with the commanding officer of his flagship. That's an important and beneficial command arrangement. It's easy to understand why Captain Geary wouldn't want to disrupt that situation and attempt to forge a similar working relationship with a new flagship commander when the fleet is in an enemy star system and facing combat."

Badaya's statement had the virtue of being absolutely true and not open to dispute. It also offered Midea an out, which she jumped on. "Of course that's so. I was expressing my concern that the fleet commander might benefit from shaking up the current command arrangement, but as you say, this is not the optimum time to do so."

The entire room seemed to relax, but then Geary spotted Rione turning an icy gaze back on Midea. He managed to catch Rione's eye and silently convey a wish for letting the matter drop. Rione gave him a stare that briefly made Geary feel cold as well, then subsided.

"That's all," Geary added quickly. "We're just under seven days from the jump point for Branwyn if the Syndics don't take the bait we're going to dangle. We'll have to see what happens and be ready to react. Thank you."

Within moments almost every virtual presence vanished, though Badaya lingered just long enough to give Geary what might have been a subtle wink. Hoping that Desjani hadn't seen that, he turned to her as Badaya left. "I'm sorry, Captain Desjani."

"It's not your fault, sir," she replied firmly. "By your leave, I need to return to the bridge." Desjani hastened out, her back stiff as she marched past Rione.

That left only Rione and the virtual presence of Captain Duellos with Geary. Duellos inclined his head respectfully toward Rione, then faced Geary. "Sorry. My fun made things a little more difficult for you."

"Yeah, I noticed. Just remember that if I die and you inherit command of this fleet, my spirit is going to be watching you and laughing as you try to deal with these people."

Duellos smiled slightly. "I'll remember that. Knowing your spirit is watching would be a comfort, even if it was mainly for your spirit's amusement." His smile faded into a look of concern. "Does everything feel too calm to you?"

"Now that you mention it, yes," Geary agreed. "I'm wondering if it's just because we expected a lot of trouble here, and it didn't materialize."

"Not yet, anyway," Duellos cautioned. "I have a premonition that our troubles in this star system won't remain confined to fleet conferences."

"We should be able to deal with anything that shows up now," Geary observed. "But I'm a bit worried, too. Speaking of troubles, though, do you have any ideas short of relieving her of command for shutting up Captain Midea?"

"I was already trying to figure that out," Duellos admitted. "Midea was Numos's executive officer before being promoted to captain and given command of *Paladin*. As we discussed back in Ixion, he knew how to keep her quiet. We could ask Numos."

"No thanks. I don't think I'd trust anything he told me. Hell, he could be getting messages to her."

"That's possible." Duellos paused to think. "Numos could actually be prodding Midea into acting like this. Hopefully he's not goading her into anything more than rash words."

"Yeah. That's definitely something to worry about, though I don't know what I can do about it." Geary gave Duellos an aggravated look. "Speaking of goading other officers, at the next conference please restrain yourself from taunting our opponents, okay?"

Duellos grinned, saluted, and vanished.

Rione was still seated, and now she turned an apparently unruffled expression on Geary. "You should let me deal with people like that Midea woman. I'm not a fleet officer and I can't debate movements of ships in these meetings, but she's playing politics, and I can run rings around her in that area."

He thought about that, then nodded. "Okay."

"And you should be more worried about placing that woman's ship any farther away from your control," Rione added. "As Captain Duellos said, she's either getting out of the habit of deferring to Numos or she's being provoked into foolish actions. She's been more aggressive and argumentative in each successive conference since Numos was arrested."

"You think that she'll act the same way in her ship?"

"I'm certain of it. You shouldn't have let her go to the other formation. She'll do something contrary to orders. I'm sure of it. And when she does, she may haul some other ships along with her."

That took Rione's assessment out of the realm of troublesome and into the area of major concern. "Damn. You may be right. I wish—" He managed to choke off the next words.

But Rione knew what they would have been. "You wish I'd expressed that during the conference? The same conference where you made a clear sign to me to sit down and shut up?"

"I didn't tell you to sit down and shut up!"

"You made it plain I should stop speaking," Rione stated in a voice lacking warmth. "I don't blame you. It would have put you between a black hole and a supernova."

"Why?" Geary asked, thinking that Rione probably qualified as the supernova.

"Because if I'd spoken up against Midea's ship going to the other formation, any agreement by you would have looked like confirmation that I, the unspeakable politician, exercise too much influence over you." Rione made an angry gesture. "But if I don't speak up, as I didn't, you don't get a perspective you *might* find worthwhile. You can't act on opinions I don't give you."

Geary sat down, thinking. "That's what my opponents in this fleet want, isn't it? To drive wedges between me and the people whose support and advice I need. You're a prime example. *The* prime example." Rione sketched a mock bow from her seat. "And those rumors are getting in the way of Desjani and me working together. How do I deal with this?"

"With Captain Desjani or with me?" Rione asked in a voice gone cold again.

"Both of you! She's my flagship captain, and you're my adviser and my . . . uh . . ."

"Lover. That's the polite term. If you call me your mistress, I promise you'll be sorry."

"Warning noted. So what do you suggest?"

"Make sure your behavior around Captain Desjani is so impeccable that it cannot be used to feed rumors any reasonable person would accept. I assume there's at least a few reasonable officers among your commanding officers? For me, continue to display your independence of me in public. I assure you that I was far from the only one to notice your command that I silence myself."

"I didn't—"

"And I'm sure most people who noticed will see it as I described it." Rione twisted one corner of her mouth up. "Evidence that you're dominating me will help calm the worries of those who think I'm controlling you."

"Dominating you?" Geary couldn't help laughing. "That's one concept that honestly never occurred to me."

Rione raised one eyebrow.

"You're not the dominatable type," Geary added.

"At least you've learned that much," she noted dryly.

"I've had a few lessons." Geary stood again. "I think I'll go to the bridge and go through some of the fleet status information again and maybe run some simulations."

"Why the bridge? You can do all of those things in your stateroom."

"That's true." He frowned slightly at her, wondering why she'd made a point of that. "Are you headed that way?"

Rione shrugged. "Eventually. I've a few things to deal with first."

"If Captain Midea is found dead with a knife in her, I'll probably have to have the knife checked for your finger-prints and DNA," Geary remarked, trying to defuse a re-newed sense of tension he couldn't understand.

She smiled in reply, her tone half-mocking, half-serious. "There wouldn't be any fingerprints or DNA on the knife, John Geary. Not if I did it."

NINE

MORE than three days gone, and the Syndics hadn't moved. As the fleet cut across Lakota Star System, the distance to the hypernet gate off to one side had gradually diminished. In another couple of hours the Alliance fleet would be at its closest point of approach to the hypernet gate (though close was a relative term when talking about a distance of three and a half light-hours), and then begin opening the range again as it proceeded toward the jump points.

Geary had kept his eye on both the Syndics and his own Formation Echo Five Five. But since arriving in the formation, Captain Midea and *Paladin* had behaved themselves, holding station near *Orion* and *Majestic*.

The only excitement that had happened was watching the kinetic barrage launched by the Alliance battleships slowly spread out across the vast distances of the Lakota Star System, scores of tracks headed on intercepts with the orbits of certain moons and planets and installations. As the barrage reached each objective, the sensors on *Dauntless* provided sharp, clear pictures of the impacts,

Syndic defense installations and fixed weaponry vanishing in fountaining bursts of plasma and debris.

"At least we've done something in this system," Desjani grumbled after they'd watched one more Syndic facility turned into craters rimmed with broken junk. Then she gave Geary an embarrassed look. "I didn't mean—"

"I understand. I'm frustrated, too."

Off to one side, the captured Syndic ore carriers were slowly converging on the Alliance formation, the two squadrons of Alliance destroyers escorting them like vigilant sheepdogs. In order to make the intercept, the lumbering Syndic merchant ships were burning almost all of their fuel cells in sustained acceleration, but since they wouldn't be going anywhere once the Alliance was done with them, that scarcely mattered.

"Seven hours until Echo Five Five meets up with those ore carriers," Desjani observed.

"Yeah. Why aren't the Syndics doing anything? They've never been this passive when we entered one of their systems."

Unfortunately, intelligence couldn't provide any answers, either, though Lieutenant Iger suggested that if Geary swung close by the habitable world, it might provoke more Syndic message traffic that could be exploited. Not wanting to burn more fuel cells by diverting the fleet from its path to go closer to that world, and not wanting to put any ships in danger from Syndic defenses mounted on the planet, Geary declined to implement the suggestion.

The Alliance fleet was almost an hour past its closest approach to the hypernet gate, with Geary seriously considering additional steps to make his auxiliaries more attractive targets for the Syndic flotilla still guarding the hypernet gate, when something finally happened. Unfortunately, it wasn't a good thing.

"Captain Geary, there's a Syndic flotilla exiting the jump point from T'negu."

By the time Geary reached the bridge of *Dauntless*, the

fleet's sensors had finished analyzing the size of the new force. Captain Desjani pointed to the display. "We ran the numbers, and it looks like this was the blocking force at T'negu, where they expected us to go. One of the HuKs watching us at Ixion surely jumped for T'negu as soon as they saw we'd jumped for Lakota. If our information on jump transit times from Ixion to T'negu, and then T'negu to here, are right, there would have been just enough time for that HuK to reach T'negu, inform the Syndics there of where we were actually going, and for them to jump here."

"We should have expected that," Geary noted, angry with himself. During its retreat so far through Syndic space, the Alliance fleet hadn't encountered many situations where that sort of space geometry applied, but that was no excuse for missing it here.

"Syndics don't usually react that quickly," Desjani pointed out. "It should have taken them a while longer to get approval to leave T'negu and come here."

Geary didn't debate the point, gazing glumly at the size of the new Syndic flotilla. "Eighteen battleships, fourteen battle cruisers, twenty-three heavy cruisers." Plus plenty of light cruisers and HuKs. The Syndic forces at the hypernet gate and this new flotilla combined now roughly equaled the size of the Alliance fleet. "The odds in this star system just evened up."

"We still have an advantage over each of those forces individually," Desjani argued.

"Yeah, if we can bring one of them to action without the other. But that new force is heavy enough to be a big problem." He thought about what would have happened if the Alliance fleet had arrived at T'negu and run into a maze of minefields plus that big Syndic flotilla. Things could definitely be worse. He took another look at the display. "They must have seen us the instant they entered the system. Why aren't they headed to intercept us?"

Desjani shook her head. "I don't know, sir. Smaller Syndic forces have been more aggressive than that when we've met them." She turned to look at him. "Maybe they're frightened of you."

He almost laughed, but Desjani appeared absolutely serious. "That'd be nice if true," he finally noted. "But—"

"They're turning!" a watch-stander called out. "Syndic Flotilla Bravo is adjusting course and speed."

Geary's eyes went back to the display. The Syndic force was a good three light-hours away. They'd seen the Alliance force over three hours before the Alliance fleet had even been aware that the Syndics had arrived. Plenty of time to plan something or to send or receive orders from the Syndic authorities in this system. Yet only now was the new flotilla apparently reacting to the presence of the Alliance fleet.

"They've turned past an intercept course," Desjani noted, surprised. "Where are they going?" Unfortunately, the answer to that became apparent all too soon. "They're heading for the jump point for Branwyn," Desjani noted sourly.

"Obviously not to jump that way," Geary added. The Syndic forces he'd encountered before this had tended to be aggressive, even when that didn't make much sense. This flotilla wasn't acting like that. "Are they just going to sit at that jump point like the other flotilla is sitting at the hypernet gate? Is this the new Syndic tactic, to wait us out until we do something dumb?"

Desjani frowned. "They were laying mines at T'negu, we think."

"Yeah." The meaning of that got through to him. "They're going to mine the jump point to Branwyn, aren't they?"

"I think so, sir. With us trying to leave this star system, they can completely block the jump point so that we can't reach it without going through part of the minefield."

"Which we'd have to slow down to do to keep from losing too many ships, thus making us vulnerable to high-speed attacks from that flotilla." The number of good options was shrinking rapidly now. "Do you think we can lure them away from the jump point for Branwyn by pointing this fleet at the hypernet gate?"

Desjani thought, biting her lower lip, then nodded. "They can't afford to let us reach that gate with superior numbers, and the commander of that new flotilla will catch hell if he or she forces the first flotilla to destroy the gate by not coming after us. But the gate flotilla can destroy it on their own if need be, and threatening the gate now would mean turning our heels to the new Syndic force. It won't look right."

"I want to get this new Syndic flotilla out of position so we can attack it," Geary pointed out.

"That's true," Desjani noted doubtfully.

"They won't attack rashly," Rione observed.

Geary turned to look, not having realized that Rione had joined them. "Why not?"

"Because even Syndics learn eventually if hit hard enough." Rione looked at Geary. "How many Syndic warships has this fleet destroyed under your command? How many battles have you won? Not only won but done so in a one-sided manner not normally seen. You've done this again and again." She waved toward the depiction of newly designated Syndic Flotilla Bravo on the display. "The Syndics have learned. They doubtless have orders to engage you only under favorable circumstances, to force you into a bad position. They can wait us out, but we don't have the luxury of trying to wait them out."

"They're frightened of Captain Geary," Desjani repeated triumphantly. "But the only way they can stop this fleet from using the jump point for Branwyn is by full-scale battle."

Geary studied the situation. Everything important was pretty much in the plane of the star system right now, neither significantly up nor down relative to each other. The Alliance fleet, taking an arcing path through space, had traveled more than halfway to the new jump point and was now heading outward through Lakota Star System, its ships' bows pointing toward deep space. The Syndic hypernet gate and the enemy flotilla standing sentry near it were just over three light-hours away in a direction just aft of the port beams of the Alliance ships. The inhabited world orbited partway on the other side of the star Lakota, nearly a light-hour distant and totally irrelevant in terms of threats to the Alliance ships right now. The new Syndic flotilla had entered through the jump exit from T'negu about three light-hours off the starboard bows of the Alliance fleet and had turned onto a course that would take it slowly across those bows. If neither fleet changed course or velocity again, the new Syndic flotilla would cross the bows of the Alliance warship at a distance of about half a light-hour, continuing on toward the Branwyn jump point. But the Alliance fleet had to change its trajectory. It couldn't simply keep heading out into empty space. The question was, how to change it and where or what to aim for?

Make a pass at the habitable world to see if the Syndics would follow to try to keep the Alliance from bombarding it? No, he'd already seen enough in other star systems to know that the Syndic leaders wouldn't waste time worrying about the fate of civilians or even the industry on a world. More than once the Syndic leaders had actually tried to provoke such a bombardment, probably in hopes of ensuring their people remained fearful of the Alliance.

Dodge back toward the hypernet gate in hopes the new Syndic flotilla would follow? As Desjani had pointed out, there wasn't any guarantee the Syndics would cooperate. Continue on toward the jump point for Branwyn, knowing that the new flotilla would be laying mines and waiting to pounce if Geary's fleet actually tried to jump out of Lakota there? He didn't need to look at Desjani again to know she expected Geary to charge the biggest enemy force, and most of his other commanders would have the same attitude. If he turned away, some might continue on toward the jump exit, determined to force battle.

Geary's eyes went to the fleet status readouts, and in

particular the fuel cell levels on each ship. *I don't have the fuel cell reserves to go charging back and forth across this system. The Syndics don't have to react unless I actually close on the hypernet gate, and then they'd destroy it and leave this fleet out of position for reaching any of the jump points to leave Lakota. And if the gate collapsed in such a way that it released one of the higher levels of potential energy discharge, this entire star system and everything in it might be destroyed. Everything—including this fleet.*

Keep it simple. Try to avoid using up this fleet's fuel cells, so I'll have them when I really need them. I don't really have a choice. "Captain Desjani, we're going to intercept the Syndic flotilla heading for the jump exit for Branwyn." She grinned, and so did the watch-standers on the bridge. "Can you give me a recommended intercept course?"

"One three degrees to starboard, up zero four degrees," she answered immediately. "That's if we increase speed to point zero seven light to intercept the Syndic flotilla as it reaches the jump point for Branwyn. Time to intercept will be forty-one hours, twelve minutes."

"Thank you, Captain." Desjani must have already run the intercept calculations, naturally. Even though the Alliance ships were currently all oriented so they would be turning to their left, or to port, fleet maneuvering commands used the external star system as their reference. Otherwise, in space where ships might face in any and all directions, no two ships could be certain of what each other meant by left and right, up or down. The rule in a star system was that port was away from the sun, and starboard was toward it, while up and down referenced the plane of the star system. Since the intercept course required the Alliance fleet to turn a bit toward the sun of Lakota, that meant the turn was to starboard.

Rione had one hand pressed against her forehead, an expression of resignation on what of her face could be seen. "Off to battle, Captain Geary?" she asked.

"We'll see." He sat down and activated the fleetwide circuit. "All ships, turn starboard one three degrees, up zero four degrees, and increase speed to point seven light at time three three two. We intend intercepting the new Syndic flotilla. Expect combat in about three days." Hating to give the next order but unable to see any alternative after the arrival of the new Syndic flotilla, Geary spoke again. "Second and Seventh Destroyer Squadrons, set the power cores on those Syndic ore carriers to self-destruct and then rejoin the fleet at best speed. Ensure any remaining Syndic prisoners from the ore carriers are put into escape pods. I don't want to have to worry about them on your ships during the battle."

What else? Oh, yes, the lure, which hadn't attracted any Syndics. "Captain Tyrosian, ensure all resupply activity is completed and all shuttles recovered as soon as possible but no later than twenty-four hours from now. Captain Mosko, increase speed of Formation Echo Five Five as necessary to bring your formation back into position relative to the rest of the fleet."

"Three more days to wait before we close on the Syndics." Desjani grimaced, plainly wishing the fleet was already approaching engagement range. "I hate this part."

"ARE you planning on jumping the fleet out of this system or fighting those Syndic ships?" Rione demanded. She had kept quiet while they were walking back to his stateroom, but the moment the hatch sealed, she hurled the question at him.

"That depends." Geary flopped down on a seat and activated the display showing the situation in Lakota Star System. "What do the Syndics do? How do they react? I *can't* chase them with this fleet. We don't have the fuel cells to waste on that."

"There's more fuel cells on the auxiliaries. If you—"

"Not enough!" He made a face. "Sorry. I didn't mean to cut you off." Rione, whose eyes had started to blaze, relaxed slightly. "If I get every fuel cell the auxiliaries have managed to manufacture distributed throughout the fleet, it'll bring the ships up to about sixty percent fuel cell reserves by the time we reach the jump exit for Branwyn if we don't do any more maneuvering. That's not enough of a safety margin for routine combat ops. For a fleet trapped behind enemy lines, it's scary as hell."

"I thought you said the fleet would have to slow down to get through any mines the new Syndic force lays at that jump point. That'll require burning more fuel cell reserves, won't it?"

"I did, and you're right. So you see how bad it is."

Rione eyed Geary for a moment, then smiled. "I underestimated you again."

"You did?"

"Yes, Captain John Geary." Rione laughed. "Limited fuel cells so you can't race around this star system, and subordinates who would create problems if they thought you were running from the enemy. So you pretend to head for battle on the straightest course to the jump point we need, knowing the Syndics are likely to pull back and let you get this fleet out of this star system. Well done! You might make a politician yet."

He returned a crooked smile. "I'm afraid I'm not half that clever. I think the Syndics *will* fight at the Branwyn jump exit. They know we have to use it. They don't want to let us out of this system unscathed."

Rione, her smile gone, searched Geary's eyes. "Then what do you intend doing?"

"Like I said, it depends. Will the new Syndic force try a major engagement, hitting us full force? Or will they try to avoid a big battle and instead hammer at any weak points? If they want to do that, they can follow us through the jump point and be right on our tails at Branwyn."

She considered that, sitting down and bending her head. After several minutes, Rione looked up at him again. "Are you sure you want to go to Branwyn?"

"What other choice do I have? It's not like T'negu is a good option."

"You're getting into a situation where you have to fight this Syndic force."

"I know." Geary sat up a bit and called up something on the display above the table that he had only rarely consulted. "Recognize this?"

Rione stared at the display grimly. "The Syndic home system. I'm not likely to ever forget it."

"The Alliance fleet suffered awful losses when it got ambushed there." Geary pointed to where a long list of ship names shone in red. "The leading elements were annihilated and the rest mauled as they fought their way through the ambush."

"You don't have to remind me of that!" Rione looked away, her face pale. "Just the memories are bad enough."

Geary nodded. "Sorry. But as you pointed out on the bridge, we've been winning some one-sided victories of our own. Not a one of them comes close to what the Syndics did to this fleet in their home system, but taken together, they've inflicted very heavy cumulative losses."

Her eyes intent, Rione studied the display again. "And if you destroy this Syndic force in the same way, you'll have come close to evening the score. Is that what this is about? Revenge? I thought better of you, John Geary, though I admit the idea of getting even with the Syndics is a pleasant one."

"It's not just revenge. Hell, it's not really revenge. We've had to run like crazy because the ambush in the Syndic home system left the Syndics with a big numerical advantage over the Alliance."

Her expression shifted again. "You're erasing that advantage."

"Right. We've come quite a way to doing that, which is why the Syndics had to employ barely trained crews and brand-new ships at Ixion. If I wipe out the new Syndic force that's arrived in this system, the ability of the Syndics to meet us with equal force at any new star system will be severely impaired. They'll have to spread out their remaining forces, so we'll have the numerical advantage in any particular star system, which should give us the time we need to get the auxiliaries restocked again and all our ships loaded out with full inventories of fuel cells, specters, and grapeshot."

Rione spent a while thinking about that, too, then turned a questioning gaze on Geary. "And if you get hurt as badly as the Syndic force?"

"Then we're in trouble."

"It's a big risk."

"Yeah. But we're already in trouble. We've been in trouble since this fleet got mangled in the Syndic home system and ended up stuck deep in enemy territory. The big risk here comes with a potentially big payoff. I can easily lose by trying to play it safe, but I can't win unless I throw the dice."

IN zero gravity dice never stop tumbling, and for the next day Geary felt like he was watching a pair endlessly rolling and never coming up with a result. Then another day dragging by. Nerves on edge, he snapped at Rione, and she snapped back harder. They spent half an hour arguing so heatedly that Geary wondered why the bulkheads in his stateroom didn't melt. He finally left and wandered the passageways of *Dauntless*, trying to maintain a facade of confidence as sailors and junior officers greeted him with possessive pride. He might be the fleet commander, but this was Black Jack's flagship, and they believed that made this ship and this crew special.

He ended up in the conference room again and morosely ran through possible battles with Syndic Flotilla Bravo at the jump point for Branwyn. But there was too much he didn't know, like what the Syndics would do, to make the simulations meaningful.

Eventually he went back to his stateroom, determined not to be exiled from his own quarters even by Victoria

Rione. She was waiting for him and pulled him to the bed without a word.

It helped the time pass but left him baffled again.

THE third day. Geary sat on the bridge of *Dauntless* and glared at the display. The Syndics were still acting as if the Alliance fleet weren't even there. "Any guesses for how we can get any Syndics in this system to react to us?" he finally asked Captain Desjani.

She gave him an apologetic look. "No, sir." Desjani gestured toward the habitable planet. "Every Syndic military asset has surely received orders from the senior Syndic leadership in this star system, and Syndics follow orders slavishly." She said it dismissively, and certainly that was a big difference between the current Alliance fleet and the current Syndic fleet. Geary had spent a good deal of his time in command convincing his ship commanders, with varying degrees of success, that following orders could be a good thing. The irony was that by this stage of the war, the rigid control of the Syndics and the rush-to-battle mob approach of the Alliance had produced the same results, both sides adopting bloody head-on clashes decided by attrition.

"I'm afraid Co-President Rione was right," Geary replied. "This time they're not going to engage this fleet until they're good and ready."

"Most likely," Desjani agreed, her experience in the fleet generating a look of disdain at such an intellectual approach to battle before she remembered that Geary was teaching the Alliance fleet to act that way. "They're learning, or starting to think, aren't they?"

"Looks like it. Or maybe just losing a dangerous level of self-confidence." Whichever it was, it was bad for the Alliance fleet.

"They'll have to fight us at the jump point for Branwyn."

Time to intercept with what had been labeled Syndic

Flotilla Bravo now rested at twelve hours, if nobody maneuvered before then. The Syndic flotilla had been in a rectangular box-shaped formation since arriving and showed no signs of wanting to change that. But twelve hours from contact was still too early to start messing with the Alliance fleet's formation.

He reviewed the status of the fleet's supplies again. Ran out the projections for how many more fuel cells the auxiliaries could manufacture using the materials they had on hand. Simulated distributing that among the fleet. Not enough.

Stockpiles of mines were low, specter missile inventories on the warships ranged from low to moderate, but at least grapeshot load-outs were high. No surprise there, since metal ball bearings were pretty easy to manufacture.

Food stocks were okay, but that would be a problem, too, if he didn't find more. The food brought from the Alliance was effectively gone, with the fleet subsisting mostly on Syndic rations looted from mothballed facilities or storage locations in Sancere. The Sancere stuff wasn't too bad, for Syndic food, but when that was gone, all that would be left would be food regarded by the Syndics as not worth bringing with them when they abandoned facilities. He'd had some of that food, and even for someone accustomed to the dubious nature of military rations, it had been hard to stomach. It would keep a person alive, but that was its only virtue.

"Estimate twelve hours to combat. Please ensure your crews get plenty of rest," Geary ordered his ship captains, then went off to pretend to rest himself.

FIVE hours to intercept.

"They're sprinting, sir," Desjani reported unhappily. "To get to the jump point for Branwyn before us. They started accelerating about an hour ago, but we just saw it. We can send some battle cruisers ahead to try to still make the intercept before the Syndics get to the jump point, but the entire fleet can't accelerate fast enough to do it."

Throw unsupported battle cruisers at that Syndic formation? He could add in some light cruisers and destroyers as well, but that would still leave the battle cruisers badly outgunned. "No. We can't risk the battle cruisers that way."

Desjani stiffened, her affronted pride clear. "Sir, battle cruisers are proud of their role as the fast-moving strike force of the fleet. We can hit the enemy fast and repeatedly while the rest of the fleet catches up."

We, of course. *Dauntless* being a battle cruiser, too. "I appreciate that, Captain Desjani, but in this case we'd have to divert the Syndic flotilla from their current course in order for it to make sense to separate the battle cruisers from the rest of the fleet. Our battle cruisers simply don't have enough firepower to achieve that against a force the size of the Syndic flotilla." He leaned closer to speak very quietly. "You know I couldn't send *Dauntless* with such a strike force anyway. She's the fleet flagship, and she carries something critically important." He meant the Syndic hypernet key, something that could have a decisive effect on the war if they could get it home to Alliance space. Every ship in the fleet was important, but some were more important than others. Because of that hypernet key, *Dauntless* was by far the most important of the important.

Desjani knew that and couldn't argue with it, so even though she still looked unhappy, she nodded in agreement.

Now Geary had to sit and watch the Syndic flotilla get to the jump point first. They'd timed their move right, leaving the Alliance fleet without enough time to respond. But when the two fleets closed to battle, he'd teach the Syndics a few things about timing maneuvers to discomfort the other side.

At point one light speed, the enemy flotilla covered thirty thousand kilometers per second. On the scale of a planetary surface, the speed was unfathomable. Against the size of even an average solar system like Lakota, where the orbital diameter of the farthest-out officially designated planet spanned about ten light-hours or roughly eleven billion kilometers, ships seemed to crawl against the star-filled darkness. Geary had sometimes wondered how people had been able to stand it in the early days of human space flight, when ships hadn't been able to achieve velocities of anywhere near a tenth of the speed of light and been forced to take weeks, months, or even years to reach other planets and moons in just a single solar system. But he supposed people living on planets then probably had trouble grasping that once it had taken weeks, months, or years for travelers to cross continental landmasses.

"No matter how fast we go, it's never fast enough," Geary muttered.

To his surprise, Desjani appeared taken aback by the comment. "Sir, if the fleet could do more—"

"Sorry. That wasn't about the fleet. The fleet's doing wonders, as usual. No, I was just thinking about people."

"I see, sir." No, she obviously didn't, but since the honor of her ship and the fleet wasn't at stake and there were enemies to watch, Desjani was willing to let it go.

Geary did, too, watching the Syndics reach for the jump point for Branwyn and hoping they wouldn't do what he fully expected them to do when they got there.

THEY did.

"They're finally turning toward us," Desjani announced. "They braked heavily to cross the jump point, and now they're accelerating toward us."

Geary exhaled, wishing something would start going right, partly relieved that he no longer had to dread what had finally happened and partly tense because it had happened. "I need confirmation as soon as possible. Did they lay mines when they went past the jump point?" That seemed the only possible explanation for the braking maneuver, to slow the ships down so the mines could be laid fairly close together, but it could have been a bluff as well.

"Yes, sir," a watch-stander reported. "Our sensors are still trying to evaluate the minefield's density and limits, but we're picking up many visual anomalies. It looks like they dropped a lot of mines right off the jump point."

Desjani frowned. "That close? Look at it, sir. The mines are so close the presence of the jump point will cause them to drift out of position fairly quickly."

"Fairly quickly meaning what?" Geary asked, feeling a leap of hope.

"A few weeks, maybe," Desjani offered. "The physics of an area that close to a jump point are a little weird, but we can run an analysis for a better estimate."

"Unless that estimate is a lot less than a few weeks, it won't do us much good." He took another look as the fleet's sensors painstakingly searched out the tiny visual anomalies that even the best stealth mines revealed, drawing in a depiction of where the mines were. Right on top of the jump point, just as Desjani had commented.

They would drift out of position in a few weeks, maybe, but until then couldn't be bypassed unless the Alliance fleet slowed to almost a dead stop to make a very tight turn. And if the Alliance warships did that, they'd be sitting ducks for Syndic Flotilla Bravo making high-speed firing runs. "I liked it better when the Syndics were underestimating us," Geary remarked to Desjani in a low voice.

"Once we've destroyed that Syndic flotilla, we can maneuver around those mines safely. Or maybe wait in this system until the mines move out of the way," Desjani suggested.

"Maybe." Wait a few weeks in Lakota? It didn't sound like a good idea. The longer they stayed here, the worse things seemed to get.

"Syndic Flotilla Bravo is steadying on an intercept

course with us," the maneuvering watch announced. "Still accelerating, now back up to point zero five light."

"They'll come back up to point one light for the engagement," Desjani predicted. "That's standard practice for them."

"And for the Alliance," Geary reminded her. "But I won't bring our ships up to point one light for a while yet."

"If the Syndics come up to point one light and hold it there," Desjani noted as she ran some calculations, "and we maintain point zero seven light, then we now have about one and one half hours to contact."

"Okay." Geary thought for a moment, then called all of his ships. "All units in the Alliance fleet, we expect combat in approximately one hour. Maintain your places in formation, and I promise you we'll teach these Syndics the same things we taught the other Syndic flotillas we've encountered."

He didn't expect a reply, but one came from back in the formation. "Advise time we should accelerate to engagement speed of point one light."

Geary checked the identification of the message and confirmed his suspicions. It had sounded like Captain Midea of *Paladin*, and it was. "We will accelerate prior to contact with the Syndics. I will order that and any formation changes at the appropriate times."

"She's going to ask what the appropriate times are," Desjani murmured.

"This is *Paladin*," another message came in on the heels of Desjani's prediction. "Clarify appropriate times."

Geary fought down a blistering reply. "The appropriate times will be when I issue the orders, *Paladin*." He shook his head, addressing Desjani again. "Midea's not that stupid, is she?"

"I don't think so," Desjani temporized.

"Then surely she knows I have to base my actions on what the enemy is doing. I won't know when to do what until we get closer to actual contact and see what formation they're in and how fast they're coming at us and any last-minute maneuvers they try."

"That's true, sir, but I only know that because you've taught me that," Desjani replied. "Our tactics were much simpler before you assumed command."

That was something of an understatement. With trained and experienced officer ranks repeatedly decimated by battles that increasingly resembled bloodbaths, knowledge of how to maneuver effectively, taking into account distances and time delays, had died along with those officers. After a hundred years, Geary had found tactics consisted of charging straight at the enemy again and again until one side or the other had been bludgeoned into retreat or destruction. "I hope you're not the only one learning that," he commented to Desjani.

"Of course not, sir."

Geary's eyes went back to the display, where Syndic Flotilla Bravo kept accelerating toward the Alliance fleet. Hopefully they hadn't learned too much from watching Geary's own battles.

As time passed it became apparent that while the Syndics might have learned a few things, they hadn't learned enough. They were coming at the Alliance fleet in the same rectangular box formation they'd been in since arriving in Lakota, one broad side now facing toward the Alliance as if the box were sliding sideways and down at the opposing fleet.

Geary nodded, then spotted Desjani and the watchstanders within his view smiling as they watched him. That was when he realized he was smiling, too. "We'll hold this formation. No, I'll make one modification."

The Alliance fleet had remained in the five coin-shaped subformations in which it had entered Lakota. Currently, the five coins all faced forward, aimed just as surely for the Syndic formation as the enemy was aimed at them, though Formation Echo Five Five with the damaged ships and auxiliaries was behind the main body in Echo Five Four. Geary played with the maneuvering systems to come up with the right orders, then transmitted them. "All units in Echo Five Five, increase speed to merge with Formation Echo Five Four and take up positions as indicated."

Desjani looked intrigued, checking the orders herself. "You're sort of tacking the old Five Five onto the bottom edge of Five Four."

"Right."

"With the Seventh Battleship Division sticking below the edge of the old Five Four?" She smiled again. "I can't wait to see."

With over an hour remaining until contact, the fleets now about ten light-minutes apart, Geary watched the ships of Echo Five Five slowly overtake their comrades and assume their new positions. He knew the Syndics would see the maneuver in about ten minutes and probably not worry about it since it still left the main part of the Alliance fleet and the single Syndic box on collision courses.

With half an hour until contact, Geary called out orders again. "Formations Echo Five Two and Echo Five Three"—the two coins to either side of the main body—"pivot formations on vertical axis at nine zero degrees at time five zero. Simultaneously roll formations on horizontal axis four five degrees so leading edges of your formations slant toward Echo Five Four." He couldn't have given those orders if human beings had been required to execute them. It would have simply been too complex to have that many ships swinging to new positions in both vertical and horizontal axes at the same time, even though the maneuvering systems were providing an exact picture of what Geary intended to every ship.

"Formations Echo Five One and Echo Five Four," Geary continued, "pivot formations nine zero degrees forward on horizontal axis at time five zero."

The maneuvers unfolded like an insanely complicated dance number in three dimensions, the coins of the Alliance formation shifting so that the leading thin edges of the vanguard and the main body were now pointing at the oncoming Syndics, while the two flanking formations hung off to either side, their thin edges also forward but sloping away from the main body. There was a weird beauty to watching hundreds of ships engage in such an intricate ballet.

The maneuvers were completed at fifteen minutes to contact. "The Syndics will be seeing us changing formation," Desjani noted.

"Right." Geary sat watching the display, gauging the right moment for the next move. The Syndics would see whatever he did at increasingly smaller delays, so he had to time his moves to make the Syndics react at the right times and in the wrong ways. They'd watch his first movements and not see any need to alter their course or formation, but that was about to change.

The Syndics were now only two light-minutes away, a little over twelve minutes to contact at a combined closing speed of point one seven light speed. "All units, increase speed to point one light at time one five. All formations, alter base course up zero five degrees at time one five."

The Alliance fleet accelerated and pivoted, the coins angling upward. Desjani grinned fiercely. "I get it! But their commander will see it in time to react."

"I'm counting on that." Geary paused, counting the seconds, depending on instinct for the timing of the next maneuver, watching the position of the Syndics relative to his own ships. "All formations, alter base course up one zero degrees, starboard zero one degrees at time one nine."

A minute later, Geary saw the Syndics reacting to his earlier maneuvers, pivoting their box upward so it would meet the Alliance main body head-on again, the two groups of ships passing through each other at a slight angle and a combined closing speed now just under point two light. Any faster, and relativistic distortion would seriously complicate the task of seeing where the enemy ships actually were, but below point two light, the combat systems should be able to compensate for velocities that literally changed the way the outside universe looked.

Unfortunately for the Syndics, Geary's second turn upward changed the angle of the engagement again, this time so close to the time of contact that the Syndic commander didn't have time to see it and react. "All units, engage by squadrons and divisions with grapeshot and hell lances as targets enter engagement envelopes. Open fire when in range." The order would ensure each squadron or division of Alliance ships targeted a single enemy ship, increasing the chances of getting enough hits during the instant in which the fleets would be close enough to fire on each other.

"Enemy missiles and grapeshot passing beneath us," the combat system watch reported gleefully as the Syndic barrage went where the Alliance fleet had been expected to be.

Then the moment of contact came and passed. If human eyes and nervous systems were able to react quickly enough to perceive it, they would have seen the flat surfaces of the Alliance vanguard and main body coins sliding across the upper leading edge of the Syndic box, concentrating their fire repeatedly on the relatively few enemy ships in and near the edge, while the Syndics could only fire back with those same few ships at Alliance warships flashing past one after another. The coins of the flanking Alliance formations slid past the upper corners of the Syndic box, their fire even more concentrated.

Geary blinked, wondering if he'd actually seen the flashes of weapons fire and hits during the fraction of a second in which the automated combat systems aimed and fired far faster than humans could have managed. As the Syndics and Alliance warships diverged now, watchstanders were calling out damage assessments on the enemy and damage reports from Alliance ships.

"We hurt them," Desjani noted.

On the display, the remnants of two Syndic battle cruisers were falling away from the rest of the Syndic fleet, joined by the tumbling wrecks of a battleship, five heavy cruisers, and numerous broken light cruisers and HuKs. The escort forces on the upper edge of the Syndic formation had been virtually wiped out. Hits had been scored on other Syndic ships, but none critical.

On the Alliance side, shields had been stressed and a few lighter units had taken hits. Thankfully, all of them could still keep up with the fleet.

Geary nodded, giving orders he'd already prepared. "All formations, alter base course up one two zero degrees at time two four." Less than a minute later, the Alliance formations rose up and over, bending into a partial C curve and inverting from their previous orientation.

As Geary had expected, the Syndics, making their own attempt to swing back into contact, had also come up and over in a mirror image of the Alliance maneuver. Since the two fleets were turning together, the result was to once again bring the Alliance formations across a single edge of the Syndic box, this time the bottom leading edge. Unfortunately for the Syndic warships that had been in the upper leading edge of their box formation and taken the brunt of the first Alliance firing pass, they were now on the bottom leading edge as the Syndic formation also inverted when it came around.

Once again the Alliance formations tore across the single edge and its corners of the Syndic formation, and once again the local superiority of firepower that created hurt the Syndics far more than they could hit back at the Alliance ships.

"Two more Syndic battleships!" Desjani exulted. "And another of their battle cruisers dead!"

"We took more hits that time, too." Two destroyers, *Assegai* and *Rapier*, had lost their weapons but remained able to maneuver. Several light cruisers and a heavy cruiser had been battered, and a few shots had gotten

through to some of the Alliance battle cruisers. Even as
Geary gave his next orders, his eyes were watching one of
those battle cruisers. "All formations turn down nine zero
degrees at time three five." The Alliance fleet began bending into a full S curve as the Syndics turned into them
again as well.

But one of the Alliance battle cruisers didn't follow the
maneuver, sliding out of the formation on a slowly twisting path that would take it across the path of the Syndic
formation. "What happened to *Renown*?" Geary demanded.

A watch-stander rapidly called up a re-creation of the
last firing pass, playing it back slowly enough for human
senses to observe. The Syndics had known the Alliance
fleet's path accurately this time and placed their grapeshot
barrage in the right places. *Renown*, closest to the enemy
on her side of one of the flanking formations, had caught
several volleys, which had collapsed her forward shields.
As combat systems automatically shifted power from the
stern and beam shields, Syndic missiles had veered in on
intercepts that came up *Renown*'s stern. The first three
missiles had broken *Renown*'s weakened stern shields,
then three more had totally taken out her main propulsion
systems.

Under the impacts of the Syndic hits, *Renown* fell back
and off to the side as she lost the ability to stay with the
Alliance formation.

A single battle cruiser, no longer able to use the speed
that was supposed to compensate for her weaker shields
and armor, no longer surrounded by the protection of her
comrades.

"*Renown* reports estimated time to regain limited main
propulsion is three zero minutes," the combat watch reported.

No one needed the maneuvering systems estimates to
know that *Renown* wouldn't have thirty minutes. The Syndic formation would sweep over her in only about ten
more minutes.

Geary breathed a prayer. Get the fleet around, get his ships turned so he could get back to the battle cruiser before the Syndics. He couldn't possibly do it. Physics wouldn't allow it.

"What's *Paladin* doing?" Desjani wondered aloud.

Geary's eyes jerked that way. At the very rear of the main body now, *Paladin* had seen *Renown* take hits to her propulsion system and had time to react. Now the battle-ship was arcing around in a turn so tight the inertial dampers on her must be screaming in protest.

He couldn't take the entire fleet in that tight a turn. The units at the edges of his formations had a lot farther to travel to make the turns than those near the center as the turns pivoted the ships around the formations' central axes. The only way to try to match what *Paladin* was doing was to let his formations dissolve, which would be a prescription for disaster when the Syndics were still holding their formation.

"*Paladin*," Geary ordered in a harsh voice, "return to your position in the formation immediately." He had to adjust his own fleet's course as it curved down to match a slight slide to one side by the Syndics. "All formations, come right zero two degrees, time four one."

"What can we do?" Rione asked from the rear of the bridge, her voice not demanding but pleading.

Geary didn't have to ask to know the question was about *Renown*. "Nothing," he replied in a voice barely louder than a whisper. "If I let this formation fall apart, we still probably won't get enough ships there in time to save her, and we'd definitely end up losing a lot more ships than *Renown*."

"*Renown* reports she has ordered all nonessential personnel to escape pods," *Dauntless*'s combat watch reported.

Geary nodded, not trusting himself to speak. He'd given the same order, a hundred years ago, a few months ago to him, at Grendel.

Desjani gave him an anguished look but said nothing.

Paladin kept coming around in a turn clearly aimed now at *Renown* as the rest of the Alliance fleet bent into its own down and over maneuver, turning as one to reverse the course of all of its ships except *Renown* and *Paladin*.

"*Paladin!*" Geary yelled, not caring if he sounded unprofessionally angry during the battle. "Return to the formation immediately! Captain Midea is relieved of command. Executive officer, assume command and return *Paladin* to formation!"

It was probably too late. It was certainly too late. At the velocities the ships were traveling, *Paladin* had already veered too far from the rest of the Alliance fleet, and the Syndics were coming around to cross under the main body of the Alliance fleet but directly at *Renown* and *Paladin*.

Renown volleyed out waves of escape pods and all of her remaining specters as the leading edge of the Syndic formation approached. Her last grapeshot followed, sparkling as it hit the shields of Syndic ships and vaporized. One, then two, Syndic HuKs fell silent as *Renown*'s weapons ripped into them. A light cruiser reeled away. The shields on a battle cruiser flared and failed in spots, letting some of *Renown*'s hell lances score hits on the enemy warship.

But an avalanche of fire was falling upon *Renown*. Her shields failed, her weak armor was penetrated in a hundred places, her hell-lance batteries fell silent as the stricken battle cruiser jerked and tumbled helplessly from the impacts of Syndic fire.

"No systems detected still active on *Renown*," a watchstander reported in a calm but trembling voice. "*Renown*'s emergency beacon has lit off. Her surviving crew is abandoning ship."

Geary had been there, too. Hoping a functioning escape pod still existed, racing through once-familiar passageways of his ship grown foreign from massive damage, the enemy weapons still tearing into his mortally wounded ship.

"Core overload set on *Renown*. Contact lost with *Renown*."

On the display, the battered hulk, which minutes before had been an Alliance battle cruiser, rolled silently away, her power core set to explode to deny her carcass to the enemy, the escape pods holding her crew mingling with those from the already destroyed Syndic warships.

Too late to save *Renown*, *Paladin* came tearing past and above the shattered battle cruiser. Hell lances tore out from the battleship in volleys that ripped into Syndic HuKs scrambling to escape. Two HuKs exploded under the impacts, and one more disintegrated under the blows of *Paladin*'s hell lances. Then the lone Alliance battleship was in among the Syndic light cruisers, its powerful hell-lance batteries shattering the shields on two of the light cruisers, destroying one and crippling the other.

A second later *Paladin*, her shields glowing now under an almost constant barrage of enemy fire, encountered Syndic heavy cruisers. *Paladin*'s own weapons tore open a single Syndic heavy cruiser as the battleship staggered onward directly toward a division of Syndic battleships.

"Captain Midea is crazy, but she's dying well," Desjani remarked somberly.

"Did she have to take her ship and crew with her?" Geary whispered in reply. Too late. Too late to relieve Midea. Too late to figure out how to control a reckless officer with a ship's fate in her hands.

"*Paladin*'s losing shields," the watch reported.

Geary could see that on his own display. *Paladin*'s lonely battle was far enough from the rest of the fleet by now that it took a few seconds for light from the fight to reach *Dauntless*. A lot could happen in a few seconds.

It took less time than that for *Paladin* to charge straight into the Syndic battleship division she'd been aiming for, shuddering as enemy weapons ripped into her from all sides. But *Paladin* concentrated her own fire on a single

battleship even as her hell-lance batteries started falling
silent under the Syndic barrage. As *Paladin* and that Syndic battleship flashed past each other, *Paladin* fired her
null field at the weakened bow shields of the enemy ship.
Its already-stressed shields failed, and the null field penetrated into the Syndic battleship's bow, digging a massive
crater there.

As the Syndic battleship reeled out of formation, crippled, *Paladin* shot through the rest of the Syndic formation, taking hit after hit, systems falling dead and pieces of
armor and hull being blown off under the impact of Syndic hell lances, grapeshot, and missile fire.

As Geary's fleet came over the top of its turn and
steadied on course for another pass at the Syndic flotilla,
Paladin's remains tumbled onward past the Syndics, the
only sign of life on the wreck a few escape pods popping
free.

"We'll avenge them," Geary stated as the Alliance fleet
steadied out to cross over the top of the Syndic formation
again. But he'd misjudged slightly this time, maybe rat-
tled by what was happening to *Renown* and *Paladin*, and
the two groups of warships tore past each other at extreme
hell-lance range, neither the Alliance nor the Syndics
scoring any significant damage on the other.

"We'll get the Syndics on the next pass," Desjani predicted, her face grim.

"Yeah." Geary took a deep breath, then transmitted his
next orders. "All formations, turn up one one zero degrees,
port zero one degrees at time five seven." As the fleet came
back around, it would invert again as the two formations
wove back and forth toward each other in interlinked S
curves. The Syndic commander should recognize that he
couldn't achieve a good firing pass unless he broke the pattern, but the Syndics wouldn't break contact while they
thought they had a chance to inflict damage back on the Alliance. They never had, stubbornly sticking to fights in misplaced displays of bravery and determination. In this fight,
the Syndics had already been hurt a lot more than the Al-

liance, even after counting *Renown* and *Paladin*. By the time the Syndics decided to flee, they'd be too badly hurt for any major warship to get away.

"Sir, activity at the hypernet gate!"

Alerts pulsed on Geary's display. His eyes went to the area of the Syndic hypernet gate even as a watch-stander began calling out the information in a breathless voice. "Syndic forces have been spotted emerging from the hypernet gate. Twenty Hunter-Killers. Update, twenty-eight Hunter-Killers. Twelve light cruisers. Update, forty-two Hunter-Killers, twenty-six light cruisers, eight heavy cruisers. Update, sixty-nine Hunter-Killers, thirty-one light cruisers, nineteen heavy cruisers."

Geary watched the enemy symbols multiplying madly at the hypernet gate, trying not to let his dismay show.

"They've got a substantial number of escorts," Desjani remarked with what Geary thought was remarkable calmness.

Which implied a lot of capital ships.

The display and the watch-stander confirmed that moments later. "Sixteen battle cruisers. Update, twenty battle cruisers. Twelve battleships. Update, twenty-three battleships."

Geary realized he hadn't been breathing and inhaled. At least the threat symbols had stopped growing in number. He took a long moment to read the final assessment of the new Syndic force. Twenty-three battleships, twenty battle cruisers, nineteen heavy cruisers, thirty-one light cruisers, one hundred twelve Hunter-Killers.

The odds in this star system had just gone from roughly even to very bad. In capital ships alone the Alliance fleet now had only twenty-five surviving battleships and seventeen surviving battle cruisers. The battle so far had taken out three Syndic battleships and four battle cruisers, but even after those losses, total Syndic capital ships at Lakota now added up to forty-four battleships and thirty-four battle cruisers, most of those fresh and presumably with full load-outs of expendable munitions, whereas the

Alliance ships had used up most of their missiles and
grapeshot already. Almost two-to-one odds, and no matter
what anyone else in the Alliance fleet believed, Geary
didn't think that superior fighting spirit could make up for
that kind of disparity in firepower.

TEN

"IT must be the main Syndic fleet," Desjani observed, her body tense. "Their primary strike force. The Syndics in this system couldn't have sent for reinforcements and had them show up this quickly, so they must have been headed here for some other reason."

"Lucky us," Geary muttered. The hypernet gate was almost five light-hours away now, so that Syndic flotilla they were just now seeing had arrived five hours ago. But the Syndics in that new strike force had seen the Alliance fleet the moment they arrived, and had already had five hours to size up the situation and make plans. "We need to wipe out this flotilla we're engaged with. Then we can—"

"Syndic ships are turning away," a watch-stander called in a disappointed voice.

"Son of a bitch." There wasn't any doubt. Instead of curving back in for another firing pass, the Syndics they'd been fighting were continuing outward, accelerating past point one light to open the distance from the Alliance fleet even faster. Instead of closing on the Alliance fleet, the

Syndics were now heading in another direction. "They're breaking contact."

Along with light from the hypernet gate had come orders for the Syndic ships they were engaged with. Geary was certain of it as he watched the Syndic flotilla accelerating away.

"Cowards," Desjani ground out, then shook her head. "No. They've been ordered to wait until that other big force gets close enough to engage us."

"Right." Geary took a look at the geometry of the Alliance and the Syndic forces, then at his fleet's fuel status. "We don't have enough fuel cells to catch them without going to critically low levels."

"Jump to Branwyn!" Rione suddenly cried, as if unable to understand why someone else hadn't already said that. "Proceed onward to the jump point and jump to Branwyn! We've inflicted more losses on the Syndics than they have on us, so there's no dishonor in leaving the battlefield now!"

Desjani just shook her head again.

Geary looked back at Rione. "We can't. That Syndic force that is breaking contact with us is going to stay close enough to come charging in if we head for that jump point. We have to slow down a lot to get past the minefield they laid and to the jump point. They'll wait until we're nearly at a dead stop to get around those mines, and then they'll hit us."

"We'd be easy targets," Desjani added in a tight voice.

"We can't outmaneuver them?" Rione demanded.

This time Geary shook his head. "They don't have auxiliaries with them slowing them down, and they can leave their damaged ships behind when they come at us, knowing that we can't go after them. Even if we didn't have the auxiliaries to worry about, we'd still have to keep our damaged ships with us." He pointed at the display. "The Syndics we were fighting will keep us from using the jump point for Branwyn or hurt us very badly if we try to use it. Meanwhile, the big new Syndic flotilla will head for us, knowing we can't escape through the nearest jump point without taking serious losses. When the newest force gets close enough, it and the one we were just fighting will hit us together."

Desjani nodded, her face grim.

"And you're just going to wait around for this?" Rione asked, incredulous.

"Not if I can help it." He sat down, trying to think. One thing was obvious, and that was he had to settle the fleet on a new course. "All ships, steady course up two zero degrees, starboard one zero degrees time four three."

Now what? Badly outnumbered, and things wouldn't be getting better. Maybe, maybe if he pulled off something absolutely brilliant, he could win here. But there was no way of doing so without losing the vast majority of his own ships. Any Alliance ships surviving after that would have absolutely no chance of reaching Alliance space and would be lost as well. A victory here would be purchased only with the sacrifice of his own fleet and wouldn't accomplish anything but stalemating the war again. The Syndics and the Alliance would be forced to hold off attacking each other for a while as they rebuilt their fleets; then they'd both go at it once more, continuing the apparently endless war. Perhaps until both the Syndicate Worlds government and the Alliance government collapsed and human-occupied space descended into heavily armed anarchy.

Even if I managed a total victory—and what are the odds of that when the enemy outnumbers us this badly?— against odds like that, my best efforts might just delay the inevitable and see the Syndics destroy this fleet while retaining enough strength themselves to finally go against the weak forces defending Alliance home space.

Desjani was chewing her lower lip, her expression determined. She'd do whatever Geary ordered, certain that whatever it was would produce a victory. Geary glanced around the bridge of *Dauntless* and saw variations of the same fear on every watch-stander, along with the same courage that would allow those officers and sailors to charge into battle despite that fear. These sailors would die if Geary ordered it, no doubt of that, fighting their hardest to achieve victory despite the odds.

But he'd already seen what that kind of attitude could produce. *Paladin* had possessed the same willingness to fight and die, and the end result had been death. He couldn't ask these sailors to die just because they were willing to follow his orders to do that. There had to be a reasonable hope that those deaths would accomplish something.

Okay. Options. Take out this Syndic formation before the newest one got here, then escape to Branwyn. Couldn't work unless the commander of the Syndic force they'd been fighting was an absolute idiot, and he or she didn't seem to be one. Besides, they'd clearly been ordered not to engage Geary unless the Alliance fleet tried to escape before the newest force got here.

Take out the newest Syndic force? Charge it and hope clever tactics could compensate for enemy superiority? That was a slim reed to cling to, especially since the Syndic force they'd already fought would charge right after them, and as he'd told Rione, could out-accelerate the Alliance fleet. He'd still end up facing both Syndic forces at once, and with them operating in two big formations like that, they'd probably be able to wipe out his auxiliaries, even if Geary managed to avoid the destruction of the rest of the fleet.

Just run like hell? Where? Aside from the fact that many of his captains would balk at fleeing from an enemy even under these circumstances, there were also the problems that he couldn't out-accelerate the Syndic flotillas, and the jump point for T'negu would just take this fleet into a maze of mines, with the Syndic forces here coming right behind. Running toward open space might keep the Syndics from catching them but would be slow suicide as the ships all ran out of fuel cells far from any star.

There was always the jump point back to Ixion, but the

Syndic force they'd left there would surely be coming out of that at any time and—

Okay. There's an option. Maybe not the sort of option that Black Jack would choose, but I'm not Black Jack.

So, a plan to run for the only possible safe way out of this star system, without making it obvious that he was running. Fortunately, for once the expected arrival of more enemy reinforcements offered him a way to do that and conceal his intentions for as long as possible from not only the enemy but also his own fleet.

"We need time, and we need to confront these Syndic forces individually," Geary announced, suddenly aware of how silent it was on the bridge of *Dauntless* as everyone waited to hear him speak. "The only way to do that with the ones we were fighting is to trick them into going after us. We can do that and engage the next wave of Syndic reinforcements into this system."

He pointed at the display. "We're going back to— toward the jump point for Ixion. At any time we expect the Syndic force we left at Ixion to come into this star system using that jump point. If we're close enough when they do, we can overwhelm them." Only four battleships and four battle cruisers had been in that force. "This Syndic flotilla we've been fighting will have to come to the rescue of that force, which will give us a chance to bloody it again."

"That still leaves the biggest Syndic flotilla," Rione objected.

"Yes, it does. We'll have to see how it reacts and hit it however we can." Don't lie to them. Lay the groundwork for escaping this star system. "We can't fight all of these Syndic formations at once. We need to hit them individually."

Captain Desjani studied the display herself for a moment, then smiled. "We're not retreating."

"No, Captain," Geary replied with all of the confidence he could fake. "We're changing the direction of our attack."

• • •

HE repeated the phrase to a hastily gathered conference of
fleet commanding officers about ten minutes later as the
Alliance fleet lined up on a course back to the jump point
for Ixion. "We're changing the direction of our attack."

A long silence followed, born partly of time needed for
his commanding officers to absorb the new plan and partly
of the time required for light itself to carry the information
between the different formations of the fleet. "We don't
know the other Syndic force is going to exit that jump
point," Captain Cresida argued. Loyal as she was to him,
she wanted to fight the Syndics.

"I'm hoping it will, and I think we have good reason to
believe it will." Plausible reason, anyway. "We need to
force Syndic Flotilla Bravo to voluntarily reengage with
us, because we can't run them down, given the state of our
fuel cell reserves." A number of officers turned and glared
toward the commanders of the auxiliaries, as if this were
somehow their fault. "If we force a fight with the Syndic
flotilla coming from Ixion, we'll have it badly outnumbered, and Syndic Flotilla Bravo will have to come to its
assistance or we'll be able to wipe it out."

Geary forced a confident smile. "Of course, we do
intend wiping out the flotilla from Ixion, then turning
and hitting Syndic Flotilla Bravo as it tries to save its
comrades."

Tulev nodded, even more stolid than usual. "We must
defeat these Syndic flotillas in detail, one by one, sepa-
rately. If they combine or get close enough to coordinate
their attacks, we'll be in a very difficult position."

"Now isn't the time for timidity," Captain Casia objected. "If we turn and chase the Syndic flotilla we've already fought, we can finish them off and then engage the
rest."

"They'll run us out of fuel cells, and then we can drift
until blown apart by the Syndics," Duellos stated, anger
showing. "It's called physics. Run the data yourself. You've
just lost a battleship from your division because an officer

thought being bold was the same as being smart. Didn't you learn anything from the loss of *Paladin*?"

"This fleet fights!" another officer insisted. "We don't run!"

"Tactical repositioning is not running!" Commander Gaes insisted. "We're in Lakota! We attacked a strong Syndic star system. How can you call that running?"

"We should rethink that attack," Commander Yin argued abruptly.

Geary gave Yin a questioning look, surprised that she'd drawn attention again after being relatively quiet at recent conferences. But then Captain Midea had been dominating the bad officer side of discussions in the last few conferences as she spun increasingly out of control. If only he'd recognized what she was doing, the increasing lack of discretion, and found cause to relieve Midea of command before the last battle. But he couldn't have done that if everyone else had seen it simply as Geary's attempt to silence someone saying something he didn't want to hear. So now he spoke firmly but calmly to Yin. "Explain that, please."

Yin flicked her eyes around nervously. "It's obvious that the fleet's movements are constrained by some of the ships. Some can't move as fast as the others, and that limits our ability to fight." True enough, but Geary waited, not trusting the amount of tension he saw in Commander Yin. "Some of the ships are slower by design, the auxiliaries. Others are temporarily slower due to battle damage, like my own *Orion*."

A lot of officers were giving Yin narrow-eyed looks now, wondering where this was going. Yin gulped but forged on, speaking quickly. "It's obvious. Get the slower ships to a safe place so the rest of the fleet can fight unencumbered."

"A safe place?" Duellos asked.

"Ixion. We're going that way, anyway. Get close to the jump point, let a formation including the damaged ships and the auxiliaries jump toward Ixion, and the rest of the fleet will be able to maneuver and fight better." Yin was breathing rapidly, staring down at her hands as they clasped and unclasped on the table before her.

It wasn't an entirely unreasonable proposal, if anyone had trusted Commander Yin. Her behavior made it clear that even Yin was worried about how the other officers would see it. After a long and hostile period of quiet, Duellos spoke again, his voice deceptively light. "Remarkable. It sounded just as if Captain Numos were speaking just now. The voice was Commander Yin's, but the advice and the words seem those of Captain Numos. Odd, isn't it?"

Yin flushed. "Captain Numos is an experienced officer and the veteran of many battles."

"Which he survived by running from," Captain Cresida snarled. "That's exactly what he wanted to do at the Syndic home system, too! Every ship for itself!"

Voices erupted all around the table, some shouting at Yin, some at Cresida. Geary searched his controls and punched the command override, quieting all the noise instantly. The ability to shut everyone up at times like this was about the only thing about being fleet commander that he liked. "Everyone listen. This kind of debate isn't doing us any good. Our enemies are the Syndics. Captain Cresida, it's true that Captain Numos has been charged with abandoning his responsibilities in the face of the enemy, but he has not yet been convicted of that."

Cresida looked unhappy but nodded. "I apologize for my remark about a fellow officer, sir."

"Thank you. Now, Commander Yin, Captain Numos is supposed to have only enough human contact to meet the requirements for humane treatment. He is not supposed to be giving advice on the running of your ship or of this fleet. Are you in fact consulting with him on those matters?"

Yin's eyes were everywhere but on Geary's. "No. No, sir."

If he could only contrive a way to get Commander Yin

down to the interrogation room in the intelligence section
on *Dauntless* and see how the sensors there evaluated answers like that. But then Geary was already certain Yin
was lying. Duellos was right—the words and the proposed
course of action sounded very much like Captain Numos.
Numos would have presented the words with a superior
sneer rather than obvious anxiety as Commander Yin had,
but then Geary suspected that Numos had a lot more experience with lying to his own advantage.

If Geary had needed any confirmation that Numos was
still working against him despite being relieved of command of *Orion* and arrested, he now had it.

Duellos spoke in a professionally detached tone. "I'd
recommend against doing as Commander Yin proposed.
How could we be certain we'd be able to rejoin with the
damaged ships and auxiliaries? That force would be well
enough off, since they would have all the supply capability in the fleet to themselves and would even be capable of
reaching Alliance home space with those supplies, though
I am of course speaking purely theoretically, since I know
Commander Yin would never consider abandoning the rest
of the fleet. Though of course the rest of the fleet would
be fighting to the death here, and there probably wouldn't
be many Syndic forces able to mount a rapid pursuit of the
ships that had gone ahead to Ixion. But that is, as I said,
purely a matter of theory and not something I would think
any fleet officer would consider doing."

Yin was pale as death now, staring at Duellos. His em-
phasis on her name had clearly conveyed the idea that another officer with that force might try to abandon the fleet.
Numos remained under arrest on *Orion*, but if *Orion* were
detached from the rest of the fleet, how long would he remain confined?

And despite requiring Cresida to apologize, Geary knew
damned well that Numos would run like a rabbit if he had
command of that formation and the auxiliaries and their
supplies with him.

Nobody was saying anything. Rione gave Geary an im-

patient look and jerked her head as if to remind him that
there was a fleet conference going on.

Geary studied the expressions around the table, relieved to be finding little apparent support for Commander
Yin's proposal. "Thank you, Commander," he stated flatly.
"I don't think it would be wise to adopt your proposal.
This fleet will remain together and return to Alliance
space together." He saw instantly on the faces of the others that it had been the right thing to say. "I know you are
all inspired by the sacrifices of *Renown* and *Paladin*. Let's
take out plenty of more Syndic ships in the names of those
brave warships." He felt like a hypocrite praising *Paladin*,
but her crew had died bravely enough. They shouldn't suffer in anyone's estimation because their captain had failed
them. "But let us also learn from the example of *Paladin*.
Hold together, and we can destroy the Syndics. Fail to do
that, and they can destroy us."

No one seemed ready to debate that point with the images of the death of *Paladin* still vivid in their minds, but
Captain Armus of the battleship *Colossus* frowned at the
display as if still thinking. "Captain Geary, that new Syndic strike force, the one that outnumbers us, *can* intercept
us prior to our reaching the jump exit for Ixion."

"That's true, if we hold the same course and speed.
We're going to try to throw off any attempted Syndic intercept." He indicated the display. "They're five light-
hours away from us, so they won't even know we're
headed for that jump point for another five hours. We'll
make some minor adjustments on the way to the jump
point, just enough to confuse a Syndic intercept that's reacting hours later."

Armus nodded reluctantly. "What do we do if that big
new flotilla does manage to intercept us? Especially if
Syndic Flotilla Bravo remains intact and positioned to
also engage us?"

Everyone looked at Geary, waiting for his answer to a
worst-case scenario. He couldn't really present a detailed
answer, not knowing how the Syndics would be positioned,

what their formations would be, a hundred big and little details that would make all the difference in his response. But it occurred to him that there was one thing he could say. "What do we do? We fight like hell, Captain, and make them sorry they caught up with us."

No one else spoke, so Geary nodded politely. "That's all. Captain Casia, Captain Duellos, please remain for a moment." The images of the other officers disappeared quickly, leaving Casia and Duellos giving each other challenging looks across the table. Desjani also remained, but retreated outside the range of the conference software to give Geary privacy with the other two officers. Rione just sat and watched. "Captain Casia," Geary stated formally, "my regrets for the loss of *Paladin* from your division." Casia, who looked as if he wanted to accuse Geary of being at fault in what happened to *Paladin*, nodded abruptly. "That's all."

Duellos sighed after Casia had gone. "He's probably trying to decide if getting rid of a loose cannon like Midea was worth losing *Paladin*."

"Probably. My regrets for the loss of *Renown*."

"Thank you." Duellos shook his head. "It often comes down to luck, good or bad, doesn't it? I liked *Renown*, liked her commanding officer, liked her crew. It'll be a long time before I stop expecting to see them in my formation." He sighed. "Most of the crew got off, though. That's something." Duellos saluted. "Let's hope it doesn't get worse."

"That's what I'm praying for." Geary returned the salute, and Duellos left.

Desjani came back up to Geary after Duellos had vanished, giving Rione a slightly apologetic look as the other woman remained seated, watching her. "Sir, I wanted to say . . . I could see how hard it must have been watching *Renown*. After Grendel."

Geary nodded. Of course Desjani had understood. "Yeah. It brought back some bad memories." He paused, letting them come clearly again. The battle had been only

a few months ago for him, a century old for Desjani and
Rione and the others in this fleet. "I had to give that same
order. Nonessential personnel to the escape pods. It's a
hard order to give. My executive officer wouldn't go. She
said she was essential."

He could see her so easily, the memories so recent in his
mind. Lieutenant Commander Decala. A good officer, re-
fusing to leave her post, her eyes determined and tor-
mented. "I told her to go. Ordered her directly, personally.
She wouldn't go." He took a long, deep breath, feeling it
all again. "I told her that she'd be needed. That the Alliance
would need good officers to defend itself from the Syndics,
to strike back in response to the surprise attack. I told her
that her duty required her to leave. She finally did."

Desjani nodded, her face solemn. "Do you know what
became of her?"

"Yes. A month ago I finally got up the nerve to look her
up in the Official Casualty Records." Funny how hard it
had been to type in her name, wondering and dreading
what had become of Lieutenant Commander Decala and
all the other members of his old crew who had survived
his last stand. "She died five years after Grendel when her
ship was destroyed during an Alliance assault on a Syndic
star system." Ninety-five years ago, while Geary drifted in
survival sleep.

Desjani bowed her head. "My condolences, sir. She has
surely rested with her ancestors in honor since that time."

"I like to think so." Geary composed himself. "Thanks
for asking, Tanya. It's one of those things I have to face
sooner or later."

She nodded, saluted, and left.

Rione finally stood and walked over to Geary, seeming
uncharacteristically subdued. "There are things I will never
be able to adequately understand," she stated quietly.

"There are memories no one should have to have,"
Geary replied. "But that's war for you."

She closed her eyes for a moment. "I have a few more
of those memories now, so I know exactly what you mean.

Tell me the truth, John Geary. Do you think this fleet can still make it out of this star system?"

"I don't know. On my honor, Victoria, I just don't know. But we have to try."

IT had been about seven days from the jump point where they'd arrived to the vicinity of the jump point for Branwyn. Now they were heading back the other way, the Alliance fleet's path arcing through Lakota again. Geary had deliberately first lined the fleet up on a course headed for the jump point for Seruta, holding that course for an hour to hopefully get the newest and biggest Syndic flotilla charging in that direction. Then he brought the fleet around, aiming for the vicinity of the jump point for Ixion.

As he had feared, Syndic Formation Bravo had taken up position about twenty light-minutes astern of the Alliance fleet. Close enough to watch and pounce if necessary, far enough off that the Syndic flotilla could accelerate away if the Alliance ships turned to try to bring it to battle.

The only good thing about the current situation was that at least he was regaining a little combat strength for once instead of just having it slowly whittled away. *Warrior*, *Orion*, and *Majestic* had finally completed enough repairs to regain a level of combat capability that would let them serve as escorts for the auxiliaries if necessary. Entrusting the fates of the invaluable auxiliaries to three ships with the shaky records of those battleships would be a major leap of faith, but the spirit of their crews needed to be fixed as badly as the ships themselves had.

By the end of the first day it was clear enough that Syndic Flotilla Delta, the massive strike force that had arrived through the hypernet gate, was indeed coming after the Alliance fleet full-bore. "Point one five light," Desjani remarked. "Edging up toward point two light."

Normally there would be a bright side to even that bad news. At that velocity, relativistic distortion easily created minor errors in how a ship's sensors viewed the outside universe. Across the huge distances that Syndic Flotilla Delta was covering, even a tiny error could produce a big difference. Unfortunately in this case, Flotilla Bravo hanging just astern of the Alliance fleet and matching its velocity of point one light could provide accurate information to Flotilla Delta.

"They'll definitely get to us before we reach the jump point for Ixion," Desjani continued. "It's a long haul, but they're coming on hard, and that Flotilla Bravo is letting them know when we try to fool them at long distance."

"They'll intercept us only a couple of hours before the jump point," Geary noted. He didn't add what they both knew, that those could be a very long couple of hours.

"And that's if we and everyone else continues on our current tracks. When we engage the Syndics coming out of the Ixion jump point, it will throw all of these projections off." Desjani leaned back, closing her eyes for a moment. "Sir, it may not be wise to engage Flotilla Delta, even though it doesn't look like we'll have an option."

That was a change, Desjani counseling caution. "You think so?" Geary asked, wondering what her reasoning was.

"We're not in the best position for a fight with a force that big," Desjani explained. "I'm sure you've seen that already, but it took me longer. If we could eliminate Flotilla Bravo as a threat before Flotilla Delta intercepts us, it will make a big difference, but unless that flotilla from Ixion comes in just right, I don't see that happening."

"I was thinking the same thing."

"I knew it." Desjani nodded firmly and opened her eyes again, gazing at him. "We need to fight these Syndics on our terms. You've said that many times. Seeing *Paladin* die a day ago . . . well, suddenly it seemed I was seeing fleets and fleets of Alliance warships doing the same thing for decade after decade, throwing away themselves and their crews. I mean, it's honorable and it's brave, but it hasn't been accomplishing much, has it?"

"No." Geary twisted his mouth. "Sometimes the braver course of action is to avoid a fight."

"Because others will accuse you of being scared?" Desjani's face hardened. "Yes. But then I've been accused of other things lately. We're going to jump for Ixion as soon as we can, right, sir?"

"Yeah. If I can get there without fighting Flotilla Delta, I'm going to do it."

"Good." Having shocked Geary by endorsing discretion in battle, Desjani now grinned. "We'll kill more of them if we fight them when and where we want to."

As bottom lines went, it had the virtues of simplicity and truth. "Right."

"**HOW** about Seruta?" Rione asked, her eyes on the star display in Geary's stateroom. "If we dodge that way—"

Geary shook his head, and she stopped speaking. "The biggest problem with that is that the jump point for Seruta is closer to Syndic Flotilla Delta. They'd intercept us earlier, and we'd have a longer fight to get through to the jump point." He gazed at the star. "Lesser but still significant problems are that we don't know what the Syndics have at Seruta, and the captured star system guides we have say Seruta is a very old and very poor system. No planets at all, just thin clouds of asteroids orbiting a dying red star, and not much in the way of good metals in the asteroids. All the Syndics ever had there was an emergency station that was shut down a long time back. We might find some nasty Syndic surprises at Seruta, and we know we wouldn't find any of the resources we need there."

Rione slumped back, frowning. "We just keep heading for the jump point for Ixion? Even knowing that the Syndics will catch us before we reach it?"

"I'll try some maneuvers to keep them from closing with us."

"Try?" She shook her head. "A very, very weak hope, John Geary. How did we end up stuck like this?"

"Exceptionally bad luck, for one thing. If Flotilla Delta hadn't shown up, we could have finished eliminating Flotilla Bravo as a threat, then left for Branwyn." Geary stared into the depths of the star display. "And bad judgment. My bad judgment. I made the decision to come to Lakota, and it was a very bad decision."

"Was it? Because you didn't know you'd encounter exceptionally bad luck?" Rione moved over and sat down beside him, leaning against his shoulder. "This isn't something you can blame yourself for. And I should know, being an expert on blaming oneself as I am."

"It doesn't feel right to not have you chewing me out for messing up by being too aggressive," Geary remarked.

"I've told you that I don't want to be too predictable." She sat up and made an exasperated sound. "Maybe we're not supposed to get home. Maybe what we've learned is too dangerous."

"I won't accept that."

"Good." She stood up. "I need to make peace with someone, if I can. I might not have too many more days to try."

Desjani? "Who?"

"My ancestors. I'll see you in a while."

"Do you mind if I walk with you?"

Rione frowned at him again. "You're not my husband. You don't belong in the room with me."

"I know. I wouldn't go that far. I want to talk to my ancestors, too."

Rione's face cleared. "Perhaps they'll have some good advice."

"If they don't, I've always got you."

She rolled her eyes. "Advice I have in plenty. Good advice is another thing, it seems."

"You told me that I'd be stupid and insane to bring this fleet to Lakota," Geary pointed out. "You seem to have been right about that."

For some reason that seemed to amuse her slightly. "I think I said you were stupid and Falco was insane. Fine.

Walk with me. Let the crew see their hero and his lover
being pious and proper. Then, assuming I haven't been
blasted into ashes by my shamed ancestors, we can come
back here and compare notes on whatever inspirations or
warnings we felt."

Geary stood up, laughing slightly. "That's one hell of
thing to base military planning on, isn't it? Signs and por-
tents. Like we're ancients peering up at the stars and wondering what they are."

Rione paused on her way to the hatch and gave Geary
a serious look. "The ancients thought the stars were gods,
John Geary. So do we, though in a very different way. But
we're not so different from the ancients, who lived but the
blink of an eye ago in the sight of this universe and spent
their lives trying to understand why they were here and
what they were supposed to do with the gifts of their lives.
I try never to forget that."

He nodded, wondering once again at the woman inside
Victoria Rione.

HALFWAY to the Ixion jump point, Syndic Flotilla Bravo
still hung behind them like an ancient sword poised to fall
on their necks, and Syndic Flotilla Delta, cutting a curving path through Lakota Star System, would cross the
track of the Alliance fleet at a point just two hours shy of
the jump point. Syndic Flotilla Alpha still cruised serenely
back and forth near the hypernet gate, standing sentry
against a desperate and increasingly impossible lunge for
the gate by the Alliance fleet. No sign of the smaller Syndic flotilla expected to be coming from Ixion.

Lacking omens or inspirations from his ancestors,
Geary sat and watched the slow track of the formations
across Lakota Star System. Every example he'd been able
to find of a force in the position of the Alliance fleet ended
the same way, and it wasn't a good way as far as the Alliance fleet was concerned.

He tried to ignore another stress headache building between his eyes. Why had it come to this? If only he hadn't been constantly thrown off balance and forced to change plans by the arrival of one Syndic force after another. Instead of calling the shots in this system, it seemed he'd just been reacting to a constant series of moves by the enemy.

Reacting to moves by the enemy.

The enemy was faster. Both Syndic Flotilla's Bravo and Delta could out-accelerate Geary's fleet and maintain higher velocities. That was a definite advantage, but slower-moving ships could turn tighter, though tighter didn't exactly mean a small turn radius at even point zero five light. Still, he'd been kept off balance a lot. Maybe if he figured out how to keep the Syndic flotillas off balance . . .

It wasn't a great plan, but it was a plan.

THE face of Commander Suram, acting commanding officer of *Warrior*, gazed back at Geary warily, doubtless expecting bad news. Suram had been Captain Kerestes's former executive officer, but what was he really like? No one was sure. But Geary had to give the man a chance now. "Commander Suram, *Warrior*'s crew has done an amazing job of repairing battle damage. Your shield capabilities are fully restored, and half of your hell-lance batteries are operational again."

Suram nodded. "Yes, sir. We haven't been able to repair all of the damaged armor, though, and propulsion is still at only seventy-five percent."

"That's good enough to keep up with the auxiliaries. I've got a special assignment for *Warrior*, Commander Suram. I'm putting you in command of *Orion* and *Majestic* as well."

That got a startled reaction. "Sir?"

"I need those auxiliaries protected, Commander Suram," Geary stated with grim intensity. "If we lose them, this fleet is dead. You know that. When we mix it up with the

Syndics again, those two flotillas are going to be coming at us from multiple directions. It'll be very difficult for me to make sure that *Titan*, *Witch*, *Jinn*, and *Goblin* aren't damaged or destroyed. I want *Warrior*, *Orion*, and *Majestic* to stick to those auxiliaries like you were tied to them by a short rope. I want you to physically block any Syndic fire at the auxiliaries if necessary and destroy any Syndic warships that try to get at the auxiliaries. Can you do that, Commander Suram?"

Suram's jaw set. "Yes, sir."

"You understand I'm giving you the most important job in this fleet. I don't have a single major warship to spare. No minor warships to spare either, for that matter. I need to know that you'll do whatever it takes and stick with those auxiliaries."

"*Warrior* will be destroyed before those auxiliaries are harmed," Suram stated. "We know we have something to prove," he added in a rough voice. "Myself and the crew of *Warrior*. We left *Polaris* and *Vanguard* at Vidha. We won't leave these auxiliaries, not while we have any capability left. I swear it on the honor of my ancestors."

Geary knew that anyone he asked would tell him he was insane to trust *Warrior*, let alone *Orion* and *Majestic*, but his instincts told him that no other ships had as much to prove. That didn't mean he would have given this mission to Commander Yin on *Orion*, of course. That really would have been insane. "If I didn't believe you capable, I wouldn't have given you the mission, Commander Suram. You tell your crew that. I know that *Warrior* can carry it out or die trying."

Suram nodded again, then saluted. "Thank you, sir. We will regain our honor or die in the attempt."

Geary smiled. "Do us both a favor and regain your honor without dying. I want *Warrior* back in the front of battle. Are you comfortable with the commanders of *Orion* and *Majestic*? Will they follow your orders?"

"Every officer and every sailor on *Orion* and *Majestic* will know their mission and the opportunity they've been given, sir," Suram promised. "Thank you again, sir. Our ships will justify your trust in us."

ONE day out from the jump point. He spent hours just gazing at the simulator, where a depiction of the current situation hung, the huge Syndic Flotilla Delta now arranged in what seemed a traditional Syndic box formation, though in this case the box was very shallow. The lid of the box pointed toward the Alliance fleet like a thick wall that overlapped the Alliance formation on all sides.

Syndic Formation Bravo had altered its box formation as well, making it shallow to match that of Delta and tilting it up to mimic the wall of Delta, though Bravo's lesser numbers made for a much smaller wall. Even after getting pummeled by the Alliance fleet near the Branwyn jump point, Bravo still boasted fifteen battleships and ten battle cruisers, though. Bravo had lost a lot of smaller combatants, too, but it only looked smaller compared to the twenty-three battleships and twenty battle cruisers in Delta.

Geary was surprised that Bravo hadn't made any lunges toward the Alliance fleet just to shake up the Alliance sailors and maybe cause the fleet to lose more ground as it dodged the feints. *They're confident again, aren't they? They think we're trapped, and the outcome is inevitable.*

We'll see.

ONE hour until Syndic Formation Delta intercepted the track of the Alliance fleet. Geary sat down on the bridge of *Dauntless* and nodded in acknowledgment of Desjani's greeting. Rione sat at the back, only her eyes betraying her tension.

"Syndic Flotilla Bravo is accelerating," the maneuvering watch reported.

"Planning to catch up with us at the same time Flotilla

Delta gets here," Desjani remarked, sounding as if she were commenting on a simulation rather than a real tactic by an overwhelming Syndic force.

"No doubt," Geary agreed. "Let's try to mess up their plans." He punched his communication controls. "All units in the Alliance fleet, assume Formation Omicron; execute immediately upon receipt of this message. Station assignments are being sent to you now."

"Formation Omicron?" Desjani asked. She fixed her eyes on her display, knowing that, as the flagship, *Dauntless* would be the guide for the rest of the ships to form on and wouldn't be doing any maneuvering herself right now. "Sir? A cylinder?"

"Yes, that's really it." He could understand her surprise. "We've got two advantages. As a smaller force we can make it harder for the Syndics to employ their full numbers against us all at once. Those box formations of theirs can't adjust quickly enough to counter that." *I hope.* "And since we're slower, we can turn this formation tighter."

The ships of the Alliance fleet collapsed into Formation Omicron. Instead of a number of separate subformations, Omicron held every ship in the fleet in one grouping. And instead of dispersing the warships with plenty of distance between them, Omicron used minimum safe distances. The cylinder was only small by comparison to the big Syndic formations, but most of the Syndic wall formed by Flotilla Delta wouldn't be able to engage his fleet, even if the two forces swept through each other.

Geary had also abandoned the standard practice of having the lighter escorts between the major warships and the enemy. That was what they were for, normally, but he didn't intend to fight a normal battle. The outside of Omicron's cylinder was made up of battleships at the front and back, the battle cruisers forming a belt in the middle between them. Inside the cylinder were the destroyers and light cruisers. Heavy cruisers blocked both ends of the cylinder, one end stiffened by the two scout battleships.

Also inside it, as well protected as possible, were the damaged warships and the auxiliaries, *Warrior*, *Orion*, and *Majestic* in close company.

"Thirty minutes to contact with Syndic Flotilla Delta," the combat systems watch announced. "Twenty-eight minutes to contact with Syndic Flotilla Bravo."

The last Alliance warship slid into place in the formation, the cylinder of the fleet pointed down along the track toward the jump point for Ixion.

"The commander of Delta is going to let Bravo soften us up and take the brunt of our first volleys and then move in to finish us off and get the credit," Desjani observed. "I always disliked commanders who did that sort of thing."

"This one's going to be disappointed." *I hope.* Geary sat and waited, trying to judge the right moment. "All units, reduce speed to point zero seven light."

The Syndic ships were close enough now to have seen the Alliance fleet changing formation only a few minutes after it had begun, but they'd been forced to wait until the shape of the new Alliance formation could be made out before they could make any counterchanges to their own formation. Now Geary saw the formation for Syndic Flotilla Delta compressing, the wall getting shorter and thicker so that more Syndic ships could engage the Alliance fleet at any point. But Geary's speed reduction was causing the Syndics to rush to contact faster than they'd anticipated.

"Ten minutes to contact with Bravo. Twelve minutes to contact with Delta."

That was close enough. Bravo, conducting a stern chase, was gaining slowly, while Delta came tearing in from the side, still at point two light. *He's going to have to brake now.* "All units in the Alliance fleet, pivot formation down nine zero degrees and turn starboard seven zero degrees at time three one." Another very complex maneuver, with ships simultaneously swinging the cylinder so it pointed down, and bringing the cylinder around onto a new course.

"Delta's braking," Desjani noted on the heels of Geary's order as *Dauntless* swung around to push herself onto the new heading.

At their velocity, Delta had a hard time viewing the Alliance fleet well and, already committed to a hard braking maneuver, they couldn't do much about it anyway.

Bravo, coming on behind the Alliance fleet, tried to turn to match its maneuver but swung wider, losing distance.

A blizzard of missiles and grapeshot fired by the Delta Flotilla tore through the empty space where their combat systems had predicted the Alliance fleet would be.

Delta's thick box rushed past the place where the Alliance fleet would have been, while the vertical Alliance cylinder swung by to one side at extreme hell-lance range.

"Nice," Desjani said approvingly, but she kept her eyes on the display, knowing that this was just the first move.

Geary had his eyes there, too. The Syndics would follow. *Bravo will continue around, ready to pounce when we steady out. Delta will go up or down, I think, to simplify coordinating another joint approach. That means I need to take this fleet . . . there.* "All units, turn starboard one nine zero degrees, time four four."

Delta was turning upward as Bravo once again failed to match the Alliance fleet's turn and lost yet more ground. "All units, alter course down two zero degrees time four nine. Pivot formation up seven zero degrees at time five two."

This time the Alliance cylinder came back close to horizontal relative to the system plane and raced past far beneath Delta as Bravo began braking hard to bring its own velocity down far enough to match the turn radius of the slower Alliance ships. Geary waited until he saw Delta start another strong braking maneuver as well. "All units, turn starboard nine five degrees and accelerate to point one light at time zero two."

As the Syndic formations brought down their speed and turned inward toward each other again, Delta from above and Bravo to one side, to try to grapple with the Alliance fleet, the Alliance ships tore away toward the Ixion jump point.

"That is the strangest engagement I ever fought," Desjani remarked in a wondering voice.

"It's not over," Geary replied. "They'll sort themselves out, accelerate again, and come after us."

"They'll both be in a tail chase now." Desjani ran the maneuvering solution. "But they'll still catch us before the jump point."

"Yeah."

"Do you think that will work again?" Rione asked.

"Dodging?" Geary shook his head. "We did that sort of thing sometimes, in the old days, having fun and justifying it by claiming it taught us how to anticipate the movements of other formations. Maybe it did. But it won't work next time. The Syndics will expect us to evade, and they've got enough ships to spread their formations wide enough to keep us from avoiding contact next time."

Rione looked unhappy, but Desjani got it and smiled like a cat. "Spreading out formations will mean the Syndics have less firepower at any point."

"Right. And we're going through one of those points." Geary gestured at the display, which the Syndics showed accelerating in pursuit again. "It looks like they're merging Bravo and Delta. I need an estimate for the flagship's position."

"He should be in the center," Desjani commented.

Geary nodded. The place of honor. The place most likely to catch the brunt of an enemy attack using the head-on tactics that had been common practice. It wasn't the smartest way of doing business, but just like the Syndics, he was still constrained by the practice, since everyone in this fleet would be horrified if the flagship wasn't in the center of an attack.

In the wake of the Alliance fleet, the huge combined Syndic formation spread out, thinner in all places but stretching so that the wall now reached far enough above,

below, right, and left of the Alliance fleet's track that no
feasible maneuver could evade it. *You want to catch us?
Fine. Prepare to learn what happens when you try to close
your hand on a hornet.*

ELEVEN

TIMING was critical again. Geary waited, watching as the Syndics chased after the Alliance fleet, their velocity now up to point one four light, gradually closing the distance. The jump point for Ixion was just over an hour away now, but the Syndics would be within engagement range much sooner. *When will they fire missiles and grapeshot? Wait a little longer. We're entering the outer edges of their missile engagement envelope. They'll wait a little to give a margin of error in case we try a last-minute burst of speed. Hold it . . . now.* "All units, change formation facing one eight zero degrees, turn up one four degrees, brake speed to point zero five light at time four seven. All ships open fire as the enemy enters engagement range."

As the Alliance ships swung their bows to point toward the Syndics and cut in their main propulsion systems to kill velocity, the closing speed of the enemy force grew rapidly. The Alliance ships were now moving backward at point zero five light, the Syndics tearing toward them far faster. Instead of overtaking the Alliance ships at a relative velocity of point zero four light, the Syndic speed advantage had increased to close to point one light and the two forces were now rushing together.

The Syndics, caught by surprise again and with only a short time to react, were spitting out missiles and patterns of grapeshot, but only those fired by the ships closest to the point where the Alliance fleet was aiming had good hit probabilities. The leading edges of the Alliance cylinder lit up with flashes as weapons impacted on shields.

Alliance warships fired as well, their weapons aiming for a relatively small point in the huge Syndic wall. Shields flared on Syndic warships in a ragged circle centered on the point where the Alliance cylinder was aimed. Not far from the center of that circle was the Syndic flagship. At a relative closing velocity of just under thirty thousand kilometers per second, one moment it seemed the enemy formation was far away and the next it was behind them as the Alliance cylinder went through the Syndic wall like a bullet through a board.

The moment of contact came and went. Geary let out a breath he hadn't known he was holding, feeling *Dauntless* shuddering from hits the Syndics had scored in that fraction of a second when the forces were within range of all weapons. "Shields down slightly, spot failures, minor hit aft, no system losses," the watch-standers on *Dauntless* reported rapidly.

"All units in the Alliance fleet, change formation facing one eight zero degrees, accelerate to point one light at time five nine."

"We're going back through them?" Rione asked, sounding shocked.

"That's the idea. If they brake to match our speed, we'll be in big trouble, but hopefully they'll assume we're going to keep heading away and accelerate toward us again." Geary's eyes were on the display, watching the damage readouts for both fleets as sensors tallied the results of the moment of contact.

"Two battleships," Desjani noted approvingly. "Three

battle cruisers knocked out, too. One of those was probably the flagship."

"Let's hope so."

Only ten or twenty more passes just as successful, and they'd have evened the odds in this star system. It wasn't exactly grounds for getting cocky. "We didn't take much damage, but it'll be worse next time."

The Alliance ships had swung their bows completely around again, facing the jump point for Ixion and toward the Syndic formation. Geary watched the Syndic movements, hoping they'd do the natural thing and reverse course in place to pursue his fleet.

They did, but not quickly enough.

"They're coming back at us, but we're going to pass through them at a relative speed of only point zero two light," Desjani reported.

That would mean a longer time within enemy weapon range and easier targets for the missiles and grapeshot that the enemy still had in far greater abundance than the Alliance fleet.

He didn't want to look at the state of the fleet's fuel cells after these maneuvers. It didn't really matter. He had to burn off fuel cells now or the fleet wouldn't survive to worry about low fuel states.

The Syndic formation was folding in on itself, trying to thicken where the Alliance fleet would pass through, but fortunately didn't have much time to accomplish that.

The wall of Syndics came and went, *Dauntless*'s shields going incandescent from enemy hits.

"Spot failures on bow and flank shields, minor damage from grapeshot impacts, several hell-lance hits amidships, hell-lance batteries 3A and 5B out of commission, estimated time of repair unknown, casualties unknown," *Dauntless*'s watch reported.

Geary's eyes ran over the state of his fleet. *Dauntless* had come off easy compared to the other battle cruisers. Duellos's *Courageous* had been raked badly, *Daring* had lost half its weapons, *Leviathan* and *Dragon* had taken propulsion hits but were grimly keeping up with the formation, *Formidable* and *Incredible* were torn up amidships. Even his battleships had taken hits, though none were hurt as badly as the battle cruisers. Scout battleship *Exemplar* had been hit multiple times but by luck had lost nothing serious. The heavy cruisers *Basinet* and *Sallet* were gone, one exploded under a hail of Syndic fire and the other drifting away from the formation, badly hurt and helpless, escape pods leaping from the crippled ship.

Light cruisers *Spur*, *Damascene*, and *Swept-Guard* had been destroyed or wrecked, and destroyers *War-Hammer*, *Prasa*, *Talwar*, and *Xiphos* shattered despite their protected positions within the cylinder.

Titan had been hit again. The auxiliary seemed to attract Syndic weapons like a magnet attracted iron. But the hit wasn't critical. Despite his pain at the losses, Geary felt satisfaction as he saw the state of *Warrior*, *Orion*, and *Majestic*. Their degraded shields and new damage told Geary that the three battleships had indeed done their best to protect the auxiliaries.

The Syndics hadn't come through the latest firing pass unscathed, thanks to the local firepower superiority of the Alliance fleet. Another of their battleships was a drifting wreck, and three more battle cruisers had been blown up or broken. At least a dozen heavy cruisers had been disabled or killed, and the wreckage of numerous light cruisers and HuKs littered space now.

"Another pass?" Desjani asked, her voice subdued as she dealt with the damage to her ship.

"No. We'd have to go through them twice again, and they'd blow us to hell on the fourth pass. We're less than an hour from the jump point. We head for it."

The Syndic wall formation, distorted and bent from its maneuvers and the two times the Alliance fleet had passed through it, was reversing its ships' headings again and accelerating once more in the wake of the Alliance fleet.

Should he try to hit the Syndics again anyway? Try to throw the Syndics off once more? Geary tallied up the status of his ships' shields, the few specters and small amount of grapeshot remaining, and the damage his ships had already suffered and knew his quick assessment for Desjani had been accurate; another pair of passes through the Syndics would be suicidal. He didn't have the speed advantage or the distance needed to try to hit a flank of the Syndic formation, which was thicker now, not as tall or wide, but still covered space behind the Alliance fleet.

Forty-five minutes out from the jump point, and the Alliance fleet would have to brake its velocity to get around the minefield in front of the jump point.

The Syndics were too close, coming on too fast. It wasn't going to be enough. Everything he had tried wasn't going to be enough.

Geary watched the maneuvering systems predict the outcome of current velocity and directions vectors, and he could see the Syndics overtaking the rear of the Alliance fleet. He'd have an ugly choice, then, to either abandon the ships in the rear or else slow the rest of the fleet to join them and doom every ship in the fleet in the process. Lose a third, at least, of his fleet, or the whole thing? Knowing that even if he ran and left so many ships to their fate it still wouldn't mean safety when the survivors reached Ixion, because the Syndics would be coming after them.

"Captain Geary." A small window had popped into existence, showing Captain Mosko looking calm in a numb sort of way. "My division is the farthest back in the formation, closest to the Syndics."

"Yes." The Seventh Battleship Division had taken the brunt of Syndic missiles and grapeshot on the first pass through the Syndic formation, avoided that on the second pass when warships on the front of the Alliance cylinder led the way through the Syndics, but now they'd catch hell again as the Syndics overtook the Alliance fleet. There wasn't a damn thing Geary could do about that, though.

"We need to stop the Syndics from overtaking the rest of the fleet before it reaches the jump point," Mosko continued. "Uh, that is, we, my division. I'd like to commit only *Defiant*, but she can't do it alone. With *Audacious* and *Indefatigable* alongside, we'll be able to hold them off."

He suddenly realized what Mosko was saying. "I can't order you to do that."

"Yes, you could," Mosko replied. "But I know how hard that would be, and it's not as if you haven't done the same yourself. We all grew up hearing about Grendel and vowing to do the same if we ever had to. This is one of the things battleships are supposed to do, Captain Geary." He sounded almost apologetic now. "When needed, we use our firepower and shields and armor to protect other ships. You understand. A forlorn hope. We're volunteering, my ships and my crews, because that's one of the missions we're supposed to carry out. When we have to. You don't have to order it, sir. We volunteer, in the spirit and example of Black Jack Geary."

Geary only knew the term *forlorn hope* because he'd read it being used to describe his own desperate defense at Grendel a century ago. A rear guard, one not expected to survive, one that knows it will be sacrificed to save the rest of the force. And doing it now in the name of his example.

The damnable things were that he *had* done that once, had made the same decision that Mosko was making now, and he couldn't tell Mosko not to do it. He needed those three battleships to keep the Syndics from overhauling the rest of the Alliance fleet and destroying it here at Lakota.

Words came to him, old words, ones he'd heard before but rarely. "Captain Mosko, to you and your ships and their crews, may the living stars welcome you and shine on your valor, may your ancestors look upon you and stand ready to embrace you, may the memories of your names and your deeds shine in the minds of all who come after. You are not lost and not forgotten but forever remembered among the ranks of honor and courage."

Mosko sat straighter as Geary recited the ancient blessing before an apparently hopeless battle. "May our deeds be worthy of our ancestors," he replied. "Captain Geary, when you've beaten the last Syndic, and by the living stars I now believe you will, make sure any survivors of these ships are liberated and taken care of as they deserve. I'll see you on the other side someday. Any messages?"

"Yes. If you see the spirit of Captain Michael Geary, let him know I'm doing my best." His grandnephew, almost certainly dead with his ship *Repulse* back in the Syndic home system.

"Of course. And please let my family know about me when you get the fleet home." Mosko saluted. "To the honor of our ancestors."

The window vanished, taking Mosko's image with it.

"Captain?" Desjani was gazing at him, not knowing what had happened.

Geary shook his head, took a deep breath, then pointed at the display, where *Audacious*, *Defiant*, and *Indefatigable* were pivoting around to use their main drives to slow their velocity. "The Seventh Battleship Division will be moving back to serve as a rear guard," he managed to say. "They volunteered."

She nodded, her face set. "Of course." And in that moment Geary knew that were *Dauntless* required to do such a thing, then Desjani would do it. Not gladly, not embracing death as some key to heroic salvation, but because she knew others would be counting on her. In the end, that was what it was all about. Do what was needed for those counting on you, or let them down. "I expect," Desjani continued, "that Captain Mosko will have his ships drop back to about three light-minutes behind the rest of the fleet and then maintain position there."

"Three light-minutes," Geary repeated.

Rione had come to stand beside him, bending down to speak very quietly. "Must this be?"

"Yes."

She gazed at him, and for once apparently had no trouble seeing how much he regretted having to make the decision. "Will it make a difference?"

"If anything saves this fleet now, it'll be their sacrifice."

Taken alone, a single battleship carried an awesome amount of firepower, matched by heavy shields and heavy armor. Three battleships operating close together were a force to be reckoned with even by the numbers of Syndic warships hurling themselves toward the Alliance fleet.

Captain Mosko brought *Indefatigable*, *Audacious*, and *Defiant* back toward the onrushing Syndics, the three battleships arranged in a vertical triangle with *Defiant* at the top, close enough to one another to provide mutual protection and combine their firepower. After he'd fallen back far enough, he accelerated again, trying to match the speed of the Syndics so they'd have to go past at a slow relative speed and be much easier targets.

There was no way to avoid the fact that it made the three Alliance battleships much easier targets for the Syndics, too.

The remaining specter missiles and grapeshot blasted out from the three battleships as the leading wave of Syndic light cruisers and HuKs entered their engagement envelopes. A lot of the light enemy ships evaded away, swinging far out to either side or up or down to avoid the fire of the Alliance battleships and thereby losing so much ground that they wouldn't be able to catch the Alliance fleet now.

About twenty HuKs and a half dozen light cruisers tried to charge past and through the Seventh Battleship Division. As the HuKs entered the engagement envelopes, the battleships' hell-lance batteries filled space with charged particle spears that tore into the light HuKs from multiple angles.

Space lit with impacts as shields flared and failed, then more hits tore holes in ships and their crews. HuKs and light cruisers exploded in balls of fragments and gas, broke into pieces that tumbled wildly through space, or simply went silent as their systems were knocked out, the dead hulks twisting away under the force of impacts.

None of the Syndic light units made it through, but right behind them were heavy cruisers and battle cruisers, none of those ships individually a match for a battleship, but in overwhelming numbers.

Clenching his fists, Geary gazed helplessly at the main body of the Syndic flotilla charging down on Mosko's battleships.

"Specters," Desjani stated in a clear voice.

She was right. There was one thing he could do. Combat systems confirmed that the rear guard was within extreme range for the specters remaining in the Alliance fleet. "All ships, fire all remaining specters targeted at the Syndic warships around *Audacious*, *Defiant*, and *Indefatigable*. I repeat, all remaining specters."

The missiles began launching, flinging into space, choosing targets, then accelerating toward the embattled Alliance battleships and the Syndics flaying them. Not nearly enough specters, just enough to distract the Syndic pursuers somewhat and draw some fire away from the battleships, but something. They scored enough hits on one Syndic heavy cruiser to knock it out and managed some blows against battle cruisers whose screens had been knocked low by the hell-lance fire of *Audacious*, *Indefatigable*, and *Defiant*. But there were so many more Syndic heavy cruisers and battle cruisers, with the Syndic battleships coming into range now as well.

Defiant was catching the worst of it, glowing with the force of repeated enemy hits. *Audacious* took out another heavy cruiser, then turned its hell lances on a Syndic battle cruiser. *Indefatigable* reeled under the fire of a full division of enemy battle cruisers but punched back, getting in a solid hit with its null field when one battle cruiser tried to pass by too close.

It physically hurt to watch the three battleships being pounded by increasingly overwhelming numbers of Syndic warships, but they were accomplishing their mission. The leading elements of the Syndic flotilla were slowed, hurt, or evading, and the Alliance fleet was within reach of the jump point. They'd bought the time they needed at the price of three battleships and their crews.

The Alliance fleet came at the jump point from slightly above and to one side, about to clear the Syndic minefield. "All units, reduce speed to point four light and follow *Dauntless*'s movements," Geary ordered. With every second critical, he didn't want to order exact courses now or worry about every unit maintaining its precise location in the formation.

Dauntless had pivoted around, her bow to the enemy now, and her main propulsion units kicking in again to force her velocity down. All around her, the other ships in the fleet were doing the same with varying degrees of quickness depending on the state of their propulsion units.

And the displays updated as the Syndics kept coming, getting past the reeling ships of the Seventh Battleship Division, closing faster now that the Alliance warships had been forced to slow down.

Desjani was watching the display intently as *Dauntless* crested the estimated top of the Syndic minefield to one side of the jump point. "Alter course down one eight zero degrees, port zero five degrees, now," she ordered.

Dauntless swung over and down, as if diving toward the jump point, the rest of the Alliance warships following suit in a wave.

The Syndic force that they had last seen at Ixion, built around four battleships and four battle cruisers, chose that exact moment to flash into existence and make an automated turn up, the arriving Syndics and the fleeing Alliance forces right on top of each other in an instant's time.

The only thing that prevented last-minute disaster was that the Syndics hadn't been expecting to encounter an enemy force literally the moment they arrived at Lakota. In the few seconds required for the Syndic crews to recognize what was happening, then activate and give firing approval to their weapons, the frantic Alliance warships surrounding them unleashed a firestorm of hell lances that

wiped out the lighter units and ripped open three of the
four battle cruisers.

But the four battleships blundered onward, shields
shredding under the Alliance fire but now shooting back
desperately as the heavy enemy warships headed straight
for the four auxiliaries. With only seconds before contact,
Titan, *Witch*, *Jinn*, and *Goblin* didn't have time to evade.

But *Warrior*, *Orion*, and *Majestic* were still there, still
hanging as close to the auxiliaries as they could. *Orion*
seemed to shy away in the moments before contact, and
Majestic was slightly to one side, but *Warrior* was right
between the auxiliaries and the Syndic battleships. She
held her ground, pouring hell-lance fire from her working
batteries into the enemy warships while the four Syndic
battleships pounded back at the single Alliance battleship.

If the fight had lasted for more than seconds, *Warrior*
would have been doomed, but the Syndic battleships
veered away in panicked flight, two of them riddled by Alliance fire and barely operational. *Warrior*, torn up anew
by Syndic fire, doggedly kept up as the auxiliaries fled toward the jump point with the rest of the fleet.

In a matter of moments the Alliance fleet had met the
arriving Syndic force, decimated it, then passed onward,
taking more damage itself and leaving the shocked Syndic
survivors in their wake.

There wasn't much left of the Seventh Battleship Division. The Syndic battleships had caught up with it and
were now methodically smashing *Audacious*, *Defiant*, and
Indefatigable. *Indefatigable* only had a single hell-lance
battery still firing. *Audacious* was silent, a ball of wreckage falling off to one side. *Defiant* took several broadsides
almost simultaneously and blew apart as two massive ex-
plosions erupted amidships and near the stern.

"Captain Geary? Captain Geary! The fleet is at the
jump point!"

He tore his eyes from the final moments of *Defiant*, trying not to notice the debris of battle that seemed to fill the
universe, the Syndic missiles reaching for the trailing

ships in the Alliance fleet, the crippled Alliance warships straining to keep up with their fellows, the broken wrecks of the Syndic warships that had run head-on into the Alliance fleet at the jump point tumbling away. "All units. Jump now."

The stars vanished. The blackness between the stars disappeared. The last gasps of *Defiant*, *Indefatigable*, and *Audacious* were gone. So were the distant, abandoned wreck of *Paladin* and the equally far-off constellation of debris which was all that remained of *Renown*. The hypernet gate had vanished, the Syndic flotillas gone with it. Where an instant before desperate battle had raged and the wreckage of battles littered space, now there was only the endless gray nothingness, the silence and the wandering lights of jump space.

He'd never jumped straight out of battle, never imagined fighting literally on a jump point's doorstep. Geary felt his heart pounding, his breath sounding loud in the sudden hush that filled *Dauntless*'s bridge as everyone sat stunned by the abrupt transition from combat to stillness. He closed his eyes, trying to deal with the reality of what had happened. Three more battleships gone. Four battleships and one battle cruiser lost all told. Two heavy cruisers. Light cruisers and destroyers. Dozens more warships in the fleet with significant damage. Most of the remaining Syndic fleet in hot pursuit and still far outnumbering the Alliance fleet's survivors. The Syndics would take a little while to get organized, to finish off *Defiant*, *Indefatigable*, and *Audacious*; then they'd come through that jump point. They couldn't touch the Alliance fleet in jump space. They couldn't even see the Alliance ships here, where every group of ships seemed to occupy its own drab reality.

But the Alliance fleet would come out of jump at Ixion, and the Syndics would come out behind them.

Geary stood up, feeling as if he had spent several days straight in the command seat. He looked toward Captain Desjani, who gazed somberly back at him. He should say something. "Thank you, Captain. *Dauntless* did well. Please see to your ship's damage and your crew."

Looking up, Geary saw the watch-standers gazing back at him as if they were about to drown and he were a lifeline. What to say to them? "Well done."

He started to leave, but a young lieutenant spoke desperately. "What'll we do, sir? At Ixion?"

Damned if he knew. "I'll consider my options." He forced a look of reassurance. "We're not beaten." Technically, at least, that was correct.

They nodded and looked comforted as Geary left the bridge, Rione going along silently beside him.

THE grayness of jump space seemed to have invaded his soul. Geary sat in his stateroom, slumped in a seat, his mind running in endless circles while ships died over and over again in his memory.

"It's been a full day," Rione said in a hard voice. She was sitting nearby, her face looking like she'd aged a decade or maybe two in that day. "Get over it. We have to prepare for Ixion."

"Ixion?" Geary didn't bother laughing scornfully. "Just what am I supposed to do at Ixion?"

"I don't know. I'm not the commander of this fleet. And if you don't do something, you won't be the commander much longer either."

"If that's an oblique reference to the fact that this fleet's destruction at Ixion seems inevitable—"

"No!" Rione made a choking motion with her hands. "It's not. That's a major problem and one I can't help you with, because I don't know how to command a fleet. But it's not just the Syndics you have worry about," Rione stated. "Your fate, your standing, is bound up in the fate and condition of this fleet. Right now this fleet is wounded, and that means you are, too. What happens to a wounded stag, John Geary?"

The vision that brought up wasn't comfortable, but he

recognized the truth of her words. "It becomes an attractive target for wolves, who gather, attack, and pull it down."

"You know some of the wolves in this fleet but not all of them. They've been testing you since you took command, looking for weaknesses, trying to trip you up. But you kept winning, kept guessing right, so they couldn't attract enough support. Now there's blood in the water, and at the next opportunity, they'll go after you."

"You're mixing your prey and predator metaphors," Geary noted sourly.

"The results are the same for the prey regardless of the nature of the predator. The first opportunity your opponents in this fleet get after we arrive in Ixion, they will move against you, and because of what happened at Lakota, you will get little support from the disillusioned and the frightened."

Geary managed to work up enough feelings to glare at her. "If this little speech of yours is supposed to be inspiring me to get going again, I have to let you know that your motivational skills could use some work."

She glared back. "Do you think you'll be the only target then? I'm known as your ally and your lover. At least some of your opponents in this fleet have learned that my husband was still alive when captured. Yes, I'm certain of it. They've been waiting to use that information for when it will do the most damage. They will employ it at Ixion, where your lover will be exposed as an opportunistic whore lacking in honor and you will either share that stain by defending me or look weak by letting me be shunned and isolated. Not every weapon aimed at you will strike you directly."

There wasn't anything he could think to say except the weakest possible thing. "I'm sorry."

"Should I be grateful for that?" Rione shot at him, then stood up, turned, and paced angrily. "I don't need you to defend me. I chose to come to you. Any shame is mine."

"I'll defend you."

"Spare me the chivalry!" She thrust an angry forefinger at him. "Defend this fleet! It needs you! I can't save it. I can tell the men and women of this fleet how much I admire and respect them, I can tell them how the Alliance honors their service and sacrifice, but I cannot command them! I don't know how. Nor can any of your allies in this fleet. I know you expect Captain Duellos to assume command, but he will be in a far weaker position than you and likely fail."

Now he was getting angry, too. "I'm indispensable? Is that what you're saying? I'm the only one who can command this fleet? Ever since we first exchanged words, you've been telling me that I don't dare ever actually believe that! That if I do, I'll be dooming this fleet and myself and the Alliance. And believe it or not, Victoria Rione, I do listen to what you say and consider it very carefully. I'm not Black Jack."

"Yes, you are." Rione came close, held his head in both hands so she could gaze straight into his eyes. "You're Black Jack. You really are. Not a myth, but the only person who can save this fleet and the Alliance. I didn't believe that for a long time. I didn't believe the myth. Maybe you're not that myth, but the legend gives you the ability to inspire and lead. You haven't misused that. Just as important, you brought knowledge with you of how to fight, which has saved this fleet several times already and hurt the Syndics badly. And you can do it again, because so many believe you are Black Jack and because you've done the sorts of things only Black Jack was supposed to be capable of."

"I can't—"

"You *must*!" She stepped back again. "I'm not saying the right things. We've shared a bed and known each other's bodies, but our souls remain hidden from each other. You need someone whose words you'll believe, someone who can speak to you in the terms you know as a fleet officer."

The anger was gone, replaced by weariness again.

"Words aren't going to make a difference, no matter who speaks them." Words could not change the state of this fleet, change the losses and damage suffered at Lakota, change the size of the Syndic force coming after this fleet.

"We'll see." Rione left, only the automatic closing mechanism on the hatch keeping it from slamming behind her.

Some indeterminate amount of time later, his hatch alert chimed, which at least meant it wasn't Rione back to give him another pep talk since she could have walked in on her own. "Come in."

"Captain Geary, sir?" Captain Desjani stood in the entry, betraying uncertainty.

Geary struggled into a more upright sitting position and straightened his uniform a bit. "Sorry, Captain Desjani." He ought to say something else. "What brings you down here?"

"I . . . may I sit down, sir?"

She never asked that. This wasn't routine business. Well, he should have known that. "Certainly. Relax." *Ask about her ship, you idiot.* "How is *Dauntless*?"

Desjani sat but of course didn't relax. "We've got all of our hell lances back online. Only a single partial volley of grapeshot left in our ammo lockers, and no specters. Hull damage won't be totally repaired by the time we reach Ixion, but we'll patch things up well enough to fight." She paused. "We lost seventeen personnel and had another twenty-six wounded badly enough to be out of service for a while."

Seventeen dead. He wondered how many of those seventeen he would have recognized. Probably most. "I'll be at their services. Tell me when." The funerals couldn't be until they reached Ixion. No one's remains were ever consigned to jump space.

"Of course, sir." Desjani looked away from Geary for a moment, then spoke quickly. "Sir, Co-President Rione asked me to speak with you. She said you'd taken our losses at Lakota very hard and that I might be able to discuss that with you."

Great. As if he wanted Desjani to see him depressed. Why couldn't Rione let sleeping dogs lie? Or in this case let a depressed dog stay depressed? "Thank you, but I don't think that's necessary."

Desjani's eyes came back to Geary, flicking over his face and uniform, then lowered. "Sir, with all due respect, it doesn't look that way."

He could get mad at Desjani, but that would be unfair and probably too much work. "Point taken. Okay."

She paused again as if waiting to be sure he'd agreed, then spoke with sudden intensity. "I knew you'd feel the losses, sir. That's who you are. It's one of the things that makes you such a great commander. But you're also someone who understands the need to keep fighting. I've seen that so many times. You don't really need my words or anyone else's. You'll come around, and you'll figure out what to do, and then we'll beat the Syndics again."

He had to say it. "We didn't beat them this time."

Desjani frowned and shook her head. "That's not true, sir. They wanted us trapped and destroyed. They didn't achieve that. We wanted to get out of Lakota. We did."

That made Geary frown, too, because Desjani was right. Seen that way, the Syndics had lost, and the Alliance fleet, by surviving and escaping, had won. Still . . . "Thank you. But . . . Tanya, we lost a lot of ships. A battle cruiser. Four battleships—"

"I know, sir," Desjani interrupted. "I wish this victory had been like your others, with our losses negligible. But every battle can't be like that, especially when we're facing those kinds of odds."

He shouldn't need her to tell him that. Geary let his real feelings show for a moment, his sorrow and anguish, and saw Desjani react. "They trusted me to get them home. Now they won't get home."

"Sir." Desjani leaned forward, her face lit with the intensity of her feelings. "Not everyone returns from battle.

We all learn that early on, and we've all lost many friends and comrades in action, as did our fathers and mothers and their fathers and mothers before them. But you were sent to save us. I know that. So do most of the officers and almost every sailor in this fleet. You are on a mission from the living stars to get this fleet home and save the Alliance, and that means you *cannot* fail. We all know that. Soon you'll remember that, and you'll figure out what to do next."

Her belief was almost terrifying to him, because he knew how fallible he really was and couldn't really believe that someone like him could be on a mission for any greater power. "I'm as human as you are, Tanya."

"Of course you are! The living stars and our ancestors work through the living! Everyone knows that!"

"This fleet doesn't need me. The Alliance doesn't need me. I'm not—"

"Sir, yes we do!" Desjani almost pleaded this time. "I don't know what I—what this fleet would do if you weren't here, what would happen to the Alliance without you. You came to us when you did for a *reason*. Because if you hadn't been there with us in the Syndic home system, then this fleet would have been wiped out and the Alliance lost. We followed you because we trusted you, and you have shown us again and again by your deeds and your words that you deserve that trust."

Geary opened his mouth to protest again, then understood as if one of his ancestors had whispered it into his ear. He had let down the crews of the ships lost at Lakota. That was an awful thing. But it would be far more awful to let down the crews of all the surviving ships still in the fleet, to break faith with their belief in him when that faith was what was keeping them going. They were counting on him, and he knew it, just as the crews of *Audacious*, *Defiant*, and *Indefatigable* had known the rest of the fleet was counting on them. He had to come through, and Desjani and Rione were both right that it had to be him.

Because that faith others had in him meant only he had

a halfway decent chance of keeping this fleet together, though keeping it from being destroyed would be just as hard a task. But he had to do it. And that meant he had to figure out what to do next.

So he sat a bit straighter, nodded, and spoke in a firmer voice. "I do have a responsibility." *Like it or not, and I don't like it one bit.* "Thank you for helping me remember that."

She sat back, smiling with relief. "You didn't need me."

"Yes, as a matter of fact, I do." He started to force a smile, then felt it become real. "Thank you. I'm very glad I'm on your ship."

Desjani smiled at him again, then swallowed and looked uncertain before standing abruptly. "Thank you, sir. I should get back to the bridge."

"Sure. If you see Co-President Rione, tell her I'm okay."

"I will, sir." Desjani saluted quickly and then hastened out the hatch.

Geary sat for a while, thinking, then reached slowly for the controls of the display. The image of Ixion Star System appeared, the Alliance fleet on it in the tangled disposition it had been in when it entered jump at Lakota, and in which it would be when it arrived at Ixion. *I have to think of something. But what?*

TWELVE

"**SIR,** this is Lieutenant Iger in intelligence. We have something important that we need to brief to you."

Geary, feeling depression creeping up again as good options in Ixion eluded him, took a moment to consider whether he should answer, but duty sat on his chest and glared at him until he reached out to acknowledge the message. "What does important mean?" he asked.

"I . . . it's hard to judge, sir. It's something very unexpected, and we really don't know what it means, but it could be critically important."

Intelligence loved modifiers like "could be," but it was unusual to have them frankly admit to not knowing what something meant.

"We have everything ready to show you down here, or I can come up there and brief you, sir," Iger continued, "whenever it's convenient."

Geary looked around. Facing the crew of *Dauntless* again after the desperate retreat out of Lakota still felt, well, daunting. But he'd increasingly felt as if this stateroom were a prison, one that he had locked himself inside.

It was long past time he got out there and tried to be a fleet commander again. "I'll come down there. Is right now okay?"

"Yes, sir. I'll be waiting, sir."

Standing up, Geary checked his appearance, grimaced, then took a while to clean up and put on a fresh uniform. No matter what had happened at Lakota, he couldn't look defeated.

The members of *Dauntless*'s crew who he encountered wore expressions of worry, which lit with hope when they saw him. Geary tried to project confidence despite the gloom filling him and apparently fooled most or all of them. He'd learned as a junior officer dealing with superior officers that if you acted like you knew what you doing, everyone else assumed you really did know it.

"What will we do at Ixion?" an anxious sailor blurted at Geary. "Sir?"

"I'm still considering options," Geary replied, as if there were a lot to choose from and any of them were good. But the sailor smiled, reassured, and saluted briskly.

As he reached the intelligence section, sealed behind multiple high-security hatches, Geary pondered the fact that an intelligence officer had been able to motivate him out of his stateroom, something that neither combat officer Desjani nor politician Rione had succeeded in doing. That had to rank high on the irony scale.

Lieutenant Iger awaited Geary, looking nervous as Geary took a seat and waited. "Sir, we've been analyzing the messages passed among the ships of the Syndic flotilla that arrived via the hypernet gate while we were in the Lakota Star System."

"How much of that can you intercept and break?" Geary asked.

"Not a lot, but some stray signals always leak, and if we remain in the star system long enough for them to reach us, we can record them and then try to break the encryption," Iger explained. "It's not even remotely a source of real-time intelligence, though if we ever broke an

enemy message in time to influence an ongoing engagement, we'd certainly bring it to your attention."

"I assume you'd let me decide if the message could influence the engagement?" Geary asked, knowing that the
intelligence types were probably making such calls themselves.

"Uh, yes, sir," Lieutenant Iger assured him, doubtless
already planning to make sure that was done in the future.

"I take it there was something important about the signals you picked up at Lakota?"

"Yes, sir," Iger repeated. "Unusual. Very unusual." He
paused, licked his lips, then spoke quickly. "Sir, it's our
assessment that the Syndics were as surprised by their arrival in Lakota as we were."

Geary wondered if he had heard right. "You mean the
Syndics already in the star system were surprised by the
arrival of reinforcements?" Why would that conclusion
bother the intelligence officer?

"No, sir. The only interpretation that matches the messages we've been able to break is that the Syndic ships
that arrived via the hypernet gate were totally surprised to
be at Lakota. They thought they'd be arriving in Andvari
Star System."

It took a moment for Geary to realize he was staring at
the lieutenant. "How often does that sort of thing happen
with hypernet travel?" No one had ever mentioned to him
ships getting lost in the hypernet.

"It *doesn't*, sir," Lieutenant Iger insisted. "The use of a
key is exceedingly simple. On the control panel you
choose the actual name of the star system you're going to.
Once you're on your way between gates, the key still displays the destination star. It would take multiple acts of
extreme stupidity or denial to avoid knowing which star
you were going to. As far as our files go, and they're very
detailed, no ship using the hypernet has ever gone to any
star system except the one it intended going to. The process
is too simple for even an idiot to mess up."

"Don't underestimate idiots, Lieutenant. Could something have been wrong with their hypernet key?"

Iger made a frustrated gesture. "Again, sir, as far as we know, any problem with the key serious enough to cause that kind of error should have led to it not operating at all."

Geary sat back, thinking, while Lieutenant Iger waited, looking unhappy. *He probably expects me to start tearing him and his analysis apart. So why would he brief it to me unless he believes it must be true?* "Assume your analysis is correct," Geary began, drawing a clear look of relief from Iger. "How could the destination of those ships have been different from what they keyed in?"

Iger shook his head. "According to our experts, there isn't any way."

"Did you talk to Captain Cresida?"

This time Iger looked surprised that Geary knew Cresida was one of the fleet's experts on the hypernet system. "No, sir, we couldn't get that long and complex a message to her ship while the fleet was in jump space. But we did call up a learning simulation based on the teachings of several of the Alliance's leading experts on hypernet, presented it as a theoretical situation, and asked if it were possible. The avatars of the experts in the simulation were all positive that it couldn't happen."

"There's no way to change a destination in midjourney on the hypernet? None at all?"

"No, sir," Iger stated firmly. "But there's only one alternative to that having happened. That's if the Syndics were trying to deceive us and deliberately broadcast a lot of misleading messages knowing we'd pick up some of them and eventually break some of those we intercepted."

"Why don't you think they did that?"

Iger grimaced this time. "Occam's razor mostly, sir. A deliberate deception in this case would be a very complex and uncertain operation. The simplest explanation, that the messages are real, is the best. And the messages *feel* real, sir. Nothing about them seems deceptive. Everything about them matches our experience with valid Syndic communications. And we can't think of any explanation why the Syndics would try to fool us that way."

"To keep us from using their own hypernet? Sow doubt that it was reliable?"

"But they couldn't know we would pick *those* signals, sir. Some of them were flying as soon as the Syndics arrived at Lakota, before they even could have absorbed the news that our fleet was there as well."

Geary nodded. "How confident are you of your assessment that the Syndic fleet that came out of the hypernet gate at Lakota didn't intend going to Lakota?"

"It's the only assessment that matches the message traffic, sir," Iger stated miserably. "We wanted to find something else to explain it. But nothing else matches."

"Fair enough." Geary stood up. "Good job on the analysis and good job on telling me the truth as you think it is. But you did miss something."

Iger looked even more worried. "What was that, sir?"

"You told me that there's no way to change the destination of ships in a hypernet in midjourney. If the intelligence you collected is right, and I know of no reason to doubt it, then there must be such a way. We just don't know what it is."

Iger looked startled, then nodded, then appeared puzzled. "But if the Syndics know a way to do that, why were they so surprised to arrive in a different star system?"

"Maybe the Syndics don't know how to do it, either, Lieutenant." Geary paused to give Iger time to absorb the implications of that. "Is there anything you have that I don't have access to? Any information deemed too sensitive for me to see?"

"No, sir," Iger stated immediately. "As fleet commander you have access to everything. I can't speak for files off of this ship, but anything on this ship is available to you, regardless of classification and other restrictions."

There was a star display floating near one bulkhead. Geary went over to it and gazed into its depths. "Lieutenant, are you aware of any information that indicates or speculates that another intelligent species exists on the far side of Syndic space from the Alliance?"

He turned back to see Iger staring at him. "No, sir," Lieutenant Iger stated in a surprised voice. "I've never seen anything like that."

Geary nodded again. "Do me a favor, Lieutenant. Pull up the data that we've captured that provides information on the far side of Syndic space. Plot in occupied star systems, abandoned star systems, and hypernet gate placements. Then tell me what you think."

Iger was staring at the star display now. "Have you already done that, sir?"

"I have. I want to see if you reach the same conclusion I did."

RIONE was in his stateroom when Geary returned. She stood and gave him a searching look. "It didn't quite feel the same in here without you slouched in a chair radiating gloom. Are you all right?"

"Yeah. I think so."

"So Captain Desjani was able to give you something I couldn't."

"That's . . . she helped. You and she both helped."

"Uh-huh." Rione sat back down, looking tired. "Good, anyway. Whatever did it. I was about to the point of standing over you and slapping you until you moved."

"I might have started to like it," Geary replied.

"A joke? You've gone from immobility to jokes?"

"Not really." He sat down near her and made an uncertain gesture. "I don't really understand how it worked, but responsibilities can weigh you down, or they can make you move. Sometimes both. Does that make sense?"

"Yes, it does," Rione agreed, her voice uncharacteristically gentle. "Where were you?"

"I just came from the intelligence offices." Geary called up a star display and explained what Lieutenant Iger had told him, Rione listening but giving little clue to her reactions. "How do you think that large formation of Syndic ships arrived in Lakota via hypernet in time to nearly destroy us?" he asked at the end.

Rione sat silently for a few moments, her eyes on the star display. "So it wasn't exceptionally bad luck. It seems our unknown aliens have chosen to side with the Syndics. I warned you they wouldn't let you win."

"I'm not getting any closer to winning! I'm still focused on survival and not sure how long I can manage that."

"Have you considered all of the implications of this?"

"Of course I have!" He glared at her, then paused to think. "Which implications?"

Rione gestured to the star display. "How did our increasingly less-hypothetical alien intelligences know that this fleet was headed for Lakota so that they could divert that Syndic fleet to there?"

Geary felt his guts tighten. "Either they have some means of detecting the movements of fleets in roughly real time across interstellar distances, or they have a spy in this fleet. Do you think they look human enough to pass?"

"If they aren't indeed human. Or perhaps they've hired agents to spy for them. Or maybe the spy isn't even living but a worm inserted in fleet systems to report on our activities."

Geary nodded. "Those are possibilities, and frankly more believable for me than anything that can see across light-years of distance without any time delay. If those . . . whatever they are can do that, then the human race is very seriously outclassed in technology. Unpleasant though the thought is, I prefer believing that some kind of spy is providing that information." He paused to think. "Obviously your spies in this fleet have never found signs of alien spies, or I'm sure you would have told me."

Rione uttered a heavily exasperated sigh. "My spies are aware of many different spies working for many different people. But many informants remain unseen, I'm sure, and the identities of most of the employers of those spies we know of remain uncertain at best. Now, the next implication. How did this spy get the information to the aliens in time for them to act?"

Geary stared at her. "I should have thought of that. The only way they could've is if these beings have a means of faster-than-light communications that doesn't involve using a ship to physically transport the message."

"We've speculated the hypernet gates could allow that somehow."

"Yeah . . . but there wasn't a hypernet gate in Ixion, which is where we decided to go to Lakota. We haven't been in a star system containing a hypernet gate since Sancere, and that gate was destroyed before we left."

"True." Rione made a face. "A faster-than-light transmitter small enough to remain undetected on one of our ships. How much more technologically advanced than we are these alien intelligences?"

Geary was staring at the starscape when another realization hit. "Damn."

"What?"

"The worst implication of all, maybe. We've been hoping to find a Syndic hypernet gate poorly enough defended to allow us to use it to get close to Alliance space."

She nodded.

"But now we can't, not even if one is sitting totally undefended."

Rione got it then, digging her fingernails into her palms. "If we enter the Syndic hypernet system, and these aliens can redirect any ships within that system . . ."

"We could end up anywhere. Instead of arriving in our planned destination next to the border with Alliance space, we might come out on the opposite side of Syndic space. Or in a system where the entire Syndic fleet is gathered waiting for us again."

"Or somewhere not even on the Syndic hypernet?" Rione wondered. "That's not supposed to be possible, but it seems a number of impossible things must already be happening."

Geary sat down, leaning back in his seat and trying to get his mind around all of the things that it seemed must be true. "I don't get it. Say they've got those capabilities, and they must have some of that. Why would they tip their hands this way? Let us know they have those abilities?"

"Perhaps because the highest levels of the Syndic leadership already know about them and will know who caused their fleet to arrive at Lakota instead of Andvari." Rione shook her head. "As for us, the aliens don't expect us to survive or perhaps even guess what really happened. But I'm still surprised they gave away knowledge of such capabilities to us."

"Maybe because it doesn't do us any good? We're still trapped." Geary felt anger growing. With all the problems he faced already, it wasn't fair to have aliens jump in and make things worse. That was ridiculous grounds for being mad, but it just wasn't fair, and it made him mad as hell. "This fleet must get home the hard way or not at all. And it *is* going to get home."

Rione gave him a disbelieving look, then smiled. "From despairing to determined. This has been a good day for mood changes as far as you're concerned." The smile faded, and she frowned slightly. "There's a possibility we haven't considered."

"What's that?"

"Perhaps the aliens deliberately let us know of their capabilities with the hypernet system. Perhaps they expected you to somehow escape from that star system just as you have successfully escaped from others. Perhaps they aren't helping the Syndics but trying to tell us something."

Geary stared at the star display, letting the idea filter through his mind. "I have enough humans who think I can do the impossible. I don't need aliens piling on, too. Why would they do that?"

"I don't know," Rione stated with open frustration. "We don't know what the goals of these mysterious opponents are. We don't know how they think, assuming they're not human. What do they want? Humanity tricked into endless war? Are they waiting for some optimum number of hypernet gates to be built before they cause all of them to collapse and liberate enough energy to sterilize every part of space colonized by humanity? Or are the gates simply insurance if we ever threaten them? Or is it something totally different, a goal based on some alien concept we can't even put a name to?"

"You're telling me they may not be hostile? Even though they redirected that Syndic flotilla to Lakota so we were almost trapped there?"

"That's exactly what I'm saying. If an alien fleet appeared before us tomorrow, what would you do?"

Geary paused to think. "I'm not sure. If they opened fire, my decision would be easy. But if they just appeared . . . I guess the smart thing to do would be to talk. Find out what they want."

"And then," Rione added, her eyes hard, "decide if what they want is something humanity can live with."

"Whoever or whatever they are, they owe us for the loss of *Audacious*, *Indefatigable*, and *Defiant*," Geary replied, his own voice harsh. "They better have a *really* good justification for that."

THREE more days of thinking, three more days of not finding answers. As the fleet exited into normal space back at Ixion, Geary felt a bitter taste in his mouth. No minefield awaited them at this jump exit from Lakota, so Geary just watched as the Alliance warships flashed into existence around *Dauntless*. He kept his eyes on the ship status readouts as reports came in, seeing updates on damage and repairs, fuel cell reserves, and expendable munitions remaining. Everything looked bad. Worse yet, a number of ships were still trying to get some of their main propulsion drives repaired. Until they did, the fleet couldn't even run at a good pace without leaving those ships behind.

Leaving them behind to the Syndic wolves that would be coming out of this same jump point in pursuit. Geary had no trouble imagining the scene, because he'd already run some worst-case simulations. The Alliance fleet fleeing for another jump point, the faster Syndics coming on after them, swarms of swift light cruisers and Hunter-Killers picking off those Alliance ships too badly damaged to keep up, then harassing the main body of the fleet itself, hitting the ships in the rear of the Alliance formation and one by one causing them to lose ground and be caught by the main body of the Syndic pursuers.

He'd tried simulations of what would happen if he tried to re-form his fleet here and fight the superior numbers of Syndics who'd be coming through that jump exit in pursuit. With many damaged ships, low fuel reserves, and expendable ammunition stocks almost exhausted, the results were always total destruction for the Alliance fleet.

Assuming he retained command after the fleet conference that would have to be held. Now, when the external threats were so critical, he knew that he had to deal with an even greater level of internal threat.

They couldn't linger in Ixion for even an extra moment, and they wouldn't get out of Ixion without losing a lot more ships. Beyond Ixion, if any Alliance ships made it out, there seemed no way to throw off the Syndic pursuit this time, no way to justify the sacrifice of all of the ships lost at Lakota. All around him on the bridge of *Dauntless* he could see the watch-standers gazing at each other with helpless expressions, looking scared and beaten as they absorbed the current condition of the fleet.

They couldn't stand, and they couldn't run.

And just like that, Geary realized what the Alliance fleet had to do. *To hell with the fleet conference. I've made up my mind, and everyone's going to follow orders.*

He took a deep breath, took a long look at the battered ships of the fleet fleeing the jump point, then calmly pressed his controls. "All ships in the Alliance fleet, this is Captain Geary. Reverse course, immediate execute. I say again, all ships reverse course by turning up and over immediately."

Captain Desjani gave the orders to her crew automatically, then turned to stare at Geary with a baffled look. He didn't have to see anyone else's face to know they were reacting the same way. "Sir?" Desjani asked. "Reverse course? If we're going to try to plant the mines left in the fleet—"

"We're not planting mines," Geary stated. "There's not enough left in our inventories to make a difference."

"Captain Geary," a message came in, "this is Captain Duellos on *Courageous*. Please confirm your last order."

"Confirm. All ships, reverse course, immediate execute. Let's move it."

Geary wondered if any of his ships would keep going, fleeing farther into Ixion Star System, but no place offering refuge or hiding could be seen, only the vast emptiness around Ixion, and it seemed no one wanted to risk being left alone in that emptiness by ignoring the order. He saw his ships curving up and around. They weren't in much of a semblance to any formation now, but he didn't have time to try to reorganize them. Even at the relatively slow speed with which the fleet had exited the jump point, it took far longer than Geary liked, but eventually the fleet was pointed back toward the jump exit.

"This is *Colossus*. What are your intentions, Captain Geary? Shouldn't there be a fleet conference as soon as possible? There are critical command issues to address."

"This is *Conqueror*. Concur with *Colossus*."

"Thank you for your input," Geary replied. "There's no time for a conference. We're leaving this star system." He paused just long enough for everyone to hear that and wonder what he meant. "All ships in the Alliance fleet, this is Captain Geary. We're not going to retreat even one more kilometer. This fleet has unfinished business at Lakota. We're going to jump back toward Lakota, and when we get there, we're going to kick in the teeth of any Syndic flotilla present there and then see how many of the crew members of *Indefatigable*, *Audacious*, *Defiant*, *Paladin*, *Renown*, and the other ships we left back there can be recovered, and then this fleet will continue on its way back to Alliance space no matter what the Syndics throw at us."

He took another deep breath, wondering what everyone was thinking right now. "We'll go through jump right like this to save time and ensure we surprise the Syndics. On exit at Lakota, all ships are to turn starboard immediately eight zero degrees and be ready for combat. We won't be leaving Lakota again until we've given the Syndics a lesson they'll never forget on how the Alliance fleet can fight." And maybe provide a lesson about how hard humanity could be to defeat for the unknown aliens as well. Even if they had spies all over this fleet, those spies wouldn't have much chance to tip off their bosses with the fleet going right back into jump. The battle would be a little more even this time without the aliens helping the Syndics.

"Yes, *sir*!" Desjani was grinning and thrusting one fist high in the air. The watch-standers Geary could see on the bridge of *Dauntless* were yelling and punching each other's arms. He could hear a low roar that he gradually realized was the sound of the crew of *Dauntless* cheering their lungs out.

Geary looked back and saw Victoria Rione staring around as if she had suddenly found herself in an insane asylum. "Captain Geary," Rione protested in a strangled voice, "your fleet is low on ammunition, low on fuel cells, and has many damaged ships. And you're taking it back to Lakota?"

"That's right," Geary stated. "We can't stand and fight here, we can't run and get away, so we're attacking."

Rione looked from Geary to the celebrating crew members of *Dauntless*, her expression horrified. "But that's madness! What if there's a superior Syndic force still awaiting us at Lakota?"

"I guess that'll be too bad for them," Geary replied,

knowing that whatever he said would somehow find its way around the fleet. It wasn't a moment for caution or reflection or doubt. *I need to* lead *this fleet. May the living stars grant that I'm not leading it to destruction, but if so, we're going to die fighting, not running.* Desjani was smiling proudly at him as the ships of the Alliance fleet reached the jump point again. Another fleet officer, and a very good one, she understood something that Rione probably never could. "All ships," Geary transmitted, "I'll see you in Lakota.

"Jump now."

THE ULTIMATE

IN SCIENCE FICTION

From tales of distant worlds to stories of tomorrow's technology, Ace and Roc have everything you need to stretch your imagination to its limits.

Alastair Reynolds
Allen Steele
Charles Stross
Robert Heinlein
Joe Haldeman
Jack McDevitt
John Varley
William C. Dietz
Harry Turtledove
S. M. Stirling
Simon R. Green
Chris Bunch
E. E. Knight
S. L. Viehl
Kristine Kathryn Rusch

penguin.com

RoC ACE

Penguin Group (USA) Online

What will you be reading tomorrow?

Tom Clancy, Patricia Cornwell, W.E.B. Griffin,
Nora Roberts, William Gibson, Robin Cook,
Brian Jacques, Catherine Coulter, Stephen King,
Dean Koontz, Ken Follett, Clive Cussler,
Eric Jerome Dickey, John Sandford,
Terry McMillan, Sue Monk Kidd, Amy Tan,
John Berendt...

You'll find them all at
penguin.com

Read excerpts and newsletters,
find tour schedules and reading group guides,
and enter contests.

Subscribe to Penguin Group (USA) newsletters
and get an exclusive inside look
at exciting new titles and the authors you love
long before everyone else does.

PENGUIN GROUP (USA)
us.penguingroup.com